Volk

Other *PULPLESS.com, inc.* by Piers Anthony

Realty Check

Volk

Piers Anthony

PULPLESS.COM, INC.
10736 Jefferson Blvd., Suite 775
Culver City, CA 90230-4969, USA.
Voice & Fax: (500) 367-7353
Home Page: http://www.pulpless.com/
Business inquiries to info@pulpless.com
Editorial inquiries & submissions to
editors@pulpless.com

First Pulpless.Com™ Paperless Editions, June 1996.
First Pulpless.Com™, Inc. Edition September, 1999.
Library of Congress Catalog Card Number: 99-63061
ISBN: 1-58445-159-9

Book and Cover designed by CaliPer, Inc.
Cover Illustration by Billy Tackett, Arcadia Studios
© 1999 by Billy Tackett

Table of Contents

CHAPTER PAGE

Foreword "The War That Never Ends" by Brad Linaweaver 7

Prolog 11

1. America 17
2. Germany 33
3. Spain 53
4. SS 69
5. England 87
6. Berlin 107
7. France 131
8. Felix 155
9. Gibraltar 175
10. Tiergarten 189
11. Nietzsche 213
12. Götterdämmerung 237
13. Krista 259
14. Rheinberg 273

Author's Note 287

About the Author 295

Foreword

The War That Never Ends

by Brad Linaweaver

Piers Anthony is a writer of passion. Something has been growing in his work for years — and this is not a reference to fecundity. His best sellers occupy whole shelves in the chain bookstores! The largeness to which I refer is a special kind of empathy. He sees the universe from a variety of points of view but always with an emphasis on youth. Adults know all about the pain of loss. The young still feel the pain of longing.

There is no literature without passion. Yes, I said *literature.*

Academic snobs automatically discount a writer who has the temerity to be popular with teenagers. Their attitude seems to be that Piers Anthony is the guy who made a fortune selling puns to adolescents. They are immune to the cleverness of the *Xanth* books. Word play offends people who do not want to play. Nor are the old at heart likely to appreciate his best science fiction and fantasy.

So when Piers Anthony turns to historical subjects, and produces Serious Novels by any conceivable standard, he faces the challenge of finding the right audience. It helps to educate young readers who then grow up to read the author's major work. William Morrow published such a novel, *Tatham Mound*, about Native Americans. The publicity campaign was virtually non-existent compared to the treatment afforded his genre series. At least *Tatham Mound* was published in hardback and attracted critical attention.

For me, it created a hunger for another historical novel by Piers Anthony. Nothing satisfies this appetite better than what you now have in your possession thanks to Pulpless.Com. Anthony has turned to one of history's true turning points to tell an unforgettable story. *Volk* is a masterpiece, a love story set during World War II. It is certain to arouse controversy because it is not a hate story. Without giving away any of the carefully developed plot, the theme may be safely discussed in this foreword. *Volk* brings together three people who become close friends despite profound differences in belief. Quality is a Quaker who volunteers to help the sick and needy in war-torn Spain. She is a woman who in her quiet way demolishes the insults of those who doubt the courage of a true pacifist. Lane is an American patriot who wants to go to England and be a fighter pilot with the R.A.F.. He anticipates eventual hostilities against the Third Reich. After all, the Spanish Civil War was the warm-up act for the most horrible war in history. There were a number of prescient Americans like Lane who couldn't help but see the handwriting on the wall. So far, so good. Right?

The remaining member of the trio is Ernst, a Nazi. No, I don't mean the cliched "good German" who often appears in fiction set during this period. Ernst is a party member, a true believer in National Socialism. A Nazi. There is no deception between these good comrades. Lane and Quality know what Ernst is. So how can a woman in the Society of Friends be friends with two warriors, one of whom serves a perfidious regime? It takes a writer with the skill of Piers Anthony to provide the answer. Sometimes it is the person who feels emotions most deeply who is willing to think through a situation to its logical end, and act accordingly.

Anthony's characters are not reworkings of stock characters from other people's fiction. He draws on life and a close study of personality, a sure way to get into trouble. *Volk* is the kind of novel Victor Hugo would write if he'd lived in our times. A true Romantic can make a personal possession into a symbol of anything he chooses, inverting or reinforcing the original intent of the symbol, baptizing or exorcising a symbol, reinterpreting it as befits the ideology of the human heart. So it is that Ernst's silver swastika takes on a meaning undreamed of by Adolf Hitler.

Another way to get into trouble.

Come to think of it, Victor Hugo might have had trouble placing a novel this honest about material normally treated with a host of considerations taking precedence over characterization. Piers Anthony did his homework. The historical figures ring true. For example, no movie has come close to capturing the real Reinhard Heydrich whose style was both urbane and sinister. Generally, the movies give us interpretations that would barely achieve credibility in a cartoon. When Anthony insists on reality here it bodes well for believability in the rest of the narrative.

Which leads to another problem. Some readers may find *Volk* too convincing. A doctorate in history shouldn't be necessary to figure out that in a war there will be good people and bad people on all sides. Common sense should be enough. But as the night follows the day, and black markets follow Total Victory, so too does ill treatment of prisoners of war happen no matter who is in charge.

Sometimes the losers die. That's why it's better to win. *Volk* shows us that for some German prisoners at the end of hostilities, it was better to fall into British hands than American or French or Russian hands.

Hold on. Did I say American? We all know Germans didn't want to surrender to Russians. That's well documented. Besides, we've seen this acted out in uncounted numbers of Hollywood films. That's where most of us get our history. But as already noted, Piers Anthony did his homework. *Volk* would be a great novel even without the unpleasant history lesson about certain American-run camps at the end of the war. There will probably be critics who complain that the British come off too well.

The research and expert story telling combine to make *Volk* a modern classic. Thanks to Pulpless.Com TM, we finally get to read this important book.

(Brad Linaweaver is author of the critically acclaimed *Moon of Ice*, about what the world might be like if the Nazis had won World War II. He is also author of fifty short stories, some radio and film scripts, *Sliders: The Novel* and is co-author with Dafydd ab Hugh of the best selling *Doom* novels based on the popular video game from id Software. His new novel, *The Land Beyond Summer*, is available exclusively from Pulpless.Com, Inc.™)

Prolog

It was a pleasant spring day. The sun shone brightly on village and farms; the sheep grazed contentedly on the outlying slopes. Soon the sheep would be herded to the high summer pastures; already some of them had been dabbed with bright colors on their backs, the dye showing specific ownership. At the moment a number of ewes and lambs stood close to the gray stone walls of the houses, feeling most comfortable there.

The nearby town was swollen with country people, because it was market day, but many others remained at work in their fields and houses. Someone had to watch the animals, regardless of the day.

There was the sound of motors. Men and women paused from their labors, listening nervously. There had been fighting in the region, and it had been coming closer as the Basque line was turned by the better equipped enemy. But defeat was unthinkable. The four insurgent generals—they'd all be hanging, as the song had it.

Soon airplanes loomed on the horizon, as they did more frequently these days. The country was at war; young men from the village had enlisted and disappeared into the labyrinth of training and dispositioning, and every family tried to suppress the hideous fear that not all those young men would survive. Normally the younger sons, unable to inherit, went elsewhere to seek their fortune, but now there might be need of them here. This was really a foreign war, but it was forging nearer to this town, like a poisonous snake that writhed and cast about randomly in search of a target.

A woman looked up from the letter she had been writing. Her house was near the main bridge across the river. Her attention had been attracted more by the cessation of song in the neighborhood than by the distant motors. These people were always singing. Young shepherds would bawl out melodies without words. Children sang together as they walked home. Young men regaled each other in groups, hurling songs back and forth. In bad times older people sang dirges, and the troubadour was highly regarded. But suddenly all song had ended.

She went to the window, looking out at the cluster of houses in the near distance. Some had whitewashed walls, and all had orange tiled roofs. She could just see the spires of the church. Beyond it were the airplanes.

No wonder the singing had stopped. Those machines were coming *here*! Not passing obliquely, but heading directly for the village. Yet of course that was probably coincidence; they would pass over harmlessly. There was after all nothing to interest a war machine.

She tried to see what kind of airplanes they were. The Russian ones were all right; they certainly wouldn't stop. But the others—

These were German planes; the Nazi emblems were plain. There were the heavy black and white truncated crosses on the undersurfaces of the wings, and the grim tilted swastika on the tail. They were traveling north toward the industrial region. There had been increasing activity there as the Nationalists closed on that prize.

Apprehension had caused her to look up the aircraft that had passed before, and now she recognized them at sight, as she recognized a particular species of bird she had labored hard to identify. There were three Italian medium bombers, and a greater number of German bombers, JU 52s, considered obsolescent. But these were nevertheless death-dealing machines, the horror of the civilized world. It was incongruous to see them here over the peaceful countryside.

She had thought she had escaped such violence by retreating here to the pastoral hinterlands. She was a pacifist, opposed to any war, but especially to this one that was ravaging her beloved country to no purpose she could approve. When the opportunity came, she had prevailed on her husband to remove his practice from the big city and set up here, albeit it at a financial sacrifice. He had been one of those younger sons who had done considerably better in the outside world than his elder brother who had been in line to inherit this farmstead. But that brother had died relatively young, creating the need for a changed inheritance, and she had begged her husband to accept it.

But the senseless destruction of war seemed to be following them. No region was safe any more.

What was that? There was a plane she didn't recognize. Smaller than the others, with heavyset, molded wheel casings, making it look almost like a sea-plane. But it wasn't; it was some sort of bomber, for she could see the bomb-assembly between those wheels.

It must be an experimental model. The Germans were dismayingly inventive in such dread matters.

The woman returned to her letter, since she had identified the aircraft as well as she was able, and there was nothing she could do about them anyway. In moments they would pass overhead and continue on to wreak destruction of the factories to the north. She approved of none of this, but was selfishly relieved that the bombs would fall on other heads than hers.

Her missive was addressed to a correspondent in distant America with the unusual name Quality, who was working to master the language she had studied in school by corresponding with a native. Actually, in this region the natives had their own separate language that dated back millennia; most of the villagers spoke it rather than the national tongue. Which was one reason the woman was glad to correspond; it kept refreshing her own language. She liked the isolation, physically, but not intellectually or linguistically, so the letters were valuable.

Quality was another pacifist, and seemed like the sort of person whom it would be worthwhile to meet despite her youth. It was easy to write to her about the futility of revolution and war, the senseless savagery. Yet at this moment the war mocked them both; the devastating machines that were its minions were passing almost overhead. Adolf Hitler, the self-styled *Führer*, was testing his new toys, in violation of international treaties. Yet the community of the world clucked its tongue and did nothing. Who was most culpable, then: the bully, or those who let the bully have his way? Yet here was a moral trap: how could the bully be stopped, except by more violence? It was a difficult point. Pacifism had no easy answer to the problems of international aggression.

There was a series of explosions. Oh, no! The bombs were falling *here*!

The woman dashed to the door. Her husband emerged simultaneously from the goatshed, staring at the carnage, his black beret clinging to his head. The Nazis were bombing the town, this town! Debris was flying up, smoke roiling, and fire bursting in the dry bracken that was used for animal bedding. The stone houses were tough, but some direct hits were tumbling the walls, and the slate tiles were flying from the roofs. What hideous devastation even a single bomb could do!

"Why are they doing this?" she cried. "There are no soldiers here!"

Her father ran in from the field—technically her father-in-law, but she had adopted the fine old man—clasping his gnarled walking stick. This was still his farm, until he died; every aspect of it was his personal responsibility. He yielded chores only grudgingly, beginning with those his late wife had done. He was not fleeing the bombs, he was coming to protect his house.

A fighter-plane swooped low on a strafing run. The bullets kicked up little gouts of dust. The man cried out and fell, face down, his beret flying from his head. Even from this distance she could see the blood.

Her husband, ordinarily of sedentary bent, caught up a pitchfork and hurled it at the passing plane. The gesture was pathetically futile. The craft took no notice; it was strafing the sheep in the pasture. The animals milled about and fell, bleating in bewilderment.

She screamed, somehow feeling the horror of the pointless slaughter of the sheep more than that of the man. She was numb to her father's fate; her emotion could not yet compass it; it wasn't real. But the sheep—their deaths were real, if incomprehensible.

Dully she watched the bombs falling on the town. Every house was being hit, systematically. She heard the screams of the people caught in collapsing homes. Her neighbors, her friends...

Yet more terror came plunging out of the sky. It was the strange, small plane, diving down in a collision course with the ground. It must have gone out of control—but it was falling directly toward her own house!

She ran outside. The noise of the descending plane became deafening. A bomb sundered the house, behind her. Stones, plaster, slate and burning wood showered about her. That strike had been intentional! She was a pacifist, yet she felt primitive rage.

The plane's motor sputtered even as the bomb scored. The machine tilted, dangerously near the ground. The pilot tried to pull it up, to level it, but could not quite succeed. The plane stalled; then with seeming slowness it dropped to the ground beyond the sheep, bounced, plowed a furrow in the turf, and came to rest almost intact.

The woman ran toward it. It would be a miracle if the pilot survived, and a part of her mind marveled that God should allow such miracles to such undeserving people. She knew that airplanes were apt to burst into flames because of surplus fuel. Panting, she caught up to the smoldering craft. The pilot was moving slowly, dazed. She scrambled up on the broken wing and to the open cockpit, amazed that the man hadn't been cut to pieces when that bubble cracked apart. She caught hold of one of his arms and half-hauled, half-urged him out. Like a child he came, a uniformed German, the swastika on his left arm. No—that was bright red blood; her imagination had transformed it into the dread symbol of Nazism.

"Why are you helping me?" the pilot asked. He spoke in German, a language she hardly understood, but she grasped his meaning. What else would he be asking? "I was aiming for the bridge, but lost control."

And she found herself baffled. This man, this foreign criminal, had bombed her house, destroying it. One of his companions had killed her father and decimated their herd of sheep. She had every reason to hate the Germans! Why did she try to help this monster? It was not that she valued life, even of enemies, though she did; she should have run first to her father-in-law, far more deserving of aid. Why aid the enemy?

Then she realized what it was. She had a correspondence with a foreign person, one she respected. The pilot was a foreign person. There was really no similarity between the two; her correspondent was a pacifist woman while this pilot was a killer in the notorious Kondor Legion. In the stress of horror, her emotion had made a wrong connection, identifying the foreign enemy with the foreign friend.

Now the surviving villagers were charging toward the downed plane, carrying staves, pitchforks and kitchen knives. Innocent victims had been transformed by the brute alchemy of violence into savage remnants; here was the only possible object of their vengeance.

The German pilot, his head evidently clearing, looked at the horde. He glanced down at his arm as if considering whether to run. How fast could he proceed while his strength was being drained by that wound? Where could he go without leaving a telltale red trail? "*Donnerwetter*!" he muttered.

He brought out his wallet and gave it to the woman; perhaps she could notify his next-of-kin. He thumbed it open and showed her where his name was: Hans Bremen. She nodded to show she understood.

Then Hans Bremen drew his pistol, put it to his head, and fired. His body crumpled silently. Vengeance had been denied the villagers. The woman stood, somehow unsurprised. War was madness; why would she expect otherwise? Sanity had departed when the first bomb fell on this village.

As the villagers arrived, one more airplane came. It dived out of the sky and planted a bomb in their midst. Bodies flew wide, and one of them was that of the woman. The German airman's wallet tumbled through the smoke and was lost in the debris. There would be no notification of the next-of-kin by this route.

At last the remaining planes lifted away and departed to the south, leaving the smoldering ruin of the village. This was merely another incident in the year 1937, in the course of the civil war in Spain, in which Germany, Italy and the Soviet Union tested some of their equipment. The headlines of the world never reported this test run against a Basque town, and the dead were lost among the three quarters of a million that were the final toll of this vicious civil war.

But this incident foreshadowed, in significant respects, the greater conflagration soon to come. The hundreds who perished needlessly here would be eclipsed by the millions who would die in World War Two. This was in fact an omen, a warning—that was ignored.

Chapter 1
America

The drive between Boston and New York was never much fun, and this rainy June night it was worse than usual. A disproportionate number of oncoming vehicles maintained their beams adamantly on high, not caring about anyone's vision but their own. Lane Dowling began to mutter with irritation, then to swear.

"Lane..." the girl murmured.

He flicked his glance across to her. Even in the gloom of the car, she was comely, her brow and nose and mouth finely chiseled in silhouette. "Sorry, Quality," he said. She was a Quaker girl, and she really did object to bad language. That was part of her allure, for him; her informed innocence. Quality Smith was far from ignorant—she was an honors student—but her background was extremely straight-laced. If anyone in this world, he thought, was pure in body and spirit, it was Quality. Therefore she was a treasure, like a hoard of gold: after remaining sequestered for years, the beauty and value were undiminished. She was smart, pretty and chaste.

Another high-beam cowboy loomed. Lane gritted his teeth. It would be so satisfying to let fly one pungent cussword!

"Perhaps I should take a turn," his friend said from the back seat. "I do have an American driving license, and since you are kind enough to convey me—"

"Forget it, Ernst," Lane said. "You don't know these roads the way I do."

"True," Ernst agreed, chuckling. "Neither do I have your experience flying, as shows in the velocity of your machine. Yet I would not have you tire yourself unduly because of me." The German accent was almost imperceptible, but he still tended to speak formally and not too rapidly in English. "It is a very great favor that you do for me."

"If I were in Germany without a car," Lane said, gratified by his friend's expressed appreciation, "and had to make it in a hurry from Berlin to—" He paused, unable to think of a suitable city. The geography of Germany was not as clear to him as that of New York State.

"From Berlin to Hamburg," Ernst filled in obligingly. "Yes, friend, I would drive you there." He smiled in the dark, highlights from passing headlights reflected in his even teeth. "But I do not think you have business in the Fatherland at this time."

"Not while the Nazi's are there, for sure!" Lane agreed. "How you can go along with the fascists—"

"Please," Quality said.

"Oh, don't worry, girl. We're not going to fight. Ernst and I are friends, though I can't say the same for our countries." He shrugged, then directed a remark at the back seat. "What the hell do you see in Hitler?"

"Please," Ernst said this time. "I am prepared to defend the government of my country, but this distresses the lady." Quality made a murmur of agreement.

"Look, Quality," Lane said. "You always get tight about politics, but they're part of today's reality. The thing to do is not to take them seriously. Not between friends. Ernst just happens to be the single solitary Nazi fascist in the world that I can get along with, and we both damn well know—"

"Lane!" she protested, a really sharp note in her voice.

"Nazi, yes. Fascist, no," Ernst corrected him. "The distinction—"

"And if war comes we'll be on opposite sides," Lane continued. "We both know that too. It's like the Civil War, where brother fought against brother—"

"The Spanish Civil War?" Ernst asked. "That is not—"

"The American Civil War, idiot! Or as the text puts it, the War of the Rebellion. But this is peace, and we are friends—and even war isn't going to change that."

"Can't we drop the subject?" Quality pleaded.

"No," Lane said, made ornery by the strain of night driving. The drizzly, dirty rain had quickened after a tantalizing intermittence, fouling the windshield and making the road surface treacherous. That was all he needed! "We have to have this out sometime."

"Friend, it should be let go," Ernst said. "I comprehend her feeling."

But now Quality, despite her best intention, was angry. "How can a Nazi comprehend the feeling of a pacifist?"

"Approximately," Ernst said with a half-twisted smile. "You abhor me as I would abhor a Jew."

"I don't abhor Jews!" she exclaimed indignantly.

"Of course not," Ernst agreed, with another unseen smile. "You are extremely tolerant of lesser races."

"There *are* no lesser—"

"You do not share our concept of the Master Race."

"I certainly don't! How anyone can believe that trash—"

"Quality," Lane murmured with a smile of his own, in the same tone she had used on him. "He's teasing you. Ernst doesn't hate Jews. That's just part of what he has to say to keep out of trouble with his government. There's a Jew on our team, and Ernst was assigned to work with him, and taught him how to—"

"Ach, swine, you betray me!" Ernst muttered, chuckling. This time he pronounced the W with the sound of a V, in the German manner. Lane had picked up a number of interesting sidelights in the course of his association with Ernst, and remained intrigued by them. Most fun was the fact that the word "folk," to which the Germans attached a special meaning, was spelled with a V and capitalized: *Volk*. So the German W was pronounced V, and the V was pronounced F. Lane hadn't figured out how the F was pronounced.

Quality was stricken. "Oh, I'm doing it! I'm making foolish assumptions, letting my temper run away with me, and using pejorative language." She inhaled deeply, exhaled, then turned to face the German. "Ernst, I apologize—"

"Accepted," Ernst said immediately. "We have mutually exclusive views, but there need be no rancor."

"Yes," she agreed faintly.

"But I believe I do understand. The mention of the war in Spain reminded me. One of my companions in the Hitler Youth, which is an organization that parallels your Boy Scouts but is more thorough, was older than I and went on to become a flyer like Lane. He was not listed as such, for political reasons, but he served in the Kondor Legion—you might spell it with a C—in Spain last year. He flew an experimental aircraft called a dive-bomber, and it crashed. When I learned of his death, I cursed the futility of war."

"Spain..." she echoed.

"I lived in Spain, in my youth; my father was stationed there for a time. I learned to speak the language there. It is a nice country, almost as pretty as Germany. Now that memory of Iberia is spoiled, for the blood of my friend seeped into that soil. Yet all would have been well, but for the idiocy of war."

"Another pacifist!" Lane said in mock wonder. But he found himself touched. He had not known about Ernst's loss of a flying friend. Ernst had always refused to be taken for a ride in a small plane, and now the reason was coming clear.

"I, too, lost a friend in Spain," Quality whispered. "I never met her, but I knew her well. A woman who lived in a Basque village."

"Ah, the territory of the Basques!" Ernst said. "That was the Republican stronghold where—"

"I know that was where!" she cried, her voice shrill again. "That awful Condor Legion bombed her town!"

"Ah, no! You do not suppose—?"

"They could have met?" she said acidly. "You think he said 'Here, my dear Spanish lady, is ein gift from der Führer,' as he dropped his bomb on her head?"

"Gift in German means poison," Ernst said. "But I take your meaning. Yet if he crashed, he might not have bombed anyone. He had no animosity to others; he did not mean to hurt. He merely liked to fly, and the experience of diving out of the sky in seeming suicide, to pull out only a few feet from the ground—"

"That I can understand," Lane murmured. "The exhilaration of falling through space, like parachuting—"

"It is not for me," Ernst said somewhat abruptly. "His name was—"

"No! No names!" Quality cried. "How terrible, if—"

"Yes, it is terrible," Ernst agreed soberly. "If I could wave a magic wand and abolish the Spanish war, then and now—for the slaughter continues there to this day—and save the lives of your friend and mine, I would certainly do so."

"The war continues." Now Quality faced straight forward, her face set. "No wish of yours or mine can change it. But I confess you have some basis to understand my feeling."

"I'm glad that's settled," Lane said. He was driving more slowly now, for the rain had continued to intensify, and the edge of the road was getting flooded. "I thought for a moment we were going to re-enact the war here in this car. Let's let the sword be a plowshare, and a gift not be poison. I want you two to get along."

"Why?" Ernst inquired after a pause. "The lady has reason to avoid me, and this I understand. Had her friend been a pilot bombing my friend's town, I would feel the same."

"No, it's not that," Quality said. "We are not our brothers' keepers in quite that sense. But as long as you support the brutal Nazi regime—"

"The American regime is far from gentle," Ernst said. "One has but to look at history, at the way your country caused Panama to revolt from Colombia, and sent her gunship to balk the Colombian troops, so that a separate deal could be made on the Canal Zone America wanted—"

"Touché!" Lane exclaimed.

"And my country's dealings with Mexico, no more savory," Quality said. "I support none of this. Yet—"

"There is evil enough to go around," Lane cut in, surprised at both Ernst's and Quality's conversance with the skeletons in America's closet. No gunship had appeared in his own history text. "We know that. And each person must support his country, his system, even if it isn't perfect. No one respects a traitor. You two should be able to tolerate each other's governments for a day."

Now it was Quality who asked "Why?"

"Because I want Ernst to be the Best Man when you and I get married."

Quality gasped. Ernst made a guttural snort of derision.

"No, I'm serious," Lane insisted. "You're the best man I know, Ernst."

After a moment the German recovered enough to protest. "Nevertheless, in the circumstances—"

The car jerked and slowed. The left front wheel had hit a pothole concealed by filling water. For a moment the vehicle veered toward the opposing traffic.

Quality made a little shriek. Ernst grunted and jumped forward. Then Lane wrestled the wheels back to the right. The scare was over.

"What?" Quality asked, startled. For Ernst's muscular left forearm was across her front, pressing her back into the seat.

"Apology," the German muttered, drawing quickly away.

"That proves it," Lane said, pulling the car into a lighted roadside area. "You want to know what he was doing, Quality? I'll tell you what he was doing. He was throwing his arm around you to prevent you going head-first through the windshield if I cracked us up. Because he has the mass and muscle and reaction-speed you don't, and he knows how to hang on during a fall. He couldn't help me, because I was driving, and anyway I'm pretty tough myself. But you're something else."

Quality considered. "I fear I misjudged thee, Ernst," she said faintly.

"Because politics don't matter in the crunch," Lane continued. "There was no time for thought, only reaction. As in wrestling or self defense. Ernst did what was needed to be done, instantly, without even thinking. He could have saved your life, Quality, if I had messed up."

"Yes," she agreed. "I apologize to thee again, Ernst."

"A natural misunderstanding—" the German demurred, embarrassed.

"So as I said: Ernst is the best man I know," Lane said. "All the rest is dross." He turned to his friend. "When she says `thee' she really means it. It's called the plain talk; she uses it at home." He turned back to Quality. "About his being—"

"I withdraw my objection," she said contritely. "Thee knows best. He shall be Best Man when we wed."

"Now let's go find something to eat," Lane said briskly. He did not try to kiss her, though he wanted to, because Quality did not do such things in public.

But the rain was still coming down. They waited in silence a few more minutes for it to diminish. Lane glanced at his face in the rear-view mirror; there was just light enough, here, because of the neon illumination of signs. He fished out his comb to straighten his tousled hair and restore the natural curl. He was what he called a bleach-blond, like Ernst: his hair was brown, quite dark when wet, but dryness and the sun made it shades lighter. On those occasions in the past when he had worn it longer, the ends turned quite fair. His mother always thought of him as blond; he had at one time taken that as evidence that she was color-blind. Now he knew better; she merely remembered him as a tow-head baby.

He leaned forward to peer at his left cheek. The scars hardly showed, but he remained conscious of them. Others had assured him that he was handsome, and that the scars might be regarded as a beauty mark. Certainly Quality wasn't bothered; she judged by other things than appearance. But he would be happier with clear skin. Maybe surgery, some day, though the notion of going under the knife did not appeal.

"If thee is quite through—" Quality said, nudging him gently. She teased him sometimes about his vanity. She never seemed to touch up her own face, yet she always looked prim. Perhaps it came with inner goodness.

The rain had finally eased. They got out of the car, emerging into a drizzle becoming too fine to heed; only the irregular puddles impeded progress. They walked toward a garishly illuminated establishment a block distant.

"That will not do," Quality said as they drew close enough to make out the neon lettering.

"Oh—beer, ale" Lane said. "You don't drink." He said that for Ernst's benefit. Germany was famous for beer, and Lane did not want there to seem to be any obscure affront.

"Sensible people do not," Ernst said tactfully. "Perhaps there is a more suitable place beyond."

They resumed walking. At that point the door to the bar burst open and four men staggered out in an ambiance of alcohol. The first almost collided with Quality. "Look at that!" he exclaimed, his beer-breath surrounding her.

Quality averted her gaze, and Lane took her by the elbow and guided her around the stranger. At this moment she reminded him of a Christian Temperance lady, and it bothered him to have her sensitivities bruised by these oafs.

"Hey!" the man cried, lurching about, reaching for Quality. The reek of his breath intensified. But Ernst's forearm intercepted him.

"Please let us pass in peace," Ernst said, gently setting the man back.

But the drunkard swung his fist instead. Ernst blocked the blow and shoved the man back again, so that he collided with his fellows. "Please let us pass," he repeated without emphasis.

The man should have taken warning, because Ernst's physical competence was readily apparent. But he had the belligerence of befuddlement. "What are you, a Communist?" he demanded.

"I am a Nazi." Ernst turned stiffly to follow Lane and Quality. If there was one thing a Nazi hated, it was Communism, Lane knew. Ernst hardly showed it, but he had been deeply insulted.

"A Nazi!" Now all four men were pressing forward aggressively, discovering the opportunity to convert their drunken ire into patriotism. It was all right to beat up a Nazi.

"That wasn't diplomatic, friend," Lane said, turning quickly around.

"No fighting!" Quality protested. But it was too late. The four drunks were wading in.

"Stand clear, girl," Lane said. "This is a job for us warmongers." She skipped back hastily.

Lane and Ernst made contact with the first two men almost simultaneously. Suddenly the two drunks were hoisted in the air, whirled about, and half-shoved, half-hurled into the remaining two. All four collapsed in a heap.

"Compliments of the two leading members of the collegiate wrestling team," Lane said, dusting himself off and clapping his friend on the shoulder. It was hard to conceal his satisfaction, but Quality's stern gaze assisted him.

The fight was gone from the drunks. Lane and Ernst turned around again and rejoined Quality.

"That would not have been a fair match even had they not been intoxicated," she reproved them. But her sympathy for brawling drunks was quite limited, and she knew the four men had not been hurt. It occurred to Lane that even a pacifist like her could appreciate certain advantages in associating with nonpacifists like him. What would she have done if she had encountered the drunks alone? But he knew the answer: she would never have gone near a bar alone.

They found a suitable place to eat. They relaxed and became college students again. They were all the same age and had many common enthusiasms, and the summer was just beginning.

By the time they returned to the car, the drunks were gone. The rain had dwindled to nothing, leaving a rather pretty nocturnal clarity.

Lane's thoughts drifted from the tedious drive. That scar on his face, glimpsed in the mirror—that had a history that returned at odd moments, especially when he was depressed or tired. He was tired now. The night road reminded him of the streets of his home region, not so very far from here. His father was a mason and a Mason—in the employment and social senses—in the Troy/Albany section of New York State. Mr. Dowling had been there most of his life and was well established. Lane had been granted material comforts from infancy, never going hungry or poorly clothed, always having the best of education and entertainment. Odd how far that missed the truth of his upbringing.

He glanced at his companions, as if fearful that his thoughts were being overheard. Both were nodding. Quality had let her head fall back against the cushion, so that her smooth neck was exposed; it was not an ideal pose, but she remained pretty, her delicately rounded chin projecting, her petite bosom heaving gently. Ernst, in back, had slumped against the window, one arm elevated to cushion his head; his neck too was exposed, showing the muscles and cords. He had a wrestlers neck, of course; he could not be choked by any ordinary person, because his neck was too strong. He was the very best companion to have, when encountering pugnacious drunks—and excellent also in intellectual conversation. The German believed in the so-called Aryan ideal, the perfect white Christian—though at times Lane doubted whether it was even Christianity the Nazis ultimately sought—physically and mentally pure by their definitions. Ernst was that ideal, as smart and strong and handsome as a man could be without being obvious.

Ernst and Quality: two unique people, his closest associates. It had been Lane's minor grief that they did not get along with each other, since each was so important to him. Yet he was well able to understand their fundamental separation. A Nazi and a pacifist? There was no way such people could enjoy each other's company! They did have certain areas of common ground, in that each could speak Spanish, but they never spoke it to each other. Ernst was the son of a minor or middling embassy official—the kind who did all the work and never got the credit—who had been assigned in Madrid for two or three years, so of course Ernst had picked it up. Since Ernst never let a talent go once he had it, he surely spoke Spanish fluently now. Quality had started Spanish as an elective course in high-school and continued it in college. She had taken French too, with what fluency Lane didn't know because he spoke no language other than English. He was good at airplanes, not tongues. But probably she was good at both French and Spanish, because she had a natural aptitude for that sort of thing. Perhaps it derived from her empathy with people; she could communicate with anyone, one way or another.

Lane pictured himself in a small airplane, with Quality beside him, passenger rather than co-pilot. They were flying high up above the clouds, and she was thrilled. She leaned over to kiss him on the cheek.

Someone spoke in Spanish. Lane could not understand the words, but he recognized the general nature of the language. It was Ernst, in a seat behind. Quality answered in the same language.

"Hey, speak English!" Lane protested.

But they ignored him, and continued their dialogue, to his annoyance. What were they saying, that was so important, that had to be hidden from him?

Well, he would show them! He swerved the plane to the left—

A horn blared, startling him. Lane blinked; headlights were flashing in his rearview mirror, alternately blinding him and leaving his vision darkened. Quality was stifling a scream. What was happening? Was the driver behind him crazy?

He pulled to the right, slowing, to let the impatient one by. "I'd like to ram you, you idiot!" he muttered.

"Peace, friend," Ernst said. "We were sleeping. He gave us warning."

"You were sleeping," Lane retorted. "I was driving." But as he spoke, he realized that he had had to pull too far to the right. His left wheel had been across the center line. He had in fact been dreaming, and his swerve to the left could have wrecked them. "Cancel that. I was drifting off." His anger was shading into retroactive consternation; this was dangerous.

"Perhaps we should stop and rest," Quality said. Her voice was strained. "Thee is naturally tired."

"Can't," Lane replied. "We have to get Ernst to New York immediately."

"We do not know that it is an emergency," Ernst protested. "Only that my father is concerned."

"If he's like you, his concern is anyone else's emergency," Lane said.

Ernst did not demur. "Yet it is not wise to drive tired. Perhaps I should after all—"

"No, I'm okay." Indeed, he was now absolutely awake. He was aware that he seemed unreasonable, and probably *was* unreasonable, but he could not help himself; to turn over the wheel now would be a sign of weakness. Of course if Quality were to make an issue, he would have to back down. But she could not drive herself; her conservative Quaker family had not yet seen the need for her to indulge in such activity. Maybe they thought that might have made her too independent. "I'll be all right."

"Certainly." Ernst nevertheless looked alert. It was evident that he intended to see that there was no more nodding while driving.

Quality cast about for a positive solution. "We were wrong to leave it all to Lane. We must maintain a dialogue."

"I do not seek to impose my words on you," Ernst said.

She turned her head to face back toward him. "I have made my peace with thee, as well as I am able. It is not thy fault that I abhor elements of thy situation. I do not seek to be uncivil."

"Nor I. But on what subjects may we maintain an dialogue that is neither dull nor objectionable?"

"Play the game of Truth," Lane said, chuckling. "We take turns asking each other questions, and the answers must be absolutely truthful, or there is a penalty."

"I always speak the truth," Quality said. "Those of my faith do not practice a double standard."

She meant that literally, Lane knew. Strict Quakers refused even to take an oath, because that implied that they might be untruthful at other times. So they did not swear, they affirmed. They did not swear in the colloquial sense, either, as Quality had already reminded him on this trip. There, again, was the essence of her appeal for him: her honor, her sheer consistency in life. She had been so aptly named that it was a marvel; she was quality.

Nevertheless, he could challenge her. "But there are questions you avoid. In this game you can not avoid them."

She nodded, reconsidering. It was Ernst who spoke. "The Nazi and the pacifist speaking truth! This game is dangerous."

Quality glanced back at him, then at Lane. Probably she was trying to decide between the risks of candor and those of a sleepy driver. Candor won. "I will play it."

"Then so will I," Ernst said. "Until it becomes unkind; then I will default."

"I'll lead off," Lane said. "And I'll state one other rule: we have to take turns answering. To ensure that, the one who answers a question will be the one to ask the next question. We don't have to go resolutely clockwise, in fact we don't want any order fixed, but if someone gets left out more that a couple of turns, he'll have to answer until he catches up." He paused, and no one objected. "First question: Quality, exactly what do you have against Nazism?"

"This is not fair of thee!" she protested.

"No, answer, then ask me to respond," Ernst suggested.

She considered. "Very well. I regard Adolph Hitler as what Lane would call a posturing pipsqueak, an accident of history who has floated to the top of the German political caldron like the froth on sewer water. The man is an unscrupulous demagogue and hideous racist, and his chief lieutenants are little more than thugs. The movement he espouses is similarly ugly. I have difficulty understanding how any person of conscience can support Nazism." She took a breath. "Now I ask thee, Ernst, for thy response."

Lane made a silent whistle. She had surprised him by really socking it to the German. She might be a pacifist, but she had fighting spirit.

"There are many answers I might give," Ernst said slowly. "I might point out that other lands have their demagogues and their racists, and that nowhere is virtue necessarily rewarded in politics. I might mention Franklin Roosevelt of America, and the mistress he keeps despite being married. But we have touched on the faults of America before; they are no worse than the faults of other nations, including my own. I will say that while I do not support everything in which the Nazi party may be involved, and that there are those who owe their positions to factors other than merit, I strongly disagree about the Führer being either inconsequential or evil. I met him, two years ago, and I believe he is a great man, the kind of leader Germany requires in desperate times. He lifted us out of our slough of despond and made us powerful again. His programs have greatly helped the youth of our nation, and I am one who has benefited. I am here at this moment because Hitler arranged it, indirectly. He sees to the welfare of the brightest of our nation. I can not do less than applaud that." He passed his hand inside his shirt and drew out a small object on a chain about his neck. It was a silver swastika. "This is why I value this symbol of Nazism, and wear it always. It represents my devotion to the Nazi ideal."

"But the racism—" she protested, staring at the swastika with a certain morbid fascination.

"Nuh-uh," Lane cut in. "No back talk. Wait your next turn."

"She merely reminds me of an aspect I had neglected," Ernst said. "The Nazis are not racists. We merely seek to promote the greatest welfare of our kind. We believe in encouraging the fittest, and in discouraging those who are detrimental to our society. Hitler discovered that the Jews, Gypsies, homosexuals, mentally unfit, Communists and some others were not contributing to the welfare of the whole. Therefore he prefers to have them go to those lands where they may be welcome. We consider this to be good management."

Quality seemed unconvinced, but did not protest again.

Ernst turned to Lane. "And how do you justify keeping company with a pacifist, when you are not?"

How, indeed! Lane watched the road ahead, trying to marshal his thoughts. It was not enough merely to swear (affirm) that he loved Quality, or that she was perhaps the prettiest coed on the campus. He needed an objective basis. So he broadened the base, addressing not this one aspect, pacifism, but her religious background which fostered it.

"I am turned off by ordinary people, which accounts for my acquaintances with both of you," he said carefully. "Quality is a loyal member of her religion. She is a Quaker, which is the common name for the Religious Society of Friends. They got their nickname because in the early days they were supposed to have quaked in the presence of God. They object to many of the follies of man, such as violence, intoxication, cigarettes, foul language, gambling and overt sexuality. They are gentle people, concerned with good works, but that does not mean they are foolish. Many Quakers are well-to-do, for good business is part of their religion. Good *honest* business, for a Friend never cheats. There's a joke that perhaps has some truth: a Quaker is the only person who can buy from a Jew, sell to a Scotsman, and make a profit."

There was a bark of laughter from Ernst, but Quality frowned. Perhaps she objected to the seeming derogation of Jews and Scotsmen. "At any rate, I understand that in Germany today, Quakers are the only people willing to do business with both Jews and Scotsmen," Lane added quickly. "As you can see, Quality is attractive both physically and intellectually, but it is her ethical core which sets her apart. She is such a good person that I could forgive many faults in her, yet do not have to, for she has none. The fault is mine, for not being more like her. How could I not love her?"

Ernst nodded. "How could you not," he murmured.

There was a silence. Quality was blushing, but could not protest, because he had indeed told the truth. He could not resist teasing her. "Do you deny it, woman?"

"No," she said. "Now thee has asked, and I have answered. There is no set length to answers. It is my turn again. Lane, why does thee seek unusual people? That is, why is thee, as thee puts it, turned off by ordinary people?"

He realized that she had turned a table on him, by taking his joke question seriously. He was stuck with another honest answer.

"That may take some time," he said. "I'm not sure you would want to listen to—"

"We are listening," Ernst said.

So he had to do it. "It dates from my childhood, right here in the state of New York. I was a wan, spindly child, lacking proper size and vitality. Naturally ordinary children picked on me. The average person seems to remember childhood as a happy time, because his memory selects for the good and the bad things fade, but I can't forget my early inability to compete. It was clear that I was both different and inferior. Everyone knew it except the adults, who didn't count.

"Then an unusual person came on the scene. He was Jed, an Australian, with his special accent setting him apart. Of course the kids started in on him, because he was new and different. Anything different was fair game, and children have no limitations of conscience. But Jed was normal in one crucial respect: he could fight. When someone got obnoxious, Jed called him out in his polite, accented way and gave him his choice: fists or wrasslin'. At first it seemed like a joke, for Jed was neither large nor muscular. But he turned out to be a well coordinated whirlwind, with a high pain threshold and considerable endurance and native cunning. Very soon it became gauche to mock Jed's accent. In fact it got so that when a boy was provoked to the point of no return about an issue, such as the shape of his nose or the pronunciation of his middle name, his voice would assume a certain Australian tinge of accent: warning of the kind of trouble that was brewing. Newcomers to the community seen learned the signal.

"Jed was victoriously different. He began looking out for others who were different. When I got in trouble, he tended to show up, his accent becoming more pronounced, as it did when he was ready to Call Out. So nobody picked on me when he was near—and after a while they stopped picking on me when he wasn't near, too. He never said why he picked a given fight, but the bullies caught on.

"I only knew him a year, before his family moved away. but since that time I've been attracted to those who are different. Especially those who are different and superior. Ordinary people are clannish and insensitive, but when I find those few who aren't—" He shrugged. "Now you know. Both of you remind me in a subtle way of Jed. And here we are in the outskirts of New York City. So here's my question for you, Ernst: how do I reach your place?"

"It is an apartment complex used by foreign nationals," Ernst said. "I will direct you."

So he did, and they wound through the night city until they reached it.

"We'll see you to your door," Lane told Ernst. "None of my business, I know, but if I can find out what made your folks call you home so suddenly—"

"You are entitled to know," Ernst agreed. "I hope there has been no misfortune in the Fatherland. All my relatives are there, and some are old." And, he did not add, his immediate family had not seen those relatives in two years, while Herr Best served his term as liaison for certain Germanic interests in the New York area. This residence had enabled Ernst to attend a good Northeastern college, where he had encountered Lane as a fellow wrestler.

Lane and Quality waited in the lobby while Ernst went up to meet his father. Lane took her hand unobtrusively, and this familiarity she consented to so long as they were alone. Such stolen contacts with her were more precious to him than considerably more emphatic gestures would have been from other girls, because everything Quality did was sincere. Only a close friend held her hand; only her fiancé kissed her.

Soon Ernst was back, his face serious. "We have been recalled to Germany," he said regretfully. "We depart within the fortnight. I must help pack and terminate our affairs in this country."

"To Germany!" Lane exclaimed. "So soon!"

"I regret I shall not after all be able to serve at your wedding."

"Maybe it's temporary," Lane said. "Maybe you'll be back next semester—"

Ernst shook his head. "In the present international climate, this must be final. I fear we shall not be meeting again—as friends."

"Oh, Ernst—I hate this! I only really came to know you this past year, when we started winning meets together. The team needs you—"

"You must continue the winning tradition for us both, friend. I fear my wrestling days are over. Perhaps I can continue my education at a University in the Fatherland, though normally I should be liable at this time for military service. But either way, we must part."

Lane's protests had been largely rhetorical, though sincere. He knew the way of these things. He had never seen Jed again after separation; probably he would never see Ernst again. All he could do was accept the situation bravely. They shook hands. "Whatever happens, we'll always be friends," he said passionately.

"Always friends," Ernst agreed. "Politics are nothing." He turned to Quality. "Lady, I differ with you, but respect your mode. Will you shake hands with me?"

Silently she offered her hand, granting him this token of respect. It was evident that she was on balance relieved to see him so conveniently out of the picture, but she knew him to be a worthy individual on his own terms.

Lane gave his friend a final friendly, half-savage punch on the shoulder, striking at the vagaries of fortune, then escorted Quality out of the building.

"But we'll stay in touch by mail," he called back at the door. "Send me your address, wherever you are."

"I shall," Ernst agreed, and sadly turned away.

Chapter 2
Germany

It was a hot summer afternoon when Herr Best and family approached his brother's city of Wiesbaden. The journey had been tedious, with delays for ship passage and train passage and assorted clearances and briefings, and Ernst was thoroughly tired of traveling. Now he admired the scenery with increasing nostalgia as the train drew closer to the familiar area. This was the Rhineland, perhaps the most beautiful region of Germany. The rivers wound through the hills and mountains, girt by lovely old castles, the remnants of medieval greatness. These were among the few things that were not tidy, orderly, and cleaned up in Germany, but it would have been a shame to modernize the ruins, which had endured for centuries. The area was thickly wooded, with vegetation threatening to overrun the edifices; Ernst's mind's eye filled in what he could not see from the tracks. Yes, Germany remained in certain enchanting respects primal; no one would take it for a modern industrial nation, from this vantage.

Then the suburban outskirts of Wiesbaden appeared, dominated by agriculture, fruit plantations, vineyards and mansions . A hundred and seventy thousand people lived here—a small number compared to the half million of Frankfurt, nearby. But Wiesbaden was still far from village status.

This had been home for Ernst during the first years of his life. Then his father had gotten the good position that took the family all around the world, and Ernst had been here only irregularly. His Uncle Karl had taken over the estate, though he was only a shopkeeper. Theoretically he maintained it for his brother; in practice it seemed to have become Karl's. But if Herr Best—to Ernst, his father would always be Herr Best, *the* important figure of the family—if he remained in Germany this time, that would change. Ernst hoped that would be the case. He was tired of getting uprooted.

Uncle Karl met them at the station and chauffeured them to the estate in the big 1936 convertible Mercedes Limousine. New cars, Ernst realized, were hard to come by these days; too much of the country's industrial capacity was going to war machines. In fact the possession of a new car might almost be considered unpatriotic, since the materials and effort squandered in its manufacture might better have been contributed to the nation's effort of improvement. But Herr Best was not an ordinary citizen, and this car would last for decades; it had been built with German pride.

"This time you must stay," Uncle Karl said genially to Herr Best. "It is no longer safe in foreign lands."

"But there is money to be made there, and there are services to be rendered there, for the good of the Fatherland," Herr Best replied with the cheerful resignation of his nature. They were speaking in German, of course; it still seemed slightly strange to Ernst, after two solid years of English. Uncle Karl knew English, but normally declined to speak it. However, Ernst knew that German, like a long disused shoe of good quality, would soon become fully natural to him again.

"Money to be made here too!" Uncle Karl exclaimed. "Since Hitler came to power, the economy is booming. My shop caters to the affluent factory workers, and business is good, very good." He turned his face to Ernst. "Do you miss the Hitler Youth, lad? There's an excellent outfit."

"I miss Germany," Ernst said. Which was true—but at the moment, the memory of his friends in America was more poignant. He had been a little afraid to make new friends after the loss of Hans Bremen, especially among flyers. But Lane Dowling, who in certain respects resembled Hans, had not been one to be denied. It was as though such people forged ahead as rapidly in social contacts as they did in the airplanes they so loved, and the targets of their attention could not be unmoved. He sincerely hoped Lane would not crash also. But Uncle Karl would never understand that sentiment, so it wasn't worth discussing.

Karl went on to other subjects, ensuring that there would be no gap in conversation. Karl was not much for silences, in contrast to Herr Best's more introspective side of the family. Perhaps it was a survival trait for shopkeepers to be loquacious, and for diplomats to be silent. "Have you kept up with current events?" he inquired meaningfully.

"You are referring to Austria?" Herr Best replied.

"Wasn't that something! This man Hitler is a marvel! Remember the terrible, degrading terms forced on Germany after the war? The bruising reparations, the occupation of Frankfurt? Right here, those misbegotten French troops passed, pillaging—"

"That is the nature of armies," Herr Best agreed grimly. "The French occupied the Saar until the end of 1930, as I recall."

"As you recall!" Karl snorted. "As if you weren't cursing the French the whole time, since the Saarland is hardly a stone's throw from here. German territory, stolen by the French!"

"But we do have it back now," Herr Best rejoined mildly. He had a more cosmopolitan outlook, having traveled far more widely and been exposed to many foreign viewpoints. Ernst, remembering the differences in attitudes about the Jews, could understand. What made sense in France or America did not necessarily make sense in Germany—and vice versa.

"And the occupation of the Ruhr," Uncle Karl continued, warming up to a favorite subject. "All because they claim we defaulted on reparations payments. How could Germany repay such huge amounts when she had six million workers out of work, with their families hungry—and that meant twenty-five million living *people* hungry—and no freedom, no equality, no territory because the French had annexed it all? The Versailles treaty was a monster; they promised us Wilson's Fourteen Points, but they betrayed us—and then they violated even that poor document! They had no honor at all!"

"True," Herr Best agreed, remembering. "Victors need no honor." He had not spoken openly of this at home, but Ernst had picked it up. Germany had been foully treated and could no longer trust the promises of enemies. Especially those who were not Aryans. What was honor to lesser races? Better to fight to the last man! Better still to make sure that Germany never lost another war.

"Those cursed payments had already destroyed the Reichsmark," Kurt continued. "The damned bloodsuckers destroyed our currency, then invaded our territory because our currency was no good!"

"Please," Ernst's mother murmured, reminding Ernst uncomfortably of the way the Quaker girl cautioned his friend Lane. Indeed, Uncle Karl's neck had grown red and his voice tight, as it did when he suffered an overload of emotion. Yet this was a righteous ire shared by many, perhaps the majority of Germans. In America, Ernst knew, people were hardly conscious of the ravages that depression and the Reparations brought to Germany. Like a starving, whipped cur, his country would have turned against its tormentors at last—but there had been no way, for Germany had also been disarmed. The Americans had never experienced this degree of humiliation, so regarded it lightly. They had suffered only a gentle backwash of the world Depression, rather than its frontal savagery. But at least America had not been closely involved in this, so the anger of the Fatherland was not directed there. France was the major culprit, and to a lesser extent England.

Uncle Karl calmed himself, turning to a more positive subject. "But Adolf Hitler changed all that. He stabilized the currency, reduced unemployment, brought law and order and restored pride to us. He made the *Volk* respectable again. He made the French return the Saarland. He rearmed us, and there was nothing the French or the British could do. He made Austria part of Germany, as it should have been long ago. Austria wanted to unite with us, but the Allies prevented it from pure spite. They wanted us to suffer! And now, soon, Czechoslovakia—"

"Czechoslovakia?" Herr Best inquired, as if he didn't catch the drift. Ernst smiled privately; his father kept a low profile, politically, but he knew precisely what was going on. He had probably known about the Czech situation long before it had come to Uncle Karl's attention.

"There are millions of good Germans settled in the Czech Sudeten," Karl assured him. "They are mistreated there, under foreign rule. There have been riots. They must be permitted to rejoin the Fatherland, and Germany itself must have Lebensraum, room to live. It is only right."

And there was a potent term, Ernst thought. *Lebensraum* was part of Hitler's *Blut und Boden* vocabulary: blood and soil. It suggested that the members of fittest races had to establish a link of blood to the soil they worked, and extend their territory to the regions governed by weaker races in order to gain more soil for the superior blood. The strong needed room to live.

"Indeed so," Herr Best agreed. But he was understandably sober. "We do not operate in a political vacuum, internationally. If such unification should provoke war—"

"Then it will be a righteous war! Besides, Germany is strong, now. No more will the French intrude on our soil with impunity."

Ernst was listening, but his eye was wandering over the familiar yet newly strange scenery beyond the road. He noted the new buildings and reduced vegetation. He had traveled through here when in the Hitler Youth.

"And what is your opinion, Ernst?" Karl inquired suddenly.

"I prefer not to express opinions on matters which are beyond my competence," Ernst said carefully.

"Then express one on a matter within your competence," his uncle said. "Demonstrate the manner your mind is maturing." It was a challenge. Karl had never said so directly, but had always managed to convey the impression that Herr Best was a relative nonentity, and his son another.

Ernst glanced at his father, who looked away. It was time for Ernst to perform for his fiery uncle, and take the consequences. If his sojourn in America had corrupted him, Karl would make him pay.

He remembered the game of Truth he had played with his American friend Lane and Lane's Quaker fiancee. This was like another episode of that. He could make of it what he chose.

"This region reminds me of my experience in the Hitler Youth," he said. "I traveled this road then. I joined at age fifteen, when the program was rapidly expanding, and I enjoyed it and believe I did well. Today boys may join at ten, serving four years in the *Jungvolk*, the junior division, then four more in the senior division, *Hitler Jugend*, which we called HJ. I was too early, so lacked those first four years; I simply crossed over from one of the other youth programs."

"Which makes you exactly like every other boy in Germany," Karl said. The implication was that Ernst had no mind of his own. But to deny it would be a trap. How could he differ from the patriotic support of his country?

Seeing the trap was tantamount to avoiding it. But he wanted to do more than that; he wanted to set his uncle back a step, to teach him some respect—without ever expressing any disrespect. There was the true challenge. So he allowed himself to walk further into the trap, seemingly.

"Perhaps so," he agreed. "There was no social pressure put on me to join; I simply liked the uniform and the programs and the camaraderie and the approval of my family. My father, working in the government, was a Nazi Party member, and of higher social status than that of the families in my neighborhood, which sometimes made for awkwardness. But in the HJ there were boys from all classes, and there were no social distinctions. In that framework, I could have any friends I wanted, including some my family might otherwise frown upon." He glanced again at his father, who continued to fix his gaze elsewhere. "All of us were united in HJ in patriotism, and excitement. We camped out, we ate well, we marched in parades, we rode horses, paddled inflated rafts across wild rivers—well, flowing streams—rowed boats, motorcycled, climbed mountains, threw dummy hand grenades, flew gliders, and indulged in many sports. We boxed, participating in tournaments, winning prizes, developing ourselves physically. We sang, both patriotically and just for fun. We loved every bit of it."

"Completely ordinary," Karl said. "No individual character at all."

"Completely," Ernst agreed. "Except in the approved manner. We had an enhanced sense of responsibility and dedication. For the Hitler Youth in my day was run by youths rather than by adults. Here, boys were no longer subservient to teachers; we were not confined to prisonlike buildings. Boys were supreme! There was an exuberance about that which was almost intoxicating. This was an escape from narrowness, and it was associated with something vital and important. This was the uplifting spirit. Here were—the *Volk*."

"The *Volk*!" Karl echoed, agreeing. He had used the word himself.

"What spirit is associated with that term!" Ernst continued. "It stands for the racially and spiritually pure and fit, the young strength and hope of the nation. In the World War we Germans lost partly because we had been deceived and betrayed by the Allies and Jews and Communists, and partly because we had not been strong. Not strong enough to withstand the kicks of the whole world. But this time our youth is being brought to its full potential, to be absolutely superior to all others. Other nations may let their youth lie fallow, to grow up into weaklings. I have seen it in America: few are strong. One in a hundred, a thousand." He thought of Lane Dowling, indeed one in a thousand. "Most Americans never approach their potential, lacking any program to bring them up to it. But here in Germany we know that a physically healthy human being with courage is more valuable than any weakling, regardless how intelligent that weakling may think himself. The *Volk* are strong, and I am proud to be one of them."

Karl eyed him appraisingly. He could not argue with this thesis without seeming false to the Fatherland, and he could not object to Ernst's attitude on the grounds of conformity. Ernst was conforming in the most patriotic possible manner. Herr Best was still gazing away, but smiling. He knew that Ernst had backed Karl off. That was a significant family event.

Then Karl changed the subject, which was his way of conceding the issue. "And what of the girls?"

"I did not go to America to socialize, I went to learn the best of what they had to offer." But now he thought of Lane's fiancee, Quality Smith. On the surface a typically decadent college creature. But she was not. She was another in a thousand, intriguing in surprising ways.

"Wait until you see the *Mädchen*," Karl said smugly. "Remember that spindly neighbor's girl Krista?"

Krista. Ernst concentrated, remembering. She had been fourteen, perhaps fifteen, in the BDM, *Bund Deustcher Mädchen*, the League of German Girls within the Hitler Youth. He had seen a lot of her because her house was adjacent and her main entertainment had been to tag along after him. Her family had not kept close enough watch on her. She had stringy yellow hair, freckles, a turned-up nose and awkward limbs.

But Krista, despite her inadequacies, had believed in the Aryan ideal. She had been convinced that proper living and proper effort would transform her, too, into a superior creature. She had had faith, determination, and precious little else.

"I remember," Ernst said.

Uncle Karl grinned. "You have an experience coming. She is most eager to see you again."

"All in good time," Ernst murmured, aware that he was the object of some sort of joke. Had Krista become an amazon? That was hard to imagine.

At last they drew up to the house. This was a fine big mansion, stone-fronted, surrounded by neatly trimmed lawns and hedges. Ernst had lived here four years, between Herr Best's Spanish and American assignments. Two of those years his father had been away on duty in Japan; the family had felt it better for Ernst to remain in civilized Germany during this important segment of his education. Thus he had had four full years in the Fatherland, and he remained grateful. It was not that he had disliked his time in Spain or America—those had in fact been rewarding years, and he had been sorry to part with his friends in those places—but he had friends here too, and continuity was important.

But now he had no time for reflection. They were swept up in the rush of moving in. Several of the old servants remained, and all had to be individually greeted by each member of the returning family. Ernst more or less turned off his mind and engaged in the necessary ritual.

Ernst had hoped to renew his acquaintance with his friends, particularly his peers of the Hitler Youth, but he was disappointed. Most of them were gone. The fittest had joined the *Wehrmacht*, the army; others had gone into Party service. The rest had found employment in the booming economy. There was virtually no one to talk to. What a change two years had made!

Then Krista showed up, as Uncle Karl had warned she would. Ernst did not at first recognize her. She had been gangling at fifteen; now she was voluptuous at seventeen, with hair that glistened like that of a harvest goddess, and startlingly blue eyes. Her freckles had abated, and her nose had assumed esthetic proportions, enhancing her facial features. In fact, she was little short of stunning.

They sat in the receiving room, decorously, and talked, for Herr Best tolerated no impropriety between the sexes. In this he was in exact accord with the stricture of the Hitler Youth. Ernst, having seen the way it was in America, now found the German system constrictive. But in due course he would be on his own; then he would see. Here, he obeyed the rules of the house. He watched while the maid delivered innocuous refreshments and retreated.

Ernst had expected conversation to be strained, for he had not really wanted to encounter the girl so soon. But Krista was charged with news and excitement, and she carried the dialogue forward at the pace of a bubbling brook.

"Oh, Ernst, you are as handsome as ever! How was it in America?

Have you forgotten how to speak German? How do you like me now?" And she inhaled, turning her profile to advantage. How well she knew what she had become, a strikingly beautiful young woman. Ernst was reminded of Lane, again, who had by his own confession been a weakling in youth, but transformed into a very fine figure of a man. Krista had certainly transformed. Maybe there was more to positive living than Ernst had supposed; more likely Krista had been fated to blossom at this time regardless of her beliefs or actions.

"I miss the Hitler Youth," Ernst said, avoiding her challenge for a compliment. She had become a forward girl, and that was not ideal.

"I'm in the BDM," she said quickly. "I'm a group leader, same as you were. We may demonstrate in Nuremberg next month."

"The Nuremberg rally," he said, remembering. "How well I recall that!"

"Yes, you were there," she agreed brightly. "Tell me how it was."

She was playing up to him deliberately, pretending a greater interest than she felt, in order to flatter him. Ernst was aware of this, and was accordingly flattered. His prior image of her was fading under the onslaught of present reality. She was one radiantly attractive girl, and the force of her prettiness was almost tangible. But he was wary of such attention. Why should this newly-bloomed creature be so fascinated with him, after two years separation? He preferred to ascertain her true motive before accepting her interest at face value. So he temporized. "How do you feel about the Youth? I mean, of course everyone attends until age eighteen, but do you really like it?"

"Of course I like it!" she exclaimed defensively.

What else would she say? To criticize the *Führer's* youth program would be unpatriotic. Yet sometimes expressed patriotism could mask a fundamental dissatisfaction with the system. Ernst had always understood that; his father's employment had made him canny about the ways of covert and overt belief. Part of the reason he had succeeded so well with his youth group was his comprehension of the motives of individuals. He had acted quietly to get the incorrigibles and incompetents transferred to other units, and had concentrated on the wavering cases that had most promise. In due course he had brought them to full belief and acceptance, so that they worked wholeheartedly for the benefit of the group. Ernst's troop had become one of the most disciplined and responsive, a model, and the rewards had been gratifying. They had made public demonstrations, and in the end had been selected to march at Nuremberg: an honor that brought lasting pride to every member.

Now he applied his subtle skill to Krista. "I liked it too. But the horses were better than *Mein Kampf.*"

"The horses!" she agreed joyfully. Of course a healthy girl liked to ride. But there was also the tacit confession that she had not been interested in the Führer's autobiography. The truth was, few youths were. Ernst himself had read it and found it fascinating—but that was because he had special interest. He was the only one he knew who had honestly gotten through it. The other boys, if they read at all, had much preferred the heroic sagas of Karl May, and Krista surely was no exception. Her body had changed remarkably in two years, but her mind had remained more constant. Copies of *Mein Kampf* were abundant—it was perhaps the most widely distributed book in Germany—and they remained clean and neat because they received almost no attention. This girl was probably a minimal reader; she read only what she had to, to set an example and qualify for a position of leadership.

"And the ghost stories were better than the propaganda," he added.

"They still are," she agreed. Then she picked up the significance and affected shock. "Propaganda?"

"Do not be naive," he cautioned her. "Propaganda is not a bad word. All countries use it. In America the people are conditioned to believe in the saintliness of Roosevelt and the sanctity of the rights of all citizens, even the Negroids and the Jews."

"The Jews!"

"And what is wrong with the Jews?" he asked, smiling.

She was so confused she splattered. "How can you—"

Ernst laughed. "All I am doing is telling you how it is in decadent America. They have almost no concept of racial purity, of *Volk*. They take pride in being a melting pot of races."

"What do they know," she said, relieved. "You shouldn't tease me so."

"Pretty girls are meant to be teased." Actually he had been trying to draw her out, to provoke her, to verify what she was now made of, so that he could come to a conclusion whether she was worthwhile to know. Ernst certainly appreciated the physical appeal, but that was superficial, like the shine on a car. More important were the fundamental attributes of personality and intellect. In addition, he was interested in exploring the currently prevailing attitude on race, for he suspected racism had been intensifying here while he had been exposed to the far more liberal attitudes of the Americans. He could make a fool of himself in Germany if he misjudged the political climate; he preferred to play it safe.

Krista, meanwhile, was blushing, pleased at the compliment. She had worked so hard for such a harvest! But she could not refer to it directly, so she continued the other subject. "So you did not associate with Jews, there?"

"I met some. I was on a college wrestling team, and one of my matches was against a Jew." Actually, a teammate had been Jewish, but Ernst deemed it inexpedient to advertise that here. "I must confess he was a strong man; he looked almost Nordic, and he fought fair. I would not have known his origin, had he not told me."

"And you touched him?"

Ernst laughed again. "It is difficult to win a wrestling match without touching your opponent! Jews are after all people, even as we are. It can be hard to blame them for the unfortunate accident of their birth. This one's grandfather was a Jew; he himself did not follow their abominable religion." Even here he was skating on thin ice, for he was not at all sure there was anything inherently abominable about the Jewish religious ritual. Was it really so different, fundamentally, from the ceremonies of Roman Catholicism? Obviously the Jews and Catholics thought so, but Ernst himself was disinterested in the various forms of religion. He believed in God, but was uncertain which forms of worship God actually favored.

"A Jew is a Jew, to the sixth generation," she said grimly. Tainted blood was extremely potent; a tiny drop of it could ruin an otherwise excellent Aryan.

"True. Yet in America it is different. Their discrimination is very subtle. Their Jews can intermarry freely with others. Some hold responsible positions; some are honored in politics or industry. To many Americans, what they term racism is a worse offense than being Jewish."

"You must be glad to be home!" she exclaimed.

"Yes, of course—but not for that reason. If I were to live in America all of the time, I would probably come to feel as they do, to accept

Jews as part of the society. Jews are people too, after all."

"Are you testing me?" she demanded, growing worried and angry.

He was, but not in the way she thought. He was verifying her horizons, which seemed not to have expanded as adequately as had her body. "Perhaps I am merely verifying my own beliefs," he said carefully. "I did not object to Jews at first. It was only after I read *Mein Kampf* that I realized their nature. How they infiltrate quietly into society, like worms in fresh apples. How they pretend allegiance, but actually conspire to hurt decent folk and dominate the world. Even now I concede that some Jews could be good people. But they are indelibly tainted by their blood and their heritage. A tame python might be a worthwhile pet, but it remains a python, and must pay the penalty of its kind."

"What penalty?" she asked.

"Well, the python caused Eve to eat the fruit of the Tree of Knowledge of Good and Evil, so that she and Adam were exiled from the Garden of Eden. For that the python is accursed among animals—"

"I meant the Jews," she said.

"The Jews? Maybe they should all emigrate to America. I do not wish them any harm. I merely want my homeland pure. A Jew-free Germany." He shrugged. He was expressing a safe attitude, rather than his own. "But this is no subject for parlor conversation! You were telling me how it is in the Youth."

"As if you didn't know!" She frowned. "You think I can't tell you anything new? I'll show you! Have you heard about Rommel?"

"I know of no Youth by that name."

"Lieutenant-Colonel Rommel, stupid—the war hero. Last year he joined the Hitler Youth."

"The war hero? Holder of the highest decoration, the *Pour le Merite*? Certainly I know of him! But the war was twenty years ago; isn't he a little old for—"

"As instructor, as advisor!" she said, laughing. "They decided to put in a real soldier, to give some practical military training. He was doing it too, organizing for sound education and character building. But our dear leader Schirach, who is no soldier, got jealous. He wants to run the Youth all by himself. Rommel told him right out that if he wanted to be the leader of a para-military force, he should first become a soldier himself. Oooo, Schirach didn't like that! So he kicked Rommel out. They called it reassignment, of course, to cover up the truth. How's that for news?"

"It's a scandal!" Ernst exclaimed. "A man like Rommel—I wish my troop had had his instruction!"

"So the Youth is not perfect," she said smugly. "There is politics there too. You thought I was too stupid to know, didn't you?"

"Well, a girl as pretty as you doesn't need to be smart." There was an art to temporizing.

Krista struggled with that statement, but finally decided it was a compliment. "*Now* will you tell me about Nuremberg?"

"Nuremberg is a famous city in the mountain's of southern Germany, in Bavaria, some two hundred and forty kilometers east-southeast of here—"

She hit him lightly with her small fist. "Will you stop that? You know I meant when you went there, four years ago."

"Oh, that. Four years is a long time to remember." Actually he owed it to her; the news she had imparted about Rommel was certainly of interest to him. What a lost opportunity for the Youth! If Ernst had to enlist in the army, he'd jump at the chance to serve under Rommel.

Of course Krista hoped to go to Nuremberg herself, for the annual festivities, and she wanted the reassurance of his prior experience. He should be happy to tell her all about it; seldom would he have a more enthusiastic audience. Yet somehow he found himself holding back. Why?

He figured it out in a moment. It was because a substantial part of Krista's interest had to be in him, rather than in the subject. That was flattering, but it was time to begin distancing himself from her, if he didn't want to be pushed into more of a commitment than he desired. It was obvious that both his family and hers thought that the two of them would be an excellent match, and so they had been put together and left alone. Krista already wanted him, and she was now the kind of girl any man would want. Propinquity was bound to have effect.

But Ernst did not want to be managed. Perhaps he had indeed been corrupted to that extent by his stay in America. He wanted to choose for himself, especially in love. Also, he had become more discriminating. He now recognized in Krista certain limitations, a narrowness of outlook, that subtly repelled him. She was beautiful, but she was not the shadow of the woman that Lane's fiancee Quality was. He did not want to be bound to her.

But how could he avoid it? It seemed that everyone, including Krista herself, was determined to do it. He could not simply decline; there would be repercussions and unpleasantness.

Then he thought of a way. He would answer her, but in a way that should discourage her from pursuing him. If he could cause her to lose her interest in him, not because of any suspicion about his patriotism but for unspecified reason, he would soon be free of her without blame.

He moved closer to her and put his arm around her shoulders. "I will be happy to tell you all about it. The very memory thrills me."

She turned into him, surprised and pleased by his action. He hoped that this was a superficial reaction. "You can imagine the excitement of preparation, the constant drilling, the competition with other units, the hope and fear of success, and of the enormous satisfaction of having your troop chosen to go to the Nuremberg Rally."

"Yes," she breathed.

He moved his hand down from her shoulder to her hip. "As you know, the city is almost three hundred kilometers by road from Wiesbaden, because the road follows the meandering river and the contours of the land, stretching out the distance. It was a longer journey than many of us had made before, which was part of the excitement."

"Yes!"

His hand moved slowly along her thigh. "It was a glorified camping excursion; we sang patriotic songs on the way. But in time boredom set in, for we were sixteen, with brief attention spans. The songs degenerated. Finally we got to the notorious ribald *Es Zittern die morschen Knochen*, 'The rotten bones are trembling,' only certain portions were changed so that it became 'the rotten bones are trembling in the ass.'"

Krista tittered. She gave no sign of objecting to the manner his hand was traveling. But she would have to, soon.

"At that point I was compelled to call off the singing," he continued. "There could have been serious repercussions if anyone in authority had overheard."

"I have heard of that song," Krista said. "I don't know the words, of course."

"Of course," he agreed with a chuckle. He gave her thigh a squeeze through the cloth of her skirt. Still she did not object. Could she be unaware?

"Then we encountered a contingent traveling south from Leipzig, and one of my boys yelled 'Beefsteak!' and almost started a pitched battle between groups. For it is known that in the larger cities a good many Communist youth groups had converted to the Hitler Youth under pressure, and many Communists had joined the Nazi storm troopers. Thus we referred to them derisively as 'beefsteak Nazis': brown on the outside, red on the inside. It takes more than a brown shirt to make a good Nazi."

"Beefsteak!" Krista exclaimed, giggling. "That's good! You should have fought them."

His hand continued past her knee and made the turn. He found the hem of her skirt and touched her bare leg. "But what kind of a marching exhibition would my troop have put on, if it had gotten beaten up by beefsteaks?" Ernst inquired. "They outnumbered us, and some were pretty large steaks." But in truth he was rather proud of the episode. He hated Communism.

"True," she said with similar regret.

"The Rally was phenomenal. It lasted almost a week, with different programs scheduled each day. There were so many people there that they filled the streets and courtyards. All day there were marches and parades, with banners and standards, the magnificent black swastika symbol of the *Volk* set in a white circle against a bright red background. There was singing and cheering in unison, a mighty chorus from thousands of throats. Bands played stirring military music; drums beat out the thrumming cadences. Emotion built up. It was terrific."

"Yes," she whispered.

His hand was now sliding back up her leg, taking the skirt with it. Still no protest. Where was her limit?

"Then the *Führer* spoke, thundering out his enthusiasm for Germany, for the great ideals of this great nation, for the thousand year empire of the Third Reich. The crowd responded passionately, and I was one with it. '*Ein Reich! Ein Volk! Ein Führer!*' over and over, louder and louder. The Nation, the People, the Leader—what inspiration! The emotion of the occasion charged the air; it was as if the very soul of the *Volk* issued forth from these massed bodies. Individual response no longer existed; there was only the passion of the moment."

"Oh," she said, her eyes shining. How could she be oblivious to the progress of his hand? He was now passing the knee again, inside her skirt. He had expected her to balk before this, to start drawing away, to be repulsed by the discovery that he was only interested in forbidden touching. That he was, in short, a typical young man. She was supposed to be turned off by this revelation, and to lose her fascination with him.

"At night there was a torchlight procession. The drumbeat grew deafening, compelling every foot, even among those who only watched. I had never experienced a more moving demonstration. The beat and image pulsed in my brain long after the marches passed. I could hardly sleep."

"Yes."

"Then came the Party Day of Unity, and the Youth Rally. This was the biggest moment of all. My troop was one of those privileged few to march in the sight of the Führer . And Adolf Hitler spoke directly to the Youth, praising the boys for their past achievements and for their attainment of the important goal of discipline. Only discipline and obedience, he said, would make us fit to issue orders later in life."

"Yes," Krista repeated. Then, as his hand crossed the top of her bared thigh and headed inside: "Someone might see."

She had finally balked! He had been getting worried.

Then she stood, adjusted her skirt, and sat sideways on his lap, her skirt falling down outside. "But now they can't," she murmured, and leaned in to kiss him.

Ernst stiffened his jaw to prevent it from dropping. She was not objecting. What was he supposed to do now?

She had to be bluffing. She was too conformist to break with convention. She was trying to make *him* back off. Where would he be, if she succeeded? So it was a contest between them, and he had to win it if he wanted to be free of her.

She was right about one thing: no one could see his hand under her skirt now. The contest would be invisible. Where would she stop? He would find out. He moved in and touched the slick satiny surface of her buttock.

But meanwhile he talked, because it was the sound of their voices that reassured family members elsewhere in the house. Silence would occasion an investigation. "I remember the very words Hitler spoke. 'We want to be a peace-loving people, but at the same time courageous,' he concluded ringingly. 'That is why you must be peaceful and courageous too. Our people must be honor-loving; you must learn the concept of honor from earliest childhood.' For all of us in the audience had learned the consequence of dishonor, as practiced by the Allies after the War. The *Volk* would set a new and perfect standard for all the world to behold and try to emulate. 'You must be proud,' the great man continued. 'Proud to be the youthful members of the greatest nation in the world. But you must also practice obedience. You must learn to overcome hardship and privations. There must be no class distinctions among our people; never let such notions take root among you.' And, with a flourish, he finished: 'All that we expect of the Germany of the future, we expect of you. We shall pass on, but Germany will live in you.'"

"Oh, yes!" Krista agreed. Ernst wasn't sure whether she meant agreement with Hitler's words, or with the progress of his hand, which was now far beyond the bounds of propriety.

He carried on. "The applause interrupted the great man frequently during his speech. Now the cheering was deafening. The Hitler Youth anthem played, and the Führer shook hands with the most favored Youths. Among those was mine. I was afraid the very bones of my fingers would shake apart as I shivered with excitement. I remember thinking *The rotten bones are trembling*, and being horribly embarrassed at the very notion. I didn't matter, but I would have hated to soil Hitler's hand with rotten bones. But his grip was firm, and mine seemed so too. 'Fine job!' the Führer murmured, giving me a brief, meaningful glance. Then he went on, leaving me half stunned. The great man had spoken personally to me, and looked me right in the eye!"

"Oh, that must have been Heaven!" Krista agreed enviously, the muscles of her legs tightening against his hand. "To shake *his* hand!"

It had been, indeed. Yet this present moment had a certain devious similarity, for her body was also having an electrifying effect on his hand. He was beginning to hope that she *wouldn't* balk.

"It was," he agreed. "I was half-dazed in off-moments for days thereafter. That was when I read *Mein Kampf* and learned about the Jews." He didn't say that he had since had cause to doubt that all Jews were of that nature.

"More," she said.

Yet again he was surprised. Did she mean more about his life, though the high point of it had passed with that meeting with Hitler, or more of what he was doing under her skirt? Or both? He was about to have to concede defeat, because there was not much farther he could afford to go without hopelessly compromising himself as much as her.

"There is not much, and I think you know it already. I graduated from the Youth at age eighteen, and was ready for my national service. But then my father was transferred to America. That was a separate experience, and one I value."

"And now you are back, and I am so glad to have you back," she said. "As I have been trying to show you."

She had indeed. "Now I am twenty, and am subject to military service," he said. "Later I can complete my education at a University, perhaps at Frankfurt." Actually the Führer despised those who studied as weaklings, unfit for the *Volk*, unless they specialized in something technical or agriculture. While Ernst would never criticize Hitler, he hoped that his own interest in higher education would not be considered too large a blemish on his character. "I will seek a term in the regular army or the SS. Unless my father is able to exert influence and get me into a university immediately. It is not that I am unpatriotic, but that I think I can best serve the Fatherland by completing my education first. So it seems likely that I will not be here at home long."

"Is this a polite riddance?" she asked.

"I thought it might be," he said, taken aback again by her candor.

Krista turned her head to face him, and spoke with intensity. "I have gone as far as you dare, right here in your straight-laced uncle's foyer. I have matched you in this game of touching, Ernst. I know you thought nothing of me before, and I knew I did not have much time to make an impression on you. But I have changed in everything but this: I still love you. I think I can be good for you, if you will let me. But I will let you go without a murmur, and not bother you again, if you can tell me right now that you will never, under any circumstances, love me back. Speak those words, Ernst, and you will be rid of me forever." She gazed into his eyes, challenging him directly. Her thighs squeezed his hand.

Ernst returned her gaze and opened his mouth. She had offered him exactly what he wanted. But he found that he could not speak the words. She was beautiful. She was ardent. His hand was captive between her legs, and his eyes were captive to hers. "You have not matched me, Krista, you have beaten me," he confessed. "I am interested in you, now, and can not say I will never love you."

"Then will I be your Mädchen ?"

He shrugged, not because of indifference, but because he had no way to deny her. "If you wish. For now."

She leaned over and kissed him. "Then I am yours. For now."

He remained surprised at this development, but oddly satisfied. His family would be pleased at the success of their ploy, but that was the least of it.

Then there was the tread of someone approaching the foyer. They sprang apart as if there had been an explosion between them, and were abruptly decorous.

Chapter 3
Spain

"I've got to do it," Lane said.

"But thee knows I can not support thee in this," Quality protested. "To go needlessly to war—"

"Would you prefer to have Hitler take over all of Europe and then threaten America?"

"I have no liking for the Nazis, as I have said. But there must be a better way than war. Even should it come, thee has better things to do than to get involved in the quarrels of others. Thee has another year to go to obtain thy degree. With that, thee could do far more good in the world than thee could ever do by pointless fighting."

"Not if Hitler overruns the world while I'm studying!"

She paced the floor of the lounge. "We do not know that Hitler truly seeks world conquest, or that he could be successful if he tried. But if war should occur, there are others already under arms. Thee has no need to seek combat."

"How does that saying go?" Lane asked rhetorically. "All that is necessary for evil to flourish is for good men to do nothing."

"But thee can do something! Thee can complete thy education, and then work with greater effectiveness for peace in the world."

He gazed somberly at her. "You can't concede that maybe prevention is better than cure?"

"It is bad education that leads to much mischief. I prefer to deal with the underlying problems of society before they lead to war. Fighting is not prevention; it is a sign that the wrongness has proceeded too far. I would have preferred to have treated other nations in such manner that they never experienced the frustration that caused them to turn to their worst elements for salvation. Perhaps even now there can be amelioration and healing."

"I think it is way too late for that. Hitler is a cancer that will kill the body of Europe. Now he must be cut out, painful as the process may prove to be."

She looked at him, shaking her head, trying to keep the tears from her eyes. "Then I fear we must agree to disagree, Lane. I can not support thee in this."

He went to her. "I love you, Quality. But this is a matter of principle."

"And I love thee, Lane. But it is principle for me too."

"I know it is. I always liked your pacifism. But I just see this business a different way. Maybe—maybe we should separate for a while, in principle, each doing what we feel is necessary, and when this ugly business is done there won't be that difference between us any more, and we can marry. I want you to keep my ring."

"Maybe that is best," she said. "I will keep thy ring."

Then they kissed, and spoke no more of war. But both knew that a fundamental break had occurred.

They finished their terms, and then drove to Canada, because there Lane could train as a pilot and later transfer to the Royal Air Force in England. He was determined to qualify, because he knew that that was where the action would be. England was right on the edge of Europe, and would soon feel the consequence of Germany's militarism. Its air force would be the first in a position to strike back at the Nazis. Though France put on a brave front and had its Maginot Line, Lane had little faith in that. The Germans could go around it or blast a hole through it. The Great Wall had not stopped the Mongols from invading and conquering China, and walled cities had not survived gunpowder. Air power was the strength of the future, and he was determined to be part of it. Quality understood all this because others had spoken of it; despite her agreement of silence with Lane, she listened to whatever she knew related to his interests. She couldn't help it. But the information only strengthened the rift between them. How much better it would have been for the Mongols simply to have lived in peace with the Chinese, and the energy expended in building the Great Wall used for the mutual improvement of life.

Lane was accepted into the program. Quality bade him a tearful farewell outside the induction station, exactly like any other girlfriend, but they both knew that their separation was deeper than physical. They would be apart, yes, and he might get killed in action, but whether apart or together, alive or dead, their difference of principle remained as a gulf between them. Would that disappear when the war did? She wasn't sure.

Now it was time for her to return home. She had a bus to catch, but did not hurry. Somehow she was loath to return home alone, as if this made her culpable. She was strangely out of sorts. Why did she feel so guilty, when she had done what she could within the bounds of propriety to dissuade Lane? There was nothing she could do to mitigate the situation of the world.

She purchased a newspaper, knowing this to be merely another excuse for delay. There she saw a picture of a bombed out city, with children crying in the street. It reminded her of Guernica, in Spain, where her correspondent had died.

Suddenly she knew what she had to do. She *could* make a difference! She made her way to the nearest Friend's Meetinghouse and found the caretaker. "I must go to Spain," she said. "To help the children."

It was arranged. She took passage on a steamer to England, where she joined the Friends' Service Council. They tried, gently, to dissuade her from her intent, because the situation in Spain was what they termed "uncertain," but she was firm, and they did need volunteers, and she spoke both French and Spanish. She was qualified.

First they taught her to drive, because she would have to do it where she went. It was a crash course, almost literally, before she got the hang of it. They had her do it in a car, a small truck, and a large truck, because she had to be able to drive whatever was available.

The British vehicles had the driver on the right side, and drove on the left side of the road. "But on the Continent it will reverse," they warned her. "Don't get confused."

"I'm already confused," she replied. But in due course she got the gearshift and clutch coordinated, and learned the international hand signals and general road signs, and was appropriately nervous about the level of petrol in the gas tank.

She wrote to Lane, c/o his Canadian unit: "I have learned how to drive! I love thee."

She learned that mail could take from two weeks to two months to reach England from Spain. Both the Republicans and the Nationalists practiced censorship of letters. Workers sometimes had to go to France to send important confidential documents. Diplomatic pouches of the American and both Spanish governments were used to expedite some mail. Important letters were sent to several offices, with requests to forward it, in order to ensure delivery of at least one.

Quality had to undergo an embarrassingly thorough medical examination. She was inoculated against typhoid and vaccinated for smallpox. She was ready.

It was not feasible to proceed directly from England to Spain, which was in the throes of its civil war. Indeed, had she tried to go there from America, she would have been refused, for international travelers were being required to sign a statement that they would not go to Spain. She had not been aware of that at the time, but in any event had started her trip from Canada, where the restriction did not exist. So now she traveled to France, where French Friends welcomed her. Already there were refugee camps just north of the Pyrenees where the Basques were fleeing the savagery of the Nationalist thrust against their homeland.

Quality visited one of the camps, helping to deliver food and supplies. She was appalled to discover that she could not understand the people at all; they spoke neither French nor Spanish. Somehow she had not realized that Basque was a different language. In fact, the Basques were a different people, looking much the same as others but separated by their culture. It seemed that their stock had been early inhabitants of the region, once far more widely spread, largely displaced by migrations and conquest. Now they were being displaced again, this time by bombs and bullets.

Spain had been a republic for several years, but there had been strife between divergent factions and general poverty, leading to unrest of increasing scale and intensity. It was exactly the type of social neglect that led to unfortunate consequences, as she saw it. In 1936 the military establishment had rebelled, supported by the Catholic Church and about a third of the people. Called the Nationalists, they had commenced a war of conquest against the Republicans who represented the formal government. It seemed unlikely that their effort would have been successful, except that they found powerful covert allies in Italy and Germany, the Fascists and the Nazis, who saw in this local war an opportunity to test their new weapons. So the Nationalists had the benefit of the most deadly modern technology, and they were gaining ground. They had taken the northern Basque region, and much of central and southern Spain, but not the great central capital city of Madrid. Now the battle line was across the north, with the western part of the nation Nationalist and the Eastern part Republican.

So here she was, a Quaker lady, going to war. But not as a combatant. Her quarrel was not with men, but with neglect, poverty and hunger.

She could not get authorization from the Nationalists to enter their territory, so she went to Barcelona, in the Republican region of the northeast. This city was not under siege, but signs of the war were everywhere. A melody was playing constantly, as if it were a hit tune, but when she listened she discovered it was of another nature. It was "The Four Insurgent Generals," and told how they had betrayed the country, concluding "They'll all be hanging, They'll all be hanging!" Quality neither endorsed violence nor chose sides, but soon she found herself humming the refrain.

Each relief station had its warehouse and its supplies, and its ragged fleet of drivers to carry the food out to where it was needed. There were volunteer missions at every village, called shelters or canteens, where most of the feeding actually occurred. The emphasis was on infants, children, and expectant and nursing mothers, because they were the least able to fend for themselves. Many of the refugees were orphaned children.

Quality had thought there would be a period of breaking in, as there had been in England, before she would be allowed to go out into the field. She was mistaken; she went out with a driver on the first day after she arrived. She rode in a small truck whose sides were plainly marked with the five pointed Quaker star and the words SERVICIO INTERNACIONAL DE LOS AMIGOS CUAQUEROS—and whose motor, suspension and tires seemed none too sure. But that was what was available.

The driver was a Spanish man who, it turned out, had no special commitment to peace or feeding children; he had his own family to support, and this was a job that paid him a living wage. So he did his job, and did it well, but he was cynical about the net effect of the relief effort.

The assignment was not far away. Quality judged that they would be able to deliver their load and be back at the warehouse by noon. But the man merely shrugged. It seemed that such trips were expected to take a day, regardless.

Today's destination was a village about thirty miles behind the front. The fighting was not close, the driver said; all the same, one had to take care. Then, approaching a bridge, he came to a stop. Quality couldn't see any reason for it; this was out in the country, and no one else was in sight.

They got out and walked up to the bridge. The far half of it was gone. There was no barrier, no warning signs; it was just out. Had they tried to cross it at speed, they would have sailed into the river.

The driver didn't say anything. He had made his point. Quality's knees felt weak. Had she been traveling alone ...

Later she realized that the driver had probably known that the bridge was out. But he had educated her in a way she would never forget—and which might save her life some day.

Quality found some debris and set it on the road to represent at least a partial obstruction to future traffic. Then they turned the truck around and looked for a detour. A few kilometers downstream they found a serviceable bridge, and continued their route, perhaps not really behind schedule.

The next time they came to a bridge, Quality was glad to get out and check. This one was intact. So they had lost time—but the caution was necessary. Too much hurry could wreck them.

Then the motor started grinding. The driver pulled to a stop. He checked under the hood. He shook his head. "I can not fix it. I must get a mechanic. There will be a phone in the nearest village." He hesitated.

"I can watch the truck," Quality said. "I assure you, I will not steal anything." She smiled, to show it was a joke.

But the driver did not smile. "It is not safe for a truck with food to be left alone. Also a young woman."

Quality realized that he was serious, and that he was probably correct. This was not contemporary America, this was a war-torn nation. "Perhaps I could go to make the call?"

He shook his head. "Even less safe. I will hurry. It should be all right."

"Yes, of course."

He set out on foot, walking rapidly. Quality sat in the truck, abruptly nervous. She almost wished that the driver hadn't warned her, but of course it would have been foolish not to be aware of the danger.

She was in luck. No one approached the truck. In due course the driver returned. "It will be several hours," he reported. "We must wait." He did not seem easy.

"There is another problem?" Quality inquired.

"Now it is known that we must remain here, with food. There are many hungry people. They will come."

And they would not necessarily be reasonable. If denied, they might turn to violence. Even had Quality not been a pacifist, that would be a problem. How could they protect the truck and themselves until the mechanic came?

Then she had an idea. "If we feed some, and enlist their support, we will use some food but may save the truck," she suggested.

"But it is supposed to be done by the local authorities. There are not facilities, here on the road."

"Then we must enlist the local authorities," she said. "And make do as we can."

He considered, and she was afraid he would reject the notion. Then he smiled. "You are resourceful. I will go back and tell them." He got out and walked back toward the unseen village.

Quality didn't wait. She thought it best to make an immediate selection of the supplies to be expended, so as to keep the rest out of sight. She let down the tailgate and shoved things to it. She soon grew sweaty handling the boxes, and her good clothing became stained. It could not be helped. She was learning, again.

In due course the driver and a local volunteer arrived, by foot. The other was an old woman.

They waited, resting, for the woman was evidently frail from hunger. Also, the driver murmured, to be sure that proper procedure was being followed. Hurry was unseemly. He was educating Quality to what she would have to be alert to when she was on her own. "There is never enough food to feed everyone in need," he explained. "We feed some infirm adults, and aged persons—if there is enough. There usually isn't. We must turn the men away. We require them to drink the milk at the station, to be sure the right ones have it. So the canteens are referred to as *Gota de Leche*, or Drop of Milk. When things are really tight, we have to do height/

weight measurements to determine the most malnourished children, and feed them first."

Quality's horror was growing as she learned the realities of the situation. She had somehow fancied that bringing food to the needy would be a positive thing. Now she saw the ugly side of it. Grim decisions had to be made, and the good she was doing had to be cynically rationed. Indeed, there were men and women appearing, and the driver was waving them away, so that they kept their distance. "They know there will be trouble, if they take the children's food," he said gruffly. "The woman is the wife of the leading man of the village; she has power, and knows what she is doing."

"But they are hungry too," Quality said.

"There is not enough for all." That was the terrible reality.

A car arrived with some necessary equipment. Its driver was a young man who looked ferocious. The woman saw Quality's concern. "My son," she said proudly. "He will keep order." Quality nodded, relieved.

The woman began opening the boxes and taking out bags of powdered milk. She mixed it with water in a large kettle and stirred patiently to get it fully dissolved. "A few lucky towns have emulsifying machinery," the driver said. "We use a lot of sweetened condensed milk, because it's nourishing and easy to mix, but it costs more. We take whatever we can get."

Then, seeing no other legitimate volunteers, the driver helped, and Quality did too, as she came to understand the process. A volunteer who had not been duly cleared might steal the food; it was better to work directly with the woman and her son. One box contained chocolate, and another cheese. Then she found one with loaves of hard dark bread. She took a knife from the truck and carved slices.

Children appeared. They were of all ages, from perhaps fifteen to toddlers. Some were unmarked but lethargic; others had sores and crude bandages. Some were missing fingers, hands, or even arms. They were subdued.

They brought cups. Now the serving began: a cupful of mixed milk for each child, and a piece of bread. Quality wished she had butter or jam for the bread, but there was none. The children did not complain. They simply took the food and ate it.

When all had been served, what was left in the opened boxes

was given to those who seemed most in need for seconds. Some was given to adults, but cautiously, according to the guidelines. Quality slipped bread to a woman who said she was pregnant, who took it without comment and disappeared. That was the way it had to be.

And this was just a random stop, because of the breakdown of the truck. Could all of Spain be like this? Quality was very much afraid that it was.

As they finished, a few of the children were acting more like children. They were running around and making noise, and some were laughing as they played impromptu games. All they had needed was some food.

The mechanic arrived. He got busy in and under the truck, doing what he could. Quality was to learn that the mechanics were geniuses of their trade. They were never held up for lack of parts; somehow they always made do, devising whatever would work.

Quality and the driver carried several additional boxes to the car, for later distribution. This might be considered a final bribe for the privilege of being allowed to depart freely—or as an act of additional compassion. Distinctions were blurring. The local children would be fed next day by the volunteers, and on the following days, while the food lasted. But what of the next week, when the truck would still be going to different villages, and these children would not have a meal?

"You will be checking to see that the food is distributed properly," the driver said. "You will have to enforce it. Hungry people can not afford honesty."

"But these ones here," she asked. "This is not a regular stop. What of them?"

"They have been fed today," he said. She knew that that was all that could be said.

When the truck was fixed, they drove on to the regular station. But it felt as if the day's work had already been done.

Quality was thoroughly tired by the time she got back to Barcelona. So she relaxed in her own fashion: she wrote a long letter to Lane, telling him all about it.

The Republicans were losing. Day by day the battle line changed, coming closer to Barcelona. The sound of the big guns and bombs grew louder, and the stream of refugees passing through the city increased.

But the relief work continued. When Quality drove out to a village near the territory of the Nationalists, there was a check point on the road. She had to stop and explain what she was doing. They were about to demand that the car be opened for inspection, suspecting contraband, but an officer put a halt to that. "Those are Quakers. They don't fight. They don't lie. The children need the food. If they bring food from other nations for our children, we will not stop them. We will send a man along to help."

"I do have some food in the car," Quality said. Because the village she was going to had not been supplied in some time, and the next truck was delayed. "Also some cloth and thread. We have workshops for refugees; the women and girls make clothing, and the boys make sandals from rope."

The car was allowed to proceed, but a Republican soldier rode his motorcycle along behind it. Quality realized that the officer was not entirely trusting; if her mission turned out to be anything other than what she had said, she would be in trouble.

But of course it was legitimate. She delivered the meager supplies she had been able to fit in the car, and helped feed the children. The soldier nodded and departed. In due course Quality returned to the city. The check point had moved during the day, and there were different soldiers, but they had been given the word. "Do you have any contraband?" the officer demanded.

"Contraband?"

"Drugs. Weapons. Subversive literature. Dirty pictures."

She laughed. "No, only milk, bread, cloth and bandages on the way out, and empty on the way back." She waited in case they decided to inspect the car, but the man simply waved her on.

After that her car was not challenged in either direction, and no soldier followed it. The word of the Quakers was good.

Personnel changed, equipment failed, and Quality had to start driving a truck. The Republican government supplied some trucks for the relief efforts, but the service was inadequate. The Quakers had to rely on their own trucks, but they did not have enough vehicles to fulfill their needs. Experience made clear that light trucks did not carry enough or stand up well enough to the constant driving on wretched roads. The best trucks were three tons or more, equipped with four rear driving wheels and double springs. But they used a lot of petrol, which was in short supply. Even so, in the course of a year they managed to distribute several tens of thousands of tons of assorted foods.

Quality's deliveries consisted variously of the three basic relief foods, milk, bread and chocolate, supplemented by preserved meat, peanut butter, cheese, egg powder, dried fish, and dried vegetables: beans, peas and lentils. Cod liver oil was also distributed as supplies allowed. From Switzerland came Farina Lactal, a mixture of cereal flours, powdered milk, sugar and malt extracts which made a nutritious porridge when mixed with water and cooked. The Friends made every effort to buy food from outside Spain, because that added to the supply instead of merely shifting it within the country, and to avoid giving foreign currency to either Spanish government. It was too likely to be used to buy weapons.

The battle line continued to change. It was evident that only months remained before Barcelona itself would be under siege and would fall. The Nationalists were too strong, and their borrowed weapons were too effective. The refugees were now a pitiful horde.

Then a wounded, bandaged man waved down the car as it returned to the city in the afternoon on a routine trip without food. "I must reach to my home," he said. "My family needs me. Give me a ride."

"But I must pass a check point," Quality protested. "You cannot go there."

"The war is lost. I must go home. I have given up my weapon. Just take me through, and let me go, and I will be with my family."

So this was a deserter. Quality didn't like this, but found herself unable to deny the man. "If they stop the car, and inspect it, you will be in trouble," she warned him. So would she. Neither side took kindly to deserters.

"They will not stop a Quaker car," he replied.

That was probably true. Most days now the soldiers at the check points simply waved the trucks and cars on by. So she let him climb into the back and hide under blankets. Ill at ease, she drove on. Probably there would be no inspection.

But as it happened, this time she was challenged. "Are you carrying any contraband?" the soldier asked.

"No," Quality said, before she thought. Then it occurred to her that the man would surely be considered contraband; she had been thinking of the usual objects. But if she told them about the man, he might be taken and killed.

The soldier was already waving her on. She was moving forward before she got her thoughts organized. But then she was horrified. She had told a lie! She had never intended to do that.

Yet if she had told them, and the man had been taken and killed, after trusting her, what then?

She mulled it over as she drove, but the conclusion was inescapable: she had lied more or less by oversight and confusion, but she would have lied outright, rather than sacrifice a life.

She came to the section of the countryside the man had mentioned, and stopped. The passenger door opened and he jumped out. "*Gracias*!" he called, waving as he moved away.

Quality sat for a moment, and shed a tear. The man had cost her her honor, without ever knowing it.

The Nationalists advanced inexorably, and the Republican retreat became a rout. Now they were fleeing not to Barcelona, but from it, for any of them caught here would be massacred. The war was ugly, and atrocities were being committed on both sides. The Nationalists bombed innocent regions, simply because they were not Nationalist; the Republicans dug the bodies of priests and nuns from their graves and put them on grotesque public display, because of the Church's support for the other side. The Republican coalition was widely divergent, including even anarchists: those who believed in no government at all, though some of them held government positions. It also included Communists, who did support it well with men and with arms from Russia, but who also sought to make of it a Communist state. "First we must win the war; then we can settle between ourselves," one leader said, but there was endless quarreling between the factions. They were not winning the war.

The International Brigade, composed of volunteer soldiers from more than fifty other countries, had fought valiantly, but had been overpowered. It retreated through Barcelona, and on north to the French border, the Nationalists in hot pursuit. There was no talk now of the four insurgent generals hanging; the generals had won. General Franco had assumed the leadership of the Nationalists, and it was apparent that he would be the new ruler of the country.

News was not always easy to obtain, or reliable. Often it was too old to be of use. They needed to know where the line was, and where the fighting was, to avoid it. They would hear the explosions of bombs, but it might be two weeks before they saw a newspaper report of any action in that region. There was also a difference between units, of either side; some were best avoided, lest they steal the food. Quality had learned to dress unattractively, even mannishly, so as to represent no obvious target. When there was danger, and he could be spared, a man would ride with her and be near, discouraging problems. Even so, it was increasingly nervous business.

In July 1938 the Republicans launched a massive counter-attack west from the Barcelona area. They had amassed almost a hundred thousand troops and improved equipment. They surged across the line, which had become relatively stable, and reconquered land in the interior. But they could not maintain their momentum, and the offensive ground to a halt in August. For three months the line stabilized again, neither side advancing. But the Quaker trucks no longer approached it; the war in this section had become uglier.

She received a letter from Lane, who had completed his training in Canada and was now in England. It brightened her week, though she was sorry he had not come to England in time to see her there.

In September the Republican government agreed to have wheat from the U.S. Government's Federal Surplus Commodities Corporation distributed under Quaker control. The Nationalist government had already agreed to this. The International Commission for the Assistance of Child Refugees in Spain was formed to administer contributions from governments, headed by a commissioner, but the actual distribution was carried out by existing organizations in the field. The Red Cross distributed it to the American Friends Service Committee, requiring affidavits to the effect that it was to be used only for the relief of the civilian population. The American Friends shared it with the British Friends. The wheat started arriving near the end of the year. The shipments were not as large as hoped, but were significant. They were, in their fashion, a godsend.

"Perhaps thee could bring some supplies in thy plane," she wrote to Lane. But the humor didn't work; there was precious little humor in war, to her mind.

One morning in November Quality drove a truck out toward a distant village near the Ebro River, southwest of Barcelona. There had been the sounds of shooting and bombing, but that had been almost continuous for months. She discovered that it had been the site of an artillery bombardment that the Friends had not known about. There was rubble across the streets, buildings had collapsed, and fires were blazing many places. A pall of smoke hung overall. It looked like a scene from Dante's *Inferno*. Or like her vision of Guernica. She had of course seen many bombed-out villages, but this was horribly fresh.

As she picked her way through the debris, she came up to the bodies. There was one in the middle of the road. She stopped and got out, thinking to help the man, but as she approached she saw that he was dead. He had to be, because half of his head was missing.

At first she couldn't believe it. But when she turned her face away, stunned, she saw an arm. No body, just the arm. Beyond it were other objects that had to be human because they were covered with blood.

Quality vomited before she even realized she was being sick. The stuff just spewed out of her and splashed on the drying blood on the road. Oddly, that made her feel better. Except that it was an unfortunate waste of food.

She wiped her mouth, then walked around the man, took hold of his feet, and hauled him off the road. Then she returned to the truck and resumed driving. She felt the diminution of her innocence. War was hell on innocence, as she was to write to Lane.

In the center of the village the people were trying to care for the survivors. The job seemed almost hopeless. Many of them were dying where they lay, and there was nothing to be done for them except to make them comfortable while their blood leaked out. There was no electric power in the village, and no running water, and whatever medical supplies were available were so phenomenally inadequate as to be a mockery. The village authorities were performing triage: determining whom to try to treat and whom to ignore because the injuries were slight or death was inevitable. It was the borderline cases that were the problem.

But through this hell came the children, hungry as they always were. Numbly, Quality helped serve them, and they were appreciative. When she had done what she could, and the main portion of the supplies were put away in the canteen she drove away, taking along three who could probably be saved by more competent bandaging and care in Barcelona. There was nothing else to do.

The battle line had been stable; now it collapsed. Yet the children had to be served, so the trucks went out on ever more limited rounds. Even so, it was dangerous. Quality heard the sound of airplanes, and ahead the bombs exploded. She pulled over to the side, hoping to wait out the raid, but she was in the wrong place. The planes came right over her, and the bombs landed on either side. She hunched down inside the truck as the detonations shook it. She was terrified. She knew that only chance separated her from eternity.

How had she gotten into such a situation? She, who deplored war and all the artifacts of war! Here she was, literally, in the middle of it. Yet she could not retrace her life and discern where she had gone wrong. She had done what she believed was best throughout, and she knew she had helped many children to survive. If God saw fit to punish her for that, it was nothing she understood.

Then the planes passed. It had seemed an eternity, but it had been perhaps only a minute. She had been spared, in body. Only her faith had been shaken.

She started the truck and put it in gear. She moved slowly forward, watching for bomb craters. This was after all a routine day.

But it was evident that the battle line was getting too close. The trucks were no longer allowed to go out.

Quality was now trapped in Barcelona. She had not intended to leave anyway, because there was too much need for her here, but the choice had been usurped by the advancing forces. She wanted to huddle deep in the building, fearing that the shells would crash amidst the city and the power would fail, but she made herself get out and help where she could. It was no longer food she dispensed, but medicine and first aid, sadly inadequate. Refugees were everywhere, dragging themselves on through the city, sleeping huddled on the street, some of them dying there from their injuries and exposure.

In January 1939 Barcelona surrendered without a fight. The Nationalists marched in and put on a victory parade, and all the people had to come out and cheer. Because any who did not would be deemed to be enemies.

Then it was worse. The Nationalists combed through the city, routing out all enemies real or suspected, and shot them. The women and children they left alone, if they did not try to interfere. An officer recognized Quality, or perhaps her Quaker emblem, and showed her the wounded Nationalist men being trucked in who needed attention. She was officially neutral, though her private sympathy had been with the Republicans. It was her business to help whoever needed it, and so she did what she could for these men too.

Perhaps it was just as well, for her loyalty to the new order was not questioned, and she was treated well. When she sought to load her truck with what supplies remained and drive to a village where children were in need—which was any and every village!—they did not prevent her. For her it was business as usual. "But it is a tearful business," she wrote to Lane. "The need is so much greater than the ability."

Thus it was that she made the transition. In the following days and weeks the shipments of food continued to come, and the Friends Service continued to distribute it to the children. Now it was done under Nationalist auspices. There was not enough for the need, but it was far better than nothing. Quality was doing what she had come to do: helping people in a peaceful way. Yet her heart was not easy. She had never imagined that there could be so much grief in the world, so pointlessly wreaked. It was as if she were putting little bits of salve on a man who was burning to death. Sometimes that was literally the case.

But soon this became academic. The new bureaucracy caught up with this minor aspect of things, and the Quakers were no longer allowed to distribute food directly. They had to turn their supplies over to the state relief organization, *Asistencia Social.* The state had to be responsible for everything. The canteens and shelters faded away. Quality was allowed to give parcels individually, and did what she could, but it was sadly inadequate.

Where was her idealism now? She had no suitable answer.

Chapter 4
SS

There was no appropriate opening at a University at this time, as Ernst had expected; he had returned to Germany too late for a normal admission, and there were many applicants. He might have been eligible for a transfer from the American college, but his abrupt departure had rendered his credits there incomplete, and in any event they would have been regarded as inferior. So he would join military service, and he was satisfied to do this.

He did Krista the courtesy of discussing it with her. It was not that she had any better information than he did, or that there was any reason for her to have any control over his life. But he was seeing her now, and he wanted to work it out in his own mind, and she was happy to discuss anything with him. Her opinions were readily formed and fairly predictable; any exceptional thinking would have to be done elsewhere. But her actions were not at all predictable, and could be quite intriguing.

They walked through a park, having ridden their bicycles there and parked them at the edge. This was midsummer, and it was hot. They did not hold hands or otherwise touch. In America couples were frequently observed in physical contact, even kissing in public, but this was not that decadent land and the two of them were not creatures of the lower class. Both his family and hers were properly conservative. Public displays were not expected, and intimate contacts were properly reserved for marriage and privacy. Ernst had been taking a risk when he put his hand on her in the foyer, and she had been taking more of a risk by allowing it. Now their game of daring was over, and no contact since had been that extreme.

Krista was lovely in her light blouse and print skirt. He remained amazed at the transformation in her. It was not just that she had filled out spectacularly; she was hardly the only girl to do that. It was not that her face had cleared and become alluring in a way hardly hinted at before, though that certainly helped. Perhaps it was because of her change in hair style. Her fair hair now framed her face on its way to her shoulders, flattering it, almost molding it, and hiding its weaker aspects. But mostly it seemed to be her attitude. She had been eager and open; now she was more assertive and suggestive. That did wonders for her personality.

"So it must be the *Wehrmacht* or the SS," he said. "Which is better?"

"The *Schutzstaffel*," she said immediately "The SS, as it is called, the Order of the Death's Head. Its classy black uniform is wonderful, and it carries a tantalizing aura of mystery, power and terror. It is the organization that most specifically safeguards the welfare of our brave new Reich, and the very best people are members. But not the SS VT, the *Verfgungstruppe*, the troops. That's the lowest form of it. I don't think that's any better than the regular army. I don't want you marching through mud and getting your ears shot off."

He was impressed by her knowledge of the subject. He had not heard of that VT branch of the SS; it must have come into existence relatively recently. "I must admit that the notion of physical combat and random extinction on the battlefield does not appeal to me either," he said wryly. "I know that war will not be the civilized situation of a college wrestling match, wherein combatants shake hands at the finish. I prefer to serve in some capacity that utilizes my mind more than my muscles. Yet my choices are limited. If I join the elite SS, the lowly SS VT may be what they put me in. In that case, I might be better off in the Wehrmacht, the regular army, where I should qualify for officer's training."

"You could be an officer in the SS," she pointed out.

"With my incomplete education? Without NPEA or national service? I fear they would laugh me right out of the SS if I applied."

"But you have qualifications," she insisted. "Your father is a Party member with good connections. He could get you a commission."

That was possible, Ernst realized. But he wasn't satisfied. "I prefer to earn my own place, if I can."

"That's not the way it works," she argued. "You have to have connections. No one gets anywhere by merit alone. Do you think you were given command of your Youth group because of your ability or enthusiasm? Your father pulled a string, as mine did for me."

He sighed. It was true. Merit alone was not enough, because there were many meritorious young men and women. "Still, this is not an aspect of the system I like."

They entered a shelter. For the moment they were out of sight of anyone else, and unlikely to be disturbed by surprise. "You have to use what you have," she said, drawing him inside and into a corner. She pressed herself against him. "I did not like having to wheedle my father into making your father invite me to your house, but I did. I did not like letting you paw me, in order to get your attention, but I did. Because it was the only way. You don't have to like what you have to do to get your commission, but it's the only way. So do it."

"I am intrigued by your logic, but not convinced."

She took his hand and pressed it against her blouse, and the firm breast beneath. "What must I do to convince you?"

She had succeeded in startling him again, but he did not try to draw his hand away. That was a very fine and intriguing surface he felt. Her device might be crude, but it was effective. "You already have my attention, Krista; you don't have to let me paw you any more." Was she conscious of his irony? This time she was in effect pawing herself. Her objection was verbal, not literal.

"This time I want you to do what is right. I'm sure you don't want me to sully myself in the effort." She pressed his hand in more securely. The delight of that soft, intimate, suggestive contact leaped from his hand to his heart, making it beat as hard as if he were running. It was hard to maintain his equilibrium.

Was she making a promise, if he agreed to her way? It was persuasive, since he had already concluded that her course was the one he would have to follow. "Then I shall have to agree with you," he said. "But if this is your manner of persuasion, I hope to find many more differences to reconcile."

She smiled. "Perhaps, in good time." Then she gently drew his hand away and kissed him.

She had of course been trying to make a further impression on him, so that he would not be interested in other feminine company. She was succeeding. He knew better than to let himself fall in love with her, but she did excite and fascinate him, as she intended.

So it was that Ernst assembled the papers and made application for an officer's commission in the SS. Herr Best put in a quiet word where it counted, and in due course the word came: Ernst had been granted a provisional status of *Untersturmfhrer*, second lieutenant, in the SS, if he completed training successfully.

Of course it wasn't as simple as that. He still had two years of military service to do before receiving any such promotion. He would have to start in the SS VT, though he hoped not to remain there. But it did mean that his course was marked, and that it was a good one.

In July he reported to the local SS station for training. Krista gave him a most passionate embrace and kiss, straining the limits of propriety, for it was in the sight of their families as they saw him to the building. But no one was in a position to protest, for Ernst was a good Nazi young man doing his duty, and Krista was a good Nazi young woman encouraging him in that, and their families were pleased that the two of them were keeping company. Anyway, their opportunities for further physical contact would be quite limited for the next few months.

He was issued a fine black SS uniform without patches; he was thus without rank or association. His belt buckle had an eagle, a swastika, and the SS motto "My honor is loyalty."

He was given a bunk in the dormitory, and instructed in the protocol of the facility. He had no problem with it; it was similar to his experience in the Hitler Youth.

Indeed, though he entered training well along in the annual cycle, he received a provisional SS pass, and was able to comport himself well. This was because not only had he had excellent prior experience, the instructors knew that an exception had been made for him because of a Party connection. They suspected that he was marked for some special service, and they wanted him to remember them with favor if his path crossed theirs at some later time. They knew that Reinhard Heydrich, the "blond beast" who commanded the SS, had once been cashiered as a naval officer, and now was possibly the most feared man in Germany. Surely the rotten bones of certain naval officers were trembling now! So, just in case Ernst Best was going any similar direction, they took care.

There was camping and marching and discipline, and Ernst enjoyed it. He was not a squad leader, having come in too late, but he was competent and dependable, and the squad he was in did well. He had to scramble to complete the qualifications for his sports badge, being short of time. It wasn't possible simply to take the examinations; he had to be personally trained by the certified instructors. Still, he managed to do well enough, because of his prior experience.

Grenade throwing was new to him, however, because these were live. That made all the difference. One of the others armed his grenade and dropped it; the instructor immediately picked it up and hurled it into the field. That was why those in training were not allowed to proceed alone. Ernst himself performed without error, but still felt uneasy. These things were dangerous! They were called "egg" grenades, because of their shape; there was a cap to be unscrewed, which gave access to a string; when the string was pulled, detonation occurred after five seconds. The ones they used had blue caps; they were warned that if they ever saw one with a red cap, to leave it alone, because it would have a one second fuse. That was the kind left behind for the enemy to find.

He also learned the SS catechism:

Why do we believe in Germany and the Führer?

Because we believe in God, we believe in Germany which He created in His world, and in the Führer, Adolf Hitler, whom He has sent us.

Whom must we primarily serve?

Our people and the Führer, Adolf Hitler.

Why do you obey?

From inner conviction, from belief in Germany, in the Führer, in the Movement and in the SS, and from loyalty.

It was easy for Ernst, because he needed no catechism to bolster his belief and loyalty. The ritual was beautiful and true.

The only thing that bothered him was religion. Ernst belonged to the Church, and his family had always belonged. He was not a devoted member, and there were things about religion he questioned, but he preferred that membership be a matter of personal decision rather than dictated by the state. Yet the candidates were pressured to renounce the Christian messages of tolerance and reconciliation as an effeminate, un-German, and even "Jewish" doctrine.

Each day on the drill field the command was given: "Anyone who has not yet left the Church take one step forward." The first day half the candidates stepped forward, Ernst among them. They were harangued for their backwardness and given disciplinary duties.

The next day when the call was made, only a quarter of the candidates took that step. Ernst remained among them.

So it continued from day to day, until only a handful remained. Ernst knew it would be easier not to take the step, because he really did not care that much about the Church. But he still did not like being forced to renounce it.

Then one day the other five candidates were put on adverse duty, but Ernst was excused. He went to the commander and inquired. "You are marked for better things," the officer told him. "The others are hopeless."

Ernst realized that the string his father had pulled was having further effect. If the authorities bore down on him too hard, or tried to drive him out, there could be unpleasant consequences for them. So they were excepting him.

But he refused to accept this. "If the others have done wrong, I have done the same," Ernst said firmly. "I must be punished in the same manner they are."

The man gazed at him for a long moment. "It is not your prerogative to establish company policy," he said. "Dismissed."

Ernst had to go, because he could not disobey a direct order. But instead of reporting back to his unit for regular activities, he went to the punishment detail. No one questioned this; it did not occur to the sergeant in charge that anyone would seek punishment he had not been assigned.

The word must have spread, however, because next morning there was no call-out. The remaining church members were allowed to proceed with the regular program.

Later, the sergeant who had been in charge of the punishment detail came to the barracks and paused at Ernst's bunk. "You have courage," he remarked, and moved on. But Ernst caught the momentary, tiny twitch of his lips. The man was pleased.

No one else said anything to him. But the subtle respect with which Ernst was treated increased. He had won the day, in a certain fashion.

On November 7 Ernst and the other candidates from all across Germany went south to Munich for the swearing in ceremony. But something strange and significant happened while they were traveling.

"Did you hear?" another candidate on the train demanded breathlessly. "Ernst von Rath has been shot by a Jew!"

Ernst thought at first that he was being teased, because of the first name. He had no idea who the victim was. But in the course of the following day, as they reached Munich and found their barracks, it came clear: he was the third secretary of the German Embassy in Paris. He was not a nationally known figure, but Goebbels, the minister of Propaganda, was spreading the word throughout Germany. A prominent leader had been treacherously murdered by the foul Jews!

Ernst was neutral concerning the Jews. He knew that Hitler did not like them, and Hitler's logic in *Mein Kampf* was persuasive. But Ernst had seen in America that Jews could be much like any other people. So it seemed best to move them out of Germany and have no further quarrel. But if they were now murdering government officials, that made the matter more serious. So he paid attention, and learned the background of this episode.

It seemed that one Herschel Grynspan was a Jew whose parents had been forcibly relocated to the Polish border, in accordance with the program to move Jews elsewhere. Rather than accept the situation, it was suggested, he had assassinated the official who had made the decision. Of course Grynspan would be dealt with. Ernst knew that these things happened. But von Rath was in critical condition, and it was doubtful whether he would live. That was unfortunate for him.

But why was Goebbels making so much of this? It was as if the Jews had bombed Berlin and killed the Führer! Anger was building up throughout Germany. What was Goebbels up to?

However, Ernst had more important things to focus on. He had to be perfect for the ceremony on the ninth. It was the anniversary of the Munich "Beer Hall Putsch" of 1923, when Adolf Hitler and his Nazis invaded a political meeting in their attempt to seize the Bavarian government. But the people did not support the Nazis then, and the troops of the government opened fire as the Nazis marched into the heart of Munich, killing sixteen. Hitler and other leaders were tried and imprisoned. But though their effort was a failure, it attracted a great deal of attention to the movement, and thereafter it grew. So in the longer view, it really had not been a failure, but a necessary step.

Ernst was among those who watched the solemn ceremony as

the remaining survivors of the Munich Putsch silently re-enacted their march through the city. Fifteen years had passed, but the solemn memory had grown rather than fading. Today the sixteen martyrs were interred in state in the colonnaded Temple of Honor beside the ill-famed beer hall. The survivors marched by it, followed by a phalanx of those who had received the "Blood Order" award. Ernst felt a tear at his eye as the procession silently passed. This was a fitting recognition of those who had risked or given their lives on behalf of Nazism in the troubled early years.

Adolf Hitler himself was in Munich with the "Old Guard" leaders for the traditional dinner celebration in the town hall after the ceremonial re-enactment of the Munich Putsch. But in the afternoon the news came that Ernst von Rath was dead. It was reported that the Führer left the hall, visibly upset, without giving his address. Goebbels had to fill in. He gave a rousing speech urging the Old Guard fighters to start spontaneous demonstrations throughout Germany.

That evening was the official swearing in, at the Beer Hall itself. But as they marched there, they heard shouting and saw crowds roving through the streets. There was the smell of smoke. What was happening?

The commander halted the troop. "There are riots in the city," he announced. "Loyal citizens are destroying the property of the Jews." He scowled. "I have no sympathy for Jews, of course, but I dislike allowing mobs to rule. Our troops are forbidden to take any notice, either to participate or to resist the activity. Therefore we shall march on past without observing anything."

The march resumed. They went right past a store whose broad glass front had been smashed in, and whose contents had been strewn half across the street. "Looters!" the commander muttered with deep disgust, but the march did not pause.

By the time they reached the Beer Hall, the directive to restore order had gone out. The police were finally in the process of protecting Jewish property and businesses, and arresting looters. But of course it was too late; the damage of what was to become known as Crystal Night had been done.

The ceremony itself was deeply moving. It was by torchlight in front of the hall, and on each of the sixteen smoking obelisks was the name of one of the martyrs of National Socialism. A voice intoned each one of those names, and was answered by the chant of a thousand voices: "Here!"

Ernst felt the tears in his eyes again. Surely those heroes were indeed here in spirit, and had not died in vain.

> I swear to thee Adolf Hitler
> As Führer and Chancellor of the German Reich
> Loyalty and Bravery
> I vow to thee and to the superiors whom thou shalt appoint
> Obedience unto death
> So help me God

Ernst received his collar patches and permanent SS pass. Now he was ready to complete his term in the SS VT, before becoming a "full candidate" and taking the final oath to obey the law restricting marriage that the Reichführer SS had issued. He was granted leave, and went home to renew acquaintance with his family and Krista.

"You are so handsome in your dress uniform!" Krista exclaimed in the company of their families. "Let me take you out on the streets of Wiesbaden and show you off to all my friends."

But when she got him away from home, she took him instead to the park, which was deserted at this hour. In the shelter they had paused at before, she embraced him and kissed him passionately. "You really are stunning," she breathed. "We have so little time together."

He smiled. "Most of our association has been apart, anyway."

She drew her blouse from her waistband. "But much can be accomplished briefly."

What was she up to this time? "There is something to be accomplished?"

She took his hand and put it against her breast, under the loose blouse. The touch was electrifying. "There is something I want from you, Ernst."

"I fear it is something I will not want to give, or you would not be taking this approach."

She let his hand go and reached behind her back. Something loosened. Then she took his hand again and moved it to bare flesh.

She had undone her halter. "I want to marry you," she said.

Yet again she had startled him. "Marriage! I'm not ready for that!"

"When you are allowed. I know you must complete your training. But when you do—"

"Krista, I love the feel of your flesh. But that is not reason to marry. The commitment—"

"I will give you the feel of all my flesh," she said evenly. "All that you want. Immediately. Here. If you will agree."

He was suspicious of this, despite the amazing effect of her breast in his hand. "Why?"

"Because I love you, as I always have."

He gave her a little squeeze, not so much for the pleasure of it but as a negation. "Your love is qualified. I ask again: why marriage?"

"As the wife of an officer, I will have status. I will not have to endure more training or to take some dull job to support myself. I will not have to remain in this dull town."

"You could marry some other officer."

"Oh come on, Ernst!" she snapped. "I gave you a practical reason because you asked for it. You're the only man I want. I'm afraid you will go away and meet someone else, who won't be as good for you." She took his hand again and moved it down to her waistband.

"So you will make a down payment on me now, to secure me for later marriage," he said. It did make a certain sense. It was not that he might meet another woman, but that she might not meet another man who suited her fancy.

"Anything you want, if you will commit," she agreed. She used her free hand to draw the waistband out, and started his hand down under it.

"But I might get shipped far away for years," he protested. "Perhaps killed. Where would you be then?"

"Then at least I will have had your love for this moment."

He stopped his hand. "No."

"I will do it," she argued. "You do not have to take my word. Everything is yours. Only promise."

"I will not promise. I am not ready to commit to marriage."

"Let me persuade you!" She tugged at his hand.

"How do you know I wouldn't lie to you, as men do, to obtain your body without marriage?"

She laughed. "The day you tell a lie, Ernst, the sky will crash about our heads."

He laughed too, but not much. "I hope never to test it. But too much is unknown. If I were ready and able to marry now, I would consider your proposal. But I am not, so I will not. Perhaps some later day I will. I do like you, Krista, and the thought of possessing your body threatens to drive me mad. But this is not the time."

She hesitated, then made a decision. "Then I will give it to you without your commitment. It is not right to tease you. Only keep me in mind, when—"

"No. That would be a tacit commitment."

"Then without any understanding at all," she said. "Please, Ernst—"

"You don't want to do this," he told her. "You want only my commitment, express or implied, and you know it will be there if I do this. If I marry you, then I will expect the delight of your body, and I do long for that delight. But I can not do this now. I will instead give you all the commitment possible for me now: I will keep you first in mind for marriage."

"I accept that." She caught his hand once again.

"No more hands," he said. "I give you this commitment without touching your body."

"Without?" Her eyes were big.

"Without. Now put yourself back together."

She proceeded to do that, seeming relieved. "I do love you, Ernst, more than ever now."

"I find you fascinating, but—"

She quickly put her finger against his lips. "That much is enough."

They resumed their walk. Ernst hoped never to be tempted this strongly again. Krista's offer had been almost enough to destroy his better judgment.

Why was she so determined to have this commitment? She had had a crush on him when she was fifteen, but that should have passed. She certainly had discovered what effect her new body had on men; she had demonstrated uncanny competence in soliciting his desire. She could have another man if she wanted. At this stage Ernst did not see himself as the best of prospects. Yet she had fastened on him instantly and persistently. Perhaps that was part of his reason for demurring; he distrusted what he did not understand,

and he did not fathom her motive. Surely she did like him, and did want to marry him, and would deliver on any promise relating to it that she made. But that could not be the whole story.

He did not think she would lie to him if he asked her the right question. But she was capable of avoiding that question. He would have to figure out what it was. Then he could decide.

Ernst was afraid that he would be assigned to the SS Regiment "Liebstandarte Adolf Hitler" in Berlin. That unit had a bad reputation. It had been commanded by Sepp Dietrich, but had been so inefficiently run that it was completely lacking in military discipline. The inspector of the SS VT, Major General Hauser, was a former Wehrmacht General, a traditional Prussian soldier who supported proper training and competence. But he had found it hard to implement his policies in the face of Dietrich's resistance. It was common gossip among the troops that Berlin was fit only for misfits.

But to Ernst's great relief he was assigned to the "Deutschland" regiment in Munich. This was commanded by Major Felix Steiner, one of the more remarkable officers in the SS. He had been a member of a Storm battalion in the World War: one of the elite units pulled from the front lines to break the deadly cycle of trench warfare. He was convinced that the future belonged to special groups which could strike with lightning-like rapidity and force, fragmenting the opposition, and then destroy the dislocated fragments. He had resigned from the Wehrmacht in the face of opposition to his theories and come to the SS, which had been starved for good officers. He had instituted his theories of training and command there with what was beginning to look like remarkable success. Ernst knew just enough of the Major's policies to be excited.

Steiner had done away with barracks drill, concentrating instead on athletics. He was turning his soldiers into cross-country experts of the hunter-athlete type. He had reduced the distinctions between enlisted men and officers, fostering camaraderie between them in the face of hardship. Unit Spirit was highly emphasized. Men and officers competed together. Doors were left open in the barracks. All future officers had to serve two years in the ranks, as Ernst himself was doing. Certainly they would not forget the concerns of the ordinary soldiers.

Ernst threw himself into the training with a will. He soon found himself in effective charge of a battle group, which was the basic unit of Steiner's force. Such groups were supposed to be well versed in military teamwork, but still capable of functioning as regiments. The theory seemed good to Ernst, but it was apparent that the unit—indeed, all of the SS VT—suffered from a lack of officers. In the past recruitment had been severely limited, because of the competitive influence of the Wehrmacht, and most of its recruits had come from rural areas. The same was true of its officers at every level. The units compensated for this with fanatical devotion and unity, but the lack was still felt. Thus anyone with good potential promptly rose to responsibility, and Ernst quickly became important.

Instead of the Wehrmacht's regulation rifles, they trained with more mobile and effective weapons, such as submachine guns, hand grenades and explosives. They dressed in camouflage instead of regulation field service uniforms. And they learned how to deploy rapidly. They were able to cover three kilometers in full gear in twenty minutes. That made the eyes of conventional units pop.

There was other things Ernst liked about Major Steiner, though he could not say so. The man gave Heinrich Himmler no respect, refused to marry, and refused to leave the Church. Ernst knew that Himmler was second only to Hitler in importance, but he was not a tenth the man Hitler was. Himmler was a pompous functionary, barely competent, and Ernst hoped never to encounter him directly. As for marriage—it was indeed expected of officers, but they had to choose approved brides, which greatly limited the romantic aspect. Ernst had been freshly reminded of this by Krista's proposal. Sometimes marriage just wasn't right for a man, and it was good to see a key officer asserting himself in this manner. Finally the matter of the Church: there were no harassing call-outs here. How could there be, when the Major openly espoused his Church membership?

So Ernst really liked this unit, and did all he could to make it a success.

Then Major Steiner summoned Ernst to his presence. "I have what I hope is not bad news for you, candidate," he said grimly. "You have been directed to appear before Reinhard Heydrich himself. The papers for your reassignment are now being processed."

"But I have done nothing!" Ernst protested, horrified.

"You have done everything to be the best SS soldier in my command," Steiner responded. "This I have told the Commander. I have begged him to allow you to complete your training with me. He will not relent. Perhaps he has a special assignment for you. I am not allowed to inquire."

"A special assignment," Ernst echoed. But what he felt was dread.

Steiner stood and proffered his hand. Silently, they shook hands.

Reinhard Heydrich was an impressive figure, tall and fit. His nose was long, his forehead high, his mouth was wide, his lips full, and his eyes were small and restless, yet possessed of uncanny power when they fell on a person. His voice was high and his speech staccato, almost nervous. He seemed hardly ever to complete a sentence, yet his meaning was quite clear. Ernst was awed by him.

"You were in America," Heydrich said, gesturing in a vaguely westward direction. His hands were long and slender, almost spiderlike in their thinness, but his eyes were predatory. Ernst's feeling of dread intensified. "You have friends there?"

So that was it! His year overseas had made him suspect. "Yes." Ernst would not have tried to lie, even if he had thought he could get away with it. This man would not be asking questions to which he did not already know the answers.

"Who?"

"Only one, sir, actually. An American who was open minded about foreigners. His name was Lane Dowling."

"No women?"

Ernst allowed himself a limited smile. "None there, sir. The American had a girlfriend whom I got to know, but my own girl is German."

"Name them."

"The American's girl was named Quality Smith. Mine is Krista—"

"What kind of name is that? Quality?"

"She is a Quaker. A small religious sect, of pacifist inclination. I believe that some of their names reflect such concerns."

Heydrich seemed to ponder a moment, as if finding this information significant. "How do you feel about the Jews?" he inquired abruptly.

So this related to the Jews! Ernst's American contact with them must have returned to haunt him. "Sir, I am a loyal German and Nazi."

Heydrich smiled. "You are evasive. Answer in detail."

He was stuck for it. "I have no special feeling about the Jews. I knew some in America, and they appeared to be like ordinary people. I did not inquire more closely."

"You do not hate Jews?" Heydrich asked sharply.

"I neither love nor hate them, sir."

"Then how can you be a good Nazi?" Heydrich barked.

Shaken, Ernst fell back on his most private faith. "My believe in Nazism is independent of the existence of Jews. I believe in the Nazi principles of racial purity, anti-Communism, subservience of the individual to the needs of the state, and personal devotion to the Führer. As a troop leader in the Hitler Youth I met the great man himself, and he spoke to me and shook my hand. I watched *Triumph of the Will*, the greatest motion picture of all time, the perfect expression of the Nazi way. Since then, in times of private stress or doubt, I have used the swastika as my object of meditation, and it has given me spiritual renewal. It is to my mind an icon of God and a symbol of the *Volk*, the true spirit of the German people. It helped me cope with the strange customs of the Americans." He drew out the silver swastika he always wore.

"You refused to renounce the Church. You still believe in a Christian God." It was an accusation.

"I believe that God expresses His will through Hitler and the Nazi party. I see no need to renounce the Church, which also supports God and therefore the things of God, including the Nazi party."

"So you are saying you would not renounce the Church because that would have implied a partial renunciation of Hitler?"

"To a degree, sir. But I also felt that a true Nazi will not allow himself to be browbeaten by inconsequentials. I and the other Candidates were serving loyally; our Church membership or lack of it had no bearing on that."

"You would have capitulated, if it had not been for the others," Heydrich said. "You were trying to spare them."

The man had uncanny insight. "It is true."

"Your woman. Why is she so eager?"

Was there nothing this man did not know? "I am in doubt."

"Could she have Jewish ancestry?"

Ernst was startled. That had never occurred to him, but it could indeed explain Krista's attitude. If there were a suspicion of Jewishness, to be hidden behind the status of being an officer's wife—but no. It did not make sense. Because any woman an officer married would be subject to the most intense scrutiny, her family tree explored for six generations back. The prospect of marriage would increase the risk of discovery, not decrease it. "I doubt it, sir."

"But you are not sure. So you declined to marry her, until it is known."

"I declined to commit to marry her because I am not at the stage at which marriage is an option for me."

"But if she were a Jew—"

Ernst caught on. "She is not."

"How so suddenly sure?"

"Because you would not be teasing me, cat and mouse, if you did not know. You have traced her lineage and exonerated her. But I will answer: I would not condemn her were she a Jew, but I would not marry her."

"If the machine gun were in your hands, and Jews before you, would you fire?"

"I would if so ordered. But that would be a task not at all to my liking."

"There does seem to be a softness in you concerning Jews. What would you have us do with them?"

"I would have us facilitate their departure from Germany. I see no reason to harm them."

"What of the Gypsies?"

"They are harmless, but they too should leave."

Heydrich's eyes bore piercingly at him. "The fourth generation, on her mother's side. The suspicion of Gypsism, unconfirmed."

Again Ernst was startled. "Krista?"

"Would you marry a Gypsy?"

So that was what made Krista so anxious! She feared that she might have some Gypsy ancestry, and that it would make her unsuitable for a good marriage. So she wanted to seal the marriage first. "The suspicion might be unfounded."

"It might. There seems to be no way to tell, given the quality of the old records. It could be a false alarm. In any event, there is no need for anyone to know. You can marry her if you choose."

Ernst realized that the man's ploy was not finished. "What do you want of me?"

Heydrich smiled, and this time it seemed genuine. "Merely your loyalty."

"I am loyal to the *Führer* and to the—"

"Of course. And to me. For the sake of that lovely girl."

Now Ernst remembered something else that had been whispered about Heydrich. He liked to get evil information on his subordinates—perhaps on his superiors too—with which to blackmail them, so that they could not do any evil to Heydrich. That way the man could trust his people to serve his interest. He had gone to the trouble to find Ernst's vulnerability—which Ernst himself had not known about, before this interview.

"You have an assignment for me," Ernst said, realizing that this was why he had been summoned here. He felt relief rather than dread, now.

"You are quick to comprehend. That is one reason I selected you."

Ernst nodded. It was amazing that it was not his ability or dedication that had qualified him for Heydrich's attention, but his hidden vulnerability. Yet this was a far better outcome than he had feared.

"You speak Spanish."

"German, English, Spanish," Ernst agreed. "I am not truly expert in—"

"It will do. What do you know of Admiral Canaris?"

Yet another surprise. What could any mission of his have to do with that eminent person? "He is head of the *Abwehr*, the military intelligence service. I am sure he is qualified and competent."

"Certainly. But is he completely loyal to the cause?"

"I would not presume to question the loyalty of an admiral!"

"Nor would I," Heydrich responded easily. "But it seems that it does fall on me to verify it. For that I need a skilled, trustworthy, and unknown agent. One who speaks Spanish. One who is ultimately loyal to me."

"But the Admiral—" Ernst protested, aghast.

Heydrich leaned forward, and his eyes were mesmeric in their intensity. "I know the Admiral, and respect him personally. I was once under his command, on a training vessel in the Navy."

Ernst was suffering dawning horror. "And you were expelled from the Navy—"

Heydrich laughed. "I left the navy, but through no doing of Admiral Canaris's. He was a good and fair commander, and he taught me much. Perhaps I am now in Intelligence because of him. We are friends. But there is a question which must be resolved. Were there any betrayal by any person in a position as critical as his, the security of the Reich itself could be seriously compromised. We can not allow any chance of that. We must be certain."

"But I have no notion—I could not—"

"Canaris is a nice man," Heydrich continued relentlessly. "He tends to be easygoing and gentle, and he has too great an affinity for peace to be entirely trustworthy in the eyes of some." His eyes flicked upward, and Ernst felt a chill, realizing that the man was obliquely referring to his own superiors, Himmler or Hitler himself. This was truly critical! "But he is too important to be challenged without ironclad evidence against him. So we must seek that evidence, to convict him or to clear him beyond doubt."

Now those hawklike eyes bore on Ernst again. "You will be my agent in this matter. I hope you are able to exonerate my friend." But those eyes were as cold as those of the death's head itself. The man wanted the truth, whatever it was, and he would act on it.

And Ernst would have to get that truth.

Chapter 5
England

Lane felt unbearably lonely after leaving Quality. He wished there had been some other way. But he had known her attitude about violence and war from the outset, so in that sense he had brought it on himself. It was as if he had now separated from his better self.

His flight testing was in Ottawa. First he had to pass an extremely thorough physical examination. He had never enjoyed such things, but knew he would do well, because he was in excellent health. He was correct.

They brought him to an American-built plane, a bright yellow Harvard. This was heavier and faster than anything he had flown before; its top speed was 210 miles per hour, and it had wing flaps.

The instructor saw him gazing at it. "Think you can handle it, mate?"

"Oh, yes," Lane said quickly. "But not letter perfect."

"That's why I'm along. I'll take her up, then you'll try it. If you get confused, don't bluff; tell me. We want to come down safely too, you know."

Lane suspected that the man thought he would be incompetent. He hoped to refute that. But he could indeed make mistakes. He would much rather suffer embarrassment than a crash.

The plane was equipped with duel controls, so that the trainer could take over at any moment. He took off, leveled it, and turned to Lane. "Take her, mate."

Lane took it. He had been watching carefully, getting the feel of the craft. It was bigger, but not essentially different from the light sports planes he had flown. The underlying principles were the same. In a moment he had the feel of it, as if his nerves were extending out to the wing-tips and tail assembly.

"Bank her left," the trainer said.

Lane did so. Now the feel was different; the response was somewhat alien. But he was catching on to it. It was like shifting gears on a new car: it was apt to be jerky until the left foot got the precise feel of the clutch, but then it was smooth. Unless the gearbox was balky, as some were. Minimum experimentation could get it straight.

"Barrel roll."

Lane went into the slow roll; this was familiar to him, and it helped him gain further understanding of the machine.

"Chandelle."

This was a shift to the side and a climbing turn. It was a maneuver used to get out from under an attacking fighter plane, and with luck reverse the advantage.

"Can you loop the loop?" the trainer asked after routine maneuvers were done.

Lane laughed. "Maybe you could, in this plane. I wouldn't try, and I'd rather be on the ground before you do."

"Lost your nerve, mate?"

"You bet. I don't know much about this airplane, but I just don't think its built for that kind of stress. I'm not suicidal. Give me a plane I know can do it without shearing a wing, and I'll try it. I love to do tricks, if I'm sure of the limits."

"Stand by, then." The man took the controls, sent the plane into a small dive, then brought it up into the steep climb of the loop. Lane saw where he had misjudged it: this was a faster plane than he was familiar with, and it could go farther up without stalling. It could indeed do the loop.

The trainer brought it over the top and back down, completing the circle. "Your turn, mate."

Good enough. Now Lane had confidence in the craft, and he had noted the velocities and attack angles as the loop was performed. He emulated these as well as he could, and managed a somewhat less stable loop.

The man nodded. "You'll do, mate. Take her down."

Lane realized that he had already passed his flying test. Nobody wanted a fool as a pilot, but in battle there had to be nerve and competence, not argument. He had balked at the loop for the right reason, and come through when satisfied that the plane was up to it. He oriented carefully on the landing strip and started down.

"The flaps, mate."

Oh. "I've never had flaps before. Maybe you'd better—"

"I'll talk you through it."

But Lane knew the man would never have let him try the landing, if he had not been almost certain he could do it. This was a significant vote of confidence.

His landing was a trifle wobbly, because of the unfamiliar drag of the flaps, but he followed directions implicitly and made it without event. Only as the wheels touched the pavement did he become conscious of his underlying feeling. It was exhilaration.

Next he reported to the Air Ministry Headquarters in Ottawa for a series of personal interviews. He had to submit several letters of reference from officials in his home town. He had come prepared, and had them with him. The background check took several days.

"You made friends with a Nazi?" the interviewer asked him sharply.

Oops. "Ernst Best, a German exchange student. His father worked for the German Embassy here, so he took two years of college. It happened to be where I was going. I befriended him. We always did disagree on politics."

"Suppose you come up against him in another plane?"

"No way. He's not interested in flying. He does gliding, but otherwise he's landbound."

"What was your interest in a Nazi?"

"None. I didn't care about his politics. Every person is a creature of his own society. In Russia they are Communists, in Germany they are Nazis. They'd be traitors if they weren't. I don't much like either brand of politics. But when one is taken out of his culture, he's different, and my sympathy is for those who are different."

"Why?"

"It's just the way I am. My fiancee is a Quaker pacifist, and I'm not. I can get along with different people."

The interviewer gazed at him for a moment, then moved on. Lane wasn't sure whether his answer was satisfactory. He had heard that one otherwise qualified man had been booted because he had written one bad check to his father. But this was hardly criminal behavior, it was tolerance for other ways. That shouldn't disqualify him. By his reckoning, the world needed more tolerance. It was intolerance that made for trouble. Now why hadn't he thought to say that, and really make his point?

"Your face is scarred. How did this come about?"

"Childhood fight." Lane smiled. "I lost."

"The whole story, please."

"You asked for it. I was sort of weak and clumsy as a child. A friend stood up for me, but then his family moved and I was on my own. For a while the boys were cautious, afraid my friend would return to even the score if they picked on me, but gradually they got back into it. I tried to stand up for myself, and I think I gave a credible account, considering. But I simply lacked the physical power and stamina to make it stick. So I got my face rubbed in the gravel, and suffered moderate but painful lacerations, as the doctor put it."

Lane paused, but the interviewer didn't seem to be satisfied yet, so he went on. "I was unlucky. The abrasions became infected, and the left side of my face swelled up, disfiguring me. It was blood poisoning. I wound up in the hospital. I think my dislike of needles dates from then. I got every kind of blood test, along with X-rays, enemas and pills. I really got to hate that hospital! They were searching for the specific agent of disease, so they could match it to the specific treatment. And they found it. Also, serendipitously, they found a chemical imbalance in my system that accounted for my general malaise. They prescribed medication—I called it horse pills—with a complex formula relating to hormones or trace nutrients or antibodies. I didn't see how mere pills could help, but I took them. At least there was hope.

"And you know, it did work. The blood poisoning passed, my face healed, except for those faint scars, and I felt better. My body filled out and my coordination slowly improved. I was recovering from the malady that had held me back, and maybe making up for lost time, because my growth outstripped that of my peers. I came to match their average in mass and power, then to exceed it. It took them some time to catch on, but after I beat them they did." He smiled. "There's nothing like doing it *back* to a bully to teach him manners. By the time I reached college, my frailty was long gone. But I never forgot what it was like to have to scramble to be not quite as good as others, and I was always nervous about it. I had to prove myself in everything, beating others not by picking fights in the street but in track or wrestling. I got into running and weight lifting, making sure my body would never lose what it had gained."

He looked up, realizing something. "Ernst—that's where I met him. He came out for wrestling too, and I worked out with him. What got me was that he was just like me in size and complexion and hair color, but of a different culture. When he spoke, it was with that German accent, that set him right apart. Just the way my girlfriend Quality was just like any other girl, until she opened her mouth. So I guess I was attracted to each of them for the same reason. They way they spoke, which showed how different they were. Because I'm different too, inside. And I don't think I'm wrong in having those friendships. They're good people, both of them, even if they don't think much of each other."

The interviewer pondered a moment, in that mystical way of his, then went on.

In due course Lane learned that he had passed the character assessment. He was made a Pilot officer in the Canadian Royal Air Force, and his combat flight training began.

Now he got into the good stuff. His combat training was done in a Miles Master, which was a two-seater, gull-winged, all wooden plane with a top speed of 264 mph. It was the fastest trainer in the world. The pilots were trained to operate in three-plane formations called a "vic"; two vics made up a flight, and two flights were a squadron, twelve aircraft. They kept in touch by radio, but it wasn't necessarily clear. They learned that singing in a high voice generated a clearer transmission. "Let's shape up, girls!" someone would singsong teasingly.

They also learned the operative terms: "pancake" meant to land immediately. "Buster" meant to proceed at full speed. "Scramble" meant to take off for battle. "Angel X" meant they were X thousand feet high. "Trade" meant an enemy formation. And "tallyho" was the R.A.F. battle cry. This was Canada, but the R.A.F. was where they were heading, once they were ready. "The greenhouse" was the cockpit of the plane.

The plane had a machine gun, but for training a motion picture camera was substituted. When the trigger was pulled this was activated, recording hits and misses. It was a lot of fun, and Lane was pretty sure he would be able to work with a real gun as effectively when the time came.

They also did do target shooting with a stationary machine gun, and then they fired at box kites towed by Fairey Battles, a light British bomber. They had to learn to recognize both friendly and enemy aircraft. They practiced Morse Code, navigation, night flying, and blind flying. They learned meteorology and the detection of thermals, because the weather could make a big difference when flying. Lane already knew that, of course, but realized that in war he would not be able to choose his flying weather, as he had as a civilian flyer. Also radio transmission procedure, aircraft maintenance, and the care and spot repair of engines and machine guns.

Lane was issued his uniform, indoctrinated into the military routine, and got his identity tags, which were on fireproof composition fiber. He was now a combat flyer.

The other trainees celebrated their success by going out on the town and getting drunk. Lane would have gone along, but he thought of Quality, and couldn't. It was not just that such celebrations were known for womanizing, which he wouldn't do, but that Quality, as a Quaker, would neither touch liquor nor associate with anyone who did. He had not had any since knowing her, and felt it would be a betrayal of her if he did so now. So he remained clean, perforce. Of course his participation in training for combat was a betrayal of Quality's nature too, but somehow that was less personal than the small things. So he remained home, as it were, and wrote her a letter.

After two months of combat training, Lane was transferred to his permanent unit: the 242nd Royal Air Force Squadron in England, a unit flying the all metal Hawker Hurricane. This was a tough and durable fighter with a top speed of around 320 miles per hour, armed with eight Browning .303 machine guns. This was the fastest and fiercest aircraft Lane had encountered, but what fascinated him was the combat gunsight.

The gunsight was a circle with a horizontal crosshair. It had three controls. The first was a key to give power to the sight, making the circle and crosshairs glow. The second was a rheostat which controlled the intensity of the glow. The third was a dial which controlled the size of the circle. The dial could be set for the wingspan of the enemy craft that the pilot expected to engage. When the wingtips touched the edges of the circle, the craft was in range. The eight machine guns were aligned to form a small circular clump of fire at a range of 250 yards. The Hurricane's guns could fire tracer, incendiary, ball, and armor-piercing bullets at a cyclic rate of 9,600 rounds per minute.

Lane whistled. "I pity the enemy plane that gets into range!" But he realized that the enemy plane was likely to have similar firepower, and a similar range. When he got close enough for the kill, he would also be close enough to be killed.

The guns were covered with a wooden shield, to decrease wind resistance and enable the plane to fly faster, as well as to cut wind noise and keep foreign matter out of the barrels. When the guns were fired, the wooden shield was blown away, so a ground crew could immediately tell when a pilot had fired on an enemy. As if they weren't going to take the pilot's word about it?

There was further training and preparation carrying him through the year 1939. There was a permanent flying station in the R.A.F that helped establish a comfortable, homelike atmosphere. A central brick building housed the pilots' bedrooms, restaurant, bar and quiet room. There was a laundry service, and batmen in attendance. The building was surrounded by lawns and tennis courts. The ground crews assigned to each pilot were very protective of that pilot, and would fight, it seemed, at the drop of a hat if anybody said anything against him.

The "wake up" drink of the R.A.F. was tea. Lane had found this quaint at first, but soon enough settled into the habit and developed a liking for it. He also learned to respect the tray of vitamin A pills which sat in the mess with the sign "for night flying personnel only." They did seem to help, when he had night practice, though he wasn't sure whether this was real or imaginary.

The flying uniform was a thick silk-lined "teddy bear" and a fireproof coverall flying suit called a sidka. For very cold weather there was a fur-lined Irving suit. When flying, the pilot wore a parachute, silk gloves under flying mittens, a heavy helmet with earphones, a throat microphone and an attached oxygen mask. The helmet plugged into the radio. The safety belt was a Suddon harness: straps over the shoulders and across the chest to the back.

He received letters from Quality, who had gone to Spain, to his surprise, and seen the civil war there first-hand. She was not a passive pacifist, but an active one; she sought to do whatever good she could in the world. He could hardly fault her for that, but he wished she were well away from that battle-torn nation. Some of what she described horrified him; she should never have been exposed to such horrors. He was relieved when he learned that that war was over and she was all right. He had no liking for the insurgent generals who had turned against their own country and conquered it, but he just didn't like the thought of Quality possibly getting hurt.

In September, Germany invaded Poland. War had been building, and now it had come. Lane had mixed feelings. He had been training for this, and hoped to see action soon. Yet he knew it would have been better if Hitler and the Nazis had never existed, so that peace had remained. He was both eager to put that bully Hitler in his place, and guilty because of the way Quality felt about violence and war.

The 242nd Squadron was transferred to France to help bolster its defenses. Lane was in the Air Component of the RAF, known as the AC. It was stationed between the town of Lille and the river Somme in the northernmost part of the country. The planes did not go near Germany, to Lane's frustration; they did not even do a great deal of drill. They just waited. Since he was not interested in exploring the favors of the local French girls, it was a dull time.

On the ninth of April, 1940, Germany invaded Denmark and Norway. Still the squadron did not act. It was saving itself for the defense of France, and was coordinating with the French, who seemed marvelously efficient in taking no action. They depended on their fancy Maginot Line to the east, and on the sanctity of the territory of Holland and Belgium to the north, buttressed by the British Expeditionary Force. This was part of the Air Component of that Force, commanded by General Gort.

On the 10th of May, Germany invaded Holland and Belgium, on the way to France. Now at last it was time for action. The planes went out: two bomber squadrons and two fighter squadrons. Lane did not; he was in one of the fighter squadrons held in reserve for the moment. This was because the situation was so confused that the commander did not know where the greatest need would be.

It turned out to be hell out there. The moment the bombers approached the advancing German lines, they were attacked by swarming German planes. The fighters tried to engage the Germans, but were outnumbered and outpiloted. They took horrendous losses. In fact, the unit suffered 50% casualties, and it was doubtful whether they had inflicted significant casualties in return. At first it was hoped that some planes were merely late coming back, but as time passed it was obvious that they had been lost. When a plane ran out of fuel, it had to come down wherever it was. Probably that had not been the problem; they had been shot down.

Lane went out the following day. The German positions were not where he had been told; they were closer. In fact they were rushing west at an alarming rate, directly toward the Air Component base. Caught by surprise, Lane and the other planes of his squadron tried to attack the Luftwaffe bombers, but could not even get close before being engaged by the snarling ME-109's. He quickly discovered that he was up against a superior plane; the Messerschmitt could outclimb, outdive, and outspeed him. But he was able to turn inside it, and that was his one advantage. Lane wanted to make a scrap of it, but he saw two of his companions go down, and the others turned to flee. He was in danger of being isolated in the midst of the enemy, which was sure disaster. He had to turn tail himself.

And the retreat was worse than the brief battle, because the Germans pursued, shooting down two more before quitting the chase. It had been mostly chance, Lane realized, that had saved him from that fate. He just had not been among those targets chosen by the hunters.

But there was no safety back at the field. No sooner had he landed than he had to refuel and take off again—for a field farther to the south. Because it was apparent that the Germans could not be stopped, and would soon overrun this field.

That was the beginning of a continuing disaster. The unit was reinforced by several more fighter squadrons, but communications were poor and coordination with the ground forces was worse. Contact with the Advanced Air Striking force was lost; the Germans had driven a wedge between the northeast and northwest of France. The lack of ground transportation was another critical problem; many units were forced to abandon equipment and burn planes which were too damaged to fly safely. There were stories of other squadrons which would retreat one day, fly a mission the next, and retreat again that night. Lane's unit retreated to an airfield near Amiens, bedded down for the night, and woke just in time to take flight before Guderian's advancing tanks. They were shunted from one airfield to another, receiving scant welcome anywhere. It became every man for himself, with each pilot scrounging for his own food, servicing his own plane, and sleeping under its wing. They had to search for enough fuel to take off and fight. And still the Germans came on, relentlessly.

By May 19 the AC was forced to retreat entirely from the continent. The squadrons were posted to Kent in England, their pilots abandoning everything but the clothes on their backs as they fled. They had lost half of their planes at that point. It wasn't better for the land forces; they were coalescing about a town at the seacoast named Dunkirk, hard-pressed by the Germans.

They hoped to continue flying missions over France, but the range of the Hurricanes was not enough for them to fly prolonged missions across the channel. They were unable to coordinate properly with the other units. About all they could do was harass the Germans who were closing in on Dunkirk, and try to protect the boats that were carrying the allied troops across to England. That was a horrendous business; there were well over three hundred thousand stranded men, and every type of boat was being marshaled to bear them to safety.

But the fact was that none of the unit's planes were considered truly flightworthy at this point. Not one had escaped France unscathed, and the pilots were demoralized. They had given what was best described as a poor account of themselves. Seven of them had died, two were wounded, and one had a nervous breakdown. As the Dunkirk evacuation was nearing completion, because by some miracle the Germans were not bringing full force to bear, the remnant of the 242 was transferred a hundred and fifty kilometers north to Coltishall, a place so small it wasn't on the map. There they had to share quarters with the 66th Squadron. It was near Norwich, where they had to go for any big-town action.

The new Squadron leader was Douglas Bader, a man who had lost both his legs because of an accident in 1930. The pilots expected him to fly very little, because of his handicap. They were afraid that he would be just another figurehead.

Douglas Bader, they soon learned at a detailed briefing, had crashed his bulldog fighter while attempting a dangerous aerobatic maneuver. The surgeon was forced to amputate his right leg above the knee, and his left leg about six inches below the knee. They fitted him with metal artificial legs, and he proceeded to rebuild his life. His determination was amazing. He taught himself to walk again, and to dance, to play golf—exceedingly well—to play squash, and above all, to fly. In fact he flew as well as he ever had. But the R.A.F., more conservative than Bader, decided that we was medically unfit for duty and forced him to retire. Only after Britain entered the war did the R.A.F. decide to allow him back in the service. His obvious qualification finally prevailed against their prejudice.

He was posted to a Spitfire squadron, where he soon became a flight leader. But he was impatient with the R.A.F.'s tactical methods. The Fighter Command theoreticians believed that modern fighters were too fast for dogfight tactics. (At this point Lane and the other pilots burst out laughing, somewhat bitterly. They had been virtually annihilated by German fighters who had practiced dogfighting.) The only approved method for a fighter attack on a bomber formation was for each three plane vic to line up and play follow-the-leader, firing in orderly turns during the run. Bader argued that these tactics exposed the fighter's vulnerable belly to the bomber's tail-gunner. ("Now he tells us!") He favored the use of dogfight tactics similar to those found effective in the War, and the use of several fighters to gang up and join fire against a single bomber. ("*What* single bomber?") He advocated using the controlling aspects of height and sun in aerial combat.

During the evacuation of Dunkirk, Douglas Bader saw his first combat. He vindicated his views by scoring his first three enemy kills.

So it was that he was given command of the 242nd Hurricane squadron, the only Canadian squadron in the R.A.F. It was obvious that he was being safely put out of the way, just as was the squadron: a man battered into uselessness, in charge of an essentially foreign squadron battered into uselessness. It was an insult to each of them.

Lane and the other pilots were ready in one of the two dispersal huts when Bader came to take command. He was unannounced, but there wan no mistaking the lurching walk of the man. He had to kick his right stump forward to move the leg, then kick it down to straighten the hinged knee. But he did move along well enough.

No one moved. The pilots just studied him quietly. They could do this because they had not been introduced; theoretically they did not know who he was.

"Who's in charge?" Bader demanded.

A heavyset young man rose slowly. "I guess I am."

"Isn't there a flight commander?"

"There's one somewhere."

"What's your name?"

At this point the man realized that he had carried the masked insolence about as far as he dared. "Turner. Sir."

Bader turned angrily and left the hut. He lurched to the nearest Hurricane and strapped himself in. He started it, taxied out to the field, took off, and proceeded to give a display of aerobatic flying that drew them all from the hut to watch. Lane was amazed. This man was *good*!

When he landed, Bader did not take any further notice of the Canadian pilots. He walked to his car and drove off.

"I think maybe we have a commander," Lane remarked. The others nodded. The next time Bader appeared, he would be treated with proper respect.

The next morning Bader called all of them into his office. They reported with alacrity, and were absolutely respectful, but the man was unforgiving. "A good squadron looks smart. I want to see no more flying boots or sweaters in the mess. You will wear shoes, shirts, and ties." He glanced at Turner. "Do you have a problem with that?"

"Yes, sir. Most of us don't have any clothes except what we're wearing now."

Bader stared at him. "I am not a man for humor. Is this the truth?" He looked at the rest of them.

"Yes, sir," they chorused.

"How did this happen?"

They told him of their disastrous flight from France, and their treatment since. "Our requests for allowance due to loss of kit have been turned down," Lane said. Ordinarily those who had lost their uniforms and personal things in the line of duty were allowed to draw replacements.

"Well, that will change," Bader said. "Order new uniforms, all of you, from the local tailors. I will guarantee that they are paid for. Meantime, for tonight, you beg or borrow shoes and shirts from someone. I've got some shirts, and you can borrow all I've got. Okay?"

"Okay," they agreed, taking heart.

"Now I want to hear about your engagements in France."

They told him, and he listened attentively. His open and friendly manner transformed their attitude toward him; not only was he an expert pilot, he was a decent person. They had judged him by his metal legs, and he had judged them by their sloppy clothing, but those judgments had evaporated.

Next came spot flight testing. He took them up in pairs, and discovered that all of them flew well (those who hadn't, had not survived), though their formations were somewhat sloppy by his standards. The next few days took care of that. When Lane's turn came, he looked down and was amazed: the airfields were camouflaged so as to be nearly invisible from the air. This had not been the case in Canada or France—but Canada was not in immediate danger of being bombed, and France—well, everything about that had been a disaster. When landing at night an R.A.F. pilot would give the colors of the day with a flare gun, or flash the letters of the day in Morse code from an amber light in the tail assembly to authenticate his identity. This was no casual thing; an enemy plane could cause a great deal of damage if allowed to sneak in unchallenged.

Bader made good on his word about the uniforms, and they sharpened their appearance and their flying skills. Morale was restored, and the squadron began to thrive.

But there was another problem. The 242's engineer officer, Bernard West, told Bader that the ground crew's spare parts and supplies had been lost in France, and that his requests for resupply had been denied. They would be unable to keep the planes even remotely flightworthy much longer.

"Well see about that," Bader said grimly. Lane was there when he put in a call to the supply officer.

"Coltishall is a new station," the supply officer responded. "I literally haven't got enough staff to type out the forms."

"To Hell with your forms and your blankets and your blasted toilet paper! I want my spares and tools, and I want 'em damned soon."

But nothing happened. Lane and the others waited with increasing interest; they knew that Bader seldom brooked being ignored. Sure enough: a few days later Bader sent a signal to the Group Headquarters. 242 SQUADRON NOW OPERATIONAL AS REGARDS PILOTS BUT NONOPERATIONAL REPEAT NONOPERATIONAL AS REGARDS EQUIPMENT. That was pretty blunt by R.A.F. standards, and could lead to trouble.

It did. Soon Bader was ordered to report to Air Chief Marshall Sir

Hugh Dowding. Lane and the other pilots saw him off. "Sir, we just want you to know—"

"That you know I'll get those damned supplies," he finished, and drove off.

They exchanged glances. That had not been their concern, at this point. They were afraid that he was going to be relieved of command for his impertinence.

But they had underestimated him again. It was the supply officer and his superior who were replaced. Next day the 242's supplies arrived.

An anonymous cartoon appeared on the bulletin board. It showed two airplanes being shot out of the air simultaneously by one. They were labeled "Supply." Below was a scrawled "five" marker, suggesting that someone had upped his notches from three to five. If Bader noticed it, he gave no indication. That was significant, because he was a stickler for form, and would have removed anything he felt was inappropriate.

On August 13, 1940, the "Battle Over Britain" began. The Germans sent everything they had, determined to blast the British out of the sky so that they could bomb with impunity. The British met them bravely, refusing to be intimidated. Day by day, the battle in the air raged.

But the 242 squadron was stationed too far to the north to take part in that action. Its fighters were being held in reserve, to protect the northern industrial areas. Bader chafed at this, and so did Lane and the other pilots. Bader repeatedly asked for his squadron to be deployed to a more southerly base for combat duty.

He could not be denied. On August 30 the squadron was ordered to deploy to Duxford. But fifteen minutes after they took off, they were ordered back to Coltishall. Bader, furious, put in a call. An hour later they were ordered to deploy again, and this time no counterorder was issued. They arrived in Duxford by noon.

There they had lunch in the dispersal area, waiting impatiently for action. Finally, near five o'clock, the phone rang: "242 Squadron scramble!"

That was it. They were finally back in action, and this time they were far better prepared than they had been in France. The four vics, a total of twelve planes, took off in order: Red Section under Bader, called Laycock; then Yellow, where Lane was, Green, and Blue.

"Laycock Red leader calling steersman. Airborne. What height?" That was the query about the position of the enemy planes.

"Angels Fifteen. Trade approaching North Weald. Vector one-nine-zero. Buster." That meant that the enemy planes were at 15,000 feet, heading toward North Weald. The squadrons were to go ten degrees west of south, at full speed.

The sun was in the west, and the enemy liked to try to come out of the sun. Therefore Bader ignored the steersman's instruction and moved in a direction calculated to negate that advantage. His sections checked in: "Yellow Leader—in position." "Green Leader—in position." "Blue Leader—in position."

"Blue Leader to Laycock Red Leader, three bogies, three o'clock low."

Bader ordered the Blue section to investigate the three dots. The rest of the squadron continued toward North Weald on an intercept course.

"Red Two here—bandits ten o'clock level."

As they got closer, Lane was able to make out two boxes of thirty or more bombers, each moving toward North Weald at about 12,000 feet. Then he saw another group of dots above the bombers: fighters, higher than the 242.

"Green section—take on the top lot."

The Green vic climbed and peeled off to the right. That left the Red and Yellow sections—six fighters to engage the bombers. They were mostly twin-engined Dornier 17's, the so-called "flying pencils," with a few ME-110 twin-engined fighters interspersed among them. The bombers were headed northeast and were grouped in rows of four to six.

Bader's squadron headed south by southeast to intercept them from slightly above, out of the sun. He led his section on a dive through the third line of bombers. The hurricanes opened fire. The startled bombers scattered.

The Yellow Section followed, and scattered the bombers further. Then all six Hurricanes climbed up to attack the scattered Germans.

It was a piece of cake. Lane oriented on his target, and it was helpless. He fired, and scored, and the bomber went down. He oriented on another, and scored on it, but couldn't get a critical hit.

Now all the bombers were fleeing, and their fighter escort with them. The sky was clear. The Hurricanes regrouped and headed for home.

When they landed, and everyone was present, Bader quizzed his pilots. It turned out that the 242 had made twelve enemy kills, and damaged several more—without suffering a single loss. And the enemy had fled without dropping a single bomb on North Weald.

There was now no doubt: Bader's strategy was sound. He had taken the broken 242 Squadron and made it into a completely successful striking force. The way to foil the Germans was threefold: use large formations of fighters to inflict maximum damage, scramble early—as soon as the enemy was identified—so as to gain maximum height, and use the three combat principles of height, sun and close-in shooting. He argued his case before his superiors, and was given the opportunity to test his theories on a larger scale.

On September 2 Bader was given control of the 310 and 19 Spitfire squadrons at Duxford. Lane and the other 242 pilots became de facto instructors, helping to show the new pilots how to integrate the Bader way. In three days of intensive practice the three squadrons were able to scramble in just over three minutes. They were ready—they hoped.

The Battle for Britain was still being waged. The Germans seemed determined to prevail, making what seemed like suicidal sallies, and all over south Britain it was a struggle to hold them back. London was taking a beating.

On September 7, in the late afternoon, they were given the order to intercept a German bomber formation. They scrambled, but it was already late; they had not been given enough warning.

Bader was not only a good flyer and an effective leader, he was a master at disarming tension among his pilots before combat. When the unit scrambled Lane heard his voice on the radio. "Hey, Woody, I'm supposed to be playing squash with Peter this afternoon. Ring him up, will you, and tell him I'll be a bit late." "Woody" was Wing Commander Woodall, who gave them instructions from the ground. This was hardly mission business!

"Never mind that now, Douglas," Woody replied, and tried to get on with business. "Vector one-nine-zero. Angels 20."

Bader pretended to ignore that. "Oh, go on, Woody. Ring him up now." Lane was smiling, feeling the tension draining away. It was almost as if they weren't on their way to a life and death struggle with the enemy.

"Haven't got time, Douglas," Woody, the straight man, said patiently. "There's a plot on the board heading for the coast."

Still Bader pretended to ignore it. "Well, damned well make time! You're sitting in front of a row of phones. Pick one up and ring the chap."

"All right, all right, for the sake of peace and quiet I will. Now would you mind getting on with the war?"

And Lane was laughing, having gotten the war into perspective. That was just as well, because they were headed into trouble, and could afford no tension-induced mistakes.

They had reached 15,000 feet when they spotted a formation of Dorniers and ME-110's at least 5,000 feet above them, and ME-109's even higher. This was similar to what they had broken up without a loss before, but this time they lacked the critical advantages of height and surprise. Lane climbed with Bader's squadron to engage, but the Spitfires climbed more slowly than the Hurricanes and weren't there in time. Thus the Hurricanes engaged without any real support. Even so, they scored eleven confirmed kills. Bader took some cannon shells in his left wing, and the others suffered similar damage. One pilot was killed, another was shot down but survived the crash landing with a cut face, and four other planes were damaged. The Spitfires had participated only in showing a reserve force, but that had counted for something, because it convinced the Germans to break off the engagement. It was possible that there would have been heavier losses otherwise.

"We've got to scramble earlier," Bader said. "We have to gain great height before engaging." And Lane knew that he was telling exactly that to his superiors. Next time the order to intercept an enemy formation would come sooner.

It did. Two days later the scramble order came early, and the three squadrons reached 22,000 feet before spotting the enemy bomber formations. This was much better. All three squadrons engaged, and by the time it was done they recorded 20 victories at the cost of four Hurricanes and two pilots. As engagements went, it was phenomenal, because the Germans were hardly pushovers. The ragtag band of foreign flyers had become one of the outstanding R.A.F. units.

Bader still wasn't satisfied. He lobbied for a still larger group of fighters that would be able to inflict even heavier damage. Too many enemy planes were getting away, and they would only return for more mischief on other days.

He was given his chance. Air Vice Marshall Leigh-Mallory was now a convert to the Bader strategy, and other squadrons in 12 Group were being urged to mirror his tactics of breaking up enemy formations by diving through their centers. He had even nicknamed the 242 the Disintegration Squadron in honor of this technique. So on September 10 he was given two more squadrons, the 302 and the 611, and there came into existence a new outfit: the 12 Group Wing. All of the original 242 pilots felt the pride of it.

On the 15th, 12 Group Wing was scrambled twice to meet Luftwaffe attacks. The second time they were scrambled late, and forced to attack from below. They hated it, but had to make do. Still, when the engagements were reviewed and tallied that evening, 12 Group Wing claimed 52 confirmed victories and 8 more possibles. What a day!

Bader was to receive the Distinguished Service Order in recognition of his accomplishments. But they weren't done yet; the Germans were still coming, day by day, still determined to bomb Britain into surrender.

On the 18th they scrambled in the afternoon, and were cruising just below a thin layer of clouds at 21,000 feet when they spied two groups of German planes about 5,000 feet below. There were some forty planes—and they were all bombers! No fighter escort.

"Fish in a barrel," Lane murmured, hardly believing it. Apparently the Nazis were so determined to bomb that they had stopped making fighters. That was their folly.

When the action was done, they had claimed 30 bombers destroyed, plus 6 probables and two more damaged. There had been no casualties on the British side.

By the end of September the German attacks were becoming less frequent and destructive. The Battle over Britain continued, but the days of the heavy bomber raids were coming to a close. The R.A.F. was establishing its supremacy over the skies of Britain. This aspect of the war was being won.

But Lane knew that this was only the first phase. The war would not be over until the Nazis were defeated on their home soil. That would be no fish-in-a-barrel shoot.

Indeed it was not. Lane went on a routine mission, and got ambushed by a German fighter plane, and had to pancake. He brought his plane down safely, but his face had been scratched by shrapnel from an enemy round and the blood impaired his vision.

A medic came to attend to him as he climbed out of the cockpit. "I'm okay," Lane protested. "It's just a scratch. Just let me get cleaned up."

"That's no bleeding scratch," the medic said. "You've got a round in your head!"

Lane laughed. Then he passed out.

Things were hazy after that. They kept him sedated, and there was surgery. When he recovered full consciousness, his head was thoroughly bandaged and his vision blurry.

He was given leave as he recovered. Unable to stand and watch others flying when he could not, he went to London—and was surprised by the changes there. As war loomed closer to Britain, nearly everyone in London carried a gas mask. A large percentage of the people were in uniform, including the women. Newspapers carried features such as "These Are Your Weapons, and How to Use Them." Balloons attached to cables were hung at an altitude of about five thousand feet, to prevent German bombers from flying low enough to aim accurately. Lane, like other pilots, didn't much care for the balloon barrage system, because balloon officers called what they did "flying." Also, when visibility was poor, British planes sometimes got snagged on the cables. Just which side were those balloons on?

When his recovery was complete, he reported for duty, but was met by a curious diffidence. The other pilots seemed glad to see him, but were vague about plans.

Bader gave him the bad news. "Your body is fine, your brain is fine. But that wound did things we don't understand to your vision. Maybe you will recover completely, in time. But we can't risk you in a plane now."

"But I still have missions to fly!" Lane protested. "There's a war to see through!"

"You need perfect vision to fly. Otherwise you will be a risk to yourself and others in the squadron. Would *you* want to be dependent for your life on another man who couldn't see straight?"

Lane saw the way of it. "But I'm otherwise fit. There must be something I can do. I can't let a little injury wash me out."

"I understand." Bader glanced down at his own legs. He understood better than any man alive. "Your fiancee—she's in Spain?"

"Yes. Only I haven't heard from her since June. The Quakers had to leave Spain, but she wasn't with them. I've been worried sick."

Bader nodded; it was evident that he had known this. "Would you like to investigate our facilities in Gibraltar? I understand they may be expanded, to give us better leverage in the Mediterranean theater. It would be better if a battle-experienced flyer had a look."

"Gibraltar! That's near Spain!"

"Which remains an officially neutral country. Possibly a passport could be arranged."

Lane saw what the man was doing. He was giving him a chance to try to check on Quality directly. Lane reached up to shake Bader's hand.

Chapter 6
Berlin

Of course Heydrich did not send Ernst straight to Admiral Canaris. Canaris, as the head of the *Abwehr*, the military intelligence unit, was far too canny to accept unknown personnel. Instead he was provided as a routine assignment of personnel to Colonel Oster, Canaris's chief of staff. Oster was a close friend of the Admiral's, and was also under suspicion. Ernst was given the identity of Lieutenant Osterecht, who was a real man but who seemed to have been lost in some distant action; Ernst was in effect taking over the man's career, assuming verifiable credentials. If the real Osterecht ever turned up alive or dead, Heydrich would try to conceal the information until Ernst could be withdrawn. Thus he traded his black SS uniform for the gray Wehrmacht uniform.

The Abwehr offices were in a shabby apartment house beside Berlin's Landwehr Canal. The building was officially designated 72-76 Tirpitz-Ufer, but it was nicknamed the "Fuchsbau"—the Fox's Den—because of its labyrinthine passages, innumerable doors and gloomy offices. The Abwehr offices were on the third floor of Fox's Den, and were shielded from unwanted visitors by a folding metal grille.

Admiral Canaris's office was at the end of the passage and had a small outer office maintained by his serious secretary Wera Schwarte. Oster's office was down the hall, with his assistant, the civilian Dohnanyi, adjacent. Ernst was given a quick tour upon his arrival, meeting the Admiral only to shake hands, before being shunted down to what seemed like the smallest and gloomiest of the available chambers where he would be working.

Ernst had of course done his homework, and knew Oster's background. The man had been decorated for gallantry several times during The War, and was a hero. But he was also temperamental, volatile, arrogant and cynical. It was said that Canaris believed that Oster's exterior concealed a serious-minded man who subscribed to a simple and straightforward code of soldierly and Christian conduct. But others considered him to be a superficial careerist, irresponsible, careless, brash and peremptory, who would not last a moment without the Admiral's support. He seemed to be obsessed with women and horses, with an insatiable appetite for new varieties of each. His womanizing had led to the end of his army career in 1932; only Canaris's intercession had enabled him to return to the service in 1937 as an Abwehr officer.

But it was not Ernst's business to remark on any of this. It was his business to do honestly and well anything that he was assigned to do, and to make mental but no other note of whatever he learned about the ultimate loyalty of those with whom he worked. He was a little fish in an alcove of a pond which was not enormous. At a later date he would report what was relevant to Heydrich, his only concern being accuracy.

His actual assignment was in *Abteilung* II, the division of the Abwehr concerned with Sabotage, Subversions and Special Duties. Within this he was in Section II, under Lieutenant Colonel Erwin Lahousen, an Austrian who had joined the Abwehr after the Anschluss.

Lahousen was glad to see him. "We have a lot to do, and too few competent people." He lifted a brow at Ernst. "You are competent?"

Ernst spread his hands. "I hope so. I have not before done precisely this type of work, but am a quick learner. I'm still not sure why—"

"We did put out a requisition. So your training is not sabotage? That does not necessarily reflect on your competence. It may be that someone saw such promise in you that he could not let you miss this opportunity. Do you have any special abilities?"

"Some. But I have to say that it may not be competence that brought me here. I had what I prefer to term a personality conflict with my commander."

Lahousen shook his head. "We know about that sort of thing, here; if you follow orders you will be all right. What abilities?"

"I have studied both American English and Spanish, and believe I speak those languages well."

"Trilingual. That must be it." The colonel signaled a man in the hall. "Fetch Heinz."

In a moment a somewhat stout man appeared, evidently long out of training. "Heinz, we have here a man who speaks American," the colonel said.

Heinz turned to Ernst. “Good morning, comrade,” he said in accented English.

“Don’t call me ‘comrade’!” Ernst snapped in the same language. “That’s a Communist.”

Heinz smiled. “And you could pass for American,” he agreed. “You sound just like one, arrogance and all.” He turned to the colonel. “He is good, sir. Better than I am.”

“Fetch Eva.”

Soon a middle aged woman appeared. “Señora,” Ernst said, standing.

“You are from Spain!” she exclaimed in Spanish.

“No. I studied it, and I like to be competent in what I do,” Ernst explained.

She turned to Lahousen. “Like a native,” she said.

The colonel smiled. “We shall surely have good use for you. But right now we are in need of a planner for commando operations. You will be that.”

“In what theater? It makes a difference.”

“Polish.”

“But I don’t speak—”

“There will be those who do. You can get started without them.”

So it was that Ernst found himself studying maps of Poland, and researching the German/Polish border. They were planning to take Poland! He had suspected it, but had not expected such abrupt confirmation.

Ernst did his work, and knew it was good. He had organized outings as a Youth leader, and understood how things fitted together. But one thing was missing. “I’ll need to see some of the terrain personally,” he told the colonel. “There could be things the maps and reports don’t tell us. One road blocked by temporary construction, and—”

“I anticipated that need,” Lahousen said. “It is time to consult with the colonel.”

He brought Ernst to Colonel Oster’s office. There was a board bearing the proverb AN EAGLE EATS NO FLIES. Two men were there: Oster, whom Ernst had seen but to whom he had never spoken, and a civilian. Colonel Lahousen, realizing that there could be awkwardness, made a quick introduction. “Sir,” he said to Oster, “I have brought Lieutenant Osterecht to confer with you and Captain

Dohnanyi about the next stage of our operation. He needs authorization to inspect the terrain in person."

"Now that is an amusing coincidence," Oster said. "My friend was just about to travel in that direction. The Lieutenant can accompany him, in case he needs his shoes polished. I will suggest this to the Admiral."

The colonel smiled, acknowledging the humor, but Ernst could tell he didn't appreciate it. It was the type of humor directed at underlings whose opinion didn't matter. Since that was a fair description of Ernst at the moment, there was nothing to be done about it. Oster lacked the authority to make assignments, but did control access to Admiral Canaris; therein lay his power. Ernst had quickly discovered how important personality was; it seemed that almost every officer had to be polite to an obnoxious superior.

Ernst did travel with Dohnanyi, and found the man surprisingly compatible. He had a good car and a civilian attitude. "I'm not a captain," he said as they drove. "I'm actually an anti-militarist crammed into the unaccustomed uniform of a wartime supernumerary and assigned the rank of captain purely as a matter of protocol. I feel quite out of place in an Abwehr headquarters geared towards military order and efficiency."

"I am in the military," Ernst said. "But I feel out of place in the Abwehr myself. It is quite different from what I have known."

"To be sure! It must seem strange to you to hear officers cursing the military."

"I have not heard any—"

"You are too kind. A number have been cashiered from the service, and restored only because of the Admiral. They hold grudges against the system. I understand you had trouble in your prior unit; perhaps that is why you were sent to this hotbed of dissension."

"No one has said that to me," Ernst said carefully. Was the man fishing for some disloyal statement from him? Testing him, the way they had tested him in his foreign languages?

"And you do not know that many of us staunchly oppose the Hitler regime?"

Ernst was shocked. "I can not believe that! The Führer—"

"May be a madman. He is bringing us to a war that can destroy us. Do you think this present mission is for peace?"

This had to be a test! If Ernst failed to protest, he would be turned in for disloyalty to the Fatherland. Yet the man sounded sincere. "I think this mission is for war, yes. Because a great nation must be prepared for anything. If Poland attacks us—"

Dohnanyi laughed. "Scant chance of that! I am sure you are not that naive."

"I do not question the decisions of my superiors. If it is decided that Poland represents a threat to—"

"Nor that naive, either. You know we are preparing to put down Poland, which has been a nuisance for a long time. And that we are even now preparing a nonaggression pact with Russia, and will let them have the far side of Poland."

Ernst was amazed. "Poland, yes, I had gathered that there would be action there. But the Führer would never make a pact with the Communists!"

"But it is true. Hitler is doing it, and I fear disaster for our nation. But it is the regime I serve, and so like you I obey directives. Now we shall inspect the border, and I shall get us across so that you can ascertain what you need of the other side."

"Across?" Ernst asked blankly. "Just like that?"

"Why did you think Colonel Oster had the Admiral send me with you? I have connections in Poland. I am a lawyer, and a good one; I do business there. I have a pass."

So it turned out to be. The border guards allowed the car to pass, and they checked the necessary sites. Ernst had assumed that they would have to sneak across by night between roads, but they drove openly. He was amazed at the sloppiness of the border security.

Meanwhile he pondered the man's words and attitude. Was it possible that there was such a hotbed of treason that its participants were open about it? If so, they were fools. But as he talked with Dohnanyi about other things, he became aware that the man was highly intelligent and possessed of a lawyer's powers of reasoning. This was no fool.

That brought up the question whether this was a trap. Did they suspect that Ernst was really Heydrich's agent? If so, they might expect him to report Dohnanyi, and thus reveal himself. That would cause the lawyer trouble, but would protect the others, because Ernst would never get any evidence on them after his report. But if he played along, pretending to harbor subversive notions, Dohnanyi might report *him*, and they would be rid of him. Either way, no important conspirator would be endangered.

The more he pondered, the more certain he became: Neither Admiral Canaris nor Colonel Oster was a fool, and both well understood the mechanisms of secrecy and spying. They had to be testing him, and his response would determine their acceptance of them. This applied regardless whether they were loyal to the regime or traitorous. So he had to find a way to reassure them without getting himself in trouble. And gradually he worked out a way to do that.

When they returned to the Abwehr, Ernst reported to his immediate superior, Colonel Lahousen. First on the terrain: he had learned what he needed to, and could now complete the planning of commando missions to the region.

"And what of your companion?"

"Captain Dohnanyi was a pleasant companion, but careless in his speech," Ernst said. "I could not take anything he said seriously, for if I did, I would not have been able to travel with him."

The colonel nodded. "Civilians tend to be half crazy, sometimes," he remarked. "It is best to ignore them."

That was all. Ernst did not get in trouble. That was in itself significant, because his proper duty should have been to report Dohnanyi for speaking treason. Colonel Oster had to know the nature of Dohnanyi's remarks—indeed, had probably instructed the man to make them—and Ernst had elected not to report them. Not quite. He had claimed not to take them seriously, but actually he was covering up for the man. That suggested that he had some sympathy. That would have been grounds to remove him from the Abwehr—had they wished to do so. He had become their tacit accomplice in silence.

Except for his secret existence. There was a telephone in Berlin which was safe, and a time when special calls were to be made, and he used that phone at the proper time for his first report directly to Heydrich.

"The civilian Johannes Dohnanyi is anti-military and says that he staunchly opposes the Hitler regime," he said when Heydrich came on. "He speaks treason—but he may be testing me. I have not reported him, and so I may be compromised. As yet I lack evidence on Oster or Canaris."

"I know about Dohnanyi," Heydrich said. "Leave him alone. Oster will trust you if Dohnanyi does—but Dohnanyi may indeed be testing you. Stay with it."

Which was exactly as Ernst had expected. In this respect he had done right.

He could not say that he really liked this kind of intelligence work, but at least he was successful in it. So far. If he became unsuccessful, he might wish he had remained in America.

Early in May the Admiral's order came down: prepare for "Contingency White." This meant that Abwehr I was to increase espionage operations in Poland, to determine the strength and dispositions of Polish army units, while Abwehr II was to prevent the demolition of communications, industrial centers and avenues of transportation which would be of use to the advancing German troops. It was no secret now, within the unit: Poland was the target. Invasion seemed incipient.

Ernst had helped identify two strategically vital communications links: One was the bridge over the Vistual River at Dirschau which carried all rail traffic from Danzig and East Prussia to the Polish interior. The other was the Jablunkov Pass in the Beskid Mountains along its southern border, whose tunnels contained twin rail tracks and connected East Germany, Southern Poland and the Balkans. Abwehr II was supposed to attack these positions before the first shot was fired, and overwhelm their defenders by surprise during peace.

But it had been ascertained that the Dirschau bridge was set with explosives designed to destroy it. Since a defender could detonate the explosives at the first sign of trouble, this made the matter delicate. Ernst discussed it with others, and they finally worked out a suitable plan: they would infiltrate a combat team by barge at another place, whose members would travel separately to a rendezvous, abduct prominent figures among the defenders, and would force them to disclose the location of the explosives. Then they would sneak in and defuse the explosives before the overt attack on the bridge. This would require fine timing and coordination, but should be possible if they prepared well and had no unanticipated misfortunes.

The plan for the Beskids was simpler. This relied on S-groups in the area. S stood for *Spannungsagentun*—agents already established in the country. They would take the command areas, destroy the detonators, and then occupy the tunnels and remove the explosives. After that it would be a simple matter to defend the tunnels from Polish intrusions. The Poles would soon be distracted by the main attack on their country.

But there was more. There was a sizable Ukraine contingent in Poland that chafed under Polish domination. A third point of attention was to use this Ukrainian element to mount insurrections against the government as soon as formal hostilities commenced. That would divert some Polish troops, possibly saving many German lives.

Finally, there was a mysterious request by Heydrich, Ernst's true superior, with the backing of Hitler himself. This was for Abwehr assistance in carrying out a very special operation for the Reichführer SS. This was for a hundred and fifty Polish uniforms, with the proper weapons and paybooks to go with them, and three hundred and sixty four men to be temporarily attached to the SD. What was going on?

It was the civilian Dohnanyi who set Ernst straight on the matter. The man was temporarily adrift while Colonel Oster entertained a buxom young woman in his closed office. "Our vegetarian leader is a dirty player. Didn't you know? Those are the men and materials to be used in the pretense of a Polish attack on the German radio station."

"But why do anything like that? It is senseless."

"You retain a certain priceless innocence. That will be the pretext for the outrage we shall evince. We shall have to teach those vandalizing Poles a lesson. They will attack us first, giving us leave to conquer their country."

Ernst was suitably appalled. He could not believe it. But as the request was honored in detail, he realized that it was. Germany was going to manufacture a pretext for war.

In July Ernst was given a ten day leave. Perhaps the Abwehr still did not trust him, and wanted to see where he went. So he did not go home. Instead he remained in Berlin, where he happened to know that a certain group of girls who had graduated from a female Youth Group were celebrating. He went in civilian clothes and picked up a young woman he happened to see, who he knew was now eighteen.

"Ernst!" Krista exclaimed, surprised.

"Better to pretend you don't know me," he said. "I may be watched, and I am not supposed to be here."

"Then what are you doing here?" she demanded.

"My hand still tingles from your touch. I could not stay away."

She glanced down at her blouse, remembering. Then her gaze lifted. "Exactly what kind of girl do you take me for, stranger?"

"A pretty one."

After a bit of banter, she allowed him to treat her to a meal at a restaurant. They sat as a small table in a corner, and under the table, concealed by the overhanging tablecloth, her legs twined around his. "Oh, Ernst, I have thought of you every day! I would go with you in a moment, if I could."

"And I with you," he agreed. "But I have other duties I can not even tell you about."

"Training must be severe!"

"It must be. I wouldn't know."

She gazed at him, understanding that he was in no regular unit. "When will you be able to marry?"

He spread his hands. "I fear our world will change before that happens."

"And I fear you are not joking. Ernst, I know a place. We can go there, tonight—"

"How I wish I could!" he said, meaning it. "But others would know, and your reputation would be soiled. I will not do that to you."

"How can anyone know, if we do not tell?"

"I met a man who—who knows too much. He told me your secret."

She stared at him. "Secret?"

"Gypsy ancestry. But it can never be proved, and it doesn't matter to me. Only if I wished to marry you, without his approval—"

She continued to gaze into his face. "I can tell you mean it," she said. "You do know, and you do want to marry me, when you were unsure before."

He nodded. "I do. But only when it is right, for both of us."

Her legs moved against his. "I know you mean it, Ernst," she repeated. "I thank you so much for telling me. It has been a burden."

"No need to be, between us."

"At least we must find a place where we can kiss."

That much they managed to do.

On August 23 Dohnanyi's prediction about the pact with the Communists came true: Germany signed a nonaggression treaty with the Soviet Union. Ernst deeply distrusted the civilian's politics, but the man had been right about everything he had said. That suggested that he would continue to be right. But what an awful thing: a deal with the Communists!

In this time of frenzied preparations, Ernst was sent to brief the Admiral on the readiness of each aspect. Canaris was a rather short man, white haired, with bushy eyebrows and a ruddy face but a general air of frailty and shabbiness. He did not look at all like a powerful Reich officer. Even before an underling such as Ernst he seemed somewhat reserved. He was, Ernst knew, a hypochondriac who would not tolerate a sick man in his office. Colonel Lahousen had a cold, which was why he wasn't here; Ernst was healthy.

The Admiral also disliked men who were too tall. Ernst was no giant, but he was substantially taller than Canaris. He tried to diminish his height so as to avoid giving offense.

The man's desk was covered with papers. The Admiral didn't sit at it; he preferred the couch, where it was said he liked to take naps. It was clear that the stories about his lack of interest and aptitude in the bureaucratic process were true. Ernst wondered how the man had ever won the Iron Cross First Class he wore.

In addition, the admiral's two wire-haired Japanese Dachshunds were in the office. Canaris loved animals. Seppel and Sabine were the bane of the Abwehr staff, as they regularly fouled the carpet. But woe betide anyone who spoke harshly of the dogs in the Admiral's presence.

But Ernst suffered a change of awareness the moment the Admiral came to grips with the details of the assignments. He picked up on the key elements instantly. "How many combat operatives do we have in place in Poland?"

"Thirteen hundred, sir. They are spread across the country—"

"Yes, but not all are truly ours. You are counting the forestry staff of Prince Henckel-Donnersmark? They may be invaluable for local information and support, but they aren't trained operatives. You have not given them more than minimal information?"

"That is correct, sir. Only the operatives trained here have real information, and of course even they do not know our specific targets."

"At least they will know better than to waste any bombs on forests. We do not want to harm any wildlife."

Ernst started to smile, then saw that the Admiral was serious. He despised anyone who hated animals. He also did not trust anyone whose ears were too small; fortunately Ernst's were not.

His gaze strayed to the Admiral's model of the light cruiser Dresden, his shelf of books, and the trio of bronze monkeys: See All, Hear All, Tell Nothing. That was certainly the motto, here.

"The Dirschau bridge—coordinating separate groups may be impossible," the Admiral continued. "Too many things can go wrong. The people we abduct may lie to us, and there will not be time to be sure of their information. We must try to get the information separately from two, then compare notes. If the two stories differ, seek a third source. Don't risk it without confirmation—we'll only get the bridge and ourselves blown up."

"Yes, sir," Ernst said, impressed. He had spent weeks working out this plan, and Canaris had spotted its weakness without seeming to think about it.

They reviewed the other projects, and the Admiral's commentary was similarly incisive. He suggested several additional targets for sabotage which Ernst duly noted to relay to Colonel Lahousen. He demonstrated the ability to juggle many options simultaneously. Whatever doubt Ernst had had about the man's competence evaporated; now it was clear why Canaris ran the Abwehr.

In fact, Ernst found himself liking this intelligent, energetic man. What did a sloppy office mean? It was ability and dedication that counted, and Canaris had these qualities in full measure.

"Well, I must go see about fomenting insurrections in the British Empire," the Admiral said at last. "There are Irish who are extremely unhappy with their masters. I only wish Hitler hadn't made that deal with the Communists. Now we have to abandon our support for the Ukrainian independence movement. At least we can help Ukrainians flee the Russian advance. It is terrible the way they suffer under that regime."

That was the end of the session. Canaris had said nothing subversive, except for his criticism of the deal with the Communist regime. Ernst could hardly fault that; he agreed. If that was the worst to be said of the Admiral, the man was clean.

Everything was set for operations against Poland to begin on August 26. But the evening of the 25th the Führer ordered the attack delayed. This threw the Abwehr into a spin. It was too late to convey the order to all of the operatives, some of whom checked in only occasionally, for the sake of security. The fake Polish attack on the radio station was halted, but a related attack on a German border station did occur. There was some gunfire but fortunately no loss of life. Radio contact had been lost with one of the combat groups assigned to take the Jablunkov Pass. The next day they learned that the unit had made two unsuccessful attempts to take the pass, before retreating to the Slovakian border under heavy Polish fire.

"The vegetarian lost his nerve," Dohnanyi remarked cynically, referring disdainfully to Hitler. Ernst wanted to hit him, but kept his peace, knowing the man was needling him. "At least it shows that we underestimated the Polish will to resist. That must be corrected."

"Agreed," Ernst said. He talked to Lahousen about strengthening the attack units wherever possible.

On August 31 the whole thing began again. This time there was no reversal. They received the coded signal *Grossmutter gestorben*, "Grandma's dead," and the invasion was on for the first of September.

On that day Admiral Canaris assembled his senior officers and delivered an inspiring pep talk. Ernst was present only as an unofficial doorman, to see that no unauthorized personnel intruded. He was amazed at the Admiral's demeanor and delivery. He pledged them all to unconditional loyalty to the Führer, concluding with a rousing "Heil Hitler!"

Almost all of the Abwehr operations in Poland were successful.

Unfortunately the Polish defenders had been alerted by the prior attack in the Beskids, so that it was impossible to capture the tunnels before the explosives were detonated. And the Admiral's cautions about the trickiness of the Dirschau bridge mission proved to be well taken; the defenders were able to blow the bridge. But Abwehr agents did manage to occupy the rail junction at Kalthof, save many industrial operations, take nearly all the coal mines of Upper Silesia, and take Katowice before the German troops arrived.

There were further requests for Abwehr activities, and the commandos received praise from many sources. Canaris was very active. He traveled to the front every week, and intensified his plans to encourage insurrections in Ireland, India and Afghanistan. But the devastation of Poland, particularly Warsaw, affected him deeply, and Ernst and the others were aware of this. Canaris helped at least one Jewish dignitary to flee the country, and a Ukrainian Bishop to do the same. He really did care about the people.

But was this any signal of treason? Ernst doubted it.

Meanwhile, Ernst had plenty to keep him occupied. His work in the planning of commando raids put him into contact with an ugly aspect of the Abwehr: the Geheime Feldpolizei, or GFP. It had been established as a police force within the Wehrmacht during the German involvement in the Spanish Civil War. It worked closely with the Gestapo, and contained many members of the SS. The Abwehr was cooperating closely with the SS, and some units were virtually indistinguishable: a given soldier could have crossed over between the SS and the Abwehr and hardly noticed the difference. At times Ernst wasn't quite sure for whom he was working, as he met with representatives of each.

In August the SS VT had gained power; some of its units were assigned to the Wehrmacht to participate in the invasion of Poland. They had not, in general, distinguished themselves. The overall report from the Wehrmacht was that the SS units were not prepared to function as part of a division, suffered inordinately heavy losses, and that their officers were incapable of commanding them in complicated operations. A spokesman for the SS VT retorted that the Wehrmacht had starved them of supplies and refused to allocate sufficient heavy weapons to their units. But Ernst was privately pleased to learn that Steiner's units, where Ernst had been training before Heydrich had taken him for this intelligence mission, had distinguished themselves. Steiner was being proved right.

But once Poland fell, the GFP began arresting as many Poles for sabotage and insurrection as they thought fit, and turning them over to the SS for execution. The practice was so widespread that finally Heydrich himself had to intervene. "Carry out your own executions," he radioed on the twentieth of September. Ernst hoped that this would result in fewer executions, because many of them seemed unwarranted, but it didn't. He was privately disgusted with the thuglike GFP.

The SS commanders, stung by the less than ideal performance in Poland, pushed for the formation of an SS division with its own heavy weapons and supply services. But the Wehrmacht, sensing competition, opposed this. Pressure was intense, and finally Himmler authorized a doubling of the size of the SS VT by incorporating concentration camp guards into it. On November 1 the *SS Tötenkopf* or "Death's Head" division was formed. The whole was unified under a new name: the *Waffen SS*: the "Armed SS."

Then the relationship between the Abwehr and the expanding SS was strained. On November 9 there was an attempt on Adolf Hitler's life. This sparked a frenzied investigation. The Führer was convinced that British intelligence was behind the plot, though there was no evidence to support this. Admiral Canaris had been trying to institute sabotage in England, and had been establishing British connections; could there be double agents among them? The SS thought there could be; Canaris vehemently denied it.

Ernst believed the Admiral. There might be those in the Abwehr who wished Hitler ill, but not Canaris.

Meanwhile, there were frantic preparations for the next major project: the assault on France. Abwehr II was called on to formulate plans for sabotage operations in Belgium and Holland. France's formidable Maginot Line prevented a direct assault on that country, but the defenses of the small nations were much less significant and could readily be breached. Ernst had to research new places and new personnel, and was kept busy for months.

But he did get occasional breaks. He learned that Krista had become a military secretary and was working in a Berlin office. Having met her for the first time, in the guise of Lieutenant Osterecht, he could now date her more openly; their hometown connection was not obvious, and so would not give away his nature as a person other than the one he claimed to be.

She was beautiful, as always. It was a genuine pleasure to be with her. He knew she had arranged to work here in Berlin so as to be near him, and that both flattered and pleased him. His lingering doubt about marriage with her was fading; he had encountered no other woman as appealing. Yet a tiny reservation remained, and it did not relate to her possible Gypsy taint. There was something that made him unwilling to let himself go and love her completely.

So their series of dates were pleasant, and he enjoyed them. But he was for the moment satisfied that marriage was not feasible. Not until he completed his mission, and had Heydrich's leave.

In January 1940 reports from Abwehr I convinced Hitler that the British were planning to occupy Norway. Abwehr II was therefore charged with readying commando operations in Scandinavia. Ernst was suspicious that Colonel Oster was not in sympathy with this, and wished to warn Britain or Norway, but he had no sufficient evidence.

Ernst traveled with Johannes Dohnanyi again, because the lawyer had the necessary connections. He learned that the man was into various subversive endeavors, such as smuggling, illegal art deals and graft. But these connections were ideal for the Abwehr's purpose, because they were hidden. Dohnanyi was adept at covering his tracks. So Ernst reminded himself again that this was a little fish, not worth bothering with, and kept silent.

But the man was happy to talk about himself as they spent tedious hours on the highway. It was almost as if he were proud of the defects in his character. He was a brilliant lawyer (others had confirmed this) who at the age of thirty six had become a personal adviser to the Reich Minister of Justice during the Blomberg-Fritsch case. This had occurred while Ernst was in America, so he had not learned of it at the time. Blomberg had been accused of having relations with a prostitute, and Fritsch had been accused of something done by another man with a similar name; he had been cleared, but had lost his position by then. Since Fritsch had adamantly opposed the expansion of the SS VT, his removal had cleared the path for what it was now becoming. Otherwise there might have been no SS unit for Ernst to join. So he listened with flattering attention.

Dohnanyi had been assigned to review the case and recommend that the charged generals be tried by either a special court, which was Hitler's preference, or a court-martial, which was the military's desire. As it happened, he was an opponent of the Hitler regime, so he recommended for the military. That had brought him into contact with Admiral Canaris and Colonel Oster.

"But why did you oppose Hitler?" Ernst asked.

"I became an enemy of Hitler in 1936, when a rival in the Ministry of Justice discovered that I had a non-Arian maternal grandfather," the man replied bitterly. "With extraordinary effort I was able to obtain a ruling from Hitler that I should receive no detriment from the doubts surrounding my grandfather's pedigree." Ernst, listening, felt a thrill of nervous agreement; this was what Krista suffered. "That experience made me hate National Socialism. For centuries Germans have been free to have what ancestry we please. Why should some bigoted demagogue come and decide otherwise? What is wrong with being non-Arian? Are we not all the people we are? To be condemned because of nothing we have done in life, simply because an ancestor had a different belief or came from a different land—this is unconscionable." He glanced at Ernst. "You argue the other case?"

Ernst knew better than to try to debate a lawyer. He also had doubt of his own, because of Krista and the Jew he had known in America. "I neither argue nor endorse the case."

Dohnanyi smiled briefly. "You are smart. Why imperil your career foolishly? But I am committed; I am the one who was challenged. I began keeping a chronicle of the injustices and abuses of power which came to the attention of my office. As the list grew, I deciphered a system of corruption which I traced ultimately to one man: Adolf Hitler. Read *Mein Kampf*!"

"I have," Ernst said.

"Then you know how he blames everything on Jews. Do you really subscribe to his logic?"

This was dangerous territory! "I prefer not to comment."

"Smart again! Bigotry has been with us always, but he made it fashionable. Now it is institutionalized. It is not merely the Jews;

Gypsies too, and others. Anyone who is not a perfectly pedigreed Arian. Is this fair? Is this sensible?"

"No comment," Ernst repeated, thinking again of Krista. He could be getting himself into trouble by not denouncing Dohnanyi, but he had come to know the man well enough to doubt this. The man was not trying to trap him; the man was genuinely outraged. The man was also making guileful sense.

"By 1937 I was convinced that the only way to end this insidious corruption of values was to eliminate its source. I examined several possible sources of assistance for my plans before deciding that the Wehrmacht was the only force capable, and perhaps willing, to destroy Hitler's power."

"You go too far," Ernst said, now quite nervous. "You know I cannot give even tacit consent to such a notion."

Dohnanyi glanced sidelong at him. "I speak merely what I once thought. I am not advocating such a thing now. You are consenting to nothing."

Ernst was uneasily silent. Could this after all be a test? Did Canaris doubt him, and was pushing him more firmly?

"I found it difficult at first to work with the military," Dohnanyi continued. "I believed that there were ardent soldiers and ardent civilians, and I was one of the latter. I condemned the military men for their narrow outlook and cadet-ish conceptions of honor and patriotism. I was a firm opponent of war as a means of settling disputes, but not a pacifist. I was an early advocate of assassination as a means of dealing with Hitler."

"Assassination!" Ernst cried, shocked.

Dohnanyi smiled. "Now you can turn me in and have me executed. I have spoken treason."

What a dangerous game this man played! "You have spoken of the way you once felt," Ernst said carefully. "Obviously you no longer feel that way, as you are now working with the military in support of Hitler's objectives. At this moment we are on a mission to facilitate what the Führer desires."

This time Dohnanyi was silent. He knew that he had gone as far as he could without forcing Ernst to report him.

The man's contacts got them into Belgium without trouble. Ernst made his notes. Then they went on to Denmark, and from there to Norway. It was a successful mission. Ernst hoped that the man's actions in facilitating Hitler's wishes belied his treasonous dialogue. That way he, Ernst, was justified in not reporting him. But it remained extremely nervous business.

On the first of April, Canaris was promoted to full admiral. Thereafter Oster became a general. On the ninth of that month the invasion of Denmark and Norway proceeded with great success. Abwehr II distinguished itself. Ernst's work had helped facilitate the smoothness of the operation, though he was one among many.

The pace did not abate. On the tenth of May the German armies invaded Holland, Belgium and France. Once again Abwehr II received praise for its successes. But it did receive a setback in Holland. And a more subtle, but worse one in France.

Because someone had tried to warn France of the attack. Telecommunications monitoring had discovered attempts by a German officer to betray the date of the invasion. The French had been too muddled to respond to the warning appropriately; otherwise it could have been a serious matter.

Adolf Hitler himself called upon Heydrich and Canaris to join forces and determine the traitor. Lieutenant Colonel Joachim Rohleder, head of Abwehr IIIF, which handled counter-espionage, was given command of the investigation. Admiral Canaris was visibly upset; he was either acting, or he had known nothing of the betrayal.

Ernst remained clear; he had other business to attend. But he kept track of it as well as he could, because if Canaris himself should be implicated, the Admiral would of course do his best to conceal it. Since he was active in the investigation, he could probably succeed in such concealment. So Heydrich wanted to know the truth, and he was depending on Ernst for it, not the official investigation.

The intercepted telegrams pointed to Müller, Oster's agent to the Vatican in Italy, as the possible courier of the treasonous information. However, it took Colonel Rohleder some time to run this down, and in the interim Müller returned to Rome and probably removed incriminating evidence and covered his tracks. Nevertheless, Rohleder pursued the matter competently, and did determine Müller's guilt. But that was only part of it; Müller was not one who should have known the date of invasion. Who had been the source of his information?

Rohleder was both a believer in the traditional Prusso-German military ideal, and a brilliant intelligence officer. He was appalled both by this betrayal of the German homeland, and by its amateurish execution. He satisfied himself as to the identity of the traitor, and acted in forthright fashion.

He went to Abwehr headquarters in Berlin and confronted General Oster in his office. Johannes Dohnanyi was there too. There he coldly presented his facts and gave his conclusions: Müller and Oster were the traitors. "Now I am going to present my findings to Admiral Canaris," he announced. "I invite you to accompany me, in the interest of defending yourself."

Oster and Dohnanyi protested, but Rohleder was firm. He did make his report to the Admiral.

But Canaris did not accept the findings. "The evidence is inconclusive," he told Rohleder. "It is insufficient to warrant pursuing the matter further."

"But it *is* conclusive!" Rohleder protested. "Some evidence was destroyed, but my documentation indicates—"

"It is not strong enough to allow the good name of the Abwehr to be soiled," the Admiral said firmly. "Would you have us all suffer because of such a suspicion?"

"Sir, I insist that this is a blight on the Abwehr which must be cleansed! It is the Abwehr I am trying to protect! What is to stop this man from betraying us again?"

"I will order Müller to immediately sever all contact with the Vatican," Canaris said. And that was it; he refused to take stronger action.

Rohleder stalked out of the office. He was incensed at this behavior, and he expressed himself freely to others in the unit. This was how Ernst learned the details. The Admiral had to call him back on another day, because there was so much talk and conjecture about the affair. It was apparent that Canaris was not going to act against his friend Oster.

But this was the last time Canaris aided Colonel Oster, and the two were no longer as close as they had been. After this affair, the Admiral became morose and fatalistic. He gave no encouragement to any opposition to Hitler, and threw himself into his duty. But he seemed to have lost his vitality.

"Oster is guilty, but not Canaris," Ernst reported to Heydrich. "He covered for his friend, but he was severely disappointed in him, and they are friends no more. Oster betrayed him personally as well as Germany."

"I am not sure," Heydrich replied. "It may be that he values his reputation more than he values his Fatherland. He spared himself embarrassment by covering up."

"Then should he not be relieved instead of depressed?" Ernst asked. "However, he *did* cover up, for whatever reason, so he is guilty too."

"Guilt is not so readily adjudged," Heydrich said. "I am satisfied neither that he is clean nor that he is dirty. I need a clearer indication. Stay with it."

Ernst was glad to oblige. He had done what he had to, and made an honest report, but he liked the Admiral, and saw how the man had been hurt by his friend's betrayal. It was, technically, a crime to protect a traitor, but understandable when the traitor was a friend. The Admiral had done what he believed he had to, and was suffering grievously for it.

Ernst mused on that. It had become known that Hitler himself had halted the attack on the British troops massed at Dunkirk in northern France, allowing them to cross the channel to Britain and escape destruction. It was said that this was because Hitler had respect for the British, and wanted to spare them if he could, hoping they would later choose to join Germany. But had any other person made that disastrous decision, he would have been deemed a traitor to the Fatherland. Was Admiral Canaris different in principle?

Ernst received promotion to Captain Osterecht. He knew he owed it to Admiral Canaris. That made him feel even more guilty, ironically.

In July, not long after the surrender of France, a new and interesting project was initiated. It seemed that Jodl had proposed to the Führer that he undertake a bold new strategy, taking the rock of Gibraltar and closing the Mediterranean Sea to the British. Admiral Canaris was intrigued, for this gave him a chance to work once again in Spain, a country he loved.

On July 5 Canaris proposed that the assault on Gibraltar might be accomplished by the Brandenburg Regiment, which was an elite military commando unit within the Abwehr.

This was placed under consideration. Meanwhile, it was necessary to reconnoiter the situation. Ernst was dispatched to the Abwehr post in Algeciras, near Spain's southernmost point, near the British peninsula of Gibraltar. He traveled "civilian," with an assumed identity. This made him three layered, as he thought of it: the lowest layer was Ernst Best, the middle was Captain Osterecht, and now the top was a vaguely Spanish civilian.

Indeed, his instructions were to evince no interest in Gibraltar. He was to conduct himself in the manner of an officer on vacation. He was not even supposed to report to Algeciras right away, as if he were routinely checking in, almost as an afterthought. But on his way he would check the route the main party was to take, and make note of any potential problems.

He called Heydrich, because this represented a change in his locale for a while and he would be out of touch until he returned to Berlin. "So I will tour the country—I will rent a car in Spain—and then be at Algeciras to help on the mission. I will report to you when I return."

"While you are down there, you can do an incidental chore for me," Heydrich said. "There is an operation in Spain run by foreigners. They are probably harmless, but if we are to get involved in Spain, we need to be sure there are not spies among them. They have centers in Madrid and Barcelona, and contacts with the British which predate General Franco's victory."

"They could have Republican sympathies," Ernst said, remembering how other countries had generally favored that side. "But surely they have been investigated."

"Surely they have—by the Spanish," Heydrich replied with inherent contempt. "You will not have time to do much, but you can inspect their operation."

"But with only three days at the most, I will hardly be able to get started," Ernst protested. "They will know I am German."

"Of course they will know. You will tell them you have been sent directly from Adolf Hitler to learn what they are doing."

Ernst laughed. But it turned out not to be a joke. Then he realized what Heydrich was up to: Ernst would make an obvious, clumsy investigation, which would set this group's fears at rest—while some other agent, hidden from their knowledge, would do the real investigation. Ernst was a mere decoy. It would be easy enough for him to do.

"I have a contact in Barcelona," Heydrich said. "He will provide you with authority to investigate.

"But the Admiral will know that something is happening."

There was a pause. "True. He is not stupid. Very well, you will do this mission for him. I will have word sent down."

Sure enough, soon Canaris summoned Ernst to his office. "Someone got wind that we had a Spanish-speaking operative going to Spain," he said, disgruntled. "It turns out that Himmler himself has a concern there, so Keitel has directed me to do a spot investigation as long as my people are in the area." He grimaced. "As if my work counts for nothing! As if my people are to be borrowed for trifles. But it must be. You must do some work on your idle time after all."

"I am ready to serve in any capacity, to further the good of the Fatherland," Ernst replied.

"Go first to Barcelona. There is a contact there who will provide you with a car and tell you something about these Quakers there."

"Quakers?" Ernst said, surprised. "I have heard of them. They are in America." For his American friend Lane had a Quaker fiancee named Quality Smith. A really nice young woman.

"They are in Britain too. And in Spain. I have been aware of their activities. They are harmless. It is a waste of time. But Himmler may not be denied. Do this job and report to Algeciras. At least it won't interfere with our real work. It may even help conceal it."

So it was that Ernst took the train through Vichy France and came to Barcelona, in northeast Spain. There he made his contact, and got his car. Then he drove to the Quaker Relief station and introduced himself.

They seemed genuinely perplexed. "We are merely feeding the hungry children," their director explained. "We receive supplies from England."

"Show me," Ernst said. "Assign a guide to me, who will also take me to the field. To see your various routes, who will explain each part."

"But we have no extra truck to spare! Two are broken, and we are having trouble getting parts. It is all we can do to keep up as we are."

Some token of exchange would facilitate things, Ernst realized. "Perhaps I can be of assistance. I have a car; your man can ride with me. Oblige me in this, and I will put in a word for your parts."

They were quick to appreciate his meaning. They knew how much good or evil the right or wrong word could do. But there was one more complication. "We can best spare one whose truck is down. But that is a woman."

Ernst smiled. "Do you think me a barbarian? I will not molest your woman."

"Of course not," the director said without complete conviction. "But she may not wish to ride with you, even so. She is American, though she speaks Spanish, and does not appreciate Germans."

"Speak plainly," Ernst said. "You know I am a Nazi SS officer in civilian guise. It is my government she opposes."

"That is true."

"Introduce us. If she declines, we shall have to seek some other person."

And so Miss Smith made her appearance. "Quality!" Ernst exclaimed, astonished.

Chapter 7
France

"Ernst!" Quality said. She was as surprised as he. She had never imagined that the snooping German could be anyone she knew.

"You know each other?" the director asked, surprised in turn.

Ernst evidently realized that this could complicate things. "Only in passing," he said. "Think nothing of it. Find another person."

A sudden, bold, foolish notion came to her. "No, I will ride with you," Quality said. Though they were speaking in English, she was not using the Quaker plain talk. "I am surplus, at the moment."

Ernst spread his hands. "As you wish. It is a matter of indifference to me." Actually that was surely a simplification. He knew her, which might help, but she had not treated him kindly in America. Perhaps he felt alienated—or possibly he was protecting her from the stigma of being too close to a Nazi. He knew she would not lie about her work, or anything else, so he was willing to work with her.

"We do have a friend in common," she said. "I am ready to join you now."

She went with him to his car, and he put it in motion. "Had I known it was you, I would not have embarrassed you by such a request," he said. "I want neither a quarrel nor a complication for you."

"If it were another person making this inspection, I might find it more awkward," Quality said. "But though our politics are diametrically opposed, I do respect your integrity, Ernst. I know I can safely ride with you."

"On that much we can agree," he said tightly.

She cocked her head, almost quizzically. "We have one other thing in common."

He was momentarily blank. Then he remembered. "Guernica! We each lost friends there."

"Must this inspection be conducted on site, or will you accept my answers to your questions? We have nothing to hide."

"I fear you would not care to answer all my questions."

"If we played a game of truth?"

He glanced at her. "I prefer not to discuss politics with you again."

"I have a truly odd idea. Could we drive to Guernica, to see what happened there?"

"But that may be three hundred kilometers by road! We could not get there today, let alone return by nightfall."

"I do trust you, Ernst, and I want very much to see it. This may be my only chance, because the moment my truck is fixed I will resume my route. I think you could safely go there, as I otherwise might not."

His surprise was growing. "You would spend the night with me?"

"I think it does not matter what others may think. You know that this is not a social encounter." That was certain.

He considered. "I would like to visit Guernica, and I could accept your answers. They are likely to be more informative than those of others I might question."

"Then go back to the office. I will notify them, and pack some things for a two day trip."

He drove her back, and waited in the car. Still surprised at her sudden audacity in proposing this excursion, she went to explain things to the director. She found it hard to believe that she was serious, but she was doing it regardless. She had never anticipated either encountering Ernst here, or traveling with him.

She collected necessary things in a small suitcase and returned to the car. They started off. He followed her directions to get efficiently out of the city and onto a suitable road going west. The farther they drove, the more the signs of the recent war manifested. There were bombed out buildings and burned areas, and every so often a detour where the road was in rubble. But she knew the best route through, and they made good progress.

"I must confess something," she said. "Though we were not friends in America, we did know each other, and it has been some time since I have seen a familiar face from my past. You remind me of America, ironically."

"So do you," he replied. "How is it you came to be here? I thought you were in college there."

"When I saw Lane off to the air training in Canada, I found I just couldn't return to my prior life. So I joined the relief effort here. We are doing what we can to feed the children, who have suffered grievously from a war they did not make."

"War is not pretty," he agreed.

"I soon discovered how ugly it is. I had never expected to find myself in such a thing, but this is where the need was, and where the need remains. Unfortunately the Nationalist government is becoming increasingly uncooperative. The American Friends Service Committee left Spain at the end of 1939, and our British Friends Service Council is under increasing pressure."

"I respect the master you serve. I will do what I can to facilitate the acquisition of the parts you need."

"We appreciate that. Can you tell me anything of your activities?"

He hesitated, and she realized that he could be engaged in secret work. Because she had recognized him, she could give away his original identity and interfere with his mission. "I must ask a favor of you."

"You are in secret work?"

"Yes. If you tell others my true identity, my life could be in danger."

This was more serious than she had thought. "I suspected something like that. I asked the director not to talk to others of our encounter."

He glanced at her. "Is this not deception? You do not practice such."

"I have learned to compromise. I am not proud of it, but now I do practice deception when it seems necessary." That was an unfortunate understatement.

"Then I ask you to speak of me to others only as I was introduced to you, and not to mention our prior acquaintance, for the person I am supposed to be has not been to America."

"Agreed."

"I am with the SS, doing internal investigation."

"Then you have not been involved in killing or sabotage," she said, relieved.

"You exonerate me too readily. I have not personally killed or sabotaged, but I have helped formulate plans which involve these things. Poland, Norway, France—I am guilty."

"I should not have asked. Have you heard from Lane?"

"Nothing. I have not tried to write to him. I think such a correspondence would bring only suspicion and perhaps discredit on us both."

"Yes, that must be true. I have maintained correspondence. He joined the RAF, and was in France. When the German invasion came. He—he surely has killed—has downed enemy airplanes. German airplanes." She tried to mask her emotion.

"It is a thing he must do. He fights for his side, as I must fight for mine. I can only support him in that." Then he seemed to realize that he had misread the thrust of her comment. "But you—this is against your religion."

She was silent. He glanced at her, and surely saw that her face was wet with tears. She had been unable to stop them.

"I can not comfort you," he said awkwardly. "I am of the other side, in this respect also."

"Yes, you are the enemy," she murmured, oddly comforted despite this.

They drove on in silence.

But later he spoke again. "I must urge you to do something, for no stated reason. Return to America."

"But there is still so much work to do here!" she protested.

"Still I think it would be better for you to get out of Spain."

That meant that the Germans might invade Spain! He might be an advance spy for that. "I appreciate the nature of your warning, but I can not. Not while the children remain hungry."

"It was the answer I expected. Perhaps it will be all right."

"Perhaps," she agreed. "But I thank thee for thy concern."

It took her a moment to realize that she was now using the plain talk. Her attitude toward him had changed, though it was not clear to herself in quite what manner.

It was not safe to drive after dark. They came to a suitable town and sought lodging in a hotel. "I have money," Ernst said. "I will obtain a separate room for you. But—"

"I know," she said. "It will be safer if we are together. Take one room, in thy name. They will not question it."

So it was done. They found themselves sharing a somewhat spare chamber on the second floor. There was no hot water, and there were roaches under the single bed, and the bathroom was down the hall, to be shared by all the rooms, but it would do.

They went to a restaurant to eat. Quality ordered water to go with her meal. Here they discovered that water was more expensive than beer. But Quality would not touch alcohol in any form other than externally medical.

"You could have milk," he said. "I will pay—"

"No. Milk is for children. I would feel guilty."

So Ernst paid the price for water, for them both.

"I apologize for embarrassing you," she said in Spanish. They had agreed to speak only Spanish when in public, so as not to attract attention. Her plain talk did not manifest in this language. "I did not think of this beforehand."

"Please, no discussion," he said. "It is all right."

But after the meal, when they were on their way back to the hotel, she brought it up again. "I'm afraid I acted too much on impulse. I did not think through the complications. Had I done so—"

"May I speak plainly?"

She was taken aback. "Of course, Ernst."

"I treat you with diffidence because you evinced objection to me in America. You are correct in this, because I am what you take me to be. I am an enemy national, and I am carrying a gun. But this is not my impression of you. I have no objection to what you are. Rather, I respect it, the more so now that I have discovered that you are actively implementing your beliefs by putting yourself at risk to help others. I regard you as a fine woman who need never apologize for her consistency or behavior. I did not know that I would encounter you here, or that you would choose to travel with me, but I am extremely pleased that both occurred."

She was silent for a moment, her feelings in disarray. "That was a bit more candor than I anticipated."

He smiled. "I believe in the truth. Yet I live a life of deceit. I have no need to practice deceit with you."

"A life of deceit," she echoed. "I hate myself for ever deceiving another person, yet at times it seems I have to. I feel degraded, yet I alone am responsible."

"I am sure Lane feels similarly about killing. He does not like it, but circumstances compel him."

"My understanding is growing. But not my ease of conscience."

"War is not kind to conscience."

They were at the hotel. They went to the room. Ernst checked the closet and found extra blankets there. He laid these on the floor, and set his bag on them. "I will accompany you to the bathroom and check it before you enter," he said. "Then I will wait outside it until you are done, and see you back to the room. I will lock you in, and then use the bathroom myself."

"Yes." She understood why. In this war-devastated region it was necessary to be extremely cautious. There could be a man hiding in the bathroom, or ready to jump out on a single woman passing in the hall, or to enter her room while her man was away.

When he returned and unlocked the door, she was already in the bed. He turned out the light and she heard him get into his blanket-bed on the floor, and heard him set the gun beside his head. He settled down to sleep.

"I thank thee, Ernst."

"Welcome, Quality."

Next morning Quality surprised herself again. "Thy gun—I have not seen one. Only the damage they do."

He was surprised. "I mentioned this only in passing, not to cause you distress."

"I am embarrassed to confess this, but the knowledge that thee has it makes me feel safer. May I see it?"

"If you wish." He brought it out. "This is a Walther P-38, the HP model—Heeres Pistol. One of the finest service pistols available in Germany. It has an eight round magazine and automatic reloading."

She stared at the thing. It seemed huge and menacing, like the German army. "May I—?"

He reversed it, holding it by the muzzle and extending the butt to her. She took it, and was impressed by its weight; it was over two pounds. What a terrible instrument!

She quickly gave it back. "I hope the day comes when no things like this exist, anywhere in the world."

"I have never used it in action," he said. "Only in target practice. But I can not claim innocence, because I would use it if the need arose."

They said no more about it, but the matter remained in her mind. She felt as if she had done something forbidden, yet she was not penitent. What was in her mind?

They reached the town of Guernica. Most of the bomb damage

had been cleaned up, and it was now much like any other town. But not in their eyes.

"I have made a certain study of this situation," Ernst said as they drove, seeking the address of Quality's former friend. "In America it was represented as an innocent hamlet with no strategic or military value. They said it was obliterated during a market day when it was swollen with country people. That it was an experiment in terror bombing by the Kondor Legion."

"Yes, I saw those reports," she agreed tightly.

"But in fact the Basques were rugged fighters. They gave ground grudgingly. It required a lot of force to make them retreat. So air power was necessary, to avoid unnecessary sacrifice of lives." He glanced at Quality. "I am speaking tactically, not morally."

"I understand."

"By late April, 1937, the main Basque defensive line had been turned. Guernica was one of the two principal routes of retreat for the Basque forces. It was a communications center. There were three military barracks and four small arms factories there. So it was a legitimate target. That particular raid was given no special importance by the units involved. The primary objectives were a nearby bridge, and any transportation and communications facilities. The town itself was bombed as well, to block any possible retreat of Basque troops."

"And some outlying residences."

"The assault was carried out by three Italian medium bombers, that dropped approximately two tons of explosives, and twenty one German bombers, eighteen of which were obsolescent JU 52's, which dropped thirty tons of explosives. The German contingent amounted to only a third of the Kondor Legion's force, and only one bombing pass was made. It was not fully effective; they failed to take out the bridge. But many bombs struck the town, where fires spread rapidly because of wooden construction, narrow streets, loss of water pressure and the lack of fire fighting equipment."

"But what of the human cost!" she exclaimed.

"It was just one small, routine action. It is coincidental that we know some of that human cost. I do not think my friend was even listed among the casualties; I learned of it through mutual friends. The cost was great, to us personally, but small in terms of military matters."

"And that human cost is echoed all over the world," she said bitterly. "Wherever there is war."

"Wherever there is man," he said.

They searched, but could not find where her friend had lived. There were several similar outlying residences, deserted; some were in rubble. There was no sign of the downed airplane; the remnants had probably been scavenged for other uses.

They started back. "I can't even say I am disappointed," Quality said. "I just wanted to see whether there was anything to see. To pay my respects to my friend, in my fashion."

"I, too, to mine."

"It is so hard to believe that this is God's will."

"According to Nietzsche, the Christian conception of God is corrupt."

She glanced sharply at him. "Nietzsche?"

"Friedrich Nietzsche, a German who lived from 1844 to 1900, but was said to be insane in 1889 until his death."

"I should think so!"

He smiled. "No, he was an able philosopher, and is held in high regard in my country. I understand that his writings influenced the Führer."

"I rest my case."

"Perhaps you should read him. It is said that it is impossible for a person to read him carefully and remain a Christian."

"Then why should I want to read him?"

"Perhaps merely to test your faith. Perhaps to ascertain whether the God you serve truly exists. If he does not, then you have your answer: this destruction is not God's will."

"Why is he so certain that God does not exist?"

"He shows how the Christian God has been adapted from the Jewish God, but refined to make man feel sinful even when he has done nothing wrong, and to give man hope for an afterlife where justice shall be done. Thus man both needs the priest, and has no chance of fulfillment in this life. His hope in the beneficence of the afterlife is vain. Thus it is hope which is the evil of evils—the one thing left in Pandora's box."

"Hope is evil? And what of love?"

"God was made a person so that it would be possible to love Him. The saints were made as handsome young men or beautiful young women, to appeal to the romanticism of the worshipers of either sex. Love is the state in which man suffers great illusions, seeing things as they are not. Thus when man loves God, he deludes himself, and tolerates much more evil than otherwise." He paused. "Or so Nietzsche says.

"Does thee believe that, Ernst?"

"I got in trouble for declining to abandon the Church! But I must say that was because I did not like having my faith or lack of faith dictated to me. I have encountered people of faith who are good. People like you. I do not know what my belief may be, other than my faith in the power of my swastika."

"Thy swastika!" she exclaimed, appalled. She had forgotten that he wore it as a silver icon, his most cherished possession. No matter how nice he seemed, he remained a Nazi.

"For me it is an object of veneration. It has helped me, perhaps as your faith helps you."

"What a parallel!"

He shrugged, not arguing, and she felt ashamed for her narrowness. She might disagree with him, but she had no right to disparage his faith. "Now we must go to Madrid."

"Madrid?"

"Where I can seek a contact, and facilitate the shipment of your parts."

"But I haven't even answered thy questions about what we are doing here!" she protested.

"Surely you will, before we return."

So it turned out. They drove to Madrid, where she waited in the car while he saw some people and shopped for some fruit to eat along the way. In due course he brought her back to Barcelona, and the shipment of the necessary parts was being facilitated.

"If I may, I will give you this," he said, handing her a small package.

Quality was surprised. "I have not asked anything from thee, Ernst, or given thee anything. I don't—"

"About that I differ. You have given me the pleasure of your company and your trust. But this is merely a book I found in Madrid. It is in French, which I can not read, but I know what it says. I fear you will not like it—"

"A French book? I can read it, of course. But why would thee assume I wouldn't like it?"

"It is Nietzsche. One of the last he wrote before his madness overcame him. But his logic is persuasive. You do not have to agree with him, and surely you will not, but you should understand what he says."

Quality was touched. She accepted the book. "Thank thee, Ernst. Thee is right: I must not condemn without understanding. I will read it."

He smiled. "I doubt we shall meet again, but if we do, we can argue Nietzsche's case."

"I say this with a certain bemusement," Quality said as they separated. "But I rather enjoyed our trip together."

"I, too."

Then he drove away, leaving her by the front of the office. She waved to him with the book.

"I have good news and bad news," the director told her. "The good news is that we have received word that the parts for the truck are on the way, just when we had almost given up on them. The bad news is that we need someone to go to Vichy France. A trainload of refugees is supposed to be crossing into Spain, and arrangements have to be made in Spain and in France. Since you speak French—"

"Yes, of course," she said. She was surprised and glad that Ernst's word had been so immediately effective; her trip with him had justified itself, though that had not been her reason for it. But to go to Vichy France—that was distinctly nervous business. France had fallen only last month, and the horror of the German advance remained fresh. It had seemed as if the panzer divisions were never going to stop, and that they might plunge right through the mountains to Spain. Fortunately they had stopped, and then the Vichy regime had been set up, and things had stabilized for the time being.

So it was that she found herself using her repaired truck not to go out on a route, but for driving alone to France. She had to go to Paris to make the arrangements, and the state of transportation was such that it was best to drive across the border and to Toulouse in France, where she could catch a passenger train. There were risks, such as possible confiscation of the truck by the French, but there were risks in any other course of action too.

The thing was that she had to take along a considerable amount of money in both French and German denominations, because it was a reality of warfare and of travel that nothing could be done without local currency, but no money was allowed to cross international boundaries. So it had to be smuggled across. She had not been involved in this aspect before, and had for some time been naive about it, but she had learned. Her pangs of conscience had settled down to low-grade distress; there just wasn't any other way to function here. The truck's spare tire was stuffed with the money. With luck the border inspection would not be thorough enough to expose it.

The truck had been fixed, but it remained balky on hills, tending to overheat. The road to the border was mostly uphill, because the border ran along the heights of the Pyrenees. She had to drive slowly, and stop frequently to let the motor cool. She was used to it. While she waited, she thought about what she was getting into, for France was now more dubious territory than Spain.

Apparently the swiftness of the German panzer advance was deceptive: the Germans lacked the personnel to occupy the whole of France directly. Probably they were still digesting Poland, and preparing for the invasion of England. There were rumors that they were preparing to mount a phenomenal air attack on the island, to bomb it into submission so that there would be no effective resistance to occupation by troops. This might explain why they were to let roughly the southern half of France be administrated by a French puppet government whose capital was at a spa town named Vichy.

The Vichy regime had come into existence on June 16, 1940, under the leadership of Marshal Philippe Petain. He was eighty four years old, and venerated by the French population as a hero of the War—now being termed the First World War, the current one assuming the status of The Second World War. He sometimes pretended to be senile as a political ploy, but he was in excellent health and in full command of his faculties. France had not yet surrendered, but the French had evidently concluded that it was better to have one of their own in charge, than to have the Germans do it. Even spread thin, the Nazis would be vicious.

Petain was given to simple statements of the obvious, such as "The family is good. Alcoholism is bad." His first act as leader was to declare his intent to negotiate an armistice with the Germans. The French troops of the region began laying down their arms immediately. General de Gaulle made a radio broadcast from London, vowing to continue the battle against Germany, but he received almost no support. The predominant mood in France was that German victory in Europe was inevitable, and the Vichy regime was attempting to solidify a favorable position for France in the new order.

Public opinion had turned against England, because England had abandoned France when the Germans invaded. All England had seemed to care about was getting its own forces to safety, in the hasty Dunkirk evacuation. Had they stayed to fight—well, who could say? The English were lucky, the French said, to have a built-in antitank ditch. In three weeks time England's neck would be wrung like that of a chicken. So the disenchanted French had said as their own country was lost.

This anti-British attitude was aggravated on July 3 when Britain seized all French ships in British ports. At the same time the British launched a pre-emptive strike against the French fleet in the Mediterranean, based at Mers el-Kebir in Algeria. They had issued an ultimatum: either join the British war effort, sail to a British port with reduced crews, or be disarmed and possibly handed over to the Americans. The French Admiral made a conciliatory counterproposal, but it was too late; the British opened fire. Nearly 1300 French sailors were killed in the assault. In response the French launched a rather timid air assault against Gibraltar. Thus instead of unifying against the Germans, the British and French were fighting each other.

Quality shook her head, watching the steam pressure in her radiator subside in much the way of the French resistance. The follies of war were eternal. When would men ever choose a better way to settle differences?

The Germans did not seem to be too brutal, so far. They had declared the historic French provinces of Alsace and Lorraine, which were along the border, to be part of Germany. Anyone the Germans deemed to be undesirable was simply being expelled to France. It seemed that a lot of people were going to be moved. This was certainly inconvenient for them, but mild compared to what the Germans could have done.

Meanwhile the Germans seemed happy to have the cooperation of the French administrative machine in the Vichy regime. They seemed to be relying heavily on it to manage day to day activities. Quality understood that the Germans had only ten thousand police of various types available, while the French had over a hundred thousand. Already the German troops were settling down, and truck-loads of food were following them in. The folk in the Vichy regime had very little resentment about that!

Quality shook her head as she resumed driving. Was she becoming favorably inclined to the Germans, because of her recent trip with Ernst? It was not her place to take sides, and she tried to maintain an inner as well as outer attitude of neutrality. But there was no question that Germany was the aggressor here, and Germany had sent the warplanes that had done much of the bombing in Spain. She had no brief for Germany. Yet she could not condemn Ernst, who was a good man. When she had been with him, it had been easy to forget his nationality. Lane was right: her error had been in judging Ernst harshly, without knowing him.

In due course she achieved the border, which was between the Spanish town of Puigcerda and the small French town of Bourg Madame, in a lovely high valley. Not far from here, she knew, was the tiny nation of Andorra. There was a river, and both the Spanish and the French had posts on the bridge, on either side.

The guards recognized the Quaker truck, for similar trucks had passed this way before. Normally travelers and their vehicles were searched, but in this case they were content to verify Quality's identification, take a quick look in the back of the truck, which was empty, and pass her through.

She felt a familiar twinge of guilt. She had lied again, by omission. Legally, she should have declared the money in the tire. But then she would not have been able to complete her mission, rendering the whole trip pointless. How would it have been to have a trainload of refugees denied, because of her conscience? She had been forced, once again, to choose the lesser of evils. But she felt unclean.

She was in France. It did not look like a conquered land. But what would she find when she left Vichy France and entered the German-occupied section, where Paris was?

Now her progress was faster, being downhill. She had no trouble reaching Toulouse by nightfall. She paid for several day's parking in a garage, and got a hotel room for the night. So far she had had no trouble.

Once settled in, she returned to the truck and carefully transferred the money from the tire to a handbag. From here on it would remain close to her.

As she lay on the bed to sleep, she thought of the trip with Ernst again. She tried to picture him lying on the floor across the room. She had felt so *safe* with him there! She did not approve of handguns any more than cannon, but the nearness of that strong man with his gun had been very reassuring. She was almost ashamed of the sentiment.

In the morning she went to the station. The train was late, of course, and she had to wait two hours for it to arrive. Then it required another hour to board. Perhaps it was just her impression, but the French seemed horribly inefficient, as if everything had to be reconsidered at every juncture.

Quality was glad she had taken the precaution to bring along a book. It was the one Ernst had given her, *The Anti-Christ*, by Friedrich Nietzsche. She was not a proficient reader in French, and this was her chance to improve. Time was one thing she had, right now. It was a small book, hardly a hundred pages. So she read slowly, and took pains to be sure she understood it. She learned from the introduction that the man had suffered from syphilis and been ill for some time before succumbing completely and becoming a child, mentally. He had been unknown, until in an irony of coincidence, his notoriety suddenly soared during his final decade of life, when his incapacity prevented him from knowing it. Now he was more famous than ever, in Germany, Quality realized, because Adolf Hitler and the Nazis liked him and were encouraging the dissemination of his views. That might account for the presence of a French translation in Spain. She saw that it was a used book, however, so probably it was from someone's liquidated collection. New books of any type were hard to come by in Spain, after the devastation of the war.

The train moved slowly, and stopped frequently. Quality was mostly oblivious. Her feelings were profoundly mixed. She had sympathy for the author's illness, but not for the manner of it: no prudent man should have indulged himself in such a manner as to acquire such a devastating venereal disease. She was tempted to dismiss his views as madness, but they were not; they were a marvel of clarity. Nietzsche had had a fine mind and a precision of expression which came through even in translation. His Foreword was touching: "This book is for extremely few.... The reader must be intellectually honest to survive my passion.... He must desire unconditional freedom.... He must be a superior man in his soul." How could she argue with that? Yet his thesis was anathema: that Christianity and all its works were an abomination. Therefore it had to be flawed, and she would have to work to discover the exact nature of that flaw.

It was best, she knew, to be able to state the opposition's case. Only when a person could do that, could he successfully refute it. But what discipline this required of her! All of her training and belief inveighed against it. Yet what horrified her most was the sheer persuasiveness of the insidious logic. It was not hard to argue Nietzshe's case. Was she being corrupted by it? It was as if she stood before Satan—the Antichrist, literally—and found herself tempted by his deceptively fair-seeming words. His concept of the *Ubermensch*, or superman, was not at all the racist doctrine that Hitler espoused; rather it was the universal human cultural goal, toward which all men should strive, the Germans among them.

The more she read, the more she was satisfied that Nietzsche was not the man that many others claimed. His original views were well worthy of consideration. Her task was not to try to refute him, but simply to refine her thinking to the precision necessary to benefit from his logic. Nietzsche, like Ernst, was perhaps an acquired taste.

It took a day, and a change of trains, to travel the one hundred and sixty miles from Toulouse to Vichy, but she hardly noticed. The book held her attention throughout.

But when she got to Vichy, she was informed that they knew nothing about the refugees. The matter was being handled in Paris, almost two hundred miles further north. There was nothing to do but catch another train. Somehow she wasn't surprised. Perhaps Nietzsche's savage commentary on the human condition had prepared her for such complications.

Paris really did not look much changed, except for the presence of German soldiers throughout, in their gray-green uniforms. When she passed close to one, she saw that his belt-buckle had the words "*Gott mit uns.*" She realized that that meant "God with Us." She hoped not! This was no longer Vichy France, but France Proper—under full occupation. The German officials and soldiers rode public transportation free, and seemed to be having a good time. Not that it made much difference to her; she was here on business, and would retreat to Spain as soon as she had accomplished her purpose.

The SS headquarters was in the Hotel de Louvre. Quality braced herself, then went to the SS office to inquire. The sight of the black uniformed men gave her a chill. The regular German soldiers were bad enough, but the SS was worse. She was glad that Ernst had been in civilian clothes; that had allowed her to put his business at arm's length, mentally. Now there was no euphemism possible: she was dealing with the Nazis.

"*Ja, Frëulein,*" the officer said in German.

"I'm sorry, I don't speak German," she said in French.

"Then I will speak French," he said in that language. "But I think you are not French."

"No. I am American. I am here on behalf of the British Friends Service Council, in connection with a trainload of refugees bound for Spain."

"Jews?" he asked sharply.

"They may be," she said evenly. "The Spanish officials in Madrid did not inform us."

He checked through some papers. "Jews. From the Palatinate area of Germany. A train will take them from Frankfurt to Paris, but there will be a delay until we can commandeer a train to the Spanish border. We will provide the train, but there are costs of transport."

"They need to be fed," Quality agreed. "I am here to buy food for them to eat along the way."

"You have the money?"

"I have French money. I hope it is enough."

His eyes narrowed. "You smuggled it across the border, of course."

"It was the only way. The Spanish will not let any currency leave the country."

"Let me have it."

"But it is for food!" she protested.

"It is for costs of transport. We will see that it is well spent."

Quality realized that she would have to turn over the money, though she distrusted this. "You will give me a receipt for it?"

"Of course."

She brought out the packet of francs. The officer counted it and wrote her a receipt. "This should suffice. However, there are also the costs of the Frankfurt train. You have German money?"

It was apparent that the SS knew what it was doing, at least with respect to squeezing the sponge dry. She brought out her packet of marks, and got a similar receipt for it.

"You will remain in Paris until the transaction occurs," the officer said. "Here is a reservation for a suitable hotel. Check here with us daily."

She wanted to protest, but realized that it would be futile. She would have to wait on their convenience. "Thank you."

He smiled. "We can not do too much for a devotee of Nietzsche."

He had noticed the book she carried! How would he have treated her if she had not had it? The Nazis were in control here; they could have had her strip-searched or worse, and could have taken the money without giving any receipts. It was possible that Ernst had done her more of a favor than he realized, by giving her the book.

She turned and left the office, conscious of the officer's eyes on her. As she emerged to the street she experienced a great easing of her muscles. Only now did she realize how tense she had been.

But her job was hardly over. She had to hope that it would not take too long for the trains to be arranged, and that the money she had brought would indeed be spent properly. This business was already more complicated than she had anticipated.

She had some personal money in her purse, as the officer had surely known. Would it be enough to keep her at the hotel as long as she was required to stay? She simply had to hope so. There would also be the expense of food for herself, and the train tickets back to Spain.

"God will provide," she told herself. Nevertheless, she took the precaution of stopping at a store and buying some bread and cheese.

It was cheap, and it would hold her for some time. Then she had to hurry, because there was a curfew here. Already the streets were clearing of all but Germans, and the main sound was that of their boots as they went on foot patrols. Some had leashed Alsatian dogs who evidently understood only German commands. Some of the men, she saw, were on bicycles, cruising silently along the streets; those would be even more dangerous to anyone in violation of the curfew, because they were silent.

The hotel, to her surprise, was both reasonably priced and of reasonable quality. It seemed that the Nazis had pre-empted the best for themselves, and she was the beneficiary. The room was small, but it had its own bathroom and a competent lock on the door. Both were important. There was a cart in the hall with a pile of used books; it seemed that in this time of privation, reading had become quite popular. She appreciated that. She sorted through the pile and took a novel that she hoped would be diverting. She had had enough of Nietzsche for the time being.

There was even a radio. She turned it on and listened to the news in French as she chewed on the bread and cheese. Then she allowed herself the luxury of a warm bath. After that she washed her underclothing, because she had only one change. What was supposed to have been a three day trip was being indefinitely extended.

The city remained quiet at night. But now she heard the noise of rats inside the walls. She shuddered, closed her eyes, and pulled the covers up over her head.

In the morning she went to the SS office and inquired. A different officer was there, but he had the information. "The train from Frankfurt is available. The connecting train here in Paris is not, but progress is being made."

That was a relief. "I will inquire again tomorrow," she said.

"As you wish, *Mädchen.*"

She did not respond to the somewhat derogatory implication. She just departed before the man could think of anything else. The longer she stayed in Paris, the more nervous she would be. It was not just a matter of running out of money.

Meanwhile, she had a day to herself in Paris. At least she should see the sights. That much was free. That was good, because she discovered to her dismay that inflation was ravenous here; her francs bought less food than they had the day before.

Armed with a little tour booklet, she set out afoot. The Louvre was close, but it was probably closed. She had heard that even when it was open, the art treasures had been replaced by plaster replicas, including the Venus de Milo. So she would save that for another time, if time offered. The Grand Opera House was also close, but she wasn't sure how she felt about opera, and she let that also go for now. So she started with the Tuileres gardens. Perhaps they would be in ruins, but there might be something worth seeing.

The flowers were beautiful. There were more types than she could identify, and they transformed the region. She could almost forget, for the moment, that this was a cruelly war-torn country. There were also many impressive statues.

At the end of the gardens was a section called *Place De La Concorde*, where Marie Antoinette was beheaded by the guillotine. Quality sat there for a time among the flowers and contemplated the events that had taken place on this historical spot. It was a unique experience, and it made her shiver in the warm day. She deplored violence and killing, though she had to recognize their significance in the history of mankind. Yet how lovely this place was now.

Then she walked on to the Seine River, where there were many bookstalls open to browsers, but this was not her purpose at the moment. She turned left on the *Qual Des Tuileres* and proceeded about half a mile to the *Hotel De Ville*, and right across a branch of the river to the *Place de la Citi*, where she could see the Notre Dame Cathedral. It seemed that all the churches were kept open by the Germans, though their philosophy hardly supported religion. This was another wonderful step back in time. She could almost feel the burden of the world's history enmeshed within its heavy atmosphere. She was struck by the mystical gloom of the sanctuary. She wished she could turn on a light, because she could hardly make out the altar and the statues of saints.

There was no service here now, because she was here at the wrong time, but that was just as well, because she was not Catholic. Nevertheless, she went to kneel where ancient kings and queens had knelt, and found it easy to imagine that some ampere of their energy lingered there, softly vibrating in the shadows. Now she found the darkness to be an asset, because it allowed her to picture the historical figures there.

She emerged from the Cathedral and blinked in the bright sunlight. This was like man's struggle to overcome his medieval ignorance and achieve the light of modern civilization. She felt not scorn but great sympathy. Man was not to be blamed for his ignorance; it came with his existence. The effort was at times excruciatingly hard, as the present occupation by the Nazis showed.

Quality walked back across the river, retracing her route to the *Place De La Concorde*. Then she went to the *Alexandre Bridge* and crossed the *Seine* again. She went straight until she reached *Les Invalides*. She went around to the back of the building to find a church. Housed within it was *Napoleon's Tomb*, in a crypt. The tomb was several feet below, but she could stand above it on a viewing platform and get an excellent view simply by looking down. She couldn't help wondering what his remains might look like, after all this time. Then she chided herself for her morbidity.

She went back to the river and turned left before crossing the bridge. This street was the *Quai D'Orsay*. She followed it until she reached the *Le Tour Eiffel* on the left. Now this was something she had dreamed of as a girl: seeing the Eiffel Tower up close.

Then she crossed the river and visited the *Chaillot Palace*. From there she followed the *Avenue D'Iena* to the *Etoile* where she saw in the distance *Napoleon's Arch of Triumph*. And where was he, by the end of his life? But she should not begrudge him his monument.

It was enough for the day. She walked straight up the avenue *Des Champs Elysees* until it intersected the *Place De La Concorde*, which was now familiar, and followed it back to her hotel. She had walked only about three miles in all, but it seemed like centuries on another level. She was surfeit. There was just no city in the world like Paris!

On the third day the news changed. "The Paris train is now available," the officer said. "However, we have received word from General Franco's administration that he has changed his mind and will not permit the Jews to cross the Pyrenees. Therefore other arrangements will have to be made, and you are free to go home."

"But the money," she said. "I must take the money back."

"I have no authority to release funds to anyone. Appropriate application must be made and approved."

Quality felt the sinking of her heart. "How long will that take?"

"It is hard to say. Perhaps only a week."

And perhaps never. She knew what she had to do. "Then I must make the application. Do you have the proper forms?"

He rummaged in the desk. "It seems not. But you may write it out on a separate sheet. We are not such sticklers as the French for such things."

She wrote out a request, knowing that the format hardly mattered. They were now entering a different phase of the game. She gave it to him. "Is it all right to inquire tomorrow, just in case there is a quicker approval?"

"Of course, *Mädchen.*"

And tomorrow, or the day after, as her personal money ran out and she became increasingly desperate, the officer would suggest that the approval might be expedited if certain conditions were met. In this manner, without violence or even open coercion, she would become an officer's mistress. She had been warned of the way of such things in Spain. Enlisted soldiers raped, but officers had higher class methods.

She packed and went immediately to the train station. There was a train to Nantes, near the coast. That wasn't where she wanted to go, but she took it anyway. She had to be out of Paris and far away before anyone thought to check on her. That was why she had written out the application: to gain a day's time. Otherwise she could have found it impossible to leave Paris. That, too, was the way of it.

She breathed a silent sigh of relief as the train departed without challenge. She was on a legitimate mission, until someone thought to make a unilateral cancellation of it. If she cleared Nantes before tomorrow morning, she should be too difficult to trace, and they would not bother.

At Nantes she caught a train to Bordeaux, and thence to Toulouse, exhausting her money. She was hungry, being unable to buy anything more, but would survive.

But when she went to get her truck from the garage, there was another problem: she had paid for only three days, and it was now a week. She owed for four, and she had no money.

"There is a way," the garage proprietor said, understanding her plight, which it seemed was not uncommon.

"No!" she said. She did not know what she was going to do. She couldn't *walk* across the Pyrenees, even if well fed, which she was not. It was just too far.

"You misunderstand," he said. "Look at me; I am an old man. I have daughters your age. But your Quaker truck will not be challenged, no?"

"Normally not," she agreed guardedly. "But smuggling isn't—"

"It is a man. A Jew. The Boche trumped up something against him, and took his house. He barely escaped the warrant for his arrest. He must escape the country."

Now she understood. "You will let my truck go?"

"With a tank full of petrol. And I will give you a good meal. If you will get him across. You can do it, when another could not."

She realized that it was a good offer. It wasn't as if she hadn't done this sort of thing before. "Very well."

"Thank you, thank you," he exclaimed, and she realized how tense he had been. The Jew must be a friend, but it was dangerous to help anyone the authorities were after. Across the border, the Jew could make his own way. At least he would have a chance.

The garage man's stout wife gave her good hot soup, a baked potato, and some wine. She had to refuse the wine, with apology, because she did not drink. She knew it was well intended; in France everyone drank wine, and it was safer than water.

Then the man caught on. "Quaker!" he said. "I had forgotten. They do not drink. You really are one."

"I really am one," she agreed. But not as good a one as she had been before she came to Europe. Now she was well compromised around the edges.

She was given blankets on the floor of the warm kitchen, and spent her most relaxed night in a week. Early in the morning, refreshed by a breakfast of porridge, she went to the truck. "Where is the—?" she asked.

"It is better that you do not see him. I hid him in the back last night."

She was alarmed. "No drugs. No smuggling."

"I promise, no. Only an old man like me. You will never know he is there, if you do not look."

That did seem best. The garage man could have hidden the Jew without telling her, but that would have been risky, because he needed the cooperation of the driver to get across the border. Had she looked inside and found him, she might have thought he was trying to steal the truck.

She drove out of Toulouse toward the border. There was no sound from the back. But the truck overheated slightly more rapidly than before, indicating that it was carrying a bit more. She was attuned to it, and could tell.

She came to Bourg Madame. She suffered a chill of apprehension as she saw that there was now a German guard at the border, in addition to the French one. The Germans were extending their hold on the country.

"Have you any contraband?" the German barked in French.

"No," she said, her mouth dry. She hated both the risk and the lie.

"It is a Quaker truck," the French guard explained. "We let them through."

"No exceptions," the German said. "Get out, woman; we shall inspect your truck."

Quality's heart seemed to shake in her chest. But there was nothing she could do. She got out of the truck and walked around to the back.

"Open it!"

With a feeling of dread, she opened the back panel. As the light spilled in, she saw with relief that there was only a pile of old blankets there. Maybe the Jew had lost his nerve and gotten out while she waited for the motor to cool.

The German reached in and grabbed a corner of a blanket. He yanked it toward him.

There, huddled beneath, was a man.

"So the word was right," the German said. "The Jew did try to cross the border." He drew his pistol. "Out, Jew! You are under arrest." Then he turned to Quality. "And your truck is impounded, and you are also under arrest."

There it was. The worst disaster had struck. Quality had the sick feeling that this was God's rebuke for her misdeeds. She had lied, and been caught, and now she would pay the penalty.

Chapter 8
Felix

Ernst saw Quality wave as he drove away. It was a perfectly ordinary thing, probably mere habit on her part, but it touched him. She seemed like such a fragile thing, standing there in her feminine jacket and skirt, yet she had been in Spain for the end of its civil war and had seen her share of blood. She was a soft-spoken pacifist, yet tough enough to get her job done. He respected that. Lane Dowling had a better treasure in her then perhaps he knew.

Now it was time for him to move on down to the southern tip of Spain. He had used up his slack time, driving with Quality. He would not be able to report to Heydrich until he returned to Germany, because the privacy of the local phones was not to be trusted. He would of course exonerate the Quaker mission; even had he not known Quality from America, he would have seen that these people were merely doing what they claimed to be doing, feeding hungry children who would not otherwise get fed. They were simply trying to do their bit of good in the world, in contrast to the great majority who had other imperatives.

There it was, he realized: Quality was good. She stood out from others not in appearance, though she was an extremely comely woman, but in the quality of her nature. Her name was the symbol of her being: Quality. He had felt it throughout, without being quite conscious of it until now.

When she had called him "thee," in English, he had felt something odd. He knew that she used the Quaker plain talk only when among friends. There was another symbol: they called themselves Friends. Indeed they were friends to the world, with their opposition to strife and their efforts to help those in need. Yet Quality was not his friend. She was his friend's fiancee. He had treated her as such. Still—

"Thank thee, Ernst," he said, repeating her words, and felt a warm shiver. He wished he could truly be her friend. He had told her that he regarded her as a fine woman. Now he realized how nice it would be to regard her as more than that.

Fortunately there was no chance of that. Their meeting had been coincidental, and it was unlikely that he would see her again. He need have no concern about presumption in his wandering fancy.

In due course he reached Algeciras and rented a room, as if he were a tourist pausing to see the sights. He did not report directly to the Abwehr post; he was an unofficial agent. But he would be there to help when Admiral Canaris arrived to supervise the implementation of Felix.

"Felix" was the unofficial code name for this project. It was, in essence, to mount an assault on the rock of Gibraltar and take it from the British. With that fortress and seaport in German hands, the British would be severely constrained, and it might be possible to close off access to the Mediterranean Sea and isolate the British fleet. It promised to be a strategic masterstroke that would protect the otherwise vulnerable underbelly of the Axis.

On July 24 Canaris appeared, accompanied by Lieutenant Colonel Pardo of the Spanish military intelligence. They were in civilian clothing, as Ernst was, and showed no papers. They operated only by personal recognition. It turned out that the Admiral had used a false passport himself to go to Madrid and meet with Spanish representatives, and even with General Franco himself. He had explained to Spain's ruler the German proposal for a surprise assault on Gibraltar. Franco had been supportive, but had reservations about the strength of the British Navy.

So did they all! But that strength certainly would not diminish as long as Gibraltar remained to service it. With the ocean supply route cut off, the pressure of the Luftwaffe and the U-boats should be decisive. The British would have few places to hide.

Admiral Canaris set up residence in a German safe house, Villa Leon, and used two other houses to establish surveillance of Gibraltar. The town commandant's office in La Linea, adjacent to Gibraltar's access to the mainland, provided a view of the northern defenses. The lighthouse at Punta Camero gave a good view of the west face.

It was Ernst's job to work with Captain Witzig of the Abwehr to establish whether an airborne assault on Gibraltar was feasible. Witzig was a small slim man, but he had a good record: he had been a paratrooper at Eben Emael in Belgium, and had been decorated for valor. Ernst took the man to the various observation points he had located, and discussed the situation with him.

"Why not just send in overwhelming force across the peninsula connecting Gibraltar to the mainland?" Witzig demanded.

"That route is obviously mined," Ernst explained. "British guns control it from many angles. Assaulting troops will experience ruinously heavy losses, and it will not be possible to make a broad enough front to assure that any get through."

"What about siege equipment? Bring down big guns from Germany, blast out the mines and the fortifications behind them, so that the troops have clearance?"

"We would have a time getting them here at all, let alone in necessary haste and privacy," Ernst replied. "The Spanish railways use a different gauge track from the French, requiring the transfer of all supplies and shipments at the border. This is a tedious process at best, and impossible to conceal from the eyes of spies. Also, the lines to Alceciras move through Madrid, making secrecy impossible in the light of British intelligence. In addition, Spain is constrained by limited resources for road maintenance, ordinance repair, communications requirements and foodstuffs."

"This is not exactly the Third Reich," Witzig muttered appreciatively. "So then it must be landings by paratroops or gliders, bypassing the peninsula."

"The slopes of Gibraltar are precipitous," Ernst reminded him as they studied the solid silhouette of the great rock. "The winds are irregular. It might as well be a minefield of the air."

Witzig nodded regretfully. "Then it seems that we are without sufficient resources to take the rock at this time. Nevertheless we shall take pictures, in case others are able to fathom what we do not."

"That is a diplomatic way to put it," Ernst agreed. He had thought it should be possible to storm Gibraltar, until he had taken a good look at it. It would be a phenomenal prize to achieve, but the cost would be prohibitive.

They took pictures. Because they did not want to be spied in the act, they took them by night. Consequently all they could come up with was murky silhouettes. This, too was a bad job; better pictures were already on file.

Canaris, disappointed, nevertheless acceded to the logic. He ordered improved observation equipment to be sent to Algeciras. Then he settled down with his consultants to draw up a feasible assault plan, taking into consideration all the problems they had noted. He also ordered the commander of the Brandenburg's third battalion to determine whether he could take Gibraltar with a surprise attack by German troops smuggled through Spain in trucks and supported by an engineer battalion infiltrated by sea.

In due course the word came back: NEGATIVE. Canaris and his party had by then returned to Germany, but Ernst remained in Spain, signifying that the Admiral had not given up the quest.

Heydrich, evidently keeping close track despite Ernst's lack of a direct report, arranged to have a sealed letter delivered to him. He found it on the floor of his room in Algeciras, slipped under the door during his absence. It was apparent that Ernst was not the only secret agent in the area.

He opened the letter. DESTROY AFTER READING was stamped at the top of the sheet, and Heydrich's signature was at the bottom. It was authentic.

It informed him that there was a plan to abduct the British Duke of Windsor, who was in Portugal now, about to take the ship *Excalibur* to the Bahamas, where he would be governor. The Duke had been King Edward VIII of England in 1936, but had gotten romantically interested in an American divorcee. Faced with the choice between her and the throne, the King, not the brightest of men, had abdicated the throne and married the woman. He was understood to be sympathetic to the Nazi cause, and might agree to make a statement on Germany's behalf. That would be a political coup that might sway others toward the cause. Ernst was to go to Portugal immediately to assist, since he spoke English and could serve as a translator. He was to tell no one else of this, but to pretend he was merely traveling, as before. There was a name and address: his contact in Portugal.

Ernst stared at the letter. Abduct the former King of England? In the hope that he would then endorse Nazism? This was utter folly! Even if the man was sympathetic, he would surely be alienated by the abduction, and in any event he would never publicly betray his country. He might not be smart, but he could hardly be that stupid. What nitwit had hatched this scheme? It couldn't be Heydrich!

But Heydrich would not directly counter a directive from his superior. He would go along with it, then arrange to divert it before real damage was done, in such a way that he would not be blamed. So this was form without substance. Ernst would have to go to Portugal and make the contact, but he doubted that it would go much farther than that.

Sure enough, when he reported to the address two days later he was told to forget it; the plan had been canceled. He was instructed to forget that it had ever existed, and to pretend that he had never entered Portugal. He was glad to oblige. Heydrich had succeeded in diverting the insanity.

Ernst, left to his own devices, resumed traveling around Spain, awaiting further orders. Something was bothering him, and it did not take any great concentration to figure out what: he wanted to see Quality Smith again. He knew this was idiocy, because even if she were not the fiancee of his friend, what interest would she have in a Nazi SS officer? Ernst was the opposite of everything she stood for. Yet he remembered her plain talk, and the way she had waved to him at the end, and his soul was restless.

In mid August he could stand it no longer. He drove to Barcelona and went to the headquarters of the Quaker Relief there. Only to be told that all of the Quakers had left Spain, and the project had been shut down. It seemed that they had done something to annoy the government, so had been abruptly expelled.

Ernst's emotions were mixed. He was sorry not to see Quality again, but glad that she had escaped the country. Now if it should come to pass that Germany invaded Spain, she would not be caught in the crossfire. She was safe in America, where she belonged.

Meanwhile it seemed that there was intense negotiation to try to get Spain to join the Axis voluntarily. Admiral Canaris came down for a week in late August to see about that, and Ernst joined him as a driver.

This, too, came to grief. After a week of intensive dialogue with Spanish officials, Canaris formed the opinion that General Franco would not join in the war until England was beaten. They would have to wait for the big effort of the Luftwaffe to break England down. Already the bombers were crossing the channel to England daily, so the capitulation should not be long in coming.

The Admiral returned to Germany, but still Ernst was relegated to Spain. Canaris was unwilling to give up on Felix, and intended to keep his personnel "on-site" until the project could be realized. This was in effect a vacation for Ernst, because he had nothing to do except drive around Spain, remaining inconspicuous. He could not remain in any one region long, lest folk realize that he was up to something. This included the Abwehr post in Algeciras.

So he toured the country in thorough fashion, reading whatever books were handy, but finding them all boring. The nights were lonely. It had been better on the floor, with Quality Smith, than in the bed alone. He thought about Krista, whom he hoped to see again soon, and about Quality, whom he expected not to see again. The two were so different, yet now occupied similar sections in his mind. Krista was beautiful, self-possessed, and decisive, and she wanted to marry him. Quality was beautiful too, in a more ethereal way, and sure of herself in a more subtle way, and decisive in an oblique way. The two were seeming opposites in nature, yet parallel. Krista wanted what was best for Krista, and would do what she had to do achieve her ambition. Quality hardly seemed to care about herself; she wanted what was best for the world, and had been doing what she could to improve it. Of the two philosophies, he preferred the latter.

But Krista was available, and Quality was not. Quality was back in America, and she was Lane's fiancee. She was a pacifist who hated the artifacts of war and despised the Nazis. He had always known that there would never be anything between Quality and himself. Why, then, was it her face that came to his mind?

He forced his imagination to picture Krista as she might be the day he agreed to marry her. She would go with him to a private place, and take off her clothing to show her fine body, and say "I thank thee, Ernst."

The picture exploded. That had not been Krista talking, but Quality! He could not keep her out of his fancy, though every aspect of her nature was foreign to his.

Ernst shook his head. There were currents of foolishness in him he had not fathomed. But they would fade in time; it was inevitable.

The Spanish press carried news the German press did not: the Battle Over Britain was not going well. Too many bombers were not returning. By the middle of September it was obvious that air power was not going to bring England to her knees. Ernst wondered whether Lane Dowling was part of the reason. He suspected that it was.

Admiral Canaris continued to campaign behind the scenes for Felix, and Ernst continued to travel Spain. He agreed with the Admiral: it was now more important than ever to deny England the use of the Mediterranean, so that the surging British aircraft could not go there to raid Axis installations. There was only so much the British ships could do, but buttressed by air power they would be formidable. The failure over England had to be redeemed by a success here, beginning with the capture of the Rock of Gibraltar. They had to make the Mediterranean theater impregnable.

In late October Adolf Hitler himself met with General Franco, trying to charm him into joining the Axis. But Franco remained noncommittal. Did the fool think he had any other course? He had gained power because of Hitler's help; now he was stalling about returning the favor.

On October 28 Italy invaded Greece. That involved the Axis in a Balkan war, because of the "Three Power Pact" signed between Germany, Italy and Japan the month before. Ernst did not like it; to his mind the Italians had delusions of the grandeur of ancient Roman days, and were not militarily competent now. This was all too likely to become a mess for Germany to clean up. Admiral Canaris originated an armistice proposal which gained Hitler's backing, but somehow there was no follow-through, and the mess remained.

But it had one beneficial effect: it revived Hitler's interest in the Mediterranean. Two weeks later Felix was given operational status, and Canaris came to Spain again to determine how Abwehr units and combat teams could best contribute to the Felix assault. There were several code names: Felsennest, soon changed to Basta, and an Abwehr Captain worked on it under the name Roderigo. But it was really Felix.

"We need reconnaissance from the other side," Canaris said. "To pinpoint the nature and number and placement of their defenses, and to spy out any possible access route. Just a good description would be immeasurably helpful."

"I wish I could get there," Ernst said. "I can speak Spanish and English, so I might pass as an educated Spaniard."

"You know better than I that the isthmus is closed off and guarded, and the surrounding waters are mined," the Admiral said. "But if you can find a way, by all means do it." He smiled at the humor of the notion.

Ernst searched for a way. He learned that there was a local smuggler, Jorge, who made regular visits to the Rock, selling dubious goods at exorbitant prices. Could they bribe Jorge to smuggle a man to Gibraltar? Probably they could—but the rock was so small and tight that any stranger there was all too apt to be spotted and challenged. A failure would be worse than not trying, because it would betray the German interest in Gibtraltar. So he concluded that this was not a viable option. There had to be some other way to get the information they needed.

But there was one thing they could do. Ernst went into the town of La Linea, just north of the Gibraltar isthmus. "I am looking for Jorge," he said in Spanish. "I think he has something for me."

It was surprisingly easy. Jorge regarded himself as a trader. He took Spanish goods to Gibraltar, trading them for British money, which was valuable to some parties in Spain. Twice a week he loaded up his small boat and rowed down to the west shore of Gibraltar where he delivered Spanish wines, exotic condoms, rare expensive canned food, dirty pictures, spices, and items of female apparel not seen on the street. The British authorities knew about it, but ignored him as long as he smuggled no dangerous drugs or weapons. Ernst could understand why: such trade served as a certain relief valve for bored military men, and helped keep the internal peace. "I have many officers as customers," Jorge confided. "They don't come in person, but I know them by their tastes. I have the only brand of tea they really like, and the herbs to make women wild for sex."

"I don't believe that," Ernst said.

Jorge eyed him cannily. "But *they* believe, and that is what counts. What is it that you believe in?"

In other words, what did he want badly enough to pay an outrageous price for it. "I believe you could smuggle someone to or from Gibraltar, and back again on your following trip."

"You believe too much! They would have my head!"

"Who?"

"The British! They watch that rock like hawks. They look the other way when I trade, but if I ever tried to bring anyone else there, they would shoot me."

Ernst nodded. "Surely they would. And what do you think the Spaniards would do if you brought a Britisher from the rock to Spain?"

He became canny. "The Spanish don't care. They sell me the goods I trade. Anyone who comes from the Rock is here for a good time, with much money to spend. There are no women there, now; the British expelled them all. The local women know how to get it all from a man, and leave him happy."

So he did conduct some British to Spain. "And the Germans? What do you think they would do to such a visitor?"

"Oh, the Germans do not know about this."

"Are you sure?"

Jorge looked at him, beginning to catch on. "Who are you?"

"I am Captain Osterecht of the Abwehr."

"What do you want with me?" Jorge asked, alarmed.

"I want information. I want you to tell me of any future British you bring here."

"But if you take them, my business will be destroyed! I must bring them safely back, or I will not dare show my face at the Rock again."

"Let me explain what I have in mind. You will inform me of any Britisher you bring here. I will encounter him by seeming coincidence, interrogate him, and let him go. You will be blameless and he will not be harmed. Your business will not be affected."

"But why should I tell you? My business will be safer if I protect the business of my clients."

Ernst slowly drew his service pistol, the one that had impressed and horrified Quality. He hoped it would have similar effect here. "Because your business will be in trouble if you do not." He paused, letting the man's fear build as the threat sank in. "And because I will pay you generously for your cooperation."

Jorge's expression changed from fear to greed. "You will pay?"

Ernst put away the pistol and brought out a packet of bills. The threat had been a bluff, but the bribe was not. "This now, and the same again, for each one you tell me of." It was the stick and carrot approach, normally quite effective.

So it was that the deal was made. With luck, they would have a Britisher to interrogate about the defenses of Gibraltar. They had a drug that would make a person talk fairly freely, and forget what had occurred.

A week later Jorge contacted Ernst by calling the number he had been given. "There is one."

Ernst went immediately, taking pesos. Jorge told him where the Britisher was dallying, and Ernst gave him the money. Then the agents of the Abwehr closed in on the target.

But it was only a seaman, fresh in port and determined to get what he usually got in port. He would not have any worthwhile knowledge. They let him go without interrogation.

The following week there was another. Again they paid handsomely for nothing. Jorge was getting far the best of the deal.

But the third week it was different. "This time an airman," Jorge said as he took the money.

That could be good news. An airman should have seen the rock from above, and know where its main defensive emplacements were. Ernst went himself to check this one.

The man was not going to the house of the prostitutes. In fact he was not staying in town at all. He had already rented a car and was driving rapidly north. What was going on? There was nothing entertaining in that direction.

"He must be a secret agent." someone said.

Now that seemed likely. What better way to introduce one to Spain? "We must discover what he is up to," Ernst said. But he was the only one free to pursue the agent. He got his car and set off. Now it was not merely information on the Rock he was after, but a line on what the British were trying to do in Spain. This could be extremely important.

Ernst knew the roads of Spain, and could drive them at night. The British agent evidently did not. He took wrong turns and got enmeshed in the dead ends of bombed out roads. He got lost in obscure towns. But he seemed to be headed up the coast, toward Valencia. He also seemed to be in a hurry to get there, so was driving all night. But Ernst was able to catch up to him, before turning off so as not to give away his pursuit. He knew which car it was, so would not lose it.

The agent would not make it to Valencia quickly. Ernst knew of a bombed-out bridge that would surely catch him and force him to retrace a goodly segment of his route. The bridge was marked plainly, so there was no danger of driving off it and into space, but it would cause the man to turn around. Ernst drew up to the turnoff and parked his car sideways, blocking it. Now he would find out who the man was and what he was up to. It seemed pointless to follow him hundreds of miles until he reached a big city, where he could be lost. Better to brace him here, alone.

Ernst got out of his car and stood beside it, his hand on his pistol. It was quite possible that the agent would be dangerous when he saw himself trapped. But it was also possible that this was not a saboteur, but someone trying to infiltrate an office or simply to make an observation and retreat with his notes. Exactly as Ernst would have done, had it been feasible to reach Gibraltar. So he would not be too ready to use his pistol. He preferred not to reveal himself as German, if he could avoid it.

At dawn the lights of the agent's car appeared. They speared down to strike Ernst's car. This was the critical point. Would the man stop? Would he talk?

The car stopped. Its motor died; the driver did not want to waste petrol. The man came out in the early light.

"Who are you?" Ernst called in Spanish. A true agent would know the language.

"I don't speak Spanish."

Ernst was amazed. *He knew that voice*!

"Lane Dowling!" he exclaimed.

"Oh my God—is that you, Ernst?"

They walked together and embraced, after each put away his ready pistol. "I thought you were a secret agent!" Ernst said.

"I thought you were a Spanish highwayman. What are you doing here?"

"Following you." Then Ernst made a connection. "Quality! You are coming to see her! But—" He hesitated.

Lane frowned. "Have you seen her?"

"Yes. I did not know she was in Spain. I was inspecting the Quaker facilities in Barcelona, and there she was. She did not expose my cover."

Lane's attention was fixed. "When was this?"

"July tenth. We traveled together, to see Guernica. I returned her to her station July twelfth."

"She was well?" There was an intensity to Lane's question.

"Physically she seemed somewhat worn, but well. Mentally—she saw war, Lane. It hurt her."

“Where is she now?”

“Why, America, I think. When I returned to Barcelona in August they told me that all the Quakers had left Spain. You did not know?”

“She did not go to America or to England. That much I know.”

Ernst gazed at him in consternation. “Then where is she?”

“That’s why I came here. To find out. Only I haven’t been able to get papers for Spain. So I had to sneak in, hoping to reach Barcelona without being discovered.”

Ernst shook his head. “The Quakers are not there. Franco deported them. The food trucks are not moving. She would not remain if she could not help. Perhaps there was a mistake in the listing, and she is after all in America.”

“No,” Lane said grimly. “No mistake. I checked and rechecked every report. She did not leave Spain with the Quakers.”

“Lane, I know nothing of this. She—I would not want her to be hurt. When we traveled together, it was compatible. It is easy to see why you love her. Had my mission in Spain had anything to do with her disappearance, I would have known. I must conjecture that either the Spanish authorities arrested her—”

“They tell us they did not.”

“They will say what they choose to say. But surely they had no reason. She meant no harm to them.”

“So what is the other prospect?”

Ernst sighed. “That she somehow fell afoul of—criminals, perhaps. There are many desperate people in Spain.”

“But she knew enough to stay clear of them.”

“Yes. She was competent.” Ernst did not like the thought of Quality being killed by criminals much better than Lane did. He cast about for something else. “Or—the Quakers had connections in France. If she went there—”

“Would the Vichy have arrested her?”

“Things are confused in France. It is possible. Yet they should have released her when they saw her papers.”

“Suppose it was the Germans?”

“They might hold her as hostage. Because she was working with the British, and we are at war.”

Lane grinned mirthlessly. “Don’t I know it! Can you find out about her?”

“Yes. I should be able to, if she is in any Vichy or German list. But

I do not know whether I could do anything to help her. If she is in a camp—they can be very strict."

"You could surely do more than I could!"

Ernst laughed, but not with humor. "I might suggest to the commandant of the camp that she is of interest to certain parties, and must be kept healthy. But that would not get her free. At least it would help until a prisoner exchange could be arranged. But prospects for any such thing are bleak."

"You will do what you can."

"I will do what I can."

"Now I am glad we met. You know it would be no betrayal of your side to help her. She's a pacifist."

"No betrayal," Ernst agreed.

"If you learn anything, maybe you could have news sent to the Spanish authorities."

"I will try."

"Then my effort here has not been for nothing, thanks to the incredible coincidence of meeting you."

"Coincidence? I think not. It was Quality who brought us together-even in her absence."

"Must be. But I'm glad it happened, Ernst. I never expected to see you again, when the war got going. Is there anything I can do for you, in return for looking out for Quality?"

"There is one thing. My people believe that I was in pursuit of a spy. I must make a report. Can you tell me of the defenses of Gibraltar?"

Lane paused, considering. "That question tells me your mission here."

"I am afraid it does. But if I do not get the answer to my question, from the spy, they may choose not to let you return."

Lane laughed. "I know how it is. Okay, Ernst, I don't think it will materially compromise our security to tell you what you already know. Gibraltar is practically invulnerable to any attack short of a major invasion. You could beat it down by shelling it from artillery based in Spain, or by continuously bombing it. But you'd take heavy losses in planes. I'm a fighter pilot, and I looked at their ack-ack. I'd never want to go up against it. I honestly believe that unless you can base your artillery in Spain, you don't have a chance. Not by land, certainly; you know the isthmus is mined. So is the harbor. So my advice to you is give it up. Don't even try to take it."

"Can you give specifics?"

"Yeah, sure. They'll only prove my point." He went on to do so.

"I think my people will be satisfied," Ernst said. "They will know that I could have come by those details only by interrogating one who had seen the defenses directly."

"For sure."

"Then let us return to La Linea. I believe our business is done. I will follow your car, and will advise my people to let you proceed unmolested. We prefer that the British not suspect that we are observing them."

"They already suspect. But they hardly care."

"With reason, I think." Ernst stepped back.

Lane relaxed. He offered his hand. Ernst took it. Then they got in their cars and Ernst drew his out of the way, letting Lane pass.

Ernst's report was no comfort to the Abwehr. "Nothing short of a massive assault will take it. We don't have the resources. There are no weaknesses I could find."

"What about Jorge? If we smuggled soldiers—"

"He wouldn't do it. If he did, we could smuggle only two at a time. They could not do enough damage to make a difference."

However, Ernst did make sketches and write out descriptions of the defenses in fair detail. He had succeeded in defining the enemy emplacements. The problem was that this only confirmed that the notion of taking Gibraltar by assault was foolish. He suspected that his report would not be forwarded to Admiral Canaris.

Meanwhile, when he was free, he drove again to Barcelona and questioned the proprietor of the house where the Quaker office had been. "We suspect that one of them did not depart with the others."

"They all left," he was assured. "None are here now."

"Did any trucks go to France?"

"There was one, but it did not return."

That was all they knew. But it opened an avenue. Quality could have driven to France, and been caught there. But there was nothing more he could do until he returned to Germany and reviewed the lists of detainees. It was galling to have to wait, but he was on assignment in Spain and had to remain there.

In December Admiral Canaris returned to Spain to meet with General Franco. Ernst accompanied him to Madrid. The Admiral's mission was unsuccessful: Spain was "unable" to join the war, or even to give a date for entry into the war, because of the current economic and military situation. "The Führer will be annoyed," Canaris muttered. "I am here on his direct order. But if we can take Gibraltar, that may make up for it. We can still secure the Mediterranean theater."

Ernst wanted to tell him that Gibraltar was hopeless, but the man was already so depressed that he remained silent.

So the consideration of Felix continued. Despite Ernst's firsthand report of the layout of the defenses, they wanted more pictures. In order to conceal their real intent, they took them by a local brothel, with some of the girls posing in the foreground.

That was a mistake. The authorities in Germany got the idea that the Abwehr personnel were playing with harlots instead of doing their work, and demanded that it stop. Project Felix was canceled.

But later in the month it was revived, as a possible diversion to relieve the hard-pressed Italians in Greece. It didn't matter; it remained hopeless.

Felix was canceled again, resurrected again, and finally canceled for good, and the Abwehr units were reassigned. But before that, Ernst was recalled to Germany. It was a relief. Now at last he would have the chance to check on Quality—if she were a prisoner of the Vichy. He hoped she was, because otherwise there was no hope for her.

Ernst returned to Berlin. It was the Christmas season, and though the Nazis frowned on Christianity, they had no objection to festivities. So Ernst had a week's leave to visit home. He could not return directly to Wiesbaden, because of his cover, but he found a way to manage it indirectly.

The first thing he did was look up Krista, whom he had not seen in almost six months. She was getting holiday leave too. She remained almost startlingly beautiful, and her interest in him was undiminished. But Berlin was crowded, and there was no sufficiently private place for her to demonstrate her interest in her normal fashion. So their first date was quite open and chaste.

"Do you think your family would object if I accompanied you, to meet them?" he inquired.

Her eyes lighted. She understood his situation, and saw opportunity. "They do know I have been seeing someone in Berlin. I think they might appreciate learning more about him. But it may be difficult to get train tickets, this late; tickets have been sold out for weeks."

"I believe I could requisition a car for a few days."

Those were magic words. "Then we must do it!"

They did it. She understood that when they arrived in Wiesbaden they would separate, each returning home alone, to avoid awkward questions both political and personal, and that when they met again there he would be Ernst Best. She was good at secrets.

As they drove toward Frankfurt, she turned to him. "We could stop anywhere along the way, for anything." Her meaning was clear.

Ernst was sorely tempted. But he resisted. "I want it to be right between us—completely right."

"But you must let me tempt you, in case it is already right. You must play fair, Ernst."

He had to smile. When they came to an intersection with a minor road, he turned off, and turned off again, finding a deserted section in a wooded region. He stopped the car.

Krista slid over to embrace him. She kissed him. Then she opened her shirt to him. "Touch me, and tell me it is not right."

"I fear that would be too much temptation."

She loosened her bra and drew it out of the way. "If you wait too long, someone will come and see me, and then you will have much explaining to do."

She was daring him to gamble on delay! And she was right: he could not afford to have anyone see her this way, and he did need to demonstrate that he could hold his course despite her.

He reached out and took her full breasts in his hands. The whole world seemed to fade out, except for that rapturous contact. His desire for her intensified to the point of seeming madness.

Then he heard something. Was it the approach of a distant car? He slid his hands around and up, catching the straps of her bra on his fingers. He drew it down to cover her breasts, and then closed her shirt over the whole.

The sound faded. It was a car, but not coming this way. But the false alarm had enabled him to do what he should.

She sighed. "You have not changed. I think it is your constancy I love most about you, though it frustrates me horribly. When you do commit, I will know it will never change."

He nodded. He rather thought he would indeed commit, when he was free of this mission. Krista was ideal for an SS officer.

The rest of the visit home was uneventful. Four days later they returned to Berlin. Did Krista know how close she had come to overwhelming his resistance? Perhaps she did, and was satisfied merely to inflame his passion without actually doing anything forbidden.

Meanwhile, in Berlin, the Abwehr was involved in plans for the next campaign: the relief of the Italian effort in Yugoslavia and Greece. As Ernst had anticipated, the Italians were messing up the job and needed to be bailed out. The Admiral had worked out an armistice proposal which had gained Hitler's support, but the Greek Premier opposed it.

"It is essential that Germany not be drawn into this action," Canaris insisted. He seemed almost desperate. That was odd, because it was obvious that German forces, if committed, could quickly reduce both Greece and Yugoslavia. It would have been better if it had been possible to take Gibraltar from the British, thus protecting that flank, but that would not stop land action.

Then Ernst had a bright idea. "Haven't a number of foreign personnel been interned in French camps? Refugees from the International Brigade may be of any nationality. They could be interviewed by military intelligence to determine whether they possess information or contacts of potential value to Reich concerns in other areas. If we can ascertain whether any are of Greek or Yugoslavian derivation—"

Canaris paused. "Any lead we can get is worthwhile. If by chance there are any with family members in important positions in Greece who might be blackmailed, that would be better yet. But it would take time to do this, and I have no personnel free." Then he did a doubletake, looking at Ernst. "Except for you. Do it. Requisition a list of interred foreigners, and go to see them. See about translators who know the languages. If any camp directors balk, refer them to me."

That was exactly what Ernst wanted. He would check every name, and if there were any Greeks or Slavs he could certainly do his utmost to get their information. But he would also check for one particular name: an American.

Soon the lists arrived, because it seemed that Hitler himself wanted Canaris to succeed in his effort. Ernst wondered what was so important about that region, that Germany had to remain clear of it? This was unlike previous campaigns.

Ernst pored over the names, noting prospects. It was not enough to check foreign names, for a name was no certain indication of origin. He had to catch the familiar names that might nevertheless have foreign connections. Also, some might have given false name to conceal their origins. He would have to actually see them and hear them speak to be sure. It was a big job he had gotten for himself.

Then he checked Gurs, a camp along the Spanish border. The name leaped out at him. Quality Smith, American. She was there. He had found her!

But Ernst did not allow anyone else to know his excitement. He completed his review of the lists, and prepared to travel to the camps. He had to do this in such a way that his interest would not cause any possible additional trouble for Quality. For despite his excitement about this confirmation, which was evidence that she was at least alive, he knew that her situation was in other respects dire. She must have been arrested for some reason. He would have to discover what that was, without tipping his hand.

He interviewed the internees at Gurs in rigorous order: first those suspected of having any Greek or Yugoslav connection, then those of other nationalities. He had to use translators for the various languages. The results were disappointing, in terms of his official mission, but he was establishing his credits so that no one would catch on to his personal mission. One of the last was the American, deliberately, as a wrap-up of what remained.

They brought her in, clad in her worn and soiled shirt and skirt. There was no money for uniforms for internees, so armbands distinguished them. Her hair fell partly across her face, not from any artful device but because she evidently lacked pins to hold it in place. She was completely unremarkable—yet his heart leaped.

He did not give her a chance to betray their prior acquaintance. He spoke brusquely in English. "Your name is—" He paused to peer at his list of names. "Smith. Of Britain?"

Her surprise could have been taken for fear of the interrogator. She had never seen him in uniform before. "I am Quality Smith, of America."

"We are not at war with America. You were caught spying for Britain?"

"I was caught trying to smuggle a man from France into Spain."

He frowned. "A Jew?" he asked sharply.

"Yes."

He glanced at the camp commandant. "See how openly she confesses it. Americans are notoriously naive about this matter. She probably did not even think she was doing wrong." Then he fired the question directly at Quality. "Is it wrong to harbor a Jew?"

"No."

He turned again to the commandant. "It is a mistake to aggravate a noncombatant nation unnecessarily. It would be better to repatriate this one. Notify the American ambassador of her presence here, and advise him that we will deliver her there for a nominal fee to cover our costs in boarding her for this time. In the interim, she should be kept in good health, so that the Americans will have no claim against us."

He watched as she was led away. He had done all he could to safeguard her. He doubted that she would be released, but he had accomplished two things: he had verified that she was alive and in health, and he had let her know that he would help her. To whatever extent he could.

What he had not anticipated was the strength of his personal reaction to the sight of her. He had addressed her with calculated indifference, but he had wanted to take her in his arms and comfort her. The emotion was different, in subtle and unsubtle ways, from what he had felt when touching Krista's breasts, but as strong.

In fact, he realized now that Quality was the major reason he had resisted Krista's allure. It was sheer foolishness and mischief in every respect, but his heart was drawn to her. He *had* to help her, though he dreaded the price of it.

Chapter 9
Gibraltar

Lane arrived at the Rock of Gibraltar in October 1940. Because the proprietors were sensitive to any interference by outsiders, he was listed as a temporarily inactive airman sent for recuperation. He would not be allowed to fly, and would not offer any criticism of existing facilities or policies. He would serve in whatever capacity to which it was convenient to assign him, and when he completed his recovery he would return to England to rejoin his unit. In short, he was represented as exactly what he was: a disabled airman who needed to be parked somewhere away from his unit until he was able to resume full activity. That way he could not interfere with the efficiency of his unit, or endanger his fellow airmen by being too eager to get back into the air.

The fact that Gibraltar was right next to Spain was officially irrelevant. No one here knew Lane's personal motive for being here. No one except Bader, who would not tell. Lane smiled, thinking of that. Bader had done him an enormous favor, and earned his lifetime loyalty thereby. But Bader had also succeeded in making him take the inactive time required, willingly. Bader had put it all together. That was his genius.

Gibraltar was impressive from the air. It was geologically a "bill," or projection from land, the opposite of a fjord or inlet. Lane, unused to being a passenger instead of a pilot, nevertheless appreciated the chance to gaze at it with his whole attention. The thing was like a sleeping two-humped camel, its head down out of sight. The higher hump was to the north, to his surprise; he had somehow thought the rock rose to its southernmost extremity, then plunged into the sea. That was far from the case; the rise was nearly vertical at the north, just below the isthmus that connected it to the mainland, and tapered down to the sea at the south. The east side was too steep for use, but the west had roads and buildings all along its gentler slope. Several great moles reached out from the west to enclose the harbor. They served as the port for Force H, the British naval group consisting of the battle cruiser Hood, the battleships

Resolution and Valiant, the aircraft carrier Ark Royal, several other cruisers, and fleet destroyers. The Eighth Submarine Flotilla was also here. The fighter planes served to protect these assorted ships. Lane had reviewed it all, and now was seeing it come to life.

Had he likened the peninsula to a sleeping camel? No, as the angle of approach shifted he saw the sharp ridges at its top, and the slanted water catchments on the eastern slope. The ridge was after all highest at the southern part, before commencing its slant. The Rock was more like a great ship, a monstrous three-mile-long battleship, no, a carrier ship, with its superstructure off to one side to make space for the landing decks. And that was what it was, essentially: a mighty dreadnought neither battleship nor carrier, but a colossal attack ship docked for the moment at the continent, about to set off for some unimaginable voyage. If he had to be out of his airplane and on a ship, this was the ship to be on.

Historically, he had learned, Gibraltar had been reckoned as one of the Pillars of Hercules, the great rocks guarding the entrance to the Mediterranean Sea. The other Pillar was the Spanish Ceuta on the North African coast. The ancient Phoenician mariners were said to have crowned the rocks with silver columns to mark the limits of safe navigation. In the eighth century A.D. the Moslems had fortified Gibraltar after invading Spain. In the fourteenth century it was captured by the Castilians, but soon regained by the Moors, who held it for more than another century. It finally passed into the hands of the British early in the eighteenth century, who had held it against all comers. Now they had deepened the harbor and built a new airfield on it, making it more formidable than ever. Spain had wanted possession of the Rock for centuries, but was unlikely to get it.

So today the British held Gibraltar, Malta and Cyprus, and effectively controlled the Mediterranean Sea from end to end. The center of British strategy was Malta, but Gibraltar was a staging area for the convoys to that island, and its carrier-based Hurricanes protected those convoys. Oh, to be in one of those Hurricanes! But if Gibraltar were ever wrested from the British, the others would follow, and the Axis would control the region. That was why it was so important to defend the Rock; the ultimate security of the region might well depend on it.

They circled around and came down on the landing strip on the northern isthmus. It looked pitifully short; he would recommend that it be lengthened if they want to do any serious flying from it.

They drove into the town on the west slope, where Lane reported to the residence of the governor. "Here you are, sir," the driver said, pulling up at the south edge of town. "The Convent."

"There must be some misunderstanding," Lane said. "I can't go to a convent!"

The man laughed. "That's the Government House. It's always been called the Convent, because that's what it was when it started."

So it turned out to be. Lane found the necessary office within, registered, and was then taken to a temporary residence elsewhere in town.

He gazed out toward the west. The water of the bay was dark, but there were lights along the moles and along the mainland farther away. There were also small craft moving about with searchlights playing across the water. It was pretty, but he was sure they weren't doing it for fun. What were they looking for?

Then he heard muffled explosions, as if fireworks were being detonated under the water. This merely increased the mystery. They were definitely up to something.

In the morning he returned to the Convent to inquire about his assignment. He assumed that he would be put on a work detail or something similar; it might not be fun, but it would be useful. He had no special illusions about the fate of a grounded airman, and expected to be treated as something of an outcast. He had in effect asked for it, by transferring away from his home unit.

All he got was a bland assurance that something would be found; he would be notified in due course. As the days passed and no notification came, he realized that he was in bureaucratic limbo.

"What's going on here?" he asked a bunkmate. "Don't tell me there are no junk details on Gibraltar."

"The minds of administrative officials are inscrutable in their stupidity," the man said. "But my guess is that they're distracted by the chariots."

"The what?"

"It's an Italian horror. We didn't even know what was going on, until one of them washed up on the beach. A chariot is a torpedo ridden by two men in diving suits. It's got a large explosive warhead that they can detach and fix to the target ship. Then the crew rides the torpedo away before the timer blows it. Nobody's supposed to know they've been there, until it's too late. Except that one of them got stuck in silt under the harbor; it blew, and we knew something was up, and got on it and captured the men and learned all about it."

Lane did not have to inquire why the Italians had given the information. Geneva conventions were honored by both sides in word rather than deed. What was called torture when the enemy did it was called interrogation when the home team did it. It was better simply to answer the questions and come away with one's health.

"So that's why the night motor launches, and searchlights, and the small explosions," Lane said. "To get rid of the chariots. Those small charges are just enough to kill any personnel that might be down there."

"You got it. They're laying barbed wire on the bottom, too, and adding torpedo nets. It's hell down there."

Lane believed it. The appearance of the nocturnal bay was lovely, but the reality was ugly. The war was being fought here out of sight, but was as serious as it was elsewhere.

He settled in to the routine. There was nothing for him to do, so he applied for a passport to visit Spain and meanwhile explored the Rock. Could it really hold out against a real attack?

The defenses were even more formidable than he had thought. The walls of the Rock were hollowed out, forming galleries at various levels. In those embrasures were heavy cannon and antiaircraft guns. Any frontal assault would be tremendously costly, if it succeeded at all.

On the second day Lane walked the road that circled the peninsula, searching for any possible weakness in the defenses. He had already concluded that there was none, but he had the foolish notion that he might make himself useful by spotting something that had so far been missed. He enjoyed traversing the tunnels that took over when the slope was too steep to support the road.

One morning there was a solid fog, making everything clammy. "What is this, England?" Lane demanded humorously.

"It's the Levanter Cloud," one of the workers told him.

"The what?"

"The east wind, called the Levanter, prevails. It sweeps across the warm Mediterranean. The warm air strikes the rock and rises up the east face to maybe fifteen hundred feet, where it cools and forms a cloud. It's worst in summer, up to September, but it can happen anytime. Sometimes it shrouds us and spreads right across to the mainland. When it's really heavy it's like living in a Turkish bath. We say the rock is wearing its hat. Sometimes it generates gusting winds, and we get little waterspouts."

Lane's irritation with the fog was replaced by intrigue. This was a more interesting place than he had thought. This was just as well, because without a regular job to do, and without many of the amenities of civilian life, boredom was a more immediate threat than the Axis. There were no women to speak of here; they had been moved out because of concern that the rock would come under siege. The men from the naval vessels that constantly stopped here were loud in their objection to this aspect. They expected to avail themselves of the pleasures of the female flesh, as they routinely did in every port, and could not. That meant considerable discontent, which found its own expression. Fights were frequent, and drinking and gambling were heavy.

Lane climbed the heights. It wasn't as if he could fancy himself the first man there, because Rock Gun was the name of the highest point, with its gun emplacement: twin 9.2 inchers. On the other peak were the ruins of the old Moorish castle, surely no match for that artillery. So there had been plenty of action at these heights. Still, it gave him a certain feeling of freedom and accomplishment, and the view was good.

The Greeks had believed that this was the end of the world. At least that was the implication of Homer's description in the *Iliad*: "Styx in her glorious house, roofed over with long rocks, propped up to heaven all around with silver pillars." St. Michael's Cave, here, contained a large underground freshwater lake, ice cold and black, surrounded by stalactites and stalagmites. Water dripped from the rocks of the Rock, freshened by its passage through the stone. Surely word of this had reached the Greeks, perhaps by way of the Phoenicians, and it had become part of their lore. Today that internally dripping water was less romantic; aluminum Nissen huts and other prefabricated shelters were erected inside the tunnels and caverns so that the occupants did not get "rained" on.

The history of the Rock extended farther back than that, however. The first Neandertal skull was discovered on Gibraltar. It was female, and as the luck of the gender would have it, was dismissed as not a serious find. They assumed that it was merely a deformed modern skull. Nine years later there was another discovery of the species at Neander in the Rhine Valley near Dusseldorf, in Germany, and so it was named for this. Thus Gibraltar Woman missed her opportunity for fame. With the women gone from the Rock now, it was easy to suppose that it was because of that neglect: the first woman was annoyed.

The first woman. Actually the Neanthertals were not necessarily the ancestors of modern man; they might more properly be considered close cousins. But the thought of a woman, even a grotesque Neandertal one (but who could say for sure? Maybe she was cute) reminded him of his private reason for being here. It was because of a woman.

Where was Quality Smith now? Her letters had stopped, and that surely meant trouble. She would have written to him if it were humanly possible. He had to find out what had happened to her.

But it was evident that the Spanish government was not rushing to issue him a passport. He had been warned that the bureaucracy of such nations was horrendous. It might take months, or it might be never. So what was he going to do?

He asked around, unofficially, and found out. It was possible to visit the mainland. Twice a week knowledgeable and nervy and desperate seamen bought rides with a local smuggler named Jorge. Their interest was the brothels of La Linea, but the trader hardly cared what they did as long as they paid him well enough.

Jorge was a Spanish given name, a common one, the equivalent of the English George but pronounced more like Hor-hee. Lane went to meet the man, understanding that news of any of this must never reach the British officers. The officers surely knew all about it, but did not interfere as long as things were handled discreetly. Fortunately Jorge spoke enough English so that they could communicate.

They bargained, and finally agreed on a price. It was of course exorbitant, and it would leave his wallet thin, but considering the value of such a trip, it was worth it. He would pay half to take him safely out, and half to bring him safely back. The trader's greed would keep him honest; this was a good additional business for him.

He was ready on Jorge's next trading night, dressed in Spanish peasant clothing. "More dirt," Jorge said, rubbing some in. "You are the lowliest of workers, paid as little as I can get away with."

They approached the boat. "I will get out and take my money and empty boxes to my friend," Jorge said. He meant his contact in the smuggling trade. "You will be my assistant. You will carry for me. Then I will send you back to watch the boat, but in the dark you will go where you wish, and I will speak to you as I leave for my own house, as if you are there. In four days I will be here again, and call to you to stay with the boat; then you will go to it. But if you do not come, I will not wait; I will pretend you are there, so no one suspects. This is all I can do."

"If I am not there, it will be my own fault," Lane agreed.

"Now the money."

"Now half the money." Lane gave the man the sheaf of bills. "My companion will meet us when we return in three days, and he will have the other half. If I am not with you, he will not pay you." Lane was of course not going to carry the money with him; it had to be secure against betrayal.

The man nodded. It was fair.

They got into the craft, which was a stand-up rowboat. Jorge showed Lane how to do it, and they took turns rowing. There was a dim lantern hung on the bow, so that no one would mistake the craft for anything else. This excursion might be unofficial, but it was not secret; the guns of the British were not kind to secrets near their shore.

"Now be properly servile," he said as they approached the Spanish shore. "They must not suspect otherwise."

Then, as Lane rowed diligently, the trader started exclaiming. "No, no, dolt, *that* way! Keep it moving! Must I do everything myself? Have you never rowed a boat before?"

Lane smiled in the dark. He would have been angry, were he anything other than a servant—or a spy. It was the perfect camouflage.

They came to land, and a dark figure hauled them in. "You bring a friend, this time, Jorge," he remarked.

"No, I bring a British spy!" Jorge retorted. "What do you think?"

The man laughed. "Well, don't let him steal my treasures."

Jorge loaded Lane with boxes and led him to the house. The light inside was dim. He set them down on the table. Now Jorge would settle with his supplier for the value of the goods he had moved, and make a deal for more for the next trip. "Go back and watch the boat," Jorge snapped at Lane. "I will call you when I want you."

Meekly, Lane obeyed. He left the house and walked toward the shore. No one went with him; it was all a pose in case any Spanish authorities were near. When he was reasonably sure he was unobserved, he strode away from the boat and lost himself among the bushes near the shore.

He waited, and in due course the trader emerged from the house. He walked to the boat. "Push off, idiot!" he cried. "Do you think we have all night?" And it did seem as if there was a separate figure there with him. Jorge's voice continued as the boat moved away, giving insulting instructions to his assistant. The man had done his job—if he hadn't secretly betrayed Lane to the Spanish.

No one came out searching. It seemed to be all right. Lane moved out cautiously. When he found a more secure place, he opened the pack he had carried in the form of a large belly and took out the Spanish civilian worker's suit. Spain was still suffering from the ravages of its civil war; there were many men looking for work. He would be just one more of them.

First he had to rent a car. Jorge had told him where to go for black market business of any type. He went there, and got a battered but sound car. He familiarized himself with its controls, and set off. With luck he might make Barcelona in a day, and with further luck be able to run down the address of the Quaker center there. Then if he could find someone who spoke English, who knew Quality—

He closed his mind to all the luck he might need. He simply had to find out. Quality was his fiancée.

But it was a hellish drive, because of the delays. Why couldn't the Spaniards keep up their roads better? He kept having to reverse and backtrack to avoid untenable routes. Meanwhile the night was passing.

Then it got worse: on one of his backtracks, he saw another car parked sidewise across the road, blocking it. Someone was after him! But who could know he was here? Even Jorge the Smuggler hadn't known where he was going. So it was more likely some kind of highway robber, hoping to clean him out.

Lane came to a stop, turned out his lights, drew his pistol, checked it, and tucked it under his jacket where it wouldn't show. He did not want to have to use it, but he had no intention of being robbed or killed. Had something like this happened to Quality? She had been doing a lot of driving, her letters said.

He got out and approached the figure standing by the other car. The man saw him in the early light and called out a query in Spanish.

"I don't speak Spanish," Lane responded in English. He put his hand inside his shirt, grasping the pistol. If there were any threatening gesture—

"Lane!" the man exclaimed. Lane was astounded. He knew that voice. It was Ernst Best!

Amazed, they embraced. Then they talked, getting things straight. As it turned out, this was a stroke of luck for each of them, because Ernst needed to make a report to his superiors on the defenses of Gibraltar, and Lane needed someone he could trust to check on Quality. So they made a deal of sorts, and separated friends. Lane was relieved. Quality and Ernst had not gotten along well together, but Ernst did know her, and would do his best for her.

When Jorge set off again, Lane was there. He got on the boat without event, and helped row the boat back.

They were met at the other landing. Jorge was paid the other half of his fare, and was well satisfied.

Time passed. Lane's passport never did come through, though that no longer mattered. Neither did his transfer back to England. Apparently his orders had gotten lost in the shuffle of the war, and so he remained where he was. Finally he went to the Convent on his own and asked to be assigned to something useful for the duration.

"It shall be taken under advisement," the clerk informed him. And of course nothing happened. Lane had to be content with doing a lot of reading at the library. He also gave the newspapers thorough perusal. He learned a tremendous amount about the history of Gibraltar and the current progress of the war, as well as getting quite sharp on the daily crossword puzzles.

In January 1941 the German 10th Air Corps was transferred from

Norway to Sicily. Lane knew that meant trouble for Malta, because it was close to Sicily and the German pilots were highly experienced in naval warfare. They were going to try to take out that island stronghold, and stood a fair chance of doing it. Lane had a lot of respect for air power, but wasn't sure the British forces of the Mediterranean theater had enough respect for it, yet. They thought they could just shoot down any plane that came over. They were apt to receive a hard education.

In February, before the German airmen were fully established in Sicily, Force H left Gibraltar. It looked like another convoy operation, but Lane hoped it was going to make a pre-emptive attack on the Sicilian installations. Instead it avoided the Italian battle fleet, which tried to intercept it, and attacked the north Italian city of Genoa. The battleship bombarded the city with fifteen inch shells. It blasted aircraft factories, marshaling yards, and port installations, while the carrier *Ark Royal* loosed its aircraft along the shore, and mined the entrances to several ports. The operation was a huge success, and there was a tremendous ovation as Force H returned to Gibraltar.

Almost immediately after that, Force H moved out again, this time into the Atlantic to harass the German fleet. Then it settled down to work to keep the supply convoys coming. Lane wished he could have a fighter plane aboard the carrier, but he remained grounded and ignored.

The battle of Malta commenced. A hundred and fifty German bombers attempted to blast the island into rubble, while force H struggled to keep the defenders supplied. Now they had respect for air power! German bombers and Italian torpedo planes came at it, but the Ark Royal's fighters broke up the attack formations in much the way Bader's fighters had done in England.

On April 6, Germany invaded Yugoslavia and Greece. Suddenly it was getting even hotter in the Mediterranean. But Force H fought its way through, and the supplies were delivered. Malta survived.

On May 14 General The Viscount Gort assumed the Governorship of Gibraltar. He had been the commander of the British Expeditionary Forces in France, and he stressed the need for full wartime preparedness.

Lane seized his chance. He reported to the Convent again, demanding one minute with the General. "I served in France," he said. "I saw what lack of preparation cost us. Then I served in England, with Bader. I have experience. If I can't fly, at least let me do something useful."

Gort nodded. "We can use you, Airman." The interview was over.

This time there was follow-through. Lane was assigned to the group studying the situation of the northern runway. "This thing is way too short," he said. "Sure, your planes can use it now. But it's a different matter when they have to scramble in a hurry. You need more parking space to the sides, and efficient access, so that you can get full squadrons up without delay. The Germans can come without much warning, and then every second will count. The fighters have to get out fast!"

They agreed, and General Gort was advised. At last Lane was feeling useful again. He had told Ernst that the Rock was virtually impregnable, but this was one of its chief weaknesses: inadequate facilities for fast scrambling. Now he was doing something about it.

Meanwhile, the war continued. Force H went out again, to the Atlantic, and took on the great German battleship *Bismarck.* A torpedo from one of the carrier's planes finally jammed the German ship's steering gear, crippling it so that it could be dispatched May 26.

In June Germany invaded Russia. Lane and the others were amazed. It had seemed that the thrust was to be against England. Germany had signed a pact with the Communists. Why was it taking on a new enemy when it didn't have to? Adolf Hitler seemed to have shot himself in the foot.

In October General Gort received authorization to extend and pave the runway. The project turned out to be far more extensive than Lane had hoped. They extended the runway out west into the bay. This required a tremendous amount of fill material. Some of it came from rock tunneled from the interior, but most of it was taken from the slopes of the North Face. There was quarry blasting, and powerful hoses were used to bring down the sand, gravel and rock.

The work continued for a year, and the runway kept lengthening. Finally it was just over fifteen hundred yards long, and a hundred and fifty feet wide, with extensive parking areas on either side. Lane had urged better space for aircraft, but this was phenomenal. What was the general up to?

Meanwhile the German aircraft disappeared from the Mediterranean theater. There was no mystery here: they were being used in the invasion of Russia. Force H no longer had any difficulty reinforcing and supplying Malta. But when winter stalled the offensive in Russia, the German planes and submarines returned to the Mediterranean. This time the siege was to be worse than before.

The German General Rommel was moving in Africa, driving for the Suez Canal in Egypt. It seemed that Hitler was determined to destroy British power in the Mediterranean, so that Rommel could complete his mission without British harassment. Now the fury of a competent campaign manifested, in contrast to the Italians' somewhat fumbling efforts. On November 13 a German submarine sank the Ark Royal as Force H was returning to Gibraltar from a patrol. Suddenly the folk of the Rock felt the full consequence of war.

On December 11 Germany declared war on the United States of America. Lane had been in this war all along; now he knew that all his countrymen were in it too. He hoped that Quality was not in further trouble because of it; if she had been taken by the Germans, she would now be an enemy prisoner. But he tried not to think about Quality, because there was only pain and emptiness there. It was getting harder to convince himself that she remained alive. Had he not been confined to a place of no women, his constancy might have been tested.

The opening of the Pacific theater was similarly grim. The Japanese bombed Pearl Harbor, inflicting devastating losses and effectively destroying American sea power there. In February 1942 the British lost Singapore, and then Burma. There seemed to be no good news anywhere.

But it was the Second Battle of Malta that concerned the personnel of Gibraltar. General Gort was transferred to the command of Malta. Force H left to escort the force that seized Madagascar in a preventive action so that the Japanese could not establish themselves there. Force W came to the Rock instead, and it included the American carrier USS Wasp, equipped with spitfires. It was like a taste of home, for Lane.

Several convoys fought their way through to Malta during the spring and summer of 1942. That was the appropriate description: fought. The Germans were doing their best to close off that sea, and inflicted heavy losses on the merchant ships and their escorts. In one case, the American tanker Ohio finally made it through—

crewed by British sailors, held up by a destroyer lashed to either side, the sole survivor of that convoy.

But now America was mobilizing her considerable resources, and her presence was being increasingly felt. The Allied counteroffensive was developing. The plan was first to attack the soft underbelly of Europe through the Mediterranean. North Africa would be occupied, and used as a springboard to drive Italy out of the war. But before the American forces entered the Mediterranean, they wanted to be sure that Gibraltar, the guardian of the Straits, was secure. That remained the linchpin; had the Germans been able to take out Gibraltar, none of this would have been possible, and the German situation would have been virtually impregnable.

Gibraltar was also to provide air cover for the invasion fleets. Now the reason for the huge expansion of the runway became clear: Gibraltar was to be the base for Operation Torch, the invasion of North Africa. It would provide air cover for the troopships, as well as being the major port for the fleets. Nearly four hundred aircraft of various types were crammed into the dispersal areas around the Gibraltar runway. Fighters had been shipped in crates and were assembled on the airfield. One hundred sixty eight American pilots came to be housed in the RAF messes at North Front. Lane felt a curious ambivalence: he was American, but he had flown for the R.A.F., so did not really identify with his countrymen. But he was able to help orient them, because he knew the American slang and could cut through misunderstandings.

Meanwhile it seemed that the Allies were watching Spain somewhat apprehensively. Lane knew why, thanks to his background research done during his extended idleness. Spain was officially neutral, but leaned toward the Axis, and Spain could cut off the Strait at any time. They did not want to give Spain any pretext to enter the war. They knew that the Germans would be urging General Franco to do just that, cutting the Allied line and attacking Gibraltar. Spain had once had a great empire, and Spanish Morocco was the last remnant of it; if Franco thought that was threatened, he might indeed act. So the Allies did several things to discourage this: they made the Americans the major partners in the effort, because America had no territorial ambitions here; they encouraged a more generous flow of food and commodities to Spain through the Allied blockade; they attempted no occupation of Spanish territory; and they proceeded without seeming hesitation with overwhelming force. Lane knew that these were signals General Franco understood, and he did elect to remain neutral. Still, it was nervous business.

But there was one more concern. Intelligence had learned that Hitler did have a plan for marching through Spain, called *Ilona*. If Franco allowed that, then the Nazis themselves would control the Strait, and Gibraltar would be under immediate siege. So they tricked the Nazis by making it seem that the buildup at Gibraltar was for another major effort to relieve Malta. Also, Franco had agreed to enter the war only if Rommel reached the Suez Canal, which would virtually assure the Axis victory in the Mediterranean. But Rommel had not reached it, so Spain did not allow the Germans to march through Spanish territory. Since the Germans did not want to invade Spain—why antagonize a friend?—they let it go. That was to make all the difference.

Force H returned. Then in November America's General Eisenhower arrived and took over command of the Rock. On the following days the landing on the Algerian coast proceeded. The counteroffensive had begun, and Gibraltar was its key. Lane, his records seemingly lost in the bureaucratic morass, remained in the war after all.

But what had happened to Quality? Had Ernst found her, and if so, what had he been able to do to help her? This concern almost nullified Lane's satisfaction with the progress of the war.

Chapter 10
Tiergarten

Ernst's feelings were mixed as he moved on to the next camp. He had found Quality, and she was well, and now she knew that her situation was not hopeless. But how was he going to get her out of Gurs? She was a foreign national who had committed a crime by the standard of the Reich. He had spoken of repatriation, but he doubted that would come to pass. The Reich hardly cared what distant America thought, and any captives were more likely to be used as hostages than guests. So about all he had accomplished was to make her treatment better. That was a short term expedient.

But that was only part of it. What was this feeling he felt for Quality? She was his friend's fiancee, and he had searched for her at his friend's behest. He had no business entertaining any other notion. He had a girlfriend of his own, who was smart and beautiful and who offered him anything he might desire.

"Thank thee, Ernst," he murmured, remembering.

He shook his head. Perhaps he could not control the foolishness of his feeling, but he could discipline his actions. He would see that no one else ever suspected the nature of his wayward fancy.

He completed his tour of the camps, and returned to Berlin. He turned a reduced list of names over to Canaris, but his verbal report covered the situation: "As a mission, it was a waste of time. None of these are likely to be of use in the current situation."

"It no longer matters," the Admiral replied heavily. "There will be no settlement there."

Ernst did not understand what Canaris meant, but thought it best not to inquire. As it turned out, there was plenty else to occupy his attention. He had to continue to correlate incoming Spanish information, because there was a growing fear that the British would invade Spain, seeking better access to France and Germany. They could use Gibraltar as a stepping stone. It was likely to prove to be sheer disaster, leaving that rock in British hands, but it was not up to Abwehr to second guess the decision of the Führer.

But the main effort was Operation Barbarosa, which related to the boundary Germany now had with Russia. German troops were going there in such number that it was evident that an invasion of Russia was planned. It had to be a surprise, for even the Communists could make trouble if forewarned. So Abwehr had to devise false orders for troop deployment, purposely leaked to diplomatic reports and even statements of Propaganda Minister Goebbels, to decoy the British and the Russians. "The British are not our real enemies," Canaris confided. "They are Aryan like us, and perhaps will accept peace in due course. But the Communists are an abomination, and must be destroyed."

So it was made to seem to the Russians that the troop concentrations along their border were merely a decoy to hide a planned invasion of England, and it was made to seem to the British that the troops were being used to counter the Russian military presence. False reports abounded: mysterious German tourists were watching bases in French Morocco. Sixty thousand German troops were moving quietly through Spain. Eight German divisions were being withdrawn from the Russian frontier for action in the west.

"It is disaster to open a second front," the Admiral confided privately. "We must first defeat Britain, making her sue for peace. Then Spain will join us. Then, secure in the Atlantic and Mediterranean theaters, we can deal properly with the Communists. But we must do what we can to facilitate the Führer's wish. It is not my business to make policy."

Early in April Germany invaded Yugoslavia and Greece. Suddenly Ernst understood what the Admiral had meant about that theater no longer mattering: because the plans for that invasion had already been set. So Canaris had thrown himself into Operation Barbarosa, which at least had some future.

A new plan was devised to foil a British invasion through the Spanish peninsula. It was code named Isabella. It was strictly a military operation, with little direct Abwehr activity, but Ernst nevertheless was sent on several reconnaissance missions as the plans evolved. During these he made sure to check on Quality, under the guise of searching out any information she might have on Spain. He talked to her in Spanish. When he was sure that there was no one else in earshot who understood that language, he was able to speak with greater candor.

"How are they treating you, truly?"

"Well," she replied.

"You have lost weight."

"Everyone has lost weight. There is not enough food to go around. But they give me more than the others, keeping me healthy."

"And you share it with others, going hungry yourself," he said with sudden insight.

She dropped her gaze. "I have to do what I can."

He realized that she would starve herself, to help others. Conditions were worsening in all the camps, and brutality was becoming more commonplace. She had evidently escaped it so far, perhaps only because of his directive that she be saved, but that could not endure indefinitely.

Ernst dug into the deep pocket of his overcoat. He brought out a chunk of cheese left over from his hurried lunch while traveling. "Take this," he said gruffly. "Eat it now, while I interrogate you."

Meekly, she obeyed. It was the only way he could be sure that she did eat it, instead of giving it away. He had promised Lane to do what he could for her, and it was very little, but all he could manage at the moment.

On June 22 Germany invaded Russia. The Russians were caught completely by surprise, thanks to Abwehr's efforts, and suffered horrendous losses. This was perhaps the Admiral's greatest intelligence coup.

Meanwhile Krista was persistent. She was not satisfied with occasional dates; she wanted commitment. "Take me to your room for a night," she urged him. "Let me show you exactly what I can do for you."

He shook his head, smiling. "I would have no judgment at all, with you there. I am not ready to marry."

"I have told you, you do not need to marry me."

He waggled a finger warningly in her face. "I would need to, if you were with me for a night."

She caught the finger between her teeth, pretending to bite. "You are like a rat, wary of the bait."

"Very like a rat," he agreed.

He managed to check on Quality at Gurs in August, and again in October. Each time she looked thinner, and the camp looked worse. She always had a positive attitude, but he distrusted that; she was trying to persuade him that things were better than they were. The little bits of food he gave here were pitifully inadequate; only if he could do it every day could he stabilize her. That was impossible.

"You are pensive," Krista told him later in October. "Do you fear for the progress of the war?"

"I do," he agreed. For he could see that the German initiative was slowing, and that boded no good. "The Allies are building an expanded runway on Gibraltar, which means they expect to use it to attack us, and Spain still refuses to join the Axis. The Russian resistance is stiffening, and our losses there are mounting; winter could be cruel indeed."

"But there is something else on your mind."

"Perhaps so." He cursed his foolishness, but he could not rid himself of his brooding concern with a single prisoner he had promised to help.

"Is there something wrong with me?" Krista asked. "Have I given you offense, or is that shadow on my ancestry—"

"No!" he exclaimed. "There is nothing wrong with you, Krista! The more I know of you, the more I appreciate you. You are beautiful, smart and competent."

"But you will not trust me with your secret," she said.

"What secret?"

"The thing that is weighing on you, making you morose."

He gazed at her. She was right: he could not tell her what was truly bothering him. Because all she would hear would be the words "other woman." It wouldn't matter that the woman was his friend's fiancee whom he had promised to help, and that instead he was standing by to watch her slowly die.

"I wish I could marry you, and go with you to some secret garden, and forget everything else," he said sincerely.

"Tiergarten," she said brightly. "The park close by your hotel. We will go there now."

He laughed, and part of his mood lifted. "And you will get me in a private place there, and show me what maddens me. It is your way of torturing me."

"Exactly," she said, inhaling.

Late in November Admiral Canaris visited Spain again, and Ernst drove down separately to join him. The Admiral truly loved Spain;

only there did he seem happy. His mission was to sound out the Spanish government on Isabella. But it was becoming obvious that despite the Allied buildup at Gibraltar, they were not going to use the distraction of the Russian campaign to invade Spain. That meant that Isabella might prove to be unnecessary.

Canaris returned to Germany December first. That left Ernst to make another routine check on the camps, and return separately.

But before he reached Gurs, the Japanese bombed the American base at Pearl Harbor, in the Pacific Ocean. That meant that America would enter the war. It could be only a matter of days before it became formal, for Germany as well as Japan.

That meant that Quality Smith would no longer represent a neutral nation. She would represent an enemy nation. That would be the end of her preferential treatment—and surely the end of her life, from privation. Others were dying in the camps, as conditions worsened.

Distraught, he thought it through from every angle as he drove to France. It was a desperate situation, requiring a desperate measure. There was no guarantee of success, and perhaps he would only drag himself down too. But he had to try it.

Quality looked thinner then ever. She still wore her original clothing, but now it hung on her. Yet her face possessed a preternatural beauty, her eyes seeming huge, her lank brown hair smoothing the angles of her jaw.

"Japan bombed the American base on the Hawaiian Islands," Ernst told her. "They destroyed American power in the Pacific. This may not be of importance to you, because you are a pacifist—"

"The poor people!" she exclaimed. "The lives lost."

"America will rebuild. But it affects you in this way: you are an American, and Japan is allied to Germany. So very soon America will be at war with Germany, too."

"And I will become an enemy national," she said, comprehending the significance.

"I must get you out of here," he said. "This is now imperative, and there can be no delay. It must be today. But I can think of only one way to do it."

She shook her head. "There is no way. They will not release me."

"SS officers have certain privileges. I dislike deception, but see no other mechanism. If I suggested that I wished to have you for—

for my use, they would not stop me from taking you."

She stared at him.

"I would not actually use you," he said quickly. "I give you my word on that. I promised Lane to find you and to help you if I could. I wish I knew a better way. I fear for your continued detention here. I fear for your life. But still, you would have to agree to go. Others would have to be given the impression that it was so. Would you do that?"

She considered. Then she whispered, "Yes."

She had agreed! He coughed to mask his astonishment. He had feared that she would elect to die. "Then I will see to it. But—you must not appear to be willing. Your agreement is for me, not for them. You must be resigned, perhaps in despair. You understand?"

She nodded.

Ernst dismissed her, then went to the commandant. "This American woman—I think she knows more than she has told. I wish to take her for more thorough interrogation. Release her to my custody."

The man looked at him. "She is beautiful," he remarked. "Or would be, when better fed."

Ernst returned his gaze. "And what of it?"

"There must be higher authorization."

This was the risky part. "Here is a code-name for Reinhard Heydrich. Contact him and say that Ernst Best is making a requisition." He had given his true name, knowing that it was unknown here, but would be known to Heydrich.

The name of Heydrich evidently impressed the man. This was a most powerful contact. But Ernst could see the lingering doubt. Was it a bluff?

"I will wait," Ernst said firmly.

The commandant left the office. If he did contact Heydrich's office, what would happen? Heydrich was at present in Czechoslovakia, and difficult to reach, so his home office would demur. Would the commandant pursue the matter further? Ernst was betting that he would not, for fear of making a powerful enemy unnecessarily. The man believed that Ernst was simply appropriating the most attractive prisoner before some other officer did; this kind of thing was known to happen. What was the harm in it? So probably he would not risk a challenge, and would not even enter the matter in the records. It would simply be one less prisoner to feed. One who might otherwise soon be dead anyway.

Sure enough, the commandant returned in less time than it would have taken to reach Czechoslovakia. "Take her," he said.

"Have her brought to me and signed out," Ernst said.

"That will not be necessary. Authorization has been given."

So he was right: the man preferred no record. Quality would remain on the camp rolls, but would simply not be there. Soon enough she would be forgotten, or possibly her name would be put in place of another woman who died.

Ernst returned to the main camp. He saw Quality standing there, waiting. He strode toward her. "Come with me," he said gruffly, taking her arm.

She tried to hold back, but he hauled her along. He brought her to his car and shoved her roughly in. He got in himself and started the motor. Quality hid her face as if terrified or ashamed. Possibly that was true. He was passed on out of the camp without challenge.

"There is bread under the seat," he said, looking straight ahead. "Take it."

She reached under and found it. "I thank thee, Ernst."

"I will take you to my apartment in Berlin. Others will think what they will think. You must always appear afraid of me. But I tell you again: I mean to help you."

"I am afraid *for* thee, Ernst," she said. "This is a great risk for thee."

"I promised Lane." But it was more than that. He would have had to do it even if Lane had never existed. Quality was simply too good a person to allow to wither and perhaps die in such a camp, or to be brutalized or raped there.

He drove her to Germany. It was a two day journey, with a night in Paris. The hotel there had a bath adjoining the room, and he was glad for that, because Quality stank of the camp and her own forced lack of hygiene. On the way they talked, as they had in Spain, and he kept her supplied with food. Freed of the environment of the camp, she was willing to eat, and she did so voraciously. That was part of the reason he maintained the dialogue: to distract her, so that she would not feel guilty for eating, and stop.

"We can talk freely here," he told her. "But not in my apartment. Anyone might overhear, and if it became known that I am trying to save you for an American airman, it could be very bad for us both. You must seem to be a captive woman, chosen for her appearance, afraid to try to flee. Since you do not speak German, the pretense should be feasible. If anyone can hear, I will treat you with contempt, a creature of no value. You will have to do menial tasks, and after the hopelessness of your situation is apparent, you will do shopping for me. If I can arrange temporary papers for you."

"I understand," she said quietly.

"My apartment is not large, but there is an alcove where you can have privacy. I will give you my bed, as before, and—"

"No."

He glanced at her, surprised. "It is the best I can do."

"No, thee must not give me privacy," she said. "Thee would not do that for a kept woman. Neither would thee put her in thy bed, with thee elsewhere. She would share thy bed."

"But—"

"I trust thee, Ernst."

He was silent, knowing that she was right. The role had to be correctly played, or it would be obvious that it *was* a role. But how was he to share his bed with her, when already she intrigued him in a manner he needed to expunge?

They drove rapidly north through France. Ernst's Abwehr authority eliminated challenges, and there were no delays. Even so, it was late by the time they approached Paris.

"Will thee have to report to the SS headquarters here?" Quality asked.

"It is not necessary. Surely you do not wish to put in an appearance there!"

"Surely I do not," she agreed wanly. "They might recognize me. I was there to arrange for food for the Jews being transported to Spain. They took my money, but the Jews wound up in Gurs and similar camps."

"Spain would not admit them," he agreed. "I am sorry your trip was for nothing."

"It cost me more than money," she said. "That was when I was arrested. Perhaps it is God's punishment."

"I thought Quakers did not believe in that sort of thing. In a retributive God."

"We do not define our beliefs in that way. I thought I did not believe that, but I did sin."

"Sin?"

"I told a lie. It was not the first time."

"To help a man escape death," he said, catching on.

"Yes. But still a lie. A sin. I have meditated much on that. I have learned the consequence of it."

"I think I would disagree with you on much else, but I appreciate your problem. I am doing something similar by taking you from that camp. I would not do it were I not afraid that there is no acceptable alternative."

"Yes. Thee understands."

They were silent as he threaded his way through Paris to reach the hotel where his room was reserved. "You understand the way this will appear," he reminded her.

"Thee has a prisoner, nominally for questioning, actually for entertainment."

"Yes. Another lie we share."

"Is it, Ernst?"

"A half lie. I did claim you for questioning, letting them believe otherwise."

"Is it otherwise?"

He was taken aback. "You said you trusted me."

"I do, Ernst."

"Then I do not understand."

She smiled. "Perhaps I am teasing thee. I meant that possibly thee does find my company entertaining. Thee said thee enjoyed it before, in Spain."

He relaxed. "That is true. But knowing that for you this is necessity rather than pleasure, I did not think of it that way."

"It is both, Ernst."

He did not answer, again. Her words had touched him deeply, but he feared misreading their implication. She could not know that his feeling for her was verging on the forbidden. She was his friend's fiancée.

He took her to his room without ceremony or apology. Officers did sometimes take women to their rooms, and it was not wise to question them about this.

There was no need for a meal; they had been eating fairly steadily while driving. Ernst locked the door, then guided her to the bathroom. She made a little squeak of delight when she saw the fancy tub.

"Wash yourself, woman," he said gruffly in German. "But do not waste water. There is a war on."

She did not speak German. This was his reminder that they could not trust the seeming privacy of the room. "Ja," she said. That much German everyone knew.

Ernst turned on the radio fairly loud and tuned in the news to help cover the sounds of her bathing. He tried not to picture her naked. It was no business of his. He had taken her from the camp to safeguard her health and life, and he intended to safeguard her dignity too. She must never know his illicit fancy.

In due course she emerged, wrapped in a towel. She went to the bed and got in.

Ernst turned off the radio and went to use the bathroom. There were her clothes, washed and hung up to dry as well as they could. He realized that he would have to get her new ones; hers were so worn as to be on the verge of uselessness.

He stripped and washed at the sink. Then, in underclothing, he returned to the room. He saw her towel folded beside the bed. She was well over to the side, leaving space for him. He remembered what she had said about sharing the bed. That applied in Paris as well as in Berlin.

He got in and turned out the light. He would ignore her proximity as well as he could.

But in the darkness her hand came across. Her cool fingers touched his shoulder. They squeezed it, lightly, once, and retreated. It was her way of thanking him, since it was not safe for her to speak.

He closed his eyes and willed himself to sleep.

Ernst woke before dawn. He got up, used the bathroom, and dressed. He felt Quality's clothes: they remained damp. She would have to don them anyway. At least she and they were now clean; the smell was gone.

She remained asleep. He knew she was recovering from the privation of the camp. She would need more sleep and food. But now he had to rouse her, for they had a long day's drive to Berlin.

"Woman, wake," he said gruffly in German.

Her eyes opened. They were blank for a moment as her mouth tightened in apprehension. Then she oriented, and smiled up at him. She flung back the blanket and sat up before he could turn his back. He saw her small breasts against her gaunt ribs. She had lost more weight than he had realized. He should have taken her out of Gur before this.

He faced away as she got out and walked around the bed to the bathroom. In a very short time she emerged, wearing her damp clothing.

He had donned his overcoat in the interim. Now, afraid of the effect the outdoor chill of the morning would have on her, he took it off and put it around her shoulders.

She shook her head no, but he insisted. What good would it be to save her from the camp, if she died of chill? The coat fell to her ankles, protecting all of her body.

He led her out of the room and down to the lobby, where he checked out. The clerk ignored her. They went on out to the car. He started the motor, then turned on the heater. "Eat," he said in English, digging out the remnant of bread and cheese from the prior day.

"Thee is circumspect in commenting on my appearance."

"No self-respecting SS officer would settle for an emaciated woman. Not in Berlin."

She nodded. "I had not thought of that. I will try to achieve the required plumpness." She ate with a will, and later in the day slept in the seat.

He stole a glance at her. It was probably his imagination, but she seemed to look better already.

They reached Berlin late at night. He took her to his room, and she stripped immediately and got into the bed. He was tired from the long drive, and did the same. Again her hand touched his shoulder; then he slept.

It got cold in the night, and the hotel was not sufficiently heated. Ernst was used to it, and his thick blankets normally were enough. But he became aware of Quality shivering. She was lean and weak, and needed more.

He got out in the darkness and found his overcoat. He spread it over her, then got back in himself. But still she shivered. Could she have some illness? What more could he do? Insulation did not help enough; she needed heat.

"Please—may I?" she whispered. "In the camp, we protected each other from the cold."

"Ja." He hoped he understood her correctly.

She moved over toward him, then lay against him, as close as she could get, her arm and leg half across his body, her head beside his. He put his arms around her, drawing her in, and drew the covers in close. She was so light and thin! Then he lay quite still.

Her body was cool, but gradually it warmed. "Thank thee," she whispered, and slept.

He found to his surprise that he could relax. He was doing his best to safeguard her, and had found the way to secure her from the cold. He was well fed and healthy, and had body heat to spare. He was sharing it with her. In this situation he had no sexual inclination; his fear in that respect had proved to be groundless. She was not an object of sex appeal, at this time, but of pity.

In the morning he disengaged and tucked the blankets closely about her. Then he did calisthenics, unkinking his arms and warming up. It was a regular morning ritual, and he saw no reason to change it; those in the neighboring rooms were used to this morning noise. No need to alert them to any change in his situation; soon enough they would realize that he had a woman in his room.

When he finished, Quality was awake. She lay huddled in the blankets, watching him. Embarrassed, he quickly dressed.

Then he recovered his overcoat. He made a gesture of eating: he had to go out to purchase food. He brought out his key and gestured as of locking the door: he would lock her in. She nodded. She understood that she could not go out alone.

He went to a store he knew, and bought bread, cheese, milk, lettuce and as an afterthought, chocolate. The proprietor lifted an eyebrow but did not comment. An SS man could indulge himself if he chose.

He also bought a newspaper—and discovered that Germany had declared war on the United States of America the day before. He had gotten Quality out of the camp just in time.

Ernst brought the food to his room. Quality had dressed, then wrapped herself again in a blanket. Her eyes were big under the impromptu hood the blanket formed. He showed her the chocolate. "Eat," he murmured. "It will make you warm." He ate only sparingly himself, saving the food for her, because he could eat elsewhere.

Then he left for the Abwehr, locking her in again. This was the way it would have to be. This set the pattern for the following days. He found books printed in French and English and brought them to her. Several were by Nietzsche; he doubted that she wanted more of that, but there was no great assortment cheaply available in those languages. She welcomed each new book, and evidently read it. She had little else to do during the days he was at work.

The first evening when he returned he found her sitting by the window, gazing out. He set down his groceries and books and came to stand close behind her. "That is *Tiergarten*," he said in a low voice, in Spanish. "The 'Animal Garden.' A popular park. I chose this room because of that view."

"Tiergarten," she repeated. "I thank thee, Ernst, for that view. It cheers me."

"Eat," he said gruffly in German. "I must go out again."

In an hour he returned with assorted items of clothing for her. He knew the fit would be imperfect, but he couldn't leave her in her inadequate original garments. One of the items was a nightgown, so that she would not have to sleep naked again, and would have what slight additional warmth it provided. She made a pleased exclamation when she saw it, and that night she wore it. Now she seemed ethereal rather than thin, and angelically attractive. He did not dare compliment her appearance, for fear his sincerity would betray his feeling.

The days passed, and she began to recover her flesh, but Ernst knew it would be months before she was restored to full health. In the interim, there were other problems. Once a week the hotel's cleaning woman came through; she had a passkey, and he could not keep her out. So he dealt with the potential problem forthrightly: he went to the manager.

"I have a woman in my room. I rescued her from a camp. She does not speak German. I want her left alone, and I do not want word of her presence spread. There may be additional expense to the hotel because of her occupancy. I hope this will cover it." He proffered a suitable amount.

"There will be no problem," the man said, pocketing the money.

"And I would like to have a second key. Here is the deposit on it."

He got the key. Then he gave it to Quality. She was no longer a prisoner, physically, though without papers this made little difference.

Another problem was Krista. The Christmas season was coming up, and though the official Nazi line frowned on the religious aspect, the celebration was allowed. Krista would have time off, and so would he, and she expected to share it with him. She hoped to come to his room, if not for a night, at least for a few hours. That would be extremely awkward.

"Who is Krista?" Quality inquired when he tried to explain why he would be absent much of the time.

"My female friend. She would like to marry me."

"I wish you well."

He found himself uncertain. She had not said "thee." Then he realized that she meant the plural. "She is a fine young woman. Any man should be well satisfied to marry her."

"Surely so." She seemed almost amused.

It remained awkward. "But to explain your presence here—I do not think she would understand."

"Thee must bring her here, Ernst, and I will explain."

"She might feel obliged to report you. She is I fear a better Nazi than I am." He looked around the room. "She would also note that we use one bed."

She smiled. "This, too, I will explain. I do not wish to interfere in thy life, Ernst."

She had already done so, if she but knew. At night, when he held her for warmth, feeling her flannel nightgown against him, and her slender body, he imagined that she was his fiancee, and he felt guilty. Yet that fancy brought him delight, and he could not abolish it. If Krista saw Quality, she would immediately divine the truth in his heart, regardless of Quality's innocent explanation. But he could not say that without betraying the trust he had assumed for Lane. "I think it best that we not chance it."

She looked down. "Thee knows best, Ernst."

It was no easier with Krista. "This is the holiday season," she pointed out as they sat at a table in a restaurant. "The time for joy and license, yet you remain withdrawn. Let me take you somewhere where I can make you truly relax."

"I fear that is beyond your power."

"But you must give me a trial. Perhaps I will surprise you." She moved her leg so that her knee touched his. When he glanced down, he saw that she had hiked up her skirt so that he alone could see her leg above the knee. It was a fine leg, and the shadow into which it rose was indeed alluring. Her body had lost none of its appeal for him. But until he came to terms with his illicit feeling for Quality, he could not afford to take any part of what Krista offered.

Ernst wished he could get out of this. "It is not that you are in any way inadequate. It is that I know of nothing that can ease my situation."

"If only you would tell me!" she exclaimed, frustrated.

"If only I could."

"Last year we went home together. Why not—"

"This year I can not."

She gazed at him in a calculated manner. He feared her next question. But she did not ask it. "You must tell me when you can, Ernst." She did not broach the subject again. But he was not reassured.

Then in January he had a surprising and unwelcome visit at his room. It was Dohnanyi, the civilian associate of General Oster, who was notoriously anti-Hitler. Ernst had traveled with him, and found the man compatible and useful, but the last thing he needed now was the political complication that further association with him would bring. Worse, he could not hide Quality's presence.

Quality sat in a corner, facing the man without speaking. She was in one of the dresses Ernst had bought for her, and already it hung less loosely on her as she regained weight. She had done some sewing on it, and fashioned a kind of sash that helped conceal her slenderness, and her bosom was filling out again. She could have been taken for German.

"So you are keeping a woman now," Dohnanyi remarked, eyeing Quality in a manner Ernst did not like.

"That has no relevance to my work," Ernst said shortly in German.

"But I understood that you had a regular girl."

"I prefer not to discuss the matter."

Dohnanyi laughed. "You are a more ambitious man than I took you for! A girlfriend and a mistress both."

"What is your business with me?" Ernst asked evenly.

Dohnanyi got serious. "Surely it is apparent to you that Hitler is a madman. First Poland, then France—had he stopped there, perhaps it would have been all right. But then Russia, and now America. These are not pygmies! They will overwhelm us, unless we renounce this folly while we yet can. While we still have our strength."

"Our troops are at the verge of Moscow, and America is far away," Ernst retorted, noting how Quality picked up on the word "America." But privately he feared exactly what the man suggested: that Germany had assumed too great a burden, and was extended on too many fronts.

"If we depose Hitler and make peace now, we can spare ourselves much agony," Dohnanyi said. "But we need internal support before we can challenge Hitler."

"You won't get it here!" Ernst retorted angrily. "Hitler is a great man. He has made Germany great." He brought out his silver swastika on its chain. "I value this symbol of what he has made of Germany. Now go away, and we shall pretend you never came here."

Dohnanyi departed without further argument. Ernst locked the door behind him. What had possessed the man to come here like this, spouting treason? Ernst had never given him any encouragement.

"What was it about?" Quality asked quietly.

He changed to English, lowering his voice. "He wants to overthrow the Führer! He seeks to convert me to his cause. But I am loyal. He knows that. I don't know why he came here."

"Perhaps to verify my presence," she suggested.

Ernst nodded. "And now he has a hold against me. If I report him for treason, he will report you. I must be silent."

She shook her head sadly. "I did not wish to complicate thy life, Ernst."

He put his arm around her shoulders. "I would not have it otherwise." Then, realizing what he had done, he withdrew. "I meant that I must do what I must do, and you are not to blame."

She did not look at him. "Thee sleeps embracing me, but thee will not touch me by day?"

He laughed, without force. "At night there is reason. By day, it is a presumption."

"A presumption of what?"

"A presumption that what others think is true."

"And is it false?"

She had questioned him in a similarly oblique manner during their drive to Berlin, a month before. Again, it made him nervous, because his attraction to her had not abated. It was essential that he reassure her, so that she would not come to fear his intent. "If I ever touch you in a way you do not wish, there will surely be compelling reason for it," he said carefully. "I deeply regret holding you prisoner here, and would free you if I could."

"I am perhaps prisoner," she agreed. "But I would not care to take my freedom from thee."

"Not in the middle of Berlin!" he agreed. "But I hope the time will come when it is possible." Then he would marry Krista, and try to forget.

The next week the trouble was abruptly worse. There was another peremptory knock on the door, and when Ernst opened it, there was Major Stummel of the Central section, the legal department. He was young and friendly, but deadly. His report could destroy Ernst's standing in the Abwehr, or exonerate him from suspicion. "I was in the area, and thought I would pay a call," Stummel said politely. "Have you time?"

Ernst could hardly decline, knowing the significance of such a seemingly coincidental visit. "By all means, come in."

The man entered. "Freulein," he said, spying Quality.

She nodded, not knowing what to expect.

They sat down. "I see you have a view of the Tiergarten," he remarked. "That is nice."

Ernst agreed. They exchanged other pleasantries. Then Stummel began to zero in on his business. "It is such a pleasure to work with the able officers of the Abwehr. Colonel Lahousen is a fine soldier, though his loyalty may be primarily military rather than political."

"I have worked closely with Lahousen," Ernst countered. "I regard him as a fine and loyal soldier in every sense."

"And of course Admiral Canaris is a brilliant espionage officer, but perhaps not as fine an administrator or manager. Perhaps he allows himself to be unduly swayed by underlings of dubious quality."

"Such as General Oster," Ernst agreed. Now he was on safe ground. "A strutting peacock, a man so consumed with his own opinions that he questions the decisions of the Führer and speaks treason carelessly. The only reason he has not been court-martialed is that his incompetence safeguards his rashness. And his friends: Dohnanyi, that sly lawyer who knows nothing of discipline and cares nothing for the Volk, a scheming weasel who embodies everything that national socialism stands against."

"Yes, there are rumors of Jewish ancestry and black market activities." Then Stummel remarked with seeming innocence: "I noticed that you talked to Dohnanyi. I believe you have worked with the man before—or do I misremember?"

Of course his memory was perfect. "I did travel with him last year. He was a pleasant conversationalist, but I did not take him seriously."

"I believe he visited here recently. To review old times?"

"I do not wish to speak ill of an associate," Ernst said tightly.

"Ill? In what manner?"

"He remains extreme in his politics. I had to ask him to leave."

"Ah, you do not subscribe to his notions?"

"I thought I had made that clear," Ernst said wryly.

Stummel smiled. "Ah, you did; I apologize for forgetting." But Ernst knew that the man had not forgotten; he had phrased his question again, verifying that Ernst's answer remained constant. His gaze flicked about the room, touching as if coincidentally again on Quality. "Forgive me if I am once more forgetful, but I had understood you are not married, Captain Osterecht."

"I am not," Ernst agreed.

"But I see here with you a most attractive young woman. Is she your cousin, perhaps, come for a visit?"

Treacherous water! "I do have her with me. She is not my cousin. I do not care to discuss her situation."

"Of course not," Stummel said with deceptive ease. "I understand that more than one officer prefers, shall we say, the comforts of home to those of the street." He was implying that Quality was a prostitute.

Ernst knew that he should let that implication stand. Keeping a woman was an indiscretion, but an understandable one, and there was a general policy of silence in such matters. But he was unable to allow this particular lie about Quality to stand. Dohnanyi's assumption that she was his mistress had been bad enough, and probably should have been countered so as to avoid any chance of blackmail. "No. She is not that kind of woman."

"No? I would not for a moment imply that such an attractive person could be an agent of the treasonable faction, sent to corrupt a good man. Yet such things have been known."

Ernst felt a terrible chill. Stummel was springing his trap, suggesting that Quality was evidence of corruption. "I have no such relationship with her!"

"She is nothing to you? Then perhaps we could take her off your hands, so that she will not remain a burden."

There was the threat. How was he to abate it? He could claim neither prostitution nor indifference, yet to suggest that she was important to him was a worse trap. They would use her mercilessly to bend him to their will, and he would have no independence.

"She does not speak German," he said carefully. "I took her from a camp, not wishing to let such an attractive creature go to waste. What she may be to me in the future is a private matter. I prefer to have no publicity."

Stummel stood and approached Quality. "I must say that she does not look like a Jew; were she such, it would be unfortunate."

"She is no Jew," Ernst said. Would Stummel never give over?

"Then surely you will have no objection if I check for a tattoo," Stummel said. His hand shot out, catching Quality's arm.

Quality mistook the nature of Stummel's intention. She thought he had rape or removal in mind, and Ernst could not clarify it for her without revealing the closeness of their association. "No!" she cried, jerking away.

Now Stummel showed his nature. "So she is willful. This is no fit companion for an officer." He stepped toward her again, determined to break her to his will—or to make Ernst betray his true feeling for her. It was a two-edged trap, skillfully set up. Either Quality would become worthless, subject to being taken and thrown in prison or perhaps turned over to other officers for their use. Or she would be revealed as Ernst's lover, a perfect hold against him, with the implication that he was being corrupted.

Ernst acted instantly. "Silence, woman!" he shouted, striding across the room. He caught her by the shoulder himself and spun her around. Her sleeve tore, baring her arm, showing that there was no guilty tattoo. Then he struck her with his open hand across the face. He felt her nose give way under the force of his blow. He winced, inwardly; he had intended to strike her on the side of the face, relatively harmlessly.

She made a stifled scream and stumbled back, the blood flowing from her nose. She fell to the floor, sobbing. But Ernst paid no overt heed. "Never talk back to an SS officer!" he shouted. He took another step toward her, lifting his foot. She cringed away from him, whimpering, her blood dripping on the floor.

Making an exclamation of disgust, he spun about to face Stummel. "My apologies for this scene," he said curtly. "The woman has not yet quite learned her place. That will be corrected, I assure you."

"So I see," Stummel said, stepping back. He was evidently satisfied: the woman was not a Jew or other condemned person, and obviously was here for Ernst's convenience, not his love. "I shall leave you to it." He turned away with distaste, and departed.

Ernst listened until he was sure the man was not only away from the room but out of the building. Only then did he dare to look at Quality.

She, too, had remained where she was, holding her nose to stop the bleeding. Her hair was disheveled, and a bruise was forming around her left eye. There were tears on her cheeks, and blood and tears on her chin.

"Oh my love," he murmured, the horror welling up. He had exonerated Quality and himself from suspicion, but at what price? "What have I done!"

Afraid to approach her, he hurried to the bathroom and got a towel. He soaked an end in water and brought it out to her. "I am so sorry," he said. "How can I explain?"

She took the towel and dabbed at her face. There was less blood than there had seemed to be, and her nose had stopped bleeding. Her face was quickly clean, but her eye was starting to swell. "There is no need to explain, Ernst."

He put out a hand to help her up, not quite touching her. She took it and got to her feet. "Yet I must try," he said as she steadied. "I would not—I would never—you are to me so—" But that was what he must not say.

She lifted a dry corner of the towel and dabbed at his face. “Thee has explained.”

He realized that his face was wet with his own tears. “He would have taken you—” he said lamely.

She dropped the towel, put her hands to the sides of his head, and drew his face in to hers. “There must be truth between us, Ernst. We have lived a lie too long.”

“The truth is not proper,” he said.

She brought his face the rest of the way down to hers, and kissed him on the mouth.

His arms went around her body. He embraced her with infinite gentleness. Truth, at last.

She drew back slightly. “I love thee, Ernst.”

“But it may not be!” he protested.

She merely looked at him.

“It is true,” he said. “I love you, Quality. But you are not mine to love. Lane—”

“I have had time to think,” she said, in a kindly but considerable understatement. “I have realized that my feeling for Lane has diminished, and my feeling for thee has increased. I know now that I am not a perfect match for Lane, or even a suitable one. I fear I am not ideal for thee, either, but my heart has spoken. So also, I think, has thine.”

“But I had resolved never to speak of it!”

“I saw thee struggling throughout. But I wished to avoid imposing on thee beyond the minimum, until I realized that I could no longer avoid it.”

The world seemed to have faded out around them. There was only himself with his arms around Quality, her face close to his. “Yet surely when I struck you and hurt you—”

“To save me from disaster. Thee told me before that thee would never touch me in a way I did not wish, unless there were compelling reason for it. I believed thee. I knew the charade was necessary.”

“Charade!” he cried, looking at her swollen eye.

“Thee had to pretend that I was nothing to thee. Violence is not my way, and I think not thy way either, but perhaps it was required in this instance.”

“I fear it was. I hope it never is again. But how could you conclude from this that I love you?"

"Why, thee said so, Ernst. Thee said 'Oh my love, what have I done.' I knew thee meant it."

He was astonished. "I said that? I did not realize."

She smiled faintly. "Thee was evidently distracted at the time."

He shook his head. "You are more poised than I at this moment. But I must not keep you standing. You must lie down and recover, and I shall get you medicine—"

"No, Ernst. I do not feel discomfort at the moment. I will lie down, if thee will lie with me."

He shook his head ruefully. "I think your phrasing is unfortunate. The vernacular of your language—"

"I am familiar with it. This is the meaning I intend."

"But I never thought of you in such manner!"

"I am sure of my love and desire for thee, Ernst. Is thee?"

How perfectly she had framed it! He yielded, and went with her to the bed. He let her undress herself and him, still afraid to presume too much. Her body remained thin, but she had recovered considerably in the past month. Then they lay together, in the Biblical sense, and it was such a perfect union that it seemed impossible that it could ever have seemed otherwise. He found that the passion he had suppressed before had become overwhelming. His concept of her had changed dramatically. Now it seemed wholly fitting that he be inside her as well as around her.

"If I may ask," he said as they lay still embraced in the ebbing of passion but not the ebbing of love.

"Anything, Ernst."

"When, for you—?"

"When I first employed plain talk with thee."

He was astounded. "But that was in America! We argued there! We did not get along."

"It was not love, then," she agreed. "But it was the dawning of respect, which I do not give lightly. It was the first step. When we met again in Spain it was the second step. I suspect I could have retreated, then, for I did not expect to see thee thereafter. But when thee came for me in France, I took the third step, and could no longer retreat."

"But I came at Lane's behest!"

"And tried thy best to honor it. I respected that, and would not have held thee. But thee helped me more than perhaps thee realizes."

"A little food at the camp, and more here."

"Thee gave me hope at the camp. I loved thee then, and it buoyed me so that I could survive."

Now her somewhat confusing references were coming clear. She had questioned his intentions while saying that she trusted him. She had known of his growing feeling for her, and had shared it, but had given him time to work it out independently.

"Thee knew me better than I knew myself," he said, emulating her plain speech in English. There was a certain additional pleasure in that, for it seemed to bring him even closer to her.

"No, Ernst. I merely was in a better position than thee to realize the changing of my feeling. I did not have to fight myself as thee did."

"Perhaps thee did not fight because thee is a pacifist."

She laughed, and kissed him. "Perhaps one day thee will be one too."

After a time they got up and cleaned the blood from the floor and rinsed out the towel. Then they ate and returned to bed. They clasped each other much as on previous nights, but now neither tried to hide the love that went with the embrace. The appearance of their clasped bodies had hardly changed, and neither had the reality of their hearts, yet a new world had opened for them.

Chapter 11
Nietzsche

In the morning Quality woke before Ernst and got quietly out of bed. She went to the bathroom and gazed at her face in the mirror. Her nose was swollen and her eye was black, but those things would pass. Her experience in Gurs had prepared her for this; Ernst did not know that she had been struck before. She had been caught giving some of her food to a woman who was being deprived because she had objected to the amatory suggestion of a guard. Quality had learned from observation how to react. Absolute fear and subservience was the way to survive, and since the proprietors did have power, it was no deceit to acknowledge it. The situation with the interrogating officer had been similar; he had had to be appeased, and Ernst had done what he had to. She had even turned her head so that his hand struck the center of her face instead of the side as he had intended, because she had known that no token slap would do.

And in the aftermath of that episode, horrified by the damage he had done without intending, Ernst had finally spoken his heart. *Oh my love*! It had come unconsciously, and been blanked from his own awareness, but not hers. She had tried not to be seductive, and to uphold the appropriate standards of decorum, but had seen that he was interested despite his honorable resolve. At night she had imagined that he was holding her for love rather than warmth, and almost it had seemed it was true. With her returning health had come renewed interest in romantic companionship, and with her solidifying love for Ernst had come the desire to possess him. She had wanted to tell him, and to offer him whatever he might want with her. But she knew that he made no commitment lightly, and that his code was such that the woman he indulged himself with would be the one he intended to marry. That had been too much to ask of him, when he could have a licit marriage and good life with his girlfriend Krista.

Until those words had shown the pointlessness of further pretense. Ernst had lost his fight to remain true to Krista, which relationship it seemed had never been wholehearted on his part. Quality had been freed to declare her own love. She had done so, and had proceeded to the denouement of which she had dreamed: the complete realization of their love. What a joy the night had been, despite her pain of the face.

But now it was the morning after. Had she done right? She wasn't sure. The intrusion of the SS officer, the threat to her limited security here, the necessary brutality, and Ernst's revelation of his love had been in the end exhilarating, and she had done what her heightened emotion urged. She did not regret their night of love at all, for herself, but was in doubt about its appropriateness for him. She had now denied him his chance for a normal German life.

She completed her business in the bathroom, and returned to the main room to dress. Ernst was stirring. He opened his eyes and looked at her.

"Ach, your face!" he said. "I should never have done that!" He considered briefly. "And then, in your confusion, I—how could I have—"

She moved to him, and cut him off with a kiss. "I did it, Ernst," she reminded him. "I asked thee to be with me, because I love thee and desire thee."

"I, too, with you," he said. "But still, to take advantage—"

And he felt guilty for his desire! She abandoned her own second thoughts. "I seduced thee last night. If thee argues, I shall do it again."

"I must argue, because you are captive, and—"

She kissed him a second time, putting fervor into it. She felt gay and reckless, glorying in her newfound freedom of expression. "I gave thee fair warning!" She drew back enough to draw off her nightgown. Then she lay against him, on top, spreading her legs to fall down outside his. It was fun being wanton. All her dreams were coming true.

"Oh Quality, Quality, how I love thee!" he whispered, hugging her. Then his passion met hers, and they were in the throes of it, without the hesitation of the night.

"I love thee, I love thee!" she breathed as it took them. "Now at last I can tell thee!"

"If I had known before—" he gasped.

"Pay attention to thy business," she said teasingly.

"I am! My business is loving thee."

She cut off further dialogue with more kisses. Every time he tried to talk, she kissed him again. Finally he gave up, and simply accepted her love.

However, he insisted on one thing. "I must marry thee, but I have no ring to give thee. I beg thee to accept instead, as a token of this union, my most precious possession."

"I need no token," she protested.

"But I need for thee to have it. It will protect thee from harm." And he brought out his swastika, silver on a silver chain.

Quality had severely mixed feelings. To her, the swastika was an abomination, standing for everything that was evil. Yet she loved Ernst, and had to accept his gift.

She decided that the silver artifact was in this case not a symbol of Nazism, but of Ernst's love. As such, it was appropriate for her to wear. She put the chain over her head and let the swastika fall to her bosom. "I thank thee, Ernst. I will wear it always."

"I wish I could marry thee now. But—"

"It is the way of Friends to marry by declaring themselves before a Meeting, which is a gathering of Friends. We have perhaps a Meeting of two. We can imagine a silent Meeting to hear our vows."

He was uncertain. "I do not know the form of such a ceremony."

"The form is as simple as we wish. I take thee, Ernst Best, to be my husband, and I will be with thee as long as we both shall live."

"I take thee, Quality Smith, to be my wife, and I will be with thee as long as we both shall live."

She kissed him. "Normally it is a longer ceremony, but it will do."

"It will do," he echoed.

But it was morning, and he had to go to work. His work consisted of assorted technical investigations and reports for Admiral Canaris, who ran Abwehr. But there was something else, about which he did not tell her, yet she knew. Something he had to do which he did not like. Their love had been realized, but the rest of the world remained grim. She was still a virtual prisoner in his room, and he was bound by his duty. No one knew what would come of all this, so they could only enjoy the moment.

Meanwhile she continued to recover, gaining weight and strength. She suspected that love had as much to do with it as food, but she abetted it by doing whatever exercises she could manage without making too much noise. She adjusted her clothing to fit her better, and brushed her hair out, encouraging it to grow. She spent much time reading, and gazed out into the pleasant park.

Her face healed. She was almost sorry to see it happen, because she associated her black eye with Ernst's love. But she knew he had no joy in that, so for his sake she was glad to recover her beauty.

Toward the end of January Ernst brought an older officer home with him. Quality could tell by his manner that Ernst was not at ease, but had not been able to avoid this. The other man was tall and impressive, and evidently of very high status. Quality was immediately afraid of him.

The man's small restless eyes focused on her. She knew Ernst had had to tell him about her, and was helpless to prevent what this man might do. But the man did not seem hostile, merely interested. He spoke rapidly in German. Quality had been learning German, slowly, but this was way too much for her. She caught only the word "Fräulein," meaning a young woman.

Ernst responded, introducing her. "This is Quality Smith, who speaks no German." Because he spoke carefully, for her benefit, she could understand. "Quality, this is Reinhard Heydrich."

Quality felt a shiver of apprehension. She knew that name! He was the feared head of the Nazi intelligence network. Stories about him had been rife in Spain and in Gurs. He was said to be a predatory animal, capable of acting swiftly and ruthlessly, called by some the blond beast and by others Mister Suspicion, and by others a criminal of the stature of the devil himself. He was the Third Reich's evil god of death, the man with the iron heart. He was also a pathological womanizer. Of all the people she did not want to encounter, Heydrich was close to the top of the list.

"I see you know of me," Heydrich said in English. "Come now, I am not as bad as all that."

"I did not speak of you to her," Ernst said, alarmed. "I told her nothing."

Heydrich ignored him. He concentrated on Quality, to her discomfort, seeming to take in every aspect of her. "And you wear the swastika! That is good; it will protect you, as it protected him." He paused. "The bruise," he said sharply. "Who hit you?"

She felt mesmerized. She knew that even had she been one to

lie, it would have been useless to try to fool this man. She wished that the last vestige of the bruise had faded, or that she had thought to cover it up with powder. "Ernst hit me. Before he gave me the swastika."

Heydrich turned a sharp glance on Ernst. "This is not the conduct of an officer of the SS! I forbid it! You must treat this pretty young woman with the utmost courtesy at all times. Can you remember that without a memo?"

"Ja," Ernst said, abashed.

"After all, in love and in revenge woman is more barbarous than man. You do not wish her to seek your downfall." He glanced again at Quality. "Do you not agree, *Liebling*?"

"Nietzsche had no respect for women," she replied.

His brow lifted. "You recognize my quote from Nietzsche? Why do you condemn him?"

"I don't condemn him. I just don't regard him as any authority on women. He said that man thinks woman is profound, because he can never fathom her depths, but that she is not even shallow. If he had ever come to know a woman who wasn't syphilitic, he would have had a better opinion."

Ernst turned his face away, perhaps horrified by her impertinence to his superior, but Quality had already realized that Heydrich respected mind more than subservience. If he had come to take her back to an awful camp, at least he would know she had a mind.

Heydrich smiled. "Now I see why Ernst selected you. And what do you think of Wagner?"

"The composer? I love his work, but I have not heard a lot of it."

"You must listen to more. The Führer approves." His eyes flicked around the room again. Then he switched back to his staccato German, addressing Ernst, who answered reluctantly. Their dialogue continued.

Quality, evidently dismissed, retreated to a corner and sat, waiting for the conclusion. What was Heydrich's purpose here? Was he going to take her away, or was she incidental? She had the unmistakable impression that his interest in her was not casual. That chilled her, but she knew she was helpless.

Then, abruptly, Heydrich was departing. "We shall meet again, Liebling, when we have more time for Nietzsche." He was gone.

Quality felt the tension draining from her. "What does he want?"

she demanded.

"He wants the truth about Admiral Canaris," he said heavily. "And I have given it to him."

"But I thought thee worked for Canaris."

"I do. But my real job is with Heydrich. I fear I have gotten Canaris in trouble."

"Trouble? How?"

"I have learned that Canaris is employing a full Jewish agent in Tangier."

"Heydrich hates Jews?"

"No, he helped a Jewish fencing instructor to emigrate to America. He was proficient in fencing, so has respect for it. He simply regards Jews as faceless objects that must be removed from Germany, as Hitler wills. But the fact that Canaris is using Jews in his operation means that Canaris is suspect. I believe he is loyal, but this counts against him."

"Thee is a spy for Heydrich, against Canaris?"

"Yes. I wish I were not."

"So Heydrich is not going to take me away?"

"Oh, no, Quality! He doesn't care about you."

"Yes he does. But I don't know how."

"I fear I do know. I hope I am wrong."

"Then what is it, Ernst? Can I avoid it?"

"It is his way to blackmail his most important subordinates. He believes he can not trust any man completely unless he knows something about that man that must not be revealed. Now he has that hold on me. Perhaps I should feel privileged, that I am important enough to him to rate this treatment." He smiled without pleasure.

"What hold?" she asked, perplexed.

"I prefer not to say." He was obviously distressed.

"Thee must tell me, Ernst, if it concerns me."

He closed his eyes in pain. "It is my love for you. I must obey him absolutely, because if I do not, he will destroy you, and therefore me."

"Oh, my," she said, horrified.

"I think he knew all along. He was the one who sent me to Barcelona to investigate the Quaker relief effort there. He knew of you from my personnel record. He has an uncanny memory for key details. He must have known I would try to protect you, once I knew you were in Spain. I invoked his name when I took you from Gurs. I thought they did not check, but now I suspect they did, and he gave you clearance to go with me. It is the way he works."

"But he could not know we would fall in love!" she protested.

"It is exactly the kind of thing he *does* know. He is a genius in the manipulation of people and power. He wanted this hold on me, and now he has it."

"Oh, Ernst!" she cried, chagrined. "What have I done to thee!"

"No, my love, no, I would not have it otherwise! I wish only that he had not known."

"There must be truth," she said, pained. "If it is to thy commander I owe my rescue from Gurs, and my stay with thee, and the love we share, then I must thank him, though his motive be unkind. I owe him my life and love."

"Can good come of an ill motive?" Ernst inquired bleakly.

"It can, and ill can come of a good motive. We do not comprehend the ways of God."

"Certainly I do not!"

She smiled, cheering him, understanding his confusion. He had never professed the kind of faith she had, yet he was as good a man as any who had faith.

Still she was sorry that her presence placed him in this peril. She knew that there was intrigue among German officers, with each striving to get ahead at the expense of others, and she was chagrined to be the mechanism by which Ernst had become vulnerable.

A few days later there was a peremptory knock on the door. It was during the day, while Ernst was at work. She did not answer, as was her policy; Ernst had stressed that no one who lacked a key should be admitted during his absence.

"Liebling! It is Reinhard."

Quality suffered a siege of panic. That was Heydrich, Ernst's terrible superior! What could have brought him here?

"Do not fear," Heydrich called. "I have brought you something. Open the door."

She could not deny this man, for his anger could cost Ernst terribly. With dread, she unlocked the door.

The Nazi officer stood there holding a box. He was in civilian clothing, as he had been before, which meant he was not advertising his presence here. He stepped into the room. He carried the box to the table and set it down. “Lock the door again, Liebling,” he said without looking at her.

Quality’s hands were shaking as she did so. It was obvious that the man had timed his appearance for Ernst’s absence. What dreadful thing did he have in mind? She knew she was helpless to prevent it, because he could readily arrange to have her killed.

Heydrich brought out a knife as he turned to face her. Quality felt a thrill of horror. He was going to kill her right here, if she even screamed!

“Fräulein, what do you expect of me?” Heydrich asked, looking surprised.

Pleading would be useless; this was a completely cynical man. She could save only her dignity, for what little it was worth. So she gave him a direct answer. “I expect you to rape me, and to kill me if I protest.”

He laughed. “You misjudge me, Liebling. I am merely opening the box.” He proceeded to use the knife to cut the string and cardboard. “While it is true that I like women, I do not impose on those committed to other men, and I am distressed that you suppose I would deplore your being hit by Ernst while intending violence on you myself. I assure you that this is not my way. Certainly not when a lovely woman is protected by her swastika.”

She was not completely reassured. “Then what is your intent?”

“Only to charm you.” He had the box open, and put away the knife.

“I am not to be charmed into what I do not wish to do.”

He glanced at her again, smiling. “Then you have nothing to fear from me.”

“But Ernst has!” she said boldly.

“Ah, he has told you of my way.”

“It’s a terrible way!”

“It is a practical way. It obviates deceit. In my profession this is necessary. Now I can truly trust Ernst, and so there will never be any problem. As Nietzsche says, what is good is all that heightens the feeling of power.”

“And what is bad is all the proceeds from weakness,” she agreed. “Therefore I am bad.”

He laughed again. “I am not so sure of that, *Liebling.* You have the power of your faith. It shines through you, making you the envy of all women. I am a connoisseur in such matters. Now take away the box as I lift it out."

Hesitantly she took hold of the box, and pulled it free of what he held. She set it down, then looked at the thing on the table. "A Victrola!" she exclaimed, surprised.

"And a record," he agreed. "Wagner. Power is good, and music is power, and Richard Wagner is the true prince of music. You appreciate Wagner, therefore you are also good."

"This is for me?" she asked, stunned.

"And for Ernst, while the two of you are here. Have no fear: Adolf Hitler endorses Wagner. You may listen with impunity." He brought out a record. "Only his shorter pieces are here, I regret. The *Ring* is too much for a mere machine."

"But why?" Quality asked.

"I do not wish you to know me only by hearsay, which is not kind. I prefer you to know me for what I am."

"But what do you care about my opinion? I am nothing."

"Ernst has good taste. He has given up a remarkably beautiful, obliging, and well pedigreed woman, for you. I suspect you are a woman among women, when you show your nature. I shall fathom that nature."

She focused on one part of what he said. "He gave up Krista?" Somehow she had not thought of this, of the insistent girlfriend she had displaced.

"He is an honorable man. When he loved you, he broke with her. She was most annoyed."

"He said nothing to me about this!" Yet of course Ernst would have done it.

"And he said nothing to her about you. He merely told her that he felt it was better that they no longer associate. She remains suspicious of his motive."

"I never intended this!" Quality cried, though another part of her recognized it as inevitable. How could she have married Ernst, even symbolically, and expected him to continue dating another woman? Such deceit might be required for appearances, but not when that woman loved him.

Heydrich was watching her, as if he could read her thoughts in the manner of ripples across her surface. "You love him, of course."

"Yes. But—"

"As Nietzsche clarifies, love is a disguised desire for possession. The will to power."

"But I would not think of—"

"And humility is protective coloration for the will to power."

"No! I do not want to harm anyone."

"The strong woman defines her own morality."

Everything he said was quoted from Nietzsche. She gave him a direct stare. "Distrust all in whom the impulse to punish is powerful," she said, quoting another maxim of Nietzsche.

He laughed. "Ah! She fights back at last! She is not quite the pacifist she pretends."

"There is no virtue in silence; all unuttered truths become poisonous." That was more Nietzsche. "Punishment tames man, but does not make him better." But Heydrich was right; he had made her oppose him, to fight fire with fire. She was indeed not truly pacifist, in words, and had never been so. She realized that now.

"Now listen to your music. I will see you again, if you are amenable." Heydrich walked to the door and waited until she came to use her key to let him out. He departed without ceremony.

She locked the door behind him, feeling weak. She had never anticipated such a visit! Yet the man seemed sincere. He did have her in his power, and knew it, yet he had chosen to bring her a gift instead of shame.

She told Ernst of the visit, when he came back. "He is an educated and sensitive man," he said. "But also a will like steel. He is letting us know how completely we are in his power."

"But the music is nice," she said. There were several records, and the pieces were indeed pretty, with the power to move the heart and spirit.

In February came disaster for Ernst's nominal superior, Admiral Canaris. Ernst tersely explained to her what had happened: Himmler had received the word that Ernst had relayed to Heydrich about the Jew Canaris employed in Tangier. Himmler had gone to Hitler and accused Canaris of favoring Jews. Hitler, outraged, had summoned Keitel, who was the Chief-of-Staff of the German armed Forces, and ordered him to dismiss Canaris. Keitel had done so. Canaris was replaced by a Vice-Admiral within Abwehr. Thus had Ernst effectively served Heydrich, to the Admiral's cost. But he was saddened and disgusted. "It is true, there is a Jew—but he is an effective operative, working loyally for Germany. Canaris is merely trying to do the best job he can, using the best people. He is not disloyal or incompetent, and he does not deserve to be so callously cast aside."

In the following days Canaris fought back. He went to Keitel, who refused to intercede on his behalf. Finally he went directly to Hitler, and in that interview was able to get himself reinstated. But the experience nearly destroyed him.

"He is despondent and morose," Ernst reported as the situation unfolded. "He no longer pays attention to detail. He seeks solace in Roman Catholic mysticism. He visits Spanish churches. He speaks of retiring and buying a coffee shop in some little Spanish town."

"But that is a nice dream," Quality said. "Spain is a nice country, when it isn't torn by war."

"Unfortunately a dream isn't enough, right now. Heydrich is using the Admiral's weakness to coerce concessions from him. If only I had not served Heydrich so well!"

Quality was silent, knowing that Ernst had no choice. *She* was the price of his loyalty to Heydrich, whatever else he might wish politically.

However, the other officers of Abwehr acted quickly to repair the damage done to their power base. Ernst had no part in it, to their frustration, but they drafted a counterproposal which retracted nearly all of the Admiral's concessions.

Late in February Heydrich appeared once more at the room. Quality let him in, concerned about what might be on his mind. "Have no fear, Liebling," he said as he entered. "I admit I am furious because of the Admiral's bad faith, and I refuse to associate with him. But no fault attaches to Ernst, or to you. Let us relax." He opened what Quality had taken to be a small suitcase and brought out a violin. "I will play Wagner's 'Ride of the Valkyries,' and we shall forget the sordid things of this bleak world."

Amazed, Quality watched and listened as Heydrich did just that. He played his violin with exquisite skill, producing the most moving rendition of "Ride" Quality could remember hearing. This despite having only his single instrument for a piece intended for an orchestra. Quality saw with further surprise that his eyes were closed, and that tears flowed from them. He was truly feeling the music.

He finished the brief piece, and took down the violin. "Oh, please play more!" Quality begged. "It is so lovely."

"How can I refuse?" he inquired, smiling sadly. "There is such greatness in Wagner, it is an honor merely to echo it in whatever way we can."

He played for an hour, and Quality was entranced. "You said you would charm me," she said as he finally put away the instrument. "You have succeeded."

He nodded, then departed, leaving her bemused. This savagely practical man, who held her hostage against Ernst's possible independence, who schemed to topple competing officers, yet had such a wonderful side. How could she assimilate this?

Of course she told Ernst, later. "Heydrich is a remarkable man," he agreed. "He was a champion athlete, and proficient in fencing and horsemanship. But he is also a power-hungry cynic, and I wish we were far from him."

Quality agreed, yet she could not forget the beauty of the man's violin playing. Surely such a man could not be wholly evil.

In March Heydrich came again. "Come, Liebling, it is a nice day out," he said. "Walk with me in the park. In happier days I rode horseback there with Admiral Canaris."

"But I can't go outside!" she protested. "I have no papers!" For Ernst had been unable to arrange this.

"I think you can, Liebling. Here is a pass for you." He handed her a bit of paper.

Amazed, she accepted it. It was indeed an identification for Frau Smith that would probably give her freedom of the streets. "But why?" she asked.

"A bird is better free than in the cage. Ernst trusts you; can I do less?"

So it was that she left the room and the hotel for the first time in three months. They walked through the Tiergarten in the brisk but pleasant air, and they discussed Nietzsche. She had read and reread all the books Ernst had been able to bring her, in the long hours of her confinement, and struggled with the concepts, and her familiarity enabled her to hold her own in this dialogue.

"But do you not agree that mankind is led by the nose with morality?" he asked. "That this is merely the arrogance of the elect, posing as modesty? That Christianity is a fateful kind of megalomania, laying claim to the concepts of God, Truth, Light, Spirit, Love,

Wisdom and Life itself?"

"I am a Christian, a Quaker Christian," she replied. "I lay claim to no such things, only my wish to be guided by my inner light. However imperfect I may be, the end is noble."

"You have read Nietzsche, yet you still believe in religion, in God?"

"Reading Nietzsche is like walking barefoot through the pitfalls of Hell," she confessed. "But with care and humility they can be navigated. One must at least try."

"And what of the Übermensch, the Overman? Is he not Godlike? Are we not right to cultivate him?"

"You interpret the Overman as a racially pure Nordic," she retorted. "That is not what Nietzsche said. It is hardness of the will, not of the flesh, that distinguishes the ideal man. By Nietzsche's definition, a strong-willed and consistent Jew is as much an Overman as any Nazi."

"Ach, the Führer must not hear you!" But he did not seem upset by the comparison. Rather, he was delighting in the discussion.

Heydrich returned her safely to her room, and departed, once more having been a perfect gentleman.

Ernst shook his head when she told him. "It seems that he wants your respect, nothing else. But that pass—I don't know how that was possible, but he has given you your freedom. If there were a way to take you out of Germany—"

"I would not go without thee, Ernst."

In May Admiral Canaris joined Heydrich at his new base in Prague. All of the intelligence operations were being gathered together under that umbrella. Heydrich's power was still increasing. Then early in June he was assassinated.

Quality received the news with shock. "But how could he be dead? He was too clever for that!"

"He was a top target," Ernst said. "The allies wanted very much to be rid of him."

"Perhaps he had his evil side, but I shall grieve for him," she said Indeed, she felt the tears. "He was always kind to me."

"Yet his death has freed you as a hostage. No other man has that hold on me. Indeed, now I can forget that aspect of my career, and work truly for Admiral Canaris."

"I am pleased for thee." Yet she knew that every time she listened to a record on the Victrola she would think of Heydrich, and whenever she went outside, protected by the papers he had arranged. Whatever the man's motive, he had done her incalculable good. Whatever his evil, he deserved that measure of her respect.

Indeed, it was a time of relief for them both. Ernst continued with his work, which sometimes took him to Spain and elsewhere, but the pass Heydrich had given Quality remained magical in its authority, and she was now able to go out and shop on her own. The hotel personnel knew her and accepted her. She was learning German, and developing facility in conversing with others.

When Ernst was home, they made love often. They listened to records on the Victrola; Ernst bought more when he found them, including other pieces by Richard Wagner. There was an emotional intensity to Wagner's music that made it an excellent background for sexual expression.

When Ernst was away, for a day or for several days, Quality read. She was no longer restricted to English or French books; a few were in Spanish, and she was practicing on German ones too, with the help of a dictionary. She was alone much of the time, but she did not feel lonely; rather she felt that she was in a period of learning, as she prepared to be a part of German society. For she knew that her future lay with Ernst, and therefore Germany, whatever the outcome of the war.

The war itself now seemed far away. They shut it out, not speaking of it. Their world was the room, and the park, and the few stores in range. They did not read the newspaper. In this they seemed to be like other Berliners, who for their own reasons preferred to ignore the world beyond Germany.

They celebrated the Christmas season together, quietly. Ernst brought her a gift of a pretty wool sweater, the best he could afford. They spoke of their dreams for "after": a nice cottage in some mountain glade, with a forest nearby, where wild animals could be seen. They drew outlines of floor plans for such a structure, and looked at a map to find a suitable location. Perhaps by a mountain lake, where they could watch the water birds. It was idyllic. If it was unrealistic, they did not care; it was their shared fantasy.

In January came the new year, 1943, and disaster. A man with an ironically similar given name, Dr. Ernst Kaltenbrunner, replaced

Heydrich as head of the broad network of intelligence services known as RHSA. Quality never met this man, but she felt his impact immediately. Kaltenbrunner was heir to Heydrich's most private information, including the fact that Ernst Best was an SS operative who had infiltrated the Abwehr. He did not know about Quality, so did not have that special hold on Ernst, but what he did know was enough.

For Kaltenbrunner did not like Heydrich. In fact, he had nothing but contempt and hatred for rear echelon intellectuals, and despised anyone associated with them. He could not do anything to the dead man, but he could still make the living ones suffer. Ernst was one of these.

"He is transferring me to an assignment guaranteed to get me dirty," Ernst said morosely. "He doesn't need any more reports on the Admiral. I am to work with the Einsatzgruppen—the SS forces charged with racial operations."

Quality felt a chill as of death. She had heard about that organization, the worst of the SS. There was even a battalion composed entirely of convicted criminals. "Oh, Ernst!"

"I am to leave the Abwehr tomorrow. They are not revealing my true mission there, because they do not want to admit that they have been spying on their own organizations. So there is another pretext. Lieutenant Osterecht will disappear from those records, and I will revert to my true identity. But I will not be in Berlin."

"I will wait for thy return," she said, with grim humor. She could do nothing else. "Perhaps I should give thee back thy charmed swastika."

"No. You must be protected more than me."

She did not argue. She valued the swastika as the token of his love, and it did indeed seem to be protecting her. Heydrich had noticed it immediately, and thereafter treated her with courtesy and kindness.

They made hasty arrangements. Ernst used the rest of his money to pay for the room ahead and to provide her with enough for groceries. "I will come back whenever I can," he promised.

"I know thee will." Neither spoke of the horror lurking behind the assignment: he might be killed on that ugly front.

Quality pretended to herself that Ernst's absence was temporary, and that in another day or two she would hear his familiar step in the hall. She did not like deception, even of herself, but it was necessary for her emotional survival.

Then there was an unfamiliar knock. Quality's presence here was no longer secret; the hotel staff and the members of Abwehr knew of her. But none of them had told the SS authorities, being loyal to a friend though they had guessed the reason for his departure. Who, then, could this be?

She opened the door. There stood a robustly attractive young woman. "So it is true!" the woman exclaimed angrily in German. "A kept woman!"

Was this a moralistic neighbor? "Who are you?" Quality asked in German.

"I am Krista."

Astonished, Quality backed away, tacitly inviting her in. Krista was the girlfriend Ernst had broken with a year ago. Actually, it had been incomplete; he had tried to, but reported that Krista had refused to disengage completely without better reason. So they had maintained a "just friends" relationship, with no promise of marriage, and Ernst had had meals with her every month or so. Krista had seemed to accept this change, and she was good company, he had said. He hoped she was in the process of finding another boyfriend.

Now it was clear that Krista had by no means given up on Ernst. She had merely bided her time, waiting for whatever problem he had to pass. Now he was gone, and she was checking out his room—and verifying her suspicion.

"I am sorry," Quality said carefully in German. "I did not mean to hurt your life."

Krista studied her closely. Her eyes fixed on Quality's bosom. "Ach, the game is lost," she murmured.

Quality glanced down. There lay Ernst's swastika. Krista evidently understood its significance. "He gave it to me in lieu of a ring," she explained.

Krista shook her head. "I came prepared to hate you. But I see he loves you, and I cannot hate what he loves. How did it come about?"

"We met in America. I was the fiancée of his friend there. I went to work in Spain, but was—" Here she did not know the German word, so had to say it in English. "Arrested."

"*Verhaften*," Krista said. Then, in English: "I know some English, if you speak slow."

Quality elected to piece it out in German. "Arrested in Vichy France. He tried to help me, for the sake of his friend, but when America joined the war, he had to take me out of the camp. We were together, here, and it happened."

"You must be a remarkable woman, to win his love. He has such discipline he cannot be tempted unless he wills it."

"He slept embracing me naked, to keep me warm, and did not touch me," Quality agreed.

"Ja, that is Ernst!" Krista shook her head. "I will keep your secret. I would not hurt Ernst in any way, though I have lost him." She turned to go.

"Krista—must we be enemies? I am without him too, now, for I fear he will not—not return." She felt the sudden tears in her eyes.

"How can we be otherwise?" Krista asked. She walked to the door.

Quality followed her. "Please, I have injured you without ever wanting to. If there is any possible way for me to make amends—"

"Where is there another man like Ernst?" Krista asked sharply. There were tears in her eyes too.

Quality was unable to answer. She watched Krista depart, then locked the door after her. Then she went to the bed, flung herself down on it, and wept.

But two days later Krista returned. Her eyes were somewhat swollen despite a careful job of makeup. Quality knew her own were the same. "I accept what must be," Krista said. "I fear it was destined; your gray eyes match his. I am a practical woman. But it is not easy to give up a dream."

Quality welcomed her. "I am not German," she said. "I am a prisoner Ernst has been protecting. If anything happens, I will be gone. Then—"

"I would not do that!"

"Of course not. I mean that there are many ways in which my future is uncertain. Any member of the hotel staff could turn me in. Then I will be out of the picture. So you have not necessarily lost Ernst."

Krista shook her head. “I have lost him. If you were gone, he would not return to me. He would morn you.”

Quality could not argue the case. “Let me share some food with you. I do not have much variety, but there is bread and jam.”

“It will do.”

Quality fixed it, and they each had a slice.

“Now we have eaten together,” Krista said. “We can not be enemies.”

“I never wished to be.”

“Ernst was never truly mine. I threw myself at him, I tried to seduce him, because I wanted a secure situation. It was not love, it was opportunity. He understood that. He is more romantic. He wanted love. This is what you gave him.”

“Yes.”

“I am as I am. There is a shadow on my ancestry. First I must secure my position. Then love can come. I would have loved him after we married. But I could not risk love before it.”

“But you said you tried to seduce him.”

“Sex is not love. If there had been sex, he would have married me, and then there could have been love. But with you, the love came first.”

“Yes. There just seemed to be something between us.”

“It is goodness between you. I saw it in him, and I see it in you. You are both beautiful inside as well as outside.”

“I make no claim to that! My soul is sullied.”

“Surely only because you were forced to choose between evils.” Krista shrugged. “But you loved another man before Ernst.”

“Yes. Lane Dowling, an American. A fine man. I dread our next meeting, if it occurs.”

“You have had no contact with Herr Dowling, so he does not know you have left him.”

“He does not know,” Quality agreed sadly. “I have wronged him, too. Yet as with you and Ernst, I now see that we were not quite right for each other.”

“You would not love an inferior man.”

“I don’t know how you mean that. I am not concerned with pedigree or status, but with personality. Lane was special. But Ernst—”

“Herr Dowling—what does he care about ancestry?”

“He doesn’t care at all about ancestry! No more than I do. In fact he seeks unusual people. That's why he befriended Ernst, who was a foreigner in America. How I wish that friendship had not led to—" Quality spread her hands. What an irony, that Lane had introduced his friend to his fiancée, and so had lost his fiancée.

"Ja. So Herr Dowling is a good man, and he will be disappointed when he meets you again. At that point he will need another woman."

"I fear he will," Quality agreed.

"Would he consider a German?"

Quality stared at her. "You can't mean—?"

"I need security. I need a good man. One who does not care about pedigree. Herr Dowling will need a good woman. I can be a very good woman, for the right man." She inhaled.

Amazed, Quality assessed the prospect. "Lane does like—he would be interested in a body like yours. I was surprised when he became interested in me, because I am not—" She shrugged.

"Your body is slender. Your face is beautiful. You are a lovely woman, overall. But perhaps it was something else he saw in you."

"My religion," Quality agreed. "I am a practicing Quaker. A pacifist. I—some of us use a variant of the language, at times. He was intrigued."

"He is a pacifist?"

Quality laughed. "Not at all! That was part of—of what was going wrong between us. He became a fighter pilot. He was fighting in the Battle over France, shooting down German bombers, when I last heard from him. Surely in the Battle over Britain, too, later. But then I was arrested, and our correspondence was lost."

"I am a Nazi. But I would change. However I needed to. For a secure position. For a good man. The kind of man whom you could once have loved, for I respect your judgment. Does this disturb you?"

Quality shook her head. "I have learned to be practical, in the past four years. Every person must do what she has to, to accomplish what she has to."

"You would introduce me to Herr Dowling?"

"If I meet him again, and if you are there. Yes, that much I would do. But Lane—he is not one to be reeled in like a fish, any more than Ernst is. He would not reject you because of your nationality, but he would not necessarily accept you. And for all I know, he has already given up on me and found another woman. He may believe

I am dead. So this is purely speculative."

"A dream," Krista agreed. "But I need a dream, now. I fear Germany is—the war is turning—the Russians are fighting back—there will not be much security in Germany. So if Herr Dowling comes, perhaps he is for me."

"Perhaps," Quality agreed, beginning to believe. "His hair is the same color as Ernst's, and his blue eyes do match yours."

"Ah! That is ideal! The hair, the eyes—perhaps it is fated. If you will tell me about him, it will help."

"Gladly." Quality remained bemused by this development, but she was wickedly tempted by the notion. If she could in effect give Krista a man to replace Ernst, and give Lane a woman to replace herself—what a precious solution! It was preposterous, yet a worthy fantasy.

So she told Krista about Lane Dowling, practicing her German, and Krista responded, practicing her English, and suddenly the day was fading and Krista had to go.

But she came again when she had time, and they talked further. Krista was insatiably interested in everything about Lane, and Quality was glad to tell it, in this way expiating some of her associated guilt.

The following month, Krista had another surprising proposal. "It is hard living alone. The expense gets worse, and it is lonely. You are also alone. I could share with you."

Quality had been refusing to think about what would happen when her diminishing supply of Deutschmarks ran out, and the rent would be due on the room. Ernst had been away a month now, and if he did not return soon, her situation would become dire. Krista had proved to be a pleasant companion during their dialogues.

So it was that Krista moved in with her, and paid the rent, and bought the groceries. They were not sharing; Krista was covering it all. Quality had no choice but to accept.

Krista was away in the days, at her employment. Quality did the shopping and housekeeping. It worked much as it had with Ernst, even to the sharing of warmth in the cold nights. But it wasn't the same.

Early in March Quality got sick. She felt bloated, and she vomited, but it didn't help. As the day progressed, she improved. But the following day it happened again.

"We can't take you to a doctor," Krista said. "He would report you. They are required to."

"It's mild," Quality said. "It must be minor."

But it continued. Every morning she suffered, and every evening she was all right.

Then Krista stared at her. "*Gott in Himmel*! That is morning sickness!"

Quality was appalled. "It can't be! I am too thin. My periods have not returned. Only very irregularly."

Krista shook her head. "You are not thin anymore. You are a beautiful figure of a woman, slender but full. Your periods are gone because you are with child."

"No!" But her protests were in vain. She was pregnant.

Late in March Ernst reappeared. Quality was alone, with Krista away at work. He swept her into his embrace. "I have missed you so!" he exclaimed. "I knew there wasn't enough money. I must pay off your debts."

"Oh, Ernst, I have so much to tell thee," she said.

By the time Krista returned, they had made love and she had told him. She wasn't certain whether he was stunned more by Krista's involvement or the news of the baby.

The meeting between Ernst and Krista was somewhat strained, with neither knowing quite how to proceed. Quality had to take the initiative. "We are all friends. We knew each other well. We have no secrets from each other. Ernst was with one of us and now is with the other. We shall eat, and listen to records, and sleep."

"Sleep," Ernst repeated, looking warily at the bed.

She hadn't thought of that. The bed held two, but was too small for three, however they might be arranged.

"I will sleep on the floor," Krista said. There was some debate, but that did turn out to make the best sense.

Ernst had to go next day. He gave them money, enough to pay for the room for two more months and to reimburse Krista. "This thing that you are doing," he said to Krista. "I have no way to thank you."

"Just remember that had things been otherwise, I would have

been good for you."

"Better than I knew," he agreed.

Then he was gone. Krista turned away, in tears. Quality felt the burgeoning guilt again. However brave a face the woman put on it, she had loved Ernst, and the loss of him hurt her in more than a practical sense.

They agreed that Ernst had seemed reticent about his activity on the Eastern Front. They knew that the fighting there was savage. They concluded that they were probably better off not knowing the details.

Two months later Ernst came again, with more money to sustain them. Quality was now five months pregnant.

"It is difficult," Ernst said. "I can not be sure when I will return. Quality must go to a *Liebensborn* home where they will take care of her and the baby. Then it will be all right."

Quality did not dare ask why he was in such doubt about returning.

"We will wait here two more months," Krista decided. "If you have not returned by then, I will take her there. You will be able to find me, here or at home. I will tell you where she is, then."

He nodded, looking pained.

Then he was gone, and they settled in for the duration. He did not reappear in two months, and the money was running out again because of the extra food Quality had to eat.

Krista explained the nature of the Liebensborn Foundation, literally "Well of Life." "It is to foster a higher birth rate for Aryan children. There are several maternity homes for the mothers of SS children, married or unmarried, to use at little cost. They provide care before and after birth. It is the best possible place to have a—" She hesitated, evidently not wanting to speak of an illegitimate baby.

"We are married before God," Quality said, touching the swastika. "In my religion the marriage consists of a simple declaration by each party, in the presence of the Friends Meeting. We exchanged vows."

"And he gave you his most precious possession. I understand. But the state does not recognize it."

"True." Quality sighed. "It would have been better not to have a baby. Yet how can I protest, when it is his?"

"When it is his," Krista echoed, turning away. Quality was chagrined; she had forgotten how Krista herself would have wanted to have Ernst's baby.

Now it was time. "We must do it," Krista said. "We must take you to the Lebensborn home. Now, while it is safe for you to travel."

"But I am a foreigner," Quality protested weakly. "I am not German."

"You are a fine Nordic specimen, and so is he. You have papers. That is the kind of baby they want. They will take care of you."

"But what of you, here alone?"

"I think my job in Berlin is almost over. The war goes badly. I think it is time for me to go home. But I will visit you as often as I can, until he returns."

Quality hated to leave the room where she had loved Ernst. But Krista was correct: for the sake of their finances and the baby, she had to do it. They would leave the name of the home with the hotel manager, so that Ernst would be able to find her without having to search out Krista.

Yet she had a dire foreboding that he was not going to find her. Because he might be in more trouble than she was.

Chapter 12
Götterdämmerung

It had been a fool's paradise, he realized: the hope that he could simply cut off his connection with Heydrich and give his loyalty to Admiral Canaris. The Abwehr, with all its faults, remained a far better working environment for him, ideologically, than the RHSA. Even those aspects that were distasteful, such as the apparent attempt to use their section, Abwehr II, as a vehicle for the assassination of a French general, could be set aside when he was home with Quality. They had also uncovered the "Red Chapel" (Russian Orchestra) network of Russian agents operating in Germany. The Admiral had been absolutely furious that German soldiers could be involved in any such treason, and livid when one of them turned out to be an officer in Abwehr II itself. That had almost involved Quality, when Major Stummel suspected that she represented a contact subverting Ernst. But he was innocent, and further investigation had clarified that. It had nevertheless been a close call; had they thought to check Ernst's possible connection to Heydrich, they might have found another kind of traitor.

But trouble had come from the other side: Kaltenbrunner had done his homework and traced down the far-flung agents Heydrich had sent out. Now Ernst had to report to the man personally, before being shipped to the front.

Kaltenbrunner turned out to be a large man, with a body like that of a lumberjack. His face was angular, his neck thick, his chin square and his eyes small. His fingers were discolored, for he was a chain smoker. He spoke with a thick Austrian accent, and was missing several teeth, which hardly helped his appearance. He also drank excessively, Ernst learned. Yet it was evident that he had a fine analytical mind, and was fully as ruthless as Heydrich, without Heydrich's cultured side. Heydrich could be subtle and even, according to Quality, charming; Kaltenbrunner would never be either.

The interview was perfunctory. It seemed that Kaltenbrunner had wanted to meet Ernst merely so as to be able to recognize him thereafter. If he knew about Quality he clearly didn't care; perhaps he intended simply to ship Ernst far away and let those left behind fend for themselves. It was an effective punishment for those who had had the temerity to support Heydrich. But he couldn't stop Ernst from taking accrued leave time, when whatever unit he was in was not in a state of emergency. Ernst would return to help Quality in due course. He had to.

He was sent to the General Kommissariat "White Russia," well back from the front line. But it turned out to be a long train ride to Minsk, though endless snowy forests. Even when he managed to get leave time, it would require days to return to Berlin, assuming he could get transport. Ernst's hope of returning within a month faded, and he was depressed.

There were other officers traveling to this and other destinations. Time was on their hands, so they played cards and talked. Some of them had been on duty at the front, and from them Ernst received evil news. It seemed that the war was not going nearly as well as the Berlin newspapers had suggested. The initial victories of 1941 had been followed by a temporary setback in December, as the Russians counterattacked near Moscow and took advantage of the savage winter to force a retreat. When the weather eased in 1942 the German advance had resumed, but by the Führer's directive not toward Moscow but to the south. Progress had been made, of course, but this was nevertheless troublesome, because the Russian capital, so near to capture, remained functioning. Now the Russians were organizing, and real trouble was developing. The great German Sixth Army was surrounded and under siege in Stalingrad, and the winter was taking its toll, as it had the prior year. "If only we had knocked out Moscow, the hub!" one officer exclaimed. "Headless, the Russians would have given up the fight. Now there is mischief we never should have had to face."

"Mischief?" Ernst inquired.

Several others laughed. "You do not know of the partisans? Ragtag bands, but vicious. They roam the countryside, striking from hiding. Never do they stand up to fight like men, but they take many lives in their sneaky way. A man can never be sure he won't get a bullet in his back."

Which accounted for why Kaltenbrunner had sent him here, instead of to the front line. He would be more likely to die dishonorably. What a contrast to his work in the Abwehr, and his nights with

Quality. He was proceeding from relative Heaven to relative Hell. But he intended to survive, because he had to, to protect Quality. The thought of her alone in Berlin saddened him, but she could manage as long as he provided her money.

At last the train reached Minsk, where Ernst was met by a driver who took him to Major General Curt von Gottberg's unit. "Exactly what is occurring here?" Ernst inquired as the car moved along the snowy road.

"Antipartisan action, sir," the driver replied. "We have to clean them out, or they will clean us out."

"But surely there is not serious partisan activity this far behind the front line," Ernst said, knowing better. "In Berlin, we were told that this area was secure."

"Sir, the truth is that we control the cities and towns, and they control the countryside. They are getting stronger every day. Of course that doesn't get put into the Berlin newspapers."

So it was worse than he had feared. "But we came as liberators. We lifted the Communist yoke. They welcomed us."

"That they did, sir. At first. Then the Einsatzgruppen started in killing all the Jews and Gypsies any anyone else they chose not to like, and burning homes and fields and taking the food away, and that made for great recruitment for the partisans. Now we have a real problem."

"You don't approve of the Führer's policies?"

"I didn't say that, sir!" the man said quickly. "I just think that maybe if they had been a bit more subtle, the people wouldn't be rebelling, and our life would be easier."

Soon enough Ernst verified the extent of the problem. No Germans went into the countryside alone; they were always in military units. Even in the city there were daily incidents, as terrorists set bombs and snipers fired at military vehicles. No one ever seemed to know anything about the activities, but it was obvious that the natives were harboring the partisans. This might as well have been enemy territory.

The first significant artipartisan sweep in which Ernst participated was Operation Hornung. He went only as an observer, learning how it was done. "Things may not be quite as they are described in Berlin," he was tersely advised.

Indeed they were not. Ernst watched as the troops went out east of Minsk, surrounding the suspected area. There was the sound of firing, but very little obvious result. If there were partisans in the countryside, most of them must have managed to slip away before the cordon tightened. Only a few rifles were captured, and there were only five German casualties reported. But the men went through the houses, routing out their occupants, shooting any who tried to resist. These were called partisans, and in the course of the operation more than two thousand were "killed in action."

Many more were brought to a rendezvous for interrogation. They were lined up along the road, the men on one side, the women on the other. Then the translators went down the lines, addressing the women. "Point out all the men who do not belong in your village. If you do not, your own men will be killed."

The women tried to balk, to pretend that they did not know which men were which. "Then they all must be partisans," the officer said. "We shall execute them all."

At that point the women, distraught, reconsidered, and began to point out the strangers. Ernst realized that similar scenes were being enacted in all the villages of this region. The assumption was that any strangers must be partisans. But what of men with legitimate business in the village? What of partisans who happened to live here? There was the risk of executing the wrong men.

"Do you want to know the greatest irony?" another officer remarked to Ernst. "Most of those translators are Jews. Jews! We are using Jews to eliminate folk fighting for their homeland."

In due course a number of selected partisans were marched into a detention camp, and the other men, together with the women, were allowed to return to their homes. It was evident to Ernst that if those other men had not been partisans yesterday, they surely would be partisans tomorrow. Because almost any man would rather die fighting than be ignominiously executed just for being there.

The next day they went through a similar process at another village, continuing the sweep. The collection of prisoners grew. And the effective recruitment of future partisans.

After several days there were more than seven thousand prisoners. These were marched to a remote field and given spades and picks. They were required to dig large graves. Any who balked were beaten until they returned to work. The ground was hard, because of the winter cold, so the job took time, but no rest was allowed.

Ernst was appalled at the callousness of it, but he could not protest. He was only here to observe. If *he* balked, he might be required to give the cruel orders.

He looked at a group of soldiers who were seeming to have a party. They were drinking bottles of schnapps and vodka, and not even trying to conceal it. There were other officers in sight, but they seemed to be paying no attention. Apparently the soldiers were allowed this astonishing privilege of getting drunk on duty. Yet they did not look happy. What was going on?

When the graves were done, the partisans were forced to strip completely. There was snow on the ground, and they stood shivering violently, but were shown no mercy. They were required to stand facing the graves. Then the drunken soldiers came, carrying Schmeisser machine pistols. There were twelve of them.

"Fire!"

The pistols fired, in a crossfire pattern, and the bullets sprayed across the backs of the standing naked partisans. The partisans fell forward into their graves.

Now Ernst understood. No one liked the task of executing prisoners. It helped to be drunk when doing it. The soldiers were encouraged to drink so that they *could* do it. Only a few were sober. Those would be the fanatical Nazis who were satisfied to slaughter the helpless. That was no improvement.

Other soldiers took the spades and started filling in the dirt. There was a groan, and motion in the grave. One of the sober executioners walked across and used a carbine rifle to put a bullet through the head of the one who was incompletely dead.

"This is barbaric!" Ernst muttered.

"Not so," the officer beside him replied. "Barbarism is when they do not put the bullets in the heads of the survivors before covering them over."

"Or when they shoot a pregnant woman in the womb and push her into the grave alive," another added.

Ernst assumed that they were trying to shock him, in a kind of initiation. Later he learned that such things did occur. He was sickened and disgusted. This was, of course, why he had been sent here. His body might or might not survive—but would his soul?

The anti-partisan effort continued. General Warlimont, the head of the National Defense Office, issued an order stating that populations rounded up by the firing of villages which harbored partisans were to be sent to concentration camps in Poland and Russia. This was in response to the liquidation of entire villages during the anti-partisan operations. It was supposed to have a moderating effect. Ernst had already achieved enough cynicism to doubt that this would be the case. Actually, this order made it possible for almost anyone in occupied territory to be sent to a camp.

On March 18 there came a directive from the security office: "Generally speaking, no more children are to be shot." This, too, was likely to have no more than a cosmetic effect on policy. Ernst no longer had any doubt why so many local folk became partisans; he would have become one too, had he been a Russian resident.

Finally he was allowed leave time. He took the train for Germany, hoping that Quality remained in the Tiergarten room. It had been almost two months, far longer than he liked.

She was there! She was startlingly lovely, after the physical and mental horrors he had seen. Perhaps it was her nature, for he knew that Quality would never be associated with the atrocities of the eastern front. He swept her into his arms and kissed her.

"I have so much to tell thee," she said.

First they made love. Her body had filled out; she had not been going hungry. Yet her money should have run out. How had she managed?

"Ernst, I hope thee will not be upset," she said. "I am pregnant."

He lay beside her stunned. "Oh, Quality, in any other situation—"

"I agree. I did not want to be in this condition. Yet it is thy doing, and thy baby within me, and I can not help but feel joy in that."

And he had just had sex with her, not knowing! "I should not have—"

"I believe that love is healthy, at any time," she said. "I very much wanted thine at this time. I apologize for this small deceit: I did not tell thee before, so thee would not feel restricted."

He had to accept it. But there was another question. "How have you managed? I was so afraid you would not have money."

"That is the other wonderful thing I must tell thee, Ernst, though I fear it will surprise thee and leave thee with mixed feelings."

"Nothing can surprise me or mix my feelings more than your

pregnancy."

"I have a friend who has moved in with me, to share the expenses. When my money ran out, she used hers. She is the reason I am well, and not completely lonely in thine absence."

"A German friend?" he asked, amazed. "How can that be?"

"She is thy friend Krista."

The bottom fell out of his insecure equilibrium. "Krista! But she would hate you!"

"She tried to, but she did not succeed."

He looked at her. "I can appreciate how that is. But still—the resentment she must feel!"

"She is a practical woman. She says that since I have taken her man, she may take mine. She has questioned me closely about Lane."

"Lane Dowling!" Ernst laughed. Then as he thought about it, it began to make insidious sense. Lane did have an eye for poise and beauty, and Krista had both in ample measure. If she had opportunity to be with him for any length of time, and privacy to show him parts of her body, he would certainly be interested. He would not be put off by her Gypsy ancestry; he would find it intriguing. Still, the thing was farfetched. "How would she meet him?"

"If Germany loses the war, I will try to introduce her to him. Surely he will seek me, and if Krista is with me, I can do that much."

If Germany lost the war. Ernst had not allowed himself to think that thought before, but it was a prospect. The eastern front could at best be described as stagnant, and the German resources were being wasted fighting partisans. After what he had seen, he could no longer hope for German victory. The Russians might be barbarous, but they did not deliberately kill women and children.

"Then perhaps it is a fair deal," he said. "Lane is certainly a good man, and Krista is a good woman. Better than I had taken her for, since she has helped you."

"A good woman," Quality agreed.

Still, it was awkward when Krista returned. She remained beautiful, her hair still glisteningly fair. She concealed her surprise at seeing Ernst. It was evident that she still had feeling for him, but she made no attempt to impress him. She had accepted the change.

Actually, it was good that Krista had come here, he realized. Quality needed more than money, now that she was pregnant. Krista would see that she was cared for.

Before he left, he gave them all of his money he could spare, repaying Krista and providing for Quality's future food and rent. He tried to thank Krista for the generous thing she was doing, but was ineffective. He promised to return as soon as he could.

As it happened, he was able to return to them in two months, just before things really got bad at the front. Knowing that he could not speak for his own future, let alone Quality's, he told her that she would have to go to a Lebensborn maternity home. There at least she would be safe until the baby came, and perhaps thereafter. He hated to do it, but the thought of her fate if he was unable to return convinced him. At least he would not have to worry about her.

For the bad news at the front was the largest anti-partisan effort yet, Operation Cottbus. Two partisan groups had joined together and formed what they called "The Republic of Lake Palik," which extended on the southern end to within twenty miles of the Minsk-Moscow railway, and to another Moscow line in the north. There could be real trouble if the partisans started sabotaging the railways. That would interrupt the shipment of supplies and troops to the front. So this had to be dealt with, if German power in the region was to be maintained.

General Gottberg rounded up more than sixteen thousand men for the operation. Most of them were police from the Baltic states, or Russian volunteers. But it also included a civilian emergency force, part of which was comprised of ninety administrative workers from Minsk. Ernst suspected he knew how they felt: desk workers hauled out to the field, like himself. And of course there were the SS personnel.

The partisan forces were no mere ragtag bands. They now had tanks, field guns, an air strip and troop-carrying gliders under the command of a Russian Brigadier General. This had become an aspect of the front line, for that line had become dangerously porous. On the map this was pacified territory, but the map was a fiction. Ernst remembered Quality's remark: "If Germany loses the war." Out here it was unfortunately easy to recognize that possibility. The folly of not taking Moscow, thus leaving the head of the bear in place, was starkly clear. As was the folly of slaughtering the natives, for each one killed seemed to generate two more partisans.

Ernst had always regarded Adolf Hitler as a great man. Now even that belief was wearing thin. Perhaps if Hitler could come out here and see the reality, the policy would change. But Hitler, and Germany, seemed to be locked in to this course. In fact Hitler was giving ever greater support to the SS Einsatzgruppen, because its methods were more effective than those of the more fastidious Wehrmacht. It was like Götterdämmerung, the twilight of the gods, as the final battle loomed. The gods were destined to lose, and all things to be destroyed. Richard Wagner's music for this was beautiful, but the reality was grim.

Would Quality be allowed to take her books and Victrola to the maternity home, so she could continue listening to Wagner? He hoped so. She was a foreigner, but she wore his swastika, which others would misinterpret as her political statement. How could they refuse her Nietzsche and Wagner?

Operation Cottbus proceeded. The Luftwaffe supported it, bombing the suspect towns. It was full-scale war, and this time there were many partisans killed in true action. But for Ernst it was worse, because he was assigned to assist the notorious Dierlewanger Regiment, the one composed of Nazi party members who were convicted criminals. They were called "poachers," but there was no masking their nature. Ernst, as an intelligence officer, had to help interrogate prisoners and monitor the activities and attitudes of personnel assigned to "special details." In reality, the execution squads. He wished he could get drunk on vodka himself, but of course he couldn't.

As it happened, he was given no command responsibility, which was a relief. He had merely to be on hand as the work proceeded. He was in effect a spectator. But what he witnessed turned his stomach.

For the partisans had particular strongholds, and these were protected by minefields. It was folly for soldiers to march across those fields; if they managed to escape the mines, they would be picked off by the partisan sharpshooters. But the Dierlewanger men had a simple, ruthless solution: they routed out the women and children who were left behind in the towns, and forced them to march across the mine fields. The German troops followed, and the partisans could not fire on them without first gunning down their own families. As a result they held their fire, and watched their own people getting blown up by their own mines.

Ernst watched it happening, unable to turn away lest his horror be manifest. He could not help picturing Quality there, carrying his baby within her, stepping on a hidden mine and being blown apart. For each of those women were beloved by someone. He watched, and did not flinch, but his heart was turning leaden. This was the twilight of decency. What possible cause could be worth this?

He would have renounced it all, and fled the region, if he could. But he could not, because there was no honorable release from military service, and a dishonorable one would have cost him not only his life, but Quality's—and probably Krista's too. His own people remained hostage to his performance. So though he shot no partisans directly, and gave no orders to sacrifice women, he felt the blackening blood on his hands, that could never be washed off. He was part of the massive dishonor that was the SS Einsatzgruppen.

The operation began in mid May and continued through the month of June, 1943. Some fifteen thousand partisans were reported killed: six thousand in action, five thousand as suspects, and four thousand women and children used in the mine spotting. Five and a half thousand women and children were also conscripted for the labor force. Only a hundred and twenty seven Germans were killed. Thus Operation Cottbus was considered a great success. The fact that the countryside seemed to be no safer than before for Germans was ignored.

Yet there was additional irony. Ernst overheard the story of one person who had tried to follow a more civilized course. General Kube, Governor of White Russia, tried to win over the villagers in the region of Minsk so that the harvest would not be abandoned. Food was a real problem, and any fields that could be saved would help alleviate hunger. So General Kube's representative followed behind the troops in a loudspeaker van, attempting to drum up support. "The resistance is over. Return to your homes and work, and there will be no further reprisals. Cooperate, and we will work with you to restore your lives and bring food. You have everything to gain by peace."

But even as he was making his appeal, an SS colonel was giving orders to burn the village. The representative came across half-burned human bodies being eaten by pigs on the floor of a burned-out barn. Seeing the futility of his effort, he returned to Minsk and reported to the General. Outraged, Kube directed a complaint to his superiors. Nothing came of it.

Ernst knew exactly how the General felt.

In August Ernst finally got more leave time. He returned to Berlin, and to Tiergarten, but the room was empty. He inquired, and the hotel manager gave him the message Quality had left: "She is at the Lebensborn at this address." He held a slip of paper. But he did not give it to Ernst immediately. "Her account was overdue, but we did not press her for it, knowing you would make it good."

"I will make it good," Ernst agreed. He settled the account, and was given the address. He probably could have run down the address himself, but he did want to settle any debts, and preferred to keep the matter quiet.

He went there, and found the home crowded with children. In December 1942 thousands of racial German children had been forcibly removed from Poland. The maternity houses were required to be used until the children were adopted by suitable parents. Thus the nursery facilities were overflowing, for adoptions were slow. Good German families had other concerns now, such as feeding themselves.

Quality was there without Krista. She was now in her eighth month, her belly well swollen. She remained lovely to his eyes, and seemed to be in good health. The swastika shone at her bosom. He knew she did not accept its symbolism, but wore it only because it was his gift to her. Still, it had surely helped her gain entry and good treatment here, for the authorities would have taken it as evidence of her conversion to Nazism.

He kissed her chastely. "I am sorry I took so long," he said. "I settled the account."

"Account?"

"The money you owed the hotel. I paid it."

"I owed the hotel no money. We left when we ran out, assuming no debt."

Ernst realized that he had been taken. There was nothing he could do about it. "You are safe; that is all that matters."

"Krista went home to Wiesbaden. Perhaps thee should visit her, too. She was very good to me."

He shook his head. “Even if I had the time and the money, I would not care to see her alone. There is only respect between us, now.”

“Of course.” That was it. There was no privacy for any serious dialogue, and his leave was short. He had to return to the front. The truth was that there was little he would have cared to tell her about his activity. He felt unworthy to be in her company, for she was a gentle, practicing pacifist, and his hands were stained. He understood the alienation she had suffered from Lane Dowling, because now it applied to himself. He loved her, but how could he be with her?

He set himself to go, though he longed to remain. But Quality held him. “Ernst, what troubles thee?”

He shook his head. “Nothing I can speak about.”

She touched the swastika. “Does thee wish to recover thy—”

“No!” For that would signal the end of their private marriage. “Oh, Quality, never think that! I am unworthy of you, but I will love you till I die. It is just that I wish things were not as they are. That the war did not exist. That all men and all women were like you. That I could be all that you would have me be.”

She nodded. “I know thee is enmeshed in horror, Ernst. I can see it in thy face and feel it in thy hand. But this is not of thy making.”

“It stains me nevertheless.”

“I, too, am stained.”

“Not in my eyes.”

“Nor thee in mine.”

He could not argue with her. “I will come again when I can.” He kissed her again, quickly, and departed.

During the final months of 1943 the situation of the Germans grew desperate. It seemed impossible to eradicate the partisans, and the Russians were advancing. It was becoming obvious that the German tenure in Russia was ending.

This brought a new policy: scorched earth. It was necessary to destroy the ability of the land to support life, so that the partisans could not exist on it. Nevertheless, resources were diverted to exterminate the few Jews who remained unaccounted for in earlier actions. Not because they had done anything, but just because they were Jews. Hitler wanted a Jew-free Europe, even if Germany lost the war while implementing this policy.

Of course the partisans controlled much of the open countryside, so that it was hazardous to go out and actually scorch the earth. Troops would go out in the morning and return at night, claiming to have reduced a particular section, but Ernst knew that it was more likely that they had spent their time hiding from the partisans.

By the turn of the year, the Russians had advanced so far that Minsk was now not far from the front. Then the Russians broke through to the south, so that Minsk was threatened with encirclement. Retreat was mandatory, lest there be another Stalingrad disaster. The anti-partisan activity became pointless; the only concern was to extricate the German forces before they were cut off.

Ernst was transferred back to Berlin in April, 1944. By the look of it, few Germans would remain behind long.

But things were confused in Berlin, too, and he was not reassigned immediately. It seemed that the authorities were too busy trying to understand the disaster to bother with the paperwork of individual assignment. Ernst was for the moment left to his own devices.

Naturally he went to the Lebensborn maternity home to see Quality. She was there, working as a volunteer to care for the children, which still crowded the premises. She was slender again, and in good health, and she still wore his swastika in plain sight. "But the baby—" Ernst asked.

"I bore a son in September," she said. "He was healthy, but they told me that I lacked the proper qualities to raise an Aryan child, so my baby would have to join the racial Germans in awaiting adoption. I was allowed to leave and fend for myself, or to remain to work for bed and board. Since I had no money, and this was the only way I could remain close to Ernst Junior, I agreed to remain. I am, it seems, good with children, and they are shorthanded, so it is a fair compromise. It allows me to remain close to Junior, who is now seven months old. I try not to favor him too much, so as not to attract attention, but he knows me. They all know me."

"But the child is mine," Ernst protested. "He must not be adopted!"

"I had hoped thee would feel that way," she confessed demurely. "Few folk care to assume the added burden of another couple's child in these troubled times, but I quail whenever a prospective couple comes to look. I am afraid that mine will be the one they choose."

Ernst talked to the proprietors, who referred him to the higher Lebensborn authority. His application was taken for consideration. "But you are not married," the clerk pointed out.

That stopped him. If he married Quality now, legally, she would be the wife of a Nazi officer—as Germany lost the war. That was no albatross to hang on her at this time.

"But I will marry thee," Quality said as he tried to explain. "We are already married in our hearts; the outer symbol is merely confirmation." She touched the swastika.

"It is no good for you," he said. "You must be free to return unencumbered to America."

"Not without thee and our son," she said firmly.

So he applied for permission to marry. His application was taken, and lost in the shuffle. He could not marry Quality until his petition was granted, and he could not secure Ernst Junior until he married.

Months passed. Ernst was assigned to routine deskwork; it seemed that Kaltenbrunner had forgotten him. On June 6 the Allies invaded Normandy, and spread east toward Germany. Six weeks later Hitler was almost killed by a planted bomb. A month after that Paris surrendered to the Allies. The Russian advance continued. The days of the Third Reich were dwindling. Admiral Canaris, under suspicion, was investigated in connection with the bomb plot; Ernst was deeply sorry to learn of that. But the marriage permission did not emerge from the bureaucracy.

"I must do something!" Ernst said. "But if I steal you and the child from the home, we will all be illegitimate, and forcibly separated. It is time for a desperate measure."

"I am satisfied to remain here," Quality said. "The children need me."

"I do not want you here when the city comes under siege by the Allies," he said. "The bombings are bad enough; then it will be dangerous."

"It will be bad elsewhere too," she pointed out.

"Not so much in the country, away from the main bastions. If I can get you to Wiesbaden, with my family, you and the boy will be comparatively safe."

She caught the omission immediately. "And not thee, Ernst?"

"I remain in the SS. There will be no safe place for me, when the Allies come."

"But—"

"You know I will return to my family when I can. That is where you must be. I am going to try to arrange it."

She understood the rigors of the situation. "I will do what thee wishes, Ernst."

Ernst made his desperation ploy. He requested a conference with Dr. Ernst Kaltenbrunner, the head of RHSA.

It was granted. "I had thought you would prefer to remain beneath my notice," Kaltenbrunner said.

"I would have, sir. But I have a problem that perhaps you can help me with."

"The problem of too soft a life?"

"I love an American woman I rescued from a camp in Vichy France. She bore my child. I must get her away from Berlin now. I will volunteer for whatever you wish, if you will enable me to take her and my son to my family in Wiesbaden."

"I hardly need to bargain with a man I already command. Why do you think I would do you any favor?"

"Because I can be trusted to keep any bargain I make, even when there is no gun at my head."

Kaltenbrunner considered. "Very well. I will make that bargain. Give my secretary the necessary information, do your deed when you receive clearance, and return here to wait for special assignment. When I indicate it, you will volunteer."

"I will volunteer, sir," Ernst agreed. He knew he was making a pact with the devil, because only the most dangerous assignments were volunteer.

"Dismissed."

Late in September Ernst was granted leave to visit his family. He went to the maternity home—and Quality and Junior were waiting for him. She had been granted permission to take her son to his father's family. There was no explanation for this odd, sudden release, but she knew it was because of something Ernst had done. He in turn knew that Kaltenbrunner was keeping his part of the bargain. But it was sure to be a hard bargain.

He drove her there. There was an air raid on the way, and they pulled onto a deserted road and parked under the foliage of a tree, hiding. Junior, now one year old, was sleeping. Quietly, efficiently, despite the cramped quarters, they made love. It was intensely sweet, after more than a year. Then they resumed the drive.

Herr Best was amazed to see them. "We feared you would never get out of Berlin!" he said.

"This is Quality Smith, whom I will marry. This is our son. I must leave them with you, until I am free of my commitments."

"Of course," his mother said. "Krista told us."

"Krista is here?" Quality asked. "I would very much like to see her again."

"She is away today, but will return tomorrow," Herr Best said. His glance at Ernst suggested that there was a good deal more he would like to say, but not in this circumstance. His family had of course thought Ernst would marry Krista, and the change to an anonymous American woman could hardly please them. But Krista had prepared them, and Quality would explain the rest, and they would be reconciled. Indeed, as they came to know Quality, they would be more than reconciled.

He kissed Quality, and then his son. "I will visit when I can," he promised.

"I know thee will," Quality murmured, managing to keep the tears from her eyes. He knew that she feared she would never see him again.

Then he was driving back, to face what Kaltenbrunner had in mind for him. The man had honored his part of the deal, and Ernst would honor his. But it did seem likely that his life would be in peril.

On October 22 Kaltenbrunner summoned Ernst. "My classmate and friend Otto Skorzeny is organizing a special mission. He needs loyal soldiers conversant in American language and custom. The mission is challenging and dangerous."

"I volunteer for that mission, sir," Ernst said.

"I commend you on your courage and patriotism." Those were the most complimentary words Ernst was ever to hear from Kaltenbrunner, though they were protocol for the situation. "You will be transferred immediately to Otto's unit." He actually shook Ernst's hand before returning the closing salute. Apparently he was pleased to be able to forward a genuinely competent man to his friend. Possibly his attitude toward Ernst had mellowed, since Ernst had performed well in his assignments and engaged in no subversive activity.

Colonel Skorzeny turned out to be a giant of a man, four inches over six feet tall. He was a self-assured Austrian whose face was badly scarred below the left cheek and across the mouth, but who nevertheless remained handsome. He was a legitimate hero, because he had made a spectacular rescue of the deposed Italian leader Mussolini. He had also succeeded in abducting Admiral Hrothy, the Hungarian leader who was attempting to make a treacherous separate peace with the Allies. He was forming Operation Grief, literally "Grab," for sabotage. He was assembling a hand picked group of about two thousand American-English speaking commandos to train for missions behind the Allied lines. This was to complement the German offensive in the Ardennes. It certainly seemed to be important, for Germany's situation was now desperate. The Allies were massing in Belgium and Luxembourg for an invasion of Germany itself, and if they were not stopped, the war would soon be over. The only way to stop them was to go on the offensive, but German strength was insufficient. It seemed that everyone knew this, except the Führer, who refused to receive any news of weakness or retreat.

Skorzeny formed the 150th Panzer Brigade and began training at Friedenthal, near Berlin. The men were equipped with American uniforms, Jeeps, and a few Sherman tanks which had been rescued from various battlefields. They were trained in the use of American military equipment, American slang, American military rank and custom, and even the American way to open a pack of cigarettes.

Ernst had no trouble with the language and slang; in fact he helped others to get it right. But he knew nothing of American tanks, and he did not smoke. Nevertheless, he learned to open a pack of cigarettes, and to take a puff without coughing. How anybody could *enjoy* such a procedure was hard to understand. It was really easier to learn to drive a Jeep, which was an efficient vehicle for the forest terrain where they would see action, the Ardennes.

The brigade had two main objectives. On the day of the offensive, small units would penetrate the lines under the pretense of retreating from the Germans, and commence sabotage activities. They would pose as military police and misdirect Allied units. They would remove Allied warning signs from minefields, so that the enemy would march into its own trap. They would mark and report targets for German artillery fire. They would blow up ammunition depots, cut communications lines, spread false reports, block roads, and act as scouts for advancing troops.

Meanwhile Skorzeny himself would take fifty American tanks and advance to the bridgeheads across the Meuse River. He would hold these crossings without challenge from the Americans—until the bulk of the German advance reached the river. Then the commandos would identify themselves to the German troops by using pre-arranged signals with colored flashlights or similar devices. In this manner the troops would cross the river without challenge, achieving a significant advantage.

Would it work? Ernst was doubtful. The plain fact was that the Russian front had sapped Germany's power, while the Allies were growing constantly stronger. It hardly mattered whether the river was readily crossed, or depots blown up; the enemy was simply too strong for such tricks to make a sufficient difference. Also, he doubted that many of the Operation Grab personnel would be able to carry it off; the intricacies of the American ways were too devious. So this was probably a death trap—as perhaps Kaltenbrunner had known.

Ernst kept his doubts to himself. He would do his best, though this type of thing disgusted him. He was becoming in effect a partisan, doing treacherous damage behind the enemy lines, and the Americans would hold him in the same contempt that he held for the Russian partisans. It was a truly terrible mission, and one which might have no escape. Obviously any of them who were caught would be executed immediately, in the field; that was what was done with partisans. So the best hope lay in doing what the partisans did: once the mission was lost, merging with the population and pretending innocence. What an irony! He had learned how to be a partisan from fighting the partisans.

They trained through November and early December. There were no breaks, and not entirely because of the urgency of their deadline for readiness; it was because of the necessary secrecy. There had to be no hint of what was planned. Ernst understood the necessity, but wished he could have visited Quality and his son. At least then there could have been one more contact, before...

Of course they were not supposed to think of failure or death. But he knew he was not the only one. This mission was dangerous in the performance and in the aftermath. Only if it should be successful would they be heroes. Ernst simply did not believe that success was destined.

The German assault began at 5:30 in the morning on December 16, 1944 with heavy artillery shelling. German troops followed immediately behind, and a thousand paratroopers were to land behind the enemy lines. Meanwhile, the commandos would infiltrate undetected. Ernst was part of a three man group that made it through in a Jeep; in fact they didn't even see any enemy soldiers.

Once they were beyond the line, they parked the vehicle in the forest, scuffled the ground to hide its tracks, and split up, so as to achieve maximum effect. Ernst was in the uniform of an MP, the Military Police. He looked for a supply depot to destroy, but was in the wrong area; all he saw were empty trucks rushing along the road in both directions. He didn't even need to interfere with that; the Allies were already confused enough.

By day's end he had accomplished nothing. He returned to the Jeep and found his companions already there. One had managed to misdirect a truckload of troops, but he knew that they would soon enough correct their error, so it would count for little. The other had managed to drag fallen branches across a road so as to block it, but before he could complete the job an allied tank had arrived and bulldozed it clear.

In the morning they drove further on, hoping for better luck. This wonderful scheme seemed rather futile in practice, because they were almost as confused as the Allies. They heard the roar of the main German advance, and knew it would soon overtake them if they didn't get clear. That was of course pointless; they had to remain behind the enemy lines.

They came to a stalled American truck. The driver flagged them down. "Hey buddy—gimme a lift!" he called. "I'm outa gas, and I'm freezing my nuts off out here!"

"Sure," Ernst said. He had warned the others about such oddities: the Americans called petrol "gas." "Hey, corporal—get down and guard the truck for him, until he gets back."

Their third man nodded, and jumped down, making space on the cramped vehicle for the truck driver. Ernst knew he would take advantage of the time alone to clip wires so that the truck would be unable to run even when refilled.

They talked with the American, and were reassured: he had no inkling of their nature. He guided them to his depot, where they picked up two big cans of gasoline and headed back. "Damn stupidest thing," the man muttered. "I know exactly how far my tank goes, but I got distracted by this damned Heine attack and forgot. Lucky thing the Krauts didn't get me!"

"Lucky thing," Ernst agreed.

They delivered the driver to his truck. He poured in the gasoline, then started it up. The engine roared into life. "Thanks, pal!" the driver called as he pulled back onto the road. "You saved my hide!"

Ernst turned to their third man. "I thought you were going to fix the motor." He spoke in English, maintaining the pretense even when they were alone.

"Too obvious. He'd know right away that I'd done it, and then we'd have to kill him, and our presence would be known. But wait until he tries the brakes!"

"Did you fix the hand brakes too?" Ernst asked.

"Of course."

"But if he puts in it gear and turns off the motor, he can stop even on a hill," Ernst pointed out.

"Oops, I didn't think of that."

So they had probably done about as much good as harm, unless the driver panicked and went out of control. They were not turning out to be much good as saboteurs.

They drove on. "But now we know where their depot is," the second man said. "I can blow that tonight."

"Good idea," Ernst agreed. They were learning on the job.

They parked the Jeep again and split up. Ernst found a temporary military base, but there were too many soldiers, and they were too alert; he could not get close enough to sabotage anything. The point was to take advantage of the enemy's innocence and neglect. He managed to pour handfuls of dirt into the gasoline tanks of several officer's cars, so that they would in due course stall out with clogged carburetors, but he knew that was a mere nuisance, not a significant act of destruction. Finally he gave it up and returned to the Jeep for the night. He was after all a desk man; he just wasn't good in the field.

One of his companions joined him there; the third did not. They realized that they had lost a man. They had all been aware that this was a high-risk mission, but this confirmation was nevertheless sobering.

On the third day, the 18th, as they drove farther ahead of the front, they were again flagged down. Ernst noticed that one man stood in the road, while two others remained at the side, rifles ready. This was no out-of-gas situation.

"Hey, buddy—who are Dem Bums?"

Ernst nudged his companion with his hidden foot, warning him into silence. "Listen, dogface—you got something against the Dodgers, let's have it!"

"Not a thing, pal. You there, sergeant—where's the Windy City?"

"Chicago," Ernst murmured without moving his mouth. "On Lake Michigan."

"Mister, I wish I was back there on Lake Michigan right now!" Ernst's companion replied. "Chicago may not be much, but it's a damn sight better than this hellhole."

"You got that right, trooper," the man said. "Pass, friends."

But Ernst retained caution. "Now do you mind telling us why the damned interrogation? A joke's a joke, but I don't like being covered like that by my own side. Would you have shot me if I'd trashed Brooklyn?"

"No. Only if you hadn't known about it. We caught some fake soldiers, Krauts in American uniforms, sabotaging our supplies. So now we're checking all strangers. Your uniform and rank don't mean nothing; you gotta prove you're American."

Ernst made a show of relaxing. "Oh. Gotcha. Sorry I got my back up."

"Get your ass on outa here."

"Right." Ernst drove the Jeep on through the checkpoint.

"How did you know they suspected us?" his companion asked.

"I spent a year in America. Now we must be alert: it's not enough just to answer questions; we have to do it as Americans do. Pugnacious, insulting. If you are challenged with something you don't recognize, make a counter-challenge; that may put them off."

They drove on, looking for something to sabotage but still had no luck. Ernst hated the feeling of ineffectiveness but knew it would be pointless to risk exposure unless he found a target worthy of the risk. Meanwhile it was becoming evident that the German attack was faltering; there were too few troops to sustain it, and the Allied defenses were stronger than expected. The commandos' element of surprise had been nullified, and there was nothing further to be accomplished.

"We had better rejoin our troops," Ernst said. "But we can't do it in these uniforms."

His companion agreed. They drove east, toward the sound of gunfire, as far as they could without hitting a checkpoint. Then they pulled into the forest and quickly changed clothing, becoming Germans again. Then they split up, knowing that it would be easier to sneak through separately.

Alone, Ernst trudged back toward the line. There no longer was an easy avenue through; the line was stabilizing as the German thrust lost momentum. But it should be possible to get through at night.

"Halt!"

Ernst stopped. He had been spied—and now he was in German uniform. There was an American soldier bringing a rifle to bear. Ernst could have shot him with his handgun, but didn't try. He had never directly killed a man, and the thought of it sickened him.

But if he surrendered, he might be spared. He might be taken as a stray from his unit.

Slowly he raised his hands. He felt like a coward. Thus ignominiously did his career end. Just as the career of the Third Reich was ending. Götterdämmerung—the day of doom, when the good gods were slaughtered. It had come at last.

Chapter 13
Krista

Lane finally had the freedom of the continent, thanks to the understanding of his superiors. He had to find his friend, if he survived, so as to find his fiancée, if she survived. There had been no word as Germany collapsed, and now in the chaos of the war's ending there seemed to be no way to run them down through Allied or German records. He had to do it himself, his own way.

On May tenth, 1945, he came to Wiesbaden, which was where Ernst Best's family had been going. He would start his search here.

The phone service was cooperative. Yes, there were Best families here, but no phone listed for Ernst. Lane took a list of their addresses, and drove to each, inquiring for Ernst Best. On the fifteenth he found recognition. "Yes, he is my nephew," Karl Best said. "A good young man. But lost in the war."

"Lost?"

"He left his woman here with my brother's family and returned to Berlin for a dangerous mission. We have not seen him since."

"How long ago?" Lane asked anxiously.

"Seven months ago."

"How can I search for him?"

The man studied him with disconcerting lack of expression. Lane realized that to these people the British and Americans were still the enemy. They had to be polite, but they were not friendly. "Krista might know."

That must be the woman. "Where is Krista?"

"I will take you to her." The man seemed relieved.

Krista was surprisingly attractive despite her worn clothing. Her hair was blond, her features fair, and her figure appealing.

"Krista, this is Herr Dowling," Karl Best said. "He is looking for Ernst."

The woman said something in German.

Karl Best turned back to Lane. "I must translate for her," he said, with an opaque expression.

"Do it," Lane agreed.

The man spoke rapidly in German. Then Krista reacted.

She turned her blue eyes on Lane. They seemed almost to glow with recognition. "Lane Dowling!" she exclaimed.

"You know my name?" he asked, startled.

She spoke again in German.

"She says you are Ernst's American friend, are you not?" Best translated. "He spoke of you."

"Yes. I must find him. Do you know where he is?"

Again the German and translation. "I know where he worked, in Berlin. But I do not know whether he remains there. I fear he is dead."

"He must not be dead!" Lane exclaimed.

She nodded when she heard with something more than agreement. "Ja, he must not be dead. But he has not returned." The intensity of her gaze made Lane uneasy. What was in her mind?

"Tell me where he worked."

"He was in the SS. There was a special mission. Perhaps one of the other officers would know."

"What other officers?"

She shook her head. "They did not speak their names to me. I would know some by sight, however."

"Then come with me, and tell me who they are," Lane said. Then, as Best translated his words to her. "I am Ernst's friend. I will not hurt you."

"I have no money to travel," Best translated.

"I have money. I have a car. Just go to Berlin with me, and show me. Then I will bring you back. I promise."

With seeming reluctance, and something else, she agreed. "But how shall we speak to each other?" she asked through Best after a moment.

"We don't need to speak! But I will teach you a few words of English while we drive there."

She turned those great blue eyes on him again. "Ja." Then she walked away.

Lane watched her go. She had an interesting walk. "She's a strange one," he murmured.

"We are a defeated people," Karl Best said. "We are careful where we tread. Especially our young women. For a woman to go with a soldier—this has implications."

"I will bring her back unscathed," Lane said, appreciating the implication. "I'm—I'm not after the local women. I'm looking for my friend, who I hope will know where my fiancée is. Maybe Ernst mentioned her: Quality Smith?"

"He did." The man seemed to be ill at ease.

Lane's heart leaped at this confirmation. "Do you know—did he say—is she alive?"

"She is alive and well. I can not tell you more."

"That's enough!" Lane exclaimed. "All this time I've been afraid she was—thank you, Mr. Best! You have given me wonderful hope."

"I have given you very little."

Lane realized that the man, perhaps mourning the loss of his nephew, was taking a negative view. If Ernst was dead, how would Lane find Quality? Yet that assurance that she was not only alive but healthy buoyed him. Ernst must have found her and gotten her to safety somewhere. Otherwise how could Ernst's uncle have known of her? He would find her somehow.

Krista returned with a handbag. "Thank you," Lane said to Karl Best. Then he stepped to Krista, to take her bag. Evidently surprised by this minor gallantry, she yielded it, smiling. She was stunning when she smiled. They walked to his rented car.

"Do you know the way to Berlin?" Lane asked. Then, remembering that she did not speak English: "Berlin. Where?"

"Berlin," she repeated. Then she pointed her finger straight ahead.

Good enough. She knew the way. He could find it, using the map, but it would be easier with someone who had been there.

Krista guided him to Frankfurt, and then north through the mountains to Kassell. It was getting late, and he realized that it wasn't worth trying to reach Berlin in one haul. He would have to spend a night on the way. But he hadn't anticipated traveling with a woman. What was he going to do with her?

He would simply have to foot the bill for a separate room for her. If she enabled him to find Ernst, and therefore Quality, it would be worth it.

"Must stop. Night," he said. "Know place?"

She turned her head to look at him. "Place?"

"Night. Eat. Sleep. Hotel."

"Sleep?"

"Two rooms! No trouble."

She seemed to understand. She pointed to the side, where a road diverged. He took it. Soon it led to a hotel.

He parked the car and entered the lobby with her. "You have rooms?" he asked.

The clerk looked blank. Then Krista spoke in German, and the clerk brightened. It turned out that he would take American dollars. Lane paid, and picked up the room key. "But there are supposed to be two rooms," he said.

Krista took his arm and guided him away from the desk. Apparently she had told the man one room. There was no bellhop, which was unsurprising in this chaotic time. Lane was glad to make his own way.

It was not a perfect room, but it had the amenities, including twin beds, which was a relief. They could make do.

They took turns using the bathroom and changing. Then they went out to eat. Krista was now in a blue dress which accented her eyes and her figure, which was really quite good. She had combed out her hair, which was like corn silk. When he stood behind her before the mirror, he realized that their eyes matched. She smiled, seeming to realize it also. It was as if they were on a date.

She was very helpful in ordering food, too, because she knew the cuisine and the language. They had a good meal.

Something occurred to Lane. "Ernst Best—what was he to you? Ernst—Krista?"

She smiled again, and he realized that she was not just pretty, she was beautiful. "Ernst, Krista," she said, then made a kiss.

"His girlfriend!" he exclaimed, glad for the confirmation of his assumption. "That's why you're ready to go with me. To find him."

"Find Ernst," she agreed.

They finished the meal and returned to the hotel. But Lane was excited by the thought that this woman might know of Quality. "Ernst knew Quality Smith. Quality. You know Quality?"

"Quality," she repeated.

"Yes. My—my girlfriend. You know?"

She seemed to hesitate. Then she lifted the hem of her dress, showing her fine leg. "Girlfriend?"

She thought he was asking her for sex! "No, no! Not you." Apparently he would not be able to question her about this. Not until they had a better mutual vocabulary. “Let’s learn words,” he said. He pointed to himself. “Man.” Then to her. “Woman.”

“Man, woman?” she asked, lifting her skirt again.

“Oh, brother!” he muttered. Then, to her: “Forget it.” He turned away.

“I know some English,” she said.

Lane whirled around. “You know? You understand me?”

“I understand you, Lane Dowling.”

“Then why the dumb act? We could have been talking all along!”

“Because a man traveling with a woman might take advantage.”

“I’ve been trying to explain, that’s not what I’m after. I just want to find Quality.”

“Not Ernst Best?”

“Him, too. He’s my friend. But if he knows where Quality is, she’s my fiancée. I have to find her.”

She paused, evidently considering. “I must tell you, Ernst Best and I are no longer that close. Suppose your Quality has found another man?”

“In Germany?” he asked, laughing. “Let me tell you, she’s a Quaker. A pacifist. An American. How would she find a man here?”

Krista shrugged. “Do the folk of different lands never get together?”

“Of course they do! But Quality is different. If you knew her, you’d know.”

“You would never find another woman? From another land?”

“You mean if Quality found another man?” Lane shook his head, finding the question awkward. “The truth is, I last saw her in 1938. It’s been seven years. I don’t know whether I still love her. But I have to be sure she’s okay, and if she still loves me, I’ll marry her. I mean to do what is right.”

Krista nodded. “You are a good man, Lane Dowling.”

“I’m just doing what I have to do.”

She unbuttoned her dress and pulled it off over her head.

“Hey!” he protested. “Go change in the bathroom. I already told you I wasn’t after your body.”

“I apologize. I forgot.” She held her skirt in front of her and walked to the bathroom in her bra and panties. He could not help seeing how well endowed she was. All his prior impressions of her body turned out to be shy of the mark. Ernst had had good taste in girlfriends! Yet it seemed that they had broken up. What had happened?

Krista soon emerged in a gauzy nightgown. She chose one of the beds and got into it. Lane saw another flash of her leg as she did so. Was she trying to tease him?

"What happened between you and Ernst?" he asked. "Who broke it off?"

"He did. I was most annoyed."

"He found a more beautiful woman than you?"

"Yes."

"I don't believe it."

She glanced sidelong at him. "Believe it, Lane Dowling."

"Oh come on, call me Lane. We can be friends, can't we? Or at least not enemies."

"I would like to be friends." She smiled and lay back.

He went to the bathroom to strip and clean up. Then he realized that he would have to walk by her bed in his underpants, as he did not use pajamas. This was awkward.

Well, there was no help for it. He walked out, went to his bed, and turned off the light. She seemed to be asleep, which was a relief.

"You have a nice body, Lane," she said.

Next day they resumed the drive to Berlin. Krista wore a skirt and blouse. It was amazing what she had been able to pack in her single bag. The blouse was tight and translucent in bright light; he kept catching glimpses of the outline of her bosom. Finally he addressed the matter. "Please put on a jacket or something, Krista."

"But it is warm."

"Because you are driving me crazy. I promised to leave you alone, but the sight of you keeps reminding me how long it's been since I've had a woman."

"I can do that."

"So if you'll just put on something—" He broke off. "Do what?"

"You have been kind to me, Lane. You have been a gentleman. I understand your need. I can oblige it."

"What are you, a whore?"

Her face froze. Then she hid it in her hands.

Lane felt like a heel. "Oh, damn, I'm sorry! I didn't mean to say that. I apologize."

She faced away from him.

He pulled the car to the side of the road. "Krista, I said I was sorry! It's—I've been in the RAF, and the women—it's like a reflex. They do it for money. Of course you're not that kind."

She lifted her face, wiping the tears away. "I understand. I should not have spoken that way. I thank thee for thy apology."

"S'okay." He started the car again.

Then he did a mental doubletake. Could she have—no, of course not. In his confusion he must have imagined it.

But his interest in Krista increased. She was becoming fascinating in more than just her body.

They reached Berlin in the afternoon. Then Lane remembered: "The Russians hold Berlin! They aren't letting Americans or British in. We're allies, but they haven't quite caught on yet. This is no good."

"But workers go in and out," she said.

"I'm not a worker."

She smiled. "But I am. Or was, before they closed down my job. I could go in. You could pretend to be a German worker."

"I can't speak a word of German!"

"*Ja* means yes. *Nein* means no. That will be enough."

"You're crazy!"

She gave him a level stare. "Do you want to get in?"

"Yes! But not if I get shot for spying!"

"They will not shoot an ally. But I think they will not stop us. All we need is some German clothing for you, and a card. I have an extra card for you."

"Now why do I have the suspicion you are not as innocent as you look?" he asked, amazed.

"I had to survive in a defeated nation. I learned how."

She took him to a store where he bought a typical German worker outfit. This was a lot like a Nazi uniform, which made Lane wince; it had black boots, baggy brown trousers, a billed cap, and a slightly less weathered place on the arm where the red Nazi armband had been. Obviously a secondhand outfit, though he had paid the price for a new one. Then she had him take the passenger seat while she drove. But before she got in, she adjusted her clothing.

"What are you doing?" Lane asked, staring. Her skirt was now drawn up to the point of nonexistence, and her blouse was open to the naval.

"I am arranging not to be questioned closely."

"You're asking to be raped instead!"

"In public daylight? I think not."

He spread his hands. "Do it your way."

They did it her way. The Russian guard looked down into the car as Krista proffered her card, leaning toward him. His face went slack. He passed their two cards before his face and approved them without blinking. Soon they were on their way into the city.

Lane shook his head in wonder. "You're some woman, Krista!"

"Thank you."

"Were you really upset when I called you a—when I said what I shouldn't have?"

She shot him one of her sidelong glances, half smiling.

Lane made a soundless whistle. This was a woman who knew how to manage men! His eyes kept straying to her body, but this time he did not ask her to cover it.

She drove to the building where she said Ernst had worked. "He was in the SS," she explained. "I used to date him here. But he never told me his work; it was secret."

"And he found a beautiful SS woman?" Lane asked jokingly, then bit his tongue.

"She was not SS. But she was secret from me, until I came to his hotel room in his absence. Then I found her."

"That must have been a hair-pulling scene!"

"No. I tried to hate her, but could not. He had given her his swastika, so I knew the game was lost. So I moved in with her."

"You're joking!"

"No. She was very beautiful and nice. A better woman than I."

"I doubt it."

"Believe it, Lane. Ernst has a very fine taste in women."

"That much I believe. I have good taste too."

"I believe it."

They parked at the building. Krista readjusted her clothing, becoming considerably more demure.

But the building turned out to be in chaos. Those rooms which remained tight were being used to shelter the homeless. The German SS was no longer in operation. "But maybe I can inquire," she said.

Krista inquired, speaking rapid German, as she went from person to person, while Lane followed somewhat helplessly Finally she found someone who seemed to know something. "He was transferred to Skorzeny's unit," she reported. "In October."

"Who is Skorzeny?"

"They say he participated in the—you call it the Battle of the Bulge. The Ardennes campaign, in December."

"English-speaking Germans!" Lane exclaimed. "Saboteurs! Ernst wouldn't get into that!"

She looked at him. "If they threatened to kill someone you loved, to make you do their will—"

Lane clenched his teeth. "If he got into that—if he got caught, they'd have executed him."

"Can you reach the American records? To see whether that happened?"

"Maybe eventually. But this is now. Isn't there a faster way?"

"If they did not kill him, maybe they made him a prisoner of war. There are camps."

"We'll check the camps! Where are they?"

"I do not know. But your people must know."

He looked at her cannily. "Your people must know too! You can probably find them faster than I can."

"I will inquire." She did, and in due course had the locations of several recently established camps for German prisoners of war. "But we cannot get into them by showing flesh," she cautioned him as they returned to the car.

"*We* don't have to get into them at all," he said. "I will take you home, as I promised, then check with the Prisoner of War Information Bureau. If he's there, I'll find him."

"But you will need someone for the German," she said. "I will go with you."

He shook his head. "If I remain much longer in your company, Krista, I'll forget my promise to bring you back unmolested. I may even forget what I'm here for."

"You need me to get you out of Berlin."

"Sure, to take you home. I'll do that. Then—" He paused. "Uh-oh. Are you blackmailing me?"

"I would not think of it."

"Why are you so hot to travel with me? You don't know anything about me."

"I know enough."

"We'll discuss it on the way back."

To that she acceded. She got them out of Berlin in much the fashion she had gotten them in. Then they went to a hotel for the night.

This time the room had only one bed. "Damn!" Lane said. Then he looked at her. "You *asked* for this! You could have gotten twin beds or two rooms."

Krista shrugged.

"Listen, Ernst probably could've slept naked in your arms and not done a thing. But I'm not that type. You're trying to seduce me, and you have a damn good shot at succeeding. You have a loathsome disease you want to give me?"

"Oh, no!" she exclaimed. "I want nothing but good for you, Lane."

"Why? I mean, why seduce me?"

"You are a rich American. I have not gone hungry in your company."

"I'm not rich and you're no whore! And don't pull the tears act this time; you know what I'm talking about. You can get money from me without giving me sex. So why are you bothering?"

She shook her head. "I do not think you want to hear, Lane."

"I'll be the judge of that! You looked at me strangely the first time you saw me. What are you up to?"

She met his gaze. "Please, Lane, there will be real tears if we go into this. I will tell you when you are ready. You must trust me that far."

"I don't trust you at all! You have an ulterior motive. Are you a spy or something? What do you want from me?"

She spread her hands in surrender. "Then I must say it. I want to marry thee."

"Marry me!" he exclaimed incredulously. "We spend two days and nights on the road, and you want marriage?" Then before she could answer, he held up his hand in a "stop" signal. "There! You did it again. You said 'thee.' *You know Quality*!"

Krista bowed her head. "Now I must tell you, and take the consequence. Quality was the woman who took Ernst from me. The one with whom I roomed. I polished my English, talking with her, and I learned her ways."

Lane dropped to the bed, stunned. "Ernst—Quality? They would not!"

"They did not mean to. But she was fading in a prisoner camp in France, and he could save her only by taking her with him and hiding her in his room. Then he hit her, and—"

"What?"

"Another officer suspected his loyalty, and thought that she was a subversive agent. So Ernst knocked her down to show that he did not care for her, and after the other was gone, they recognized their love."

"But he would never—she would never—"

"Believe it."

He turned on her. "You—what's in it for you?"

"She took my man. I will take hers."

"In revenge? I want no part of this!"

"In understanding. She chose you first, so I knew you were a good man. You are now without a woman. You are hurting as I was hurting, but I can ease your hurt. I know you, Lane Dowling."

"You can't know me!"

"I know you from her. I know every detail of you. I know how you seek unusual friends. I know the weakness of thy childhood, and the strength of thy manhood. I know—"

"Don't *do* that!"

"I do it when I forget myself, as she does. She calls me thee."

"She calls you—*you* know where she is now!"

"She is with Ernst's family. They moved out of Wiesbaden, to better survive the war, but I see them often. She said she would introduce me to you, but you found me first."

"You could have taken me right to her!"

She shook her head. "You were not ready, Lane."

"You knew I'd never touch you if I found her!"

"I knew your heart would break if you found her too soon."

"So you're just going to patch it up. Just like that."

"I had hoped to. If I could have had enough time with you, before you learned."

"You even proposed marriage to me!"

"No. You asked me what I want of you. I told you. That is not the same. I did not want to tell you yet."

"That's right! You did everything you could to avoid telling me anything! Knowing where Quality was all the time."

"Yes."

He stared at her. "That's a really practical deal, Krista. Everything all set up in advance."

"I am a practical woman." She dabbed at her face.

"And now you make with the waterworks again."

"I said there would be real tears, this time. I meant yours. I meant mine."

"Why the hell should I believe you?"

"Because it is true."

He got up and paced the floor. "Well, you got some of it right. You did hurt me."

She did not reply.

"Tell me again: exactly why do you want to marry me?"

"I want to marry well. There is a blemish on my ancestry which prevents me from marrying well in Germany. And Germany now is not a good place to be. When I lost Ernst—"

"What do you mean by a blemish?"

"My grandmother may have been Gypsy."

Lane burst out laughing. "No, really. I want to know. What's wrong with your ancestry?"

"You do not believe?"

"That doesn't matter. I don't *care*. What does it matter whether your grandmother had two heads? *You* don't."

"A German of quality would care. I may not be pure Aryan."

He shrugged. "So?"

"So I must marry outside of Germany."

"You're serious?"

"Always."

"No love, no fun, just pedigree? That's all you care about?"

"I care about everything. But I must not love without first being practical."

"That's not how it's done in America."

"You do not understand our ways."

"Damn right I don't! What makes you think I could stand having you around all the time, with your—I'll bet you're a Nazi, too!"

"I was."

"That's all I need! A Nazi wife! That's almost as funny as Quality taking a swastika!" He looked at her. "She did do that?"

"Yes. But she was never a Nazi. She accepted it from Ernst in lieu of a ring, because it was his most cherished possession. It is Ernst she loves, not the swastika."

"You know, she *would* do that," Lane said, bemused. "She has her own values."

"She is a good woman."

"All right! You've really run me through the meat grinder, here. I admit it. You tell me my best friend ran off with my fiancée, and you want to take her place, and you've got sex on the line to prove it. I'm going to tell you one thing, and ask you one thing, and then we'll see."

She waited without seeming emotion.

"Here's what I'm telling you," he said. "I don't regard sex as a commitment. I could do it with you without marrying you. Ernst is different. So you can't rope me that way. And here's what I'm asking you: suppose we do it, and then we discover that Ernst is dead? Who do you think I'll marry then?"

"I do not want Ernst to be dead."

"Well, neither do I! But I'm not going to leave Quality stuck here in Germany, for sure! So do you want to gamble that's he's alive?"

"Oh, yes! I still love Ernst, in my way. I would never wish him dead. But I have accepted my loss of him. He loves Quality, and I want him to have her. If she died, he would not marry me, he would mourn her. And so would I. And if Ernst is dead, Quality will not marry you. She will mourn him. So do with me as you wish, Lane; I have no fear of that. And perhaps you will find that you like me."

"You're on, sister!" Lane felt lightheaded, almost euphoric after the recent storm of emotions. This was like a dream, and Krista was as beautiful a woman as he could remember, and he needed release.

In a moment they both were naked. He met her on the bed, and she matched him kiss for kiss and move for move, as passionate as he. She *did* know him, and she catered to his foibles, fulfilling him almost perfectly. And in the throes of it, he found a strange doubt looming.

"God, Krista!" he gasped. "You may be right!"

She guided him to the present residence of Ernst's family. A woman came to the door. "Frau Best," Krista said formally, "I bring

Lane Dowling."

The woman—Ernst's mother, looked at Lane. "I will tell Quality."

Then Quality came to the door. "Oh, it really is thee, Lane!" she cried, rushing out to hug him. "I have not seen thee in so long!"

"Krista brought me."

She looked up at him. "And did she tell thee, Lane?"

He knew already that it was true. Her love for him had diminished into friendship. Now he saw the bright silver swastika at her breast. He found it both appalling and fitting. "Yes. I—I understand."

"Now thee must meet my son." She turned back to the house.

"Your—?"

She picked up a child of about a year and a half. "Ernst Junior."

Speechless, Lane looked at Krista, who nodded.

Quality caught the look. "I promised to introduce thee to Krista, but it seems I am too late."

"Too late," he echoed numbly.

"The game is lost," Krista said.

"Lost," he agreed.

Quality smiled, briefly. "And how long did it take for her to conquer thee, Lane?"

He had to smile, realizing that there was a new game. "About two days."

Chapter 14
Rheinberg

Ernst lost track of the number of prisoner of war camps through which he was routed. There was such a tremendous influx of prisoners as the war ended that the camps were constantly being reorganized. Conditions were harsh, but that was to be expected; at least they were not being gunned down.

In April, 1945, he was transferred to a new camp on the Rhine River, only about two hundred kilometers from Wiesbaden. This was Camp Rheinberg, ironically close to the place where Neandertal Man had been discovered and named. It was surrounded by nine kilometers of barbed wire fencing. There were no guard towers, no tents, no shelter, no water, no cooking facilities and no latrines. It was essentially open countryside. There was not even enough barbed wire to divide the camp into separate enclosures; all the prisoners, men, women and children, were crowded in together. There were, it seemed, about one hundred thousand of them.

Ernst observed this with despair. He had seen the camps in which partisans were confined before they were killed; this was of that nature. This was an Allied death camp.

Trucks brought food, but there was little organization. The prisoners had to fend for themselves, walking up to get what they could, and retreating to allow others their turns. There was little internal strife; they knew that it was pointless. All of them had one mission: to survive.

"But where is our shelter?" a prisoner asked querulously in German.

"There is none," Ernst said.

"But what of the Geneva Convention? Prisoners of war are supposed to have shelter, to receive mail, and be visited by the Red Cross."

"Did we honor the Geneva Convention on the Russian front?" Ernst asked rhetorically.

"But they were animals! Jews, partisans, traitors."

"They were captive enemies. Now we are the captives."

The man stared at him, not willing to comprehend the implication. "The Russians—we expected no mercy from them. But the Americans are softhearted. They are merciful to enemies."

"Let's hope so," Ernst said. But his experience in American captivity the past three months gave him little hope. It did not seem to matter what the nationality of the captors was, or the nationality of the partisans; the end was the same. It was in its fashion fitting: he had not helped the Russian partisans, and now no one would help him. He had merely changed sides: from outside the barbed wire to inside. That was the only difference.

At first he had been treated decently, but as increasing numbers of German troops surrendered, the facilities had been overwhelmed. He had been shipped to ever-larger, ever worse camps. The respect of the front-line officers for enemy officers had gradually been replaced by the disrespect of the rear-echelon corporals.

Some prisoners had been treated carefully: the "Wanted." This was not a good status, for those were the war criminals: the officers who had given the orders to extirpate Jews or to commit atrocities. They were being saved out for trial. Ernst was among the unwanted, which had seemed better, at first. He had hoped he would be interrogated and released in due course, but it became apparent that surrendering to the Americans had been a grotesque mistake. He had learned from the remarks of the guards and other prisoners that the American General Eisenhower, though possessed of a German name, hated not only Nazis but all things German. He wanted to destroy the German military machine forever, and the German industrial complex. He wanted a "Carthaginian peace": the settlement the Romans made on their most formidable enemy, the Phoenician city of Carthage. Total destruction. They had plowed salt into the earth so that no crop would grow there. Germany was to be reduced to a peasant economy, as in medieval times. The destruction of its manpower was the second step in this program; the industry had already been demolished.

Ernst sat on the ground and dug into the dirt with his tin cup. He poured cupfuls of dirt to the side and his hole deepened.

"What are you doing?" the nearest man demanded.

"I am digging a hole."

"But you need to drink from that cup!"

"First I need protection from the night."

The man considered. Then he lifted his own cup. "May I join you?"

"If you dig your share. I am Ernst." Prisoners did not bother with their last names, because their acquaintances were likely to be fleeting.

"I am Ludwig."

The man began digging. Soon others, observing them, were doing the same. Holes developed, with mounds of earth between.

A woman came. "May I join you? I see that you are strong men."

Ernst looked at her. She might have been attractive once, but she was in a sad state now. Her hair was matted and her dress was so dirty that its original color could not be told. She was thin, and there was a festering sore on one arm. "You look too weak to do your share of digging."

"I have a cardboard."

Ludwig laughed, but Ernst did not. "Fetch it."

"It is here." She lifted a section of cardboard about as long as a man and somewhat wider. It had evidently been salvaged from a supply box.

"What is your name?," Ernst asked, by that token accepting her. "I am Ernst."

"Johanna."

"But what good is that?" Ludwig asked.

"It is good insulation," the woman explained. "Like a blanket."

The man nodded, suddenly appreciating its value. "Ludwig."

They dug the hole as deep as was feasible, then tried it. The two men lay down at either side in their clothes, with the woman in the middle. The cardboard covered her and part of each of them. It would have to do.

The trucks brought food in the evening, but not enough. Ernst and Ludwig got some American K rations, but Johanna was not able to forge to the front before it ran out. There was no water.

Ernst measured off a third of his portion and gave it to her. He glanced at Ludwig. The man hesitated, then did likewise.

"I will return this favor when I can," Johanna said. She did not offer anything now; it was obvious that even sex would be no reward for them in her present filthy state.

"How did you, a woman, become prisoner?" Ernst asked.

"My husband was trying to defend our house. He shot an American in the hand. They killed him, and took me." She did not need to say what they had done with her; it was obvious that after raping her they had simply put her in with the prisoners.

Someone started singing as the dusk came. They joined in, singing German folk songs. It was not great music, but it engendered a feeling of camaraderie.

The night got cold. The people walked to one side of the compound, near the barbed wire, before hunkering down in their holes. The three of them followed to the edge, and found a crude trench with a log over it. They took turns on the log, two standing at either side of the trench to hold the third steady in the middle. They did not worry about modesty; the facility was crowded, and the line of people was long. Those who needed only to urinate did so from the sides, without waiting.

They returned to their hole and settled in for the night. The cardboard blanket was a considerable help, as was their closeness; now Ernst understood with new clarity how Quality had survived in Gurs. Body warmth was precious.

He also understood how he had helped her, in that camp. Now he was echoing her experience, and his love of her welled up and gave him strength to carry on. This, too, was fitting.

A wind came up in the night, chilling them despite their limited shelter. Ernst heard the moans of those who had not made holes; they had no protection at all. Those others had to huddle together in human mounds, with the associated discomforts. Ludwig, Johanna and Ernst huddled too, but at least they were out of the wind and had the protection of the walls of their pit and their cardboard blanket.

In the morning they went to wait at the gate, so as to be ready when the food was delivered. Soon long lines formed behind them, as others realized that this was probably the only way to get fed. But the food was slow in coming. Instead a guard signaled Ernst aside. "Speak English?" he asked.

"Yes, sir." The man was a sergeant, but too much respect was a better risk than too little.

"You look strong. You're assigned to body detail."

"Sir?"

"Any dead bodies in there, you haul them out here. You get a bonus for it." The man held out two packages of food.

"Thank you, sir." Ernst tried not to show his extreme eagerness for the food, because he knew it would always be in short supply and would be a terrible tool for discipline. That had been the way of it on the Russian front. "Do you wish me to look now?"

"Get moving."

Ernst tucked one package inside his shirt and opened the other. He set off around the edge of the camp, just inside the barbed wire, eating as he walked. Others would believe that this was his only ration. He did not speak to Ludwig and Johanna, knowing that they had seen, and that it would be better for them if no one else realized that they were associated with a man who had food. The two of them might be denied it by the camp authorities, or other internees might attack them and him for it. Again, Ernst's experience as an observer in Russia prepared him; he had survival information. For that much, perhaps, he should thank Dr. Kaltenbrunner.

"Are there any dead?" he called in German.

To his surprise, he received an answer. He went to the man who had answered and squatted by the indicated body. It was an old man whose eyes stared unblinkingly at the sky. He must have been dying when unloaded here. "I will take him away," Ernst said. "Have you saved his things?"

"We would not rob the dead!" the man protested.

Ernst gave him a level stare. "If we do not save what we can, we will all die sooner. His things are of no further use to him. He would want you to have them."

The man nodded reluctantly. He bent to rifle the pockets of the dead man. There were a few coins. He offered them to Ernst.

"No. I am paid to do this work." He looked at the man's feet. "Take his shoes, also; they may fit someone. And his shirt." He got the shoes off and handed them to the man.

"This is ghoulish," the man protested.

"This is survival. I saw it on the Russian front. Now it is our turn. We may be here a long time. We can not afford pride or niceties." He turned the dead man over and worked his shirt off. He gave that, too, to the living man. "Share as you see fit; do not stain his memory by hoarding what you can not use. Then get in line for food; they will not bring it to you."

The man nodded, appalled as comprehension came.

Then he took hold of the dead man's ankles and pulled him along the ground toward the edge. The man's head left a trail in the dirt. Ernst keep hauling, and in due course got the body to the front gate.

"That's the ticket," the sergeant said. Two soldiers came to pick up the body. They tossed it unceremoniously onto the back of a truck.

Ernst went out again, looking for bodies. By noon he had found three. Then he took a break and joined Ludwig and Johanna.

"I got water," she said. She proffered her cup.

"But did you drink?" Ernst asked.

"Yes. I refilled it while I could."

Gratefully, he drank. The water tasted of dirt, but his thirst was formidable.

Then he brought out his package and shared it with the others. It was a generous ration. "It pays to have a job," he said. They had eaten in the morning, but had been given only single packages.

He looked for bodies again in the afternoon, and found two. He was rewarded by another extra package. He realized that the sergeant wanted to keep him healthy enough to continue this work, so that no American would have to do it. It was a fair deal.

So the pattern was set. They deepened their hole, and it offered protection against the heat of the day. But then it rained. The cardboard became sodden, and the icy water soaked through their clothing. The bottom of the hole formed a pool. They had to sit up to avoid the worst of it, but there was no escape. The walls of their hole collapsed. They heard exclamations as the same thing happened to others.

The woman was shivering violently. "We must get closer, before we freeze," Ernst said. "Joanna, we will embrace you from front and back."

They did so, with Ludwig behind and Ernst in front, lying on their sides with the wet cardboard on top. Slowly Johanna's body warmed, and they slept. Ernst dreamed of Quality, and that was his only comfort for the night. She had been through this, and had survived; he must do the same.

The next day more were dead from exposure. More men had to be recruited for hauling. In this manner Ludwig also got a job, because of Ernst's recommendation; he did not speak English, but Ernst gave him instructions, and the guards were satisfied. Johanna went alone for food and water, with better fortune than before.

Then the rations were cut. They weren't sure when it happened; the camp was timeless in its fashion, because there were no calendars and only a few prisoners retained watches.

Ernst learned why the hungry became apathetic: protest required energy. An increasing number of people simply sat in their holes doing nothing. Johanna was one of them. She had diarrhea, and it vitiated her. They had to almost carry her to the crude latrine trench a work group had dug, and then she lacked the strength to get her clothing down. They had to do it for her. It was the same with others. The smell intensified throughout the camp, and there was the sound of weak coughing. Disease was rampant because the resistance of the prisoners was low. The death count rose.

They dug their trench deeper, and made a cunette, a ditch within the trench, to help drainage in a storm. Even so, the sides tended to collapse. Others were also digging, and now the camp was a network of holes with narrow paths threading between them. Sometimes people slipped on the muddy surface, and fell into the holes. The holes were so deep, and the people so weak, that this could be a serious matter; they had to have help to get back out.

One night during a heavy rain they heard screams nearby: the walls of a deep trench had collapsed on its occupants, burying them, and the neighboring prisoners were too weak to dig the victims out before they suffocated. Soon the commotion faded; it wasn't as if death were uncommon, here.

Ernst and Ludwig considered, then reworked their trench so that the sides sloped. The ones that had collapsed had had almost vertical walls and were deep. That was too dangerous. But their own trench had to be made shallower, because there was no room to broaden it without overlapping the neighbors' holes. Thus the protection against the wind and sun was less.

Ludwig came down with a terrible fever. He could barely stand or walk. Light red froth showed at his mouth when he coughed. "I'm done for," he gasped. "I must get away from here, so I don't spoil our trench with my body."

"The hospital," Ernst said. "Maybe they'll take you, now." The guards had been adamant that only those on the verge of expiration be allowed access to the camp hospital.

He helped the man to walk to the gate. "This man is very sick," he told the guard in English. "His disease may spread. He needs to go to the hospital."

The guard eyed Ludwig, nothing the phlegm and blood on his chin and shirt. "Okay. Bring him out."

Amazed at this fortune, Ernst walked Ludwig through the gate and helped him into the truck. "You go along," the guard told Ernst. "We don't want to touch him."

So Ernst rode too, as the truck bumped along. Soon it stopped. "Get him out," the driver called back.

Ernst looked out. "But this is just another open field!" It wasn't even that; part of it was freshly turned dirt with bulldozer tracks on it.

"Yeah. Unload him."

Appalled, Ernst hesitated. "Do it," Ludwig said. "I will die anyway. You will have more room in the apartment." He tried to laugh, but only choked.

"Move it," the driver said.

Ernst got down and lifted Ludwig down. The man lay on the dirt. Now Ernst understood about the freshly turned earth; evidently all prior visitors had been promptly buried. "Farewell, my friend," Ludwig gasped.

"Farewell," Ernst whispered. Then he climbed back onto the truck.

Back at the camp, he was uncertain what to say. Men had gone to the "hospital" before and not returned, but it was assumed that they were taking time to recover. Now he knew that they were dead. It was a dying place, a burial ground, nothing more. The same place they took the bodies which were already dead. Was there any point in telling?

He walked back to his trench. Johanna looked up. "I thought I would be the first of us to go," she said.

"Don't go there," Ernst replied.

She nodded, understanding.

The days passed. The prisoners were assuming the likeness of walking skeletons, except for their swollen bellies. Johanna herself looked pregnant, but Ernst knew that this was a grotesque parody. It was the edema of starvation that filled her belly. She was no longer able to go for her food. But Ernst was still strong enough to haul bodies out, slowly, so he still got extra rations, which he shared with her.

"I promised to repay you, Ernst," she said. "But I think I will default."

"Just survive," he said. "That is all you need to do."

Someone must have done something to annoy the guards, because abruptly the water was cut off. Thirst became a monster. Then it rained, and throughout the camp men lay with their faces up, mouths open, their cups out to catch more. It wasn't enough, but there was no better choice. The deaths increased.

Then Ernst himself got the diarrhea. At first he went to the latrine trench, but soon that became too great an expenditure of energy, and he had to do it in his trench, and cover it up. Then he became too weak to get his pants down in time, and had to foul himself.

"I am sorry I gave you this," Johanna said.

"It is throughout the camp," he demurred. "We are so crowded, there is no way to avoid it."

She nodded. It was true.

Next day Ernst managed to drag himself up, shake out his filthy trousers, and go for food. But there was a change. Bulldozers were coming in. "Move over!" the guards shouted, forcing the prisoners to crowed to one side.

Then the bulldozers started leveling the ground, erasing the mounds and trenches.

"But Johanna is in there!" Ernst cried, trying to return.

A guard swung around, rifle ready. Other hands caught Ernst and pulled him back. "Nothing can be done," a man said. "They don't care."

Numbed, Ernst watched as the section of the camp was leveled. Johanna, and all others too weak to leave their trenches, had been buried alive.

If the Americans were now openly killing prisoners, instead of hiding it with the fiction of a separate hospital, what hope remained for the rest of them?

Indeed, there was activity outside the compound. Trucks were moving, and personnel were gathering around them. Were they going to bring out the machine guns? Was the camp being closed down the easy way? He had seen it on the Russian front.

"British," someone said. Now Ernst recognized the markings on incoming trucks. What were the British doing here?

Soon enough it was known: this Rheinburg camp was in the sector of Germany to be managed by the British, and they were now taking it over. The Americans were departing.

Was this good news or bad news? It had to be good news, because nothing could be worse than the hunger, disease, and callousness they had suffered under the Americans. Perhaps the British would have some slight compassion.

Soon enough the British soldiers entered the compound. "Line up to be counted! Line up to be counted!" a sergeant called in English.

"Line up to be counted," Ernst repeated in German for the benefit of those around him.

A British soldier overhead him. The man approached. "Who speaks English here?" he demanded.

Was this more trouble? Or a chance to get extra rations by being of use to the conquerors? What did it matter? Ernst raised his hand, and then several others who spoke English well did the same.

"Come here."

They followed the soldier to the front gate, where an officer stood.

"This is appalling!" the officer said. "You are starving and filthy, and by the look of you, diseased too."

"We meant no affront, sir," Ernst said.

"We must use you to help our survey of the prisoners," the officer continued. "You will translate our questions for the internees, and give our clerks their answers. We want names, ranks, military numbers and home cities. But as soon as you have done this, those of you in worst need will be taken to the hospital in Lintford."

"Sir, we can do what you wish," Ernst protested. "We do not need to be taken to the hospital."

"We shall be the judge of that. Sergeant, give these translators food immediately, then go with them for the survey."

It was done. Ernst had his first decent meal in a month. The British were formal but not callous.

There were repeated countings, as the orderly British got everything straight. Then Ernst, protesting as firmly as he dared, was put on a truck bound for the hospital. He did feel terrible, because the food made his diarrhea worse: now his system had something to work on. But he was not yet ready to die.

Then they came to the town, and to a building. Ernst stared, amazed: it really was a hospital, not a dying field!

The next week was something like heaven. Ernst and his companions were given food and medicine and were allowed to read and listen to the radio. Female nurses attended them. They slept in beds with clean sheets. They themselves were clean.

Some were already too far gone to be saved, but Ernst saw that the doctors were making every effort. Ernst himself recovered; his illness had been relatively new and slight.

He was returned to the camp. It had been transformed. It was larger, and there were tents throughout. The prisoners now had shelter! He saw others staring at him. He realized that he, too, had changed almost beyond recognition. He remained very thin, but he was in a clean uniform and he was reasonably healthy.

Soon he had spread the word: the hospital was real. After that, many more prisoners were willing to go. They had been struggling desperately to conceal their illnesses.

Now prisoners were being mustered out. But the processing was tedious, and Ernst was needed as a translator. It would be some time for him.

He did his work with a positive attitude. He had learned that the British had not realized how badly prisoners of the Americans and French were being treated, and were shocked by it. The British prisoners were being cared for and released, as they had assumed was the case throughout.

However, an officer advised Ernst, they had notified his family of his presence here, and it was likely that someone was coming to see him. It might be possible to advance the paperwork in his case, so that he could be released sooner.

"Sir, I sincerely appreciate this," Ernst replied. "But there are many here I can still help. I prefer to remain until I am not needed." This was not wholly generosity; he still distrusted the fate of those who departed without returning. The British seemed different from the Americans, like day after night—but were they really?

The officer nodded. Ernst was dismissed.

The following day he was summoned again. This time there was a British airman in the office.

"Ernst Best," the airman said.

"Present, sir."

"Don't you know me?"

Ernst looked at the man more closely. A familiarity dawned, then widened. "Lane Dowling!"

Then they were embracing. But almost immediately Ernst pulled back. "Lane, before we go any farther, there is something I must tell you."

Lane frowned. "That you took my girl."

Taken aback, Ernst nodded. "It was not my intention. I—we—"

"And I took yours. So we're even."

Ernst was set back again. "Krista?"

"Krista and Quality explained everything. I've got to tell you, Ernst, that in seven years it had thinned between me and Quality. I—I knew other girls along the way. But I couldn't let her be lost in Germany. Then, when I found out what you did, I was glad, and mad, and amazed, and finally relieved. I realized that it wouldn't have worked out with Quality. We're different types. But Krista, now—there's a woman I can relate with!"

Ernst had forgotten about this. Lane and Krista! But he realized that it was a good match. They were of a similar temperament. "Then there is no bad feeling between us?"

"Hell no, man! I saw your son. Krista's taking care of him now."

"Krista? But—"

"I pulled a string to get you released early," Lane said. "Let me tell you, it was hell to locate you! The American camps won't release any names at all, but after this one was transferred to British control, they got the names, and notified us. But they told me that you weren't ready to leave the camp yet. So Quality came here."

"Quality—here?" Ernst asked, dazed.

Then Lane took him down the hall to another office. There was Quality, just finishing at a desk. She was very like an angel.

She turned and saw them. "Ernst!" she cried gladly.

He embraced her. Then she explained. "Thee helped me when I was interned. Now I will help thee. I have learned some German, and I know how to help the hungry."

"It's been cleared," Lane said. "She's been deputized as an aide and assigned to you. You have been deputized as temporary staff. When you finish up here, you'll know where to go. And now *I* have to go. There're things to do in Wiesbaden, too." He stood up straight, and lifted his hand in a military salute. "Good luck, friend."

Bemused, Ernst returned the salute. Then Lane was gone, and they were walking back out to the camp to help the remaining prisoners. His life was reappearing before him.

Author's Note

I realize that there will be readers who are infuriated by the last chapter of this novel. It is considered un-American to suggest that any evil could be associated with America. Nevertheless, it is true: America, too, maintained death camps where disarmed German soldiers and even some women and children were systematically destroyed through starvation, exposure and bad treatment. This information was covered up for forty years, but now has come to light, and I think sensible Americans will prefer to explore it and try to find out how to prevent it from ever happening again.

The source of my information is *Other Losses* by James Bacque, published in hardcover by Stoddart in Canada. You should be able to order it through your bookstore, unless the proprietors, like so many others, prefer to pretend that the book doesn't exist. The truth should be known, ugly as it may be.

According to this book, approximately three quarters of a million Germans were killed in American captivity, and one quarter million in French captivity. Only the British acted with decency in this respect. Apparently it was the determination of General Eisenhower and General de Gaulle that Germany should be rendered forever impotent, and the killing of German captives was part of the process. The Red Cross tried to protest, and the Quakers, and the British and Canadian governments, but they were barred from the camps, and mail privileges were denied, so that the prisoners themselves could not describe their situation.

What of the Geneva Convention? It was claimed that these were not prisoners of war, but Disarmed Enemy Forces—DEF—who had no such protection. In fact it was a gross and deliberate violation of human rights, similar to what the Nazis and Russians did. It has been easy to ask, pointedly, how the German people could not have known what their government was doing to the Jews and Gypsies. Now the question is reversed: how could *we* not have known what our government was doing to Germans who had laid down their arms?

Well, one reason is the same as it was for the Germans: we don't know because we don't *want* to know. Even those in a position to ascertain the truth may furiously deny it. I cite as evidence a commentary by Stephen E. Ambrose in *The New York Times Book Review* dated February 24, 1991 titled "Ike and the Disappearing Atrocities." It is what is known in the trade as a "killer review" of *Other Losses*. It describes the author's thesis, then goes on to say that "when scholars do the necessary research, they will find Mr. Baque's work to be worse than worthless." The review is, in essence, a comprehensive denial of Baque's thesis, in part and in whole. Since the reviewer is the director of the Eisenhower Center at the University of New Orleans, so should know something about Eisenhower's role in the war, this is a damning indictment.

However, my assistant Alan Riggs and I had read the book. I asked Alan to do a point by point analysis of the review versus the book and ascertain, as far as possible, the truth. He spent two days on the comparison and wrote up an 1800 word report. The essence was that, on the whole, the book was correct. The reviewer had two valid points: (1) That we can not at this stage know what was in the mind of Eisenhower, so can not attribute a base motive to him. (2) The author's calculation of the number of German dead was in error. As to the first: lack of information about the secret motives of a man now dead works two ways. Eisenhower managed to hide immediate news of his adulterous love affair with his driver, Kay Summersby, but later documentation pretty well establishes it. There are significant hints that he did know and approve the death-camp policy. So Ike may indeed be innocent—but there is doubt. As to the second: the error in calculation, when corrected, still suggests more deaths than the official records admit. So it was our judgment that the death camps did exist as described.

Then came the reader response, in the Letters column of *The Book Review* for April 14, 1991. The letters covered the gamut from congratulating the reviewer, to authenticating the atrocities. Two were from actual prison guards at the camps, one was from a prisoner who had been at Camp Rheinburg and escaped for the same reason Ernst did—British intervention—and one was from an Air Force officer who had witnessed the condition of the prisoners. Another letter writer expressed a caution about Ike's supposedly benign character: he described how Eisenhower had ordered the forced transfer of hundreds of thousands of anti-Communist Russians, Ukrainians and other Eastern Europeans to Stalin's Soviet

Union, where death and slave labor awaited them. Another letter mentioned an article on the death camps that had previously been published in a Canadian magazine, which had elicited letters from former prisoners thanking heaven that at last the truth was being told. Significantly, there was no rebuttal from the reviewer. It was obvious that he was in error. So the case seems secure: like the holocaust, it did happen.

Now some background on my writing of this novel. I am known as a writer of light fantasy, but I have been moving into other areas and have been addressing increasingly serious social concerns. Thus I have written *Firefly*, related to sexual abuse, and *Tatham Mound*, about the situation of the American Indians displaced by the white man's colonization of their continent, and the *Geodyssey* series tracing the sometimes savage history of our species for several million years. *Volk* is similar in the sense that it contains provocative material, but different in other respects. It is technically a historical novel, but also an exploration of a personal interest of mine.

I started work on *Volk* in 1980, but publishers refused to take my non-fantasy efforts seriously and I was unable to place it. So I set it aside with only two chapters completed, and pursued other aspects of my career. Ten years later I took it up again, trusting that my increased leverage as a best-selling writer could enable me to get it into print this time. Originally it was to be a straight World War II novel, but in the intervening time the story of the "Other Losses" broke, and I realized that Ernst would not have ended up in an ordinary detention center, but in a death camp. Yet as the main character of my novel he had to survive, so he had to be in one of the camps that were transferred to the British.

There were other changes, because this novel, like most of mine, looked different when I was in the actual text than it did from afar, in preliminary summary. I had thought that Lane would learn that Ernst had been brutalizing Quality, and swear to kill Ernst. But I discovered in the course of research that Nazi SS men did not approve of abusing women, and could be disciplined for that sort of thing. So Ernst's terrible necessity to brutalize Quality, to prevent his superiors from realizing the real nature of their relationship, was reduced to one episode. Since Lane encountered Quality before catching up to Ernst, no desperate scene could occur with the two men. I had thought that Lane would be shot down over Germany, and be a prisoner, but with Quality already a prisoner, and Ernst destined to become one, I realized that this would be too similar. I had also intended to have a sequence in the defunct Maginot line, and had finally found a book on the subject—and then my story did not provide me the opportunity. So that setting became part of one of the GEODYSSEY novels.

Krista had a smaller part, and was going to fade out after Ernst fell in love with Quality. But the characters of novels do not necessarily resign themselves to their fates, and Krista refused to fade, and became, really, the fourth main character, interacting significantly with all three of the others. So it went, but overall, the novel is similar to the one I worked out in 1980. Except that it is, oddly, less violent. I did not see reason to put in the usual dogfaces-in-trenches battle scenes when my story did not require it; I'm sure that others have done enough of that. So this novel shows other aspects of the war, and seeks other insights than mere victory and loss in battle. I had planned to make more of the German Spanish strategy, as their position would have been significantly strengthened had they taken Gibraltar and cut the allies off from the Mediterranean theater. But that is not the way history went, and this is a novel of history, not fantasy.

What of the major characters, following the end of the novel? I believe that after doing what they can for the remaining prisoners of Camp Rheinberg, Ernst and Quality return to Wiesbaden. They seek to do something for the prisoners in other American and French camps, but are not allowed to approach any, and indeed, it is suggested that if they wish to remain free, they need to stay well clear. They return to America with their son, and again seek to change the American policy, but are rebuffed by the layered bureaucracy and secrecy. So it is that they, like other well-meaning folk, are unable to alleviate this horror. Meanwhile Lane and Krista also travel to America, where Krista is quite pleased with the relative affluence. Both couples visit Europe regularly, and their children are bilingual. Today they have disappeared into the fabric of society in much the way my own bi-national family has.

As it happened, I had a tiny bit of personal involvement in some of the events of that day. I was born in England, and lived for a while in Spain. My parents were in charge of the Quaker relief effort in north east Spain during the Spanish civil war. Quality Smith is fictional, but the work the Quakers did was real. That was shut down in 1940 when my father was arrested, apparently by mistake, and required to leave the country. We came to America on the same voyage that brought the Duke of Windsor to the Western Hemisphere, after the German plot to kidnap him had died stillborn. But for that exile of my father, I might have grown up in Spain. There is more on this in my autobiography, *Bio of an Ogre*. I was raised as a Quaker, but elected to go my own way. Thus my choice of a Quaker lady as a main character is not coincidental; I retain considerable respect for the Quaker way. I should clarify that the Quaker "plain talk" was originally an attempt to identify with the common folk, but as time passed and the language of the common folk changed, it became a distinguishing mark. Today few Quakers use it, but in the 1940's more did. Quality's practice of using it only with those to whom she was close is my adaptation; perhaps this is the policy of some Quakers, but not of most. As a general rule, Quakers do not seek to set themselves apart; their beliefs in integrity, pacifism and the "inner light" of the individual's communion with God are firm and to my mind commendable, but there is no "holier than thee" attitude. The Quakers I know have silent meetings instead of church services, and have no clergy; each person finds his own way. I understand that there are however other Quakers who have more conventional services. It is my impression that where good works are being done without demand for renown or material reward, you are likely to find Quakers. Quality was very much a creature of her religion in that respect, and if she is the type of person you would like to know, look among the Friends.

Several people helped me on aspects of this novel. One was Frances Wagner, a correspondent who introduced me to Nietzsche and reminded me of the power of Richard Wagner's music. She also described the tour of Paris, which Quality took. Another was Arne Bister, a German student who happened to write to me when I was working on this novel: In ways he seems very like Ernst Best, for he had spent a year in America, been on a wrestling team, gotten to know an American girl, and then returned to serve in the German army. Arne had help in his spot research for this novel from his friend Michael Frömmel. There was irony here, because they included detailed material on the routes and trains leading into the Wiesbaden area, establishing that one of the most beautiful trains of that time, the *Rheingold*, used Route 600 down the west side of the river, going on to perhaps the most beautiful train station in Germany at Frankfurt. The thing is palatial! But the route 610 on the east side that went directly to Wiesbaden was a lesser thing, used more for freight, and that was the one the Best family took. So we did not get treated to the first class ride on the train with the purple roof, and did not see the phenomenal Frankfurt station. Sigh. "It is not my fault that their estate is in Wiesbaden," Arne grumped. And a special credit to Alfred Jacob, my father, head of thc Friends Service Council relief effort in north east Spain. He was anonymous in the novel, but may be known here. Helpful comment was also offered by Stan Carnarius, a family friend.

One additional reason I completed the novel at this time: I had the research assistant, Alan Riggs. He was to work for me a year, and I realized that this was the time to do my research novel. Because I have found that I have been spoiled by the ease and speed of fantasy, and am no longer satisfied to take the necessary time for research. There are those who spend three years in research before starting to write a novel, but in the three years prior to *Volk* I completed thirteen novels and reworked one. Three were collaborative, and one was a movie novelization, which speeded things up; nevertheless, it is evident that I move at a good clip, and I'm just not about to take years on any one piece. So with Alan's help I was able to write *Volk* at almost the speed of a non-research novel. Alan mentions that he had help in the library, locating references, from Dan Monkhern, Drew Wojciechowski and Peg Rombach. There is surely little connection to this novel, but Drew later committed suicide, and Alan married Peg.

As I proofread the novel in 1999, 19 years after starting it and 8 years after finishing it, I was struck by the degree to which it is drawn from my own experience and that of my parents in peripheral ways. There is more of me here than mere writing effort. In Chapter 3 I drew from my mother's experience in Spain, such as her reaction to the sight of freshly dismembered bodies after the artillery barrage—but she died three months after I finished the novel, long before it saw print, and never got to read it.

You may wonder why I keep departing from the fantasy genre where I have had such success. The answer is that I started in science fiction and fantasy because that was what I liked and knew best. But I never wanted to be limited to it. I want to be free to write in any genre where I may have something to say. But since I have an easier time with fantasy, and make more money there, I don't step out of it unless I have special reason. Thus my non-genre efforts tend to have significant and perhaps controversial elements, as is the case in this novel. What is the point in breaking out of the barrier of one genre, only to be confined in another? I want to be known, ultimately, not merely as a fantasy writer, but as a writer with something to say, whatever the genre.

At any rate, I hope that it has been worthwhile for you, the reader. I hope also that those of you who object to the final chapter will do your homework before sending me angry or ignorant letters or emails. I am well aware that there is still no general public awareness in America of what happened to the disarmed German soldiers. Denial is a powerful if misdirected force. It is not me you have to refute, but history.

About the Author

Piers Anthony was born in August, 1934, in England, and became an American citizen while serving in the U. S. Army in 1958. He has two grown daughters and lives with his wife, Carol, in Florida. He sold his first story, after eight years of trying, in 1962; his first novel, *Chthon*, was published in 1967. Through 1995 he has had 102 books published, and translations have appeared in ten languages. Currently he writes three novels a year. He has had 21 books on *The New York Times* bestseller list in the span of ten years; and in one year, three of his novels placed on *The New York Times* bestseller list. His first Xanth novel, *A Spell for Chameleon*, won the August Derleth Fantasy Award for the best novel in 1977, and the Spokane Public Library gave him the Golden Pen Award for being their favorite fantasy author in 1982.

9 781584 451594